Books by Gordon Ryan

Dangerous Legacy

Threads of Honor

Upon the Isles of the Sea

Spirit of Union:
Volume 1: Destiny 1895–1898
Volume 2: Conflict 1898–1919
Volume 3: Heritage 1919–1940

SPIRIT OF UNION

VOLUME 3 1919–1940

HERITAGE

GORDON RYAN

Deseret Book Company
Salt Lake City, Utah

Library of Congress Cataloging-in-Publication Data

Ryan, Gordon
    Heritage, 1919–1949 / Gordon Ryan.
        p.   cm.
    ISBN 1-57345-577-6
    I. Title.   II. Series : Ryan, Gordon.   Spirit of union : v. 3.
    PS3568.Y32H47   1999
    813'54—dc21   99-34053
                                                                   CIP

Printed in the United States of America

10   9   8   7   6   5   4   3   2   1   18961-6519

And Moses' father in law said unto him, . . .
Moreover thou shalt provide out of all the people
able men, such as fear God, men of truth. . . .
And let them judge the people at all seasons.

Exodus 18:17–22

Dedicated to

Judge George Gene Granata Jr.
1945–1998

Not alone do I mourn your passing, dear friend, but thousands who have crossed your path. Yet He who called has need, and should you judge again in His court, I would be well served to come before your bench and once more receive of your Christlike love.

As for your priceless gift, I can but share it.

Gordon Ryan

Acknowledgments

As always, my deepest love to my beautiful Kiwi wife, Colleen, and my daughter, Kate, a true mother in Zion, who continue to support and encourage me in my writing endeavors.

A heartfelt thanks to my editor, Richard Peterson, without whose editorial skills, life and breath would have eluded these pages, and, in fact, the "spirit" would have been absent from *Spirit of Union*.

My sincere appreciation to Kent Ware, director of publishing, who designed the original artwork, and to designers Richard Erickson and Shauna Gibby, who continued to provide the highest quality art over the next two volumes. Their creative ability provided these volumes their all-important shelf appeal.

I admire the professional skills of those who work in the editorial, publication, production, marketing, and distribution departments of Deseret Book. I marvel at the range and quality of products they produce annually, taking the raw product authors and artists provide, catching and visually enhancing the concept, and producing in the end a glistening, visually appealing literary or musical product.

A special thanks also to the many gracious readers who

have written to let me know how they felt and what expectations they had for the conclusion of this series. Would that we all could have sat around a table laden with pizza and worked out the solutions together.

The author would be pleased to receive E-mail correspondence. He can be reached at GordonRyan@AOL.com

Preface

Thomas Callahan, the runaway Irish larrikin, has led a varied and oft-troubled life, hasn't he? And he has provided enough discord as a husband and father to last his family several lifetimes. If in bringing his saga to a close, I have failed to produce each reader's desired solution to Tom and Katrina's continuing dilemma . . . well, that's the nature of life, isn't it?

Perhaps even Tom Callahan isn't completely happy with how I have dealt with him. Surely Katrina would have hoped for an earlier resolution to her conundrum. Still, Tom and Katie have arrived at the later stage of their lives as we all do—increasingly aware of their mortality and their relationship to God and not entirely certain of how well they have accomplished all that was expected.

In the first volume of this series, *Spirit of Union: Destiny,* I wrote about the proposed union of three entities: first, a political union between the Territory of Deseret (later to be called the State of Utah), and the United States of America; second, the improbable marital union of Thomas Callahan, itinerant Irishman, and Katrina Hansen, well-to-do Norwegian; and third, the often uneasy union of

1

Mormon and Gentile who ended up living together in the beautiful valleys of Utah.

Now, in Volume 3, *Heritage*, each of these unions has developed in its own way. Utah indeed became a state, and in 1946, some six years after the conclusion of Volume 3, it celebrated its fiftieth anniversary of statehood. In this volume, Tom and Katrina retain and strengthen their love for one another and leave a true legacy in their children.

Of the three unions, perhaps only Mormon and Gentile continue to struggle somewhat to find perfect harmony. But I submit that my original premise still stands: that Deseret was, and is, more than merely a Mormon enclave and that many other peoples, religions, and cultures contributed— and continue to contribute—to the making of the beautiful and highly livable place we call Utah.

I have enjoyed creating the characters in this story and seeing—often to my surprise—how they have reacted to the situations the world thrust upon them. As a relatively new "immigrant" to Salt Lake City, I have also enjoyed learning about Utah and its place in American history.

I sincerely hope that *Spirit of Union* has brought a few moments of pleasure to your life. Writing it certainly has brought joy to mine.

Gordon W. Ryan
Helamano, Oahu, Hawaii
May, 1999

1

October, 1919
County Cork, Ireland

Thomas Callahan could barely see the *Obsidian* as she stood a half mile offshore. Obscured by the darkness of a cold and cloudy October night, the unlighted, rusty freighter pitched and rolled, besieged by an endless line of dark Atlantic rollers that surged in serried ranks toward the rocky Irish coast. Below the spot where Tom stood, on a ledge overlooking the cove, the waves broke on the jagged rocks and narrow beach then fell back in a froth of white foam.

Three small fishing boats bobbed and danced on the agitated sea, continuing a relay they had been running since shortly after midnight, making round trip after round trip from the ship to the rocky beach. It had been easy enough to enlist the owners of the local fishing fleet to help shuttle the contraband cargo from ship to shore, but negotiating the large swells and heavy surf in the near total darkness had proven risky, and the operators of the small boats were by now tired and testy and anxious to finish their task.

Wrapped in a thick, Aryan sweater and wearing a heavy woolen mackinaw, Tom stood with his hands in his pockets, leaning into the gale and looking out to sea, watching the work progress. The wind and salt spray burned his eyes and numbed his face, and he wondered how cold and miserable it must be for the three- or four-man crews on each of the fishing boats.

Tom's youngest brother, Seamus, stood beside him, and the two men watched without talking as the heavy wooden crates were handed ashore, lugged up the steep embankment, and then hastily loaded onto the waiting lorries. Once loaded, the heavily laden trucks quickly disappeared, each in a different direction beyond the rolling hills.

Tom had made a decision. In 1916, he had met with Michael Collins[1] in a pub in Cork and had agreed to support the Irish Brotherhood in that organization's fight to win Irish independence from England. Tom had stood by his pledge, and for three years had financed the procurement and delivery of weapons and ammunition to be used in the struggle. During those years, Seamus had made several trips to America and to Mexico, to visit Tom and to function as the middleman in the acquisition of the armaments. On three previous occasions, ships had made the run from Mexico to Ireland, transporting their contraband cargoes and delivering them under cover of darkness. Each time, the ship had rendezvoused with members of the brotherhood at a different location, at prearranged sites along the barren, remote stretches of the Irish coastline, as far north as County Donegal and now at this isolated spot in southwestern County Cork, south of the village of Kinsale.

Watching the crates come ashore, Tom wrestled with how he would tell Seamus, and Collins for that matter, that this was to be his last delivery—that he had had a change of heart and could no longer be a part of the killing and maiming that had gone on and would continue.

To the east, toward the Welsh coast, the early morning light was beginning to break over the ocean, and the fishermen who were ferrying the valuable cargo knew they had time for only one more trip each to the freighter before dawn would fully be upon them. Anxious to remove his vessel beyond the twelve-mile limit, the captain of the *Obsidian* had bellowed his orders, and the Irish fishermen knew there would be no reprieve from his determination to depart. Still, for the most part, the weapons were ashore, and the vessel had been unloaded of her cargo with only one mishap.

On the first round trip, the third fishing boat to tie up alongside the freighter had loaded her cargo too high, and on the return trip to the beach she was hit beam on by a heavy roller, causing her to list severely to port. A dozen crates of small arms had slid overboard into the sea, and only an heroic effort on the part of the crew had saved the remaining cases. After that trip, each boat limited its load and made certain to fasten it securely—resulting in the prolonged process that had lasted nearly till dawn. Other than that single incident, the long night's work had been productive, and the Irish Republican Army had increased its stockpile of weapons and ammunition considerably.

Awaiting the final load, the twelve-man beach crew was startled by an explosion and a blinding flash that erupted without warning, illuminating the cove. Caught and brightly silhouetted in the momentary glare, the men whirled toward the light and were astonished to see that one of the fishing boats had exploded and was burning brightly on the water. A second explosion then erupted in the water, some fifty meters astern of one of the other fishing boats, and a loud voice began barking orders to his men on the shore.

"Right, lads. Away with ya, and mind the major crossin's. Watch for the ambush," he hollered over the noise of the howling wind. Suddenly the man was up the cliff and standing beside Tom and Seamus. "It's a British gunboat. She's behind the point, in the lee of the weather," he said, handing Tom a pair of binoculars. "She'll be after the freighter right enough. The captain's already turned for deep water," he said. The three men peered through the gray light to the west to catch a glimpse of the freighter, her bow now pointed away from land and her stack belching smoke as she gathered steam for the run to international waters. Farther to the west, appearing as a ghostly shadow on the turbulent sea, was the dark silhouette of a trim British frigate. As quickly as Tom spotted her, she rounded the Old Head of Kinsale, slicing her way through the incoming rollers in pursuit of the fleeing invader.

"The *Obsidian's* got a four-mile start," Tom said. "They'll never catch her before she reaches the twelve-mile mark."

"They don't need to catch her," the other man said, just as another cannon shot erupted from the frigate. "They'll be content to sink her."

Tom stood silently, the rain and ocean spray continuing to buffet his face, as the chase continued. The growing light from the east brought increased visibility as the drama unfolded. Several minutes passed while the frigate continued to close the distance between the two vessels, her forward cannon rising and falling with the heave and plummet of the waves. With her Morse lamp, the frigate challenged the *Obsidian,* ordering the freighter to heave to, but she ignored the warning, steaming at full speed toward international waters.

The first shell to hit the target struck the ship on the stern, just above the railing but inflicted little damage. Having found the range, the frigate's next two shots apparently disabled the bridge crew, and the freighter lost her way, listing to starboard and beginning to slew off toward the west. With the *Obsidian* broadside on, and having received no reply to their order to halt, the frigate fired again, impacting the freighter amidships. The resulting secondary explosion was enormous. When the blinding glare died down and Tom's eyes adjusted to the predawn light, the *Obsidian* had all but disappeared.

"The bloody Brits. She was disabled and running loose," Willie Ryan, the man with Tom and Seamus said. "They could have taken her instead of sending her to the bottom."

"Aye," Tom said softly, turning on his heel and pulling Seamus's arm as they headed for the cliffs. "They must have radioed our position. We'd best be off."

The three men began to climb the cliff toward their vehicle, parked above them on the rocky outcropping above the beach. Before they reached the crest, the sound of barked orders and of the clank of military equipment above them and beyond their sight reached their ears. In moments, several British soldiers appeared at the top of the cliff, pointing their weapons down at the trio.

"We'll have you peaceful now," the man in charge shouted down the hillside, "or we'll have you dead. Keep climbing."

Tom glanced at Seamus and shook his head, trying to encourage his younger brother not to panic and bolt, but it did no good. The young man jumped behind a rock alongside the trail and began to scurry down the cliff, scrambling through the brush in his attempt to escape the soldiers. Gunfire erupted and Tom watched as his brother was struck, several times it seemed, and then fell, tumbling end over end to the rocky beach below, where he lay still.

"You, lot," the officer hollered again, "keep climbing, and put your hands in the air."

7

Tom reached the top ahead of his companion and was unceremoniously thrown to the ground, his face ground into the dirt, and his hands pulled roughly behind him. A thin rope was used to lash his wrists and then he was jerked to his feet and shoved toward the back of a canvas-covered lorry. A young British officer came to stand close to both prisoners, eyeing each of them in turn.

"Where are the guns that came ashore?"

"Forget that. See to the man that you shot," Tom demanded.

The officer looked at Tom for a moment, his facial expression and slightly cocked head revealing his surprise at Tom's American accent.

"No need. He's dead. Now where are the guns?"

"You don't know that he's dead. For God's sake, man, send someone down to see to him."

A sergeant stepped forward and thrust his rifle butt into Tom's stomach, doubling him over in pain.

"Keep a civil tongue in yer head, ye bloody Yank, when speaking to the leftenant."

"Now answer the question," the officer repeated. "Where did you take the weapons?"

Both captives remained silent.

"Well, Paddy," the young leftenant said, a smile crossing his face, "His Majesty's government hangs gunrunners for treason against the Crown. But if you tell us where the weapons are, it *might* go easier on you."

Tom Callahan and Willie Ryan, the man who had commanded the beach party, remained silent.

"Take them," the officer commanded.

Tom was lifted by two men into the bed of the truck and shoved against the back of the cab. Willie, who had remained with Tom and Seamus when the loaded trucks had carried the weapons away, was also placed in the lorry, his hands tied behind him. The engine was started and the truck bumped over the ruts in the field, reaching the road and beginning the short drive through the breaking dawn to the nearby village of Kinsale. Tom remained silent, replaying in his mind the vision of his brother's body cascading down the cliff. The bitter thought that recurred to him was the irony that Seamus should die during Tom's last delivery of weapons to Irish soil.

❖

FEBRUARY, 1920

FOUR COURTS, DUBLIN, IRELAND

"Thomas Matthew Callahan, it is the sentence of this court that you be incarcerated in His Majesty's prison at Portlaoise[2] Gaol for the term of fifteen years and that you be transported forthwith. Have you anything to say to the court?"

Stunned by the verdict, Tom stood numbly beside his legal counsel, Sir Reginald Hollister, a London barrister who had presented Tom's case and had succeeded in convincing the court that although Mr. Callahan had indeed been born in Ireland, he was now a citizen of the United States of America. Hollister had argued that as an American citizen, Callahan was perhaps guilty of gunrunning, but had not committed treason and was therefore not subject to execution under British law. Hollister had cited the example of Eamon de Valera[3], who had a few years earlier been convicted and sentenced to death for his part in the abortive 1916 Easter Rebellion, but whose sentence, in deference to his American citizenship, had later been commuted.

A plea for leniency by President Woodrow Wilson, the

9

response to Congressman Anders Hansen's request for the president to intervene, had also weighed heavily in Tom's favor, but in the end, the fact that he had been captured in the act of unloading a shipload of weapons made defending Tom a formidable task. Finally, at the urging of Tom's brother-in-law, Congressman Hansen, the London lawyer had convinced Tom to throw himself on the mercy of the court.

Fifteen years! Sir Reginald had told Callahan to expect nothing less. His Majesty's government was determined to stamp out the Irish insurrection, and putting an end to foreign gunrunning was seen by British authorities as a priority. But a sentence of fifteen years! Hearing the judge's actual pronouncement left Tom feeling numb.

"Mr. Callahan," the judge said, "do you have anything you wish to say to this court?"

Before responding, Tom closed his eyes and took a deep breath. Then, looking into the judge's eyes, he said, "I do wish to speak, your honor. I wish to express my gratitude for your willingness to recognize my American citizenship and for your leniency in waiving the death sentence. However, I also wish to state that while I am an American citizen by choice, I am Irish by birth and by temperment. The time is not far distant when this people will be free of British tyranny. May God grant that I live to see that day. That's all I have to say, Your Honor."

The magistrate shifted uncomfortably on his seat, coughed a bit, then pounded his gavel on the bench. "Yes, yes, well, we'll see about that in due course. The prisoner is remanded into custody and will be transported immediately."

As Tom and Sir Reginald shook hands, the barrister said, "This is not the end of it, you understand. I'll persist in trying to have you released and deported." The prisoner was then immediately shackled, hand and foot, by two Irish Guarda officers.

"Take heart, Tom. I shall keep working on this case at the highest levels," Sir Reginald continued.

As he was being led away, Tom said, "It's Katie I'm worried about, Reggie. Anders had a hard enough time keeping her from coming over here. Now when she hears the sentence . . . Contact her, encourage her, and keep her informed, please."

"You can count on it, Tom. Godspeed. I'll be in touch."

———— ∞∞ ————

The ride to Portlaoise Prison, located about fifty miles west of Dublin, took nearly two hours. Two other prisoners were being transported in the canvas-enclosed back of the truck and two guards sat also inside the rear, separated from the prisoners by a wire barrier. No talking was to be allowed, but the two Irishmen ignored the guards' repeated attempts to get them to shut up.

"We hear ya done well, Yank," the more burly of the two other prisoners said.

"Time will tell," Tom replied. It struck him as ironic that in his native land, on his way to prison, he was viewed as a foreigner.

"The bloody Brit's seen his best day, man. He's through in this land and he knows it. And as for the Irish traitors who sat at their feet and licked crumbs from their table," the prisoner said, looking through the wire at the guard and spitting on the floor of the truck, "there'll be no place in Ireland deep enough for him to hide."

"I said shut your gob," the guard bellowed, rapping on the wire with his billy.

The truck arrived at the prison and was driven through

an archway in the two-foot-thick stone walls. Once in the center of the compound, the truck stopped, and the guards opened the rear door and the wire cage, motioning for the prisoners to climb down. Shackled closely together, the men struggled to maintain their balance as they exited the truck. After the prisoners were all on the ground, one of the guards from the truck stepped behind the three shackled men. Suddenly the man next to Tom, the one who had derided the guard, grunted and fell to his knees from an unseen blow to the small of his back. Tom was jerked off balance by their connecting chains and went to one knee.

"Get up, Yank," the guard bellowed, "unless you want some of the same."

Tom tried to assist the downed man to his feet, but received a kick in the buttocks from the guard. "I didn't say to help him, I said get up."

Tom rose slowly, but his chains prevented him from standing fully upright while his companion remained on the ground.

"Now you, Mick. Stand on your feet."

Grimacing in pain, the other prisoner got to his feet and stood unsteadily alongside Tom. Both men remained silent as several guards gathered around. One of them, wearing a wide, polished leather belt around his waist, came to stand in front of the Irish prisoner.

"You've been granted a five-year visit with us, lad. We'll brook no mouth of yours in here. If you're to see your dear, sweet mother again, you'll do *what* you're told, *as* you're told, and *when* you're told. And that goes for the lot of you. Do I make myself clear, lads?" the man said.

The three prisoners looked down at the ground, avoiding eye contact with the warder and didn't speak.

"Right, move 'em inside."

2

United States Congressman Anders Hansen, Chairman of the House Foreign Relations Committee, argued as forcibly as he could that his sister, Katrina Callahan, should remain in Salt Lake and let government officials handle things. But Katrina was not a woman who was going to let her husband rot in a British jail while the politicians—including her brother—muddled through the morass of protocol. Her only concession to Congressman Hansen—the name she applied to her brother whenever she disagreed with him—was that she would be grateful for his company during her trip to the British Isles. She was, in fact, appreciative of his advice and possible influence. She suspected that were she to travel to Ireland alone, she would only encounter multiple levels of "pass-the-buck" bureaucracy. She hoped her brother could help steer her through the process that would see Tom released. London, not Ireland, was the place to begin, Anders had assured her, and to this bit of political savvy, she listened.

Aware of the purpose of Tom's mission to Ireland, Katrina had nevertheless been floored six months earlier by the news of his arrest, and also by the brevity of Tom's statement:

"Arrested by British authorities–Stop–Trial in January–Stop–Notify Anders–Stop–Do not come to Ireland–Stop–Love, Tom"

When Anders had finally telephoned her thirty-six hours later with the full story of Tom's arrest, Katrina's impulse was to leave immediately for Ireland. Distraught and frantic, she was only prevented from doing so by her brother's pleadings and those of his wife, Sarah. Together, they were finally able to convince Katrina to remain at home until the issue had been well considered and all political avenues explored. Four weeks later, Katrina traveled to Washington, D.C., to stay with Anders and Sarah until arrangements could be made to travel to London to meet with the proper authorities.

With the possibility of execution hanging quite literally over Tom's head, Katrina had at first been crazy with fear. But Sir Reginald's advice that Tom plead guilty and throw himself on the mercy of the court had proven sound. At least Tom wasn't going to be hanged. Still, her husband had been sentenced to fifteen years in prison, and Katrina worried constantly how it must be for him—to be so far from home, locked up in who knows what kind of conditions. A continual exchange of cablegrams between Tom's attorney and Congressman Hansen kept her sufficiently informed about the proceedings to keep her in D.C., but she was constantly agitated, sick with fear over Tom's safety and finding it difficult to eat or sleep.

When the sentence was pronounced and news came that Tom had been transported to Portlaoise Prison, Katrina renewed her badgering of Anders to intercede politically. Then, when it appeared that nothing more could be done without actually going to England, Anders agreed to accompany Katrina there in an effort to somehow win amnesty for Tom. In the interim, Sir Reginald had appealed the verdict, seeking to get his client released from prison and deported.

Six weeks after Tom's appeal to the prime minister had been denied, Katrina and Anders were seated in the outer office of Sir Reginald Hollister, barrister, waiting impatiently for their appointment. Hollister had been surprised the previous day to receive a phone call from Anders, announcing the fact that Mrs. Thomas Callahan, *and* her brother, Congressman Anders Hansen, were in London. Anders hoped his presence would open doors that would be closed to Katrina alone. It was unusual that the chairman of the United States Congressional Committee on Foreign Affairs would come to England. The political protocol attendant to such an impromptu visit, notwithstanding its unofficial nature, placed Sir Reginald in a difficult position. While he might have been inclined to merely placate Mrs. Callahan, he could not so easily avoid the level of courtesy required by the presence of a visiting legislator of Congressman Hansen's stature. As Sir Reginald ushered Anders and Katrina into his office suite and took their coats, Katrina sensed the attorney's British reserve—he was polite, but somewhat aloof.

"Please, be seated," Sir Reginald said, motioning toward two leather chairs. His office window looked out onto the Thames River and Big Ben and the British houses of parliament beyond. It was a magnificent view, but one that was largely lost on Katrina.

Anders spoke first. "Please accept our thanks for seeing

us so quickly, Sir Reginald. We know that it has been an imposition."

"Not at all, Congressman Hansen. I am very much involved in your brother-in-law's case and still hopeful of resolution."

"Has there been any change?" Katrina interjected.

Sir Reginald had always appreciated a pretty face and before responding to Katrina, he briefly studied her. She wore a dark, full-length skirt and a white, ruffled, long-sleeved blouse, buttoned to her throat. The simple ensemble, he thought, quite flattered her trim figure, and with her blonde hair pulled up on top of her head under a broad brimmed hat, she was an attractive woman. He judged her to be about forty years of age, and under any other circumstance, he might have enjoyed meeting such a woman. But now, she was understandably agitated and was struggling to manage her emotions.

Sir Reginald shook his head. "I'm afraid not. These things take time. I understand that is not much consolation, but I am *personally* attending to your husband's case."

"Perhaps that's the problem," she said abruptly.

"*Katrina!*" Anders said.

"No, Anders," she replied, glancing toward her brother, "Sir Reginald needs to hear exactly how I feel and understand my intentions."

Anders shifted nervously in his seat and gave a half-hearted smile to Sir Reginald.

"I'm not certain I understand," Sir Reginald said.

"Then let me make myself clear. I know that Tom has been most appreciative of your efforts to resolve his case and that he has full faith in your continued efforts. However, what is being done simply isn't sufficient," she said.

Sir Reginald looked toward Anders and back again at Katrina. "I'm still not certain—"

"I know you mean well, sir, but you are bound by your own traditions and protocol and probably fear offending your political peers. I have no such impediments. When all is said and done, Sir Reginald, this is a political issue, as you well know. We are not talking about criminals in the true sense, and that goes for most of the Irish military and political leaders as well. I am a Norwegian by birth, Sir Reginald, in case you weren't aware, and my own country has only recently received its independence from Sweden. Certainly you can understand my sympathy for Ireland's cause, even if Tom had *not* been born Irish."

"Mrs. Callahan, it was difficult enough to persuade the Crown to drop charges of treason—charges which would have brought a death sentence, or, at a minimum, life imprisonment, as was the case with Willie Ryan, the man captured with your husband."

"Sir Reginald," Katrina continued, smiling sweetly at the older man, "treason is most often a political charge, is it not? In the beginning of the American Revolution, I believe the Crown considered George Washington a traitor but later dealt with him as the president of his country." Katrina leaned forward in her chair and smiled again at the barrister. "In a few years, I wouldn't be surprised to see your prime minister dealing with President Michael Collins of the nation of Ireland. I know this is difficult, but I am fighting for the life and freedom of the man I love, and my resources, Sir Reginald, are considerable. Make no mistake, I will use every penny that Thomas Callahan has amassed over the past twenty years. And that, sir, will buy a lot of press—politically oriented press, if you understand my meaning."

17

"Katrina, I'll not be party to this. This is blackmail," Anders said, standing suddenly and staring down at his sister.

"Sir Reginald is doing his absolute best to free Tom. We should be grateful for that effort. He might have been hanged, you know. He admitted his guilt."

"I know that, Anders," she said, reaching for her brother's hand. "And I also know that you and Sir Reginald are trapped by the system. A political system that grinds ever so slowly. I *am* not, and *will* not, be constrained by that system. It's important that Sir Reginald, and the other British authorities, know of my resolve in this matter and that he deliver my message clearly."

"Katrina, this is not like you at all. Had I known your intentions, I would never have agreed to come along," Anders argued.

"I know that too, Anders," she smiled sweetly, "that's why I didn't tell you."

Sir Reginald leaned back in his chair and folded his hands on his ample belly. A grin slowly formed on his face. "What would you have me do, Mrs. Callahan?" he asked.

"Sir Reginald, I want an immediate appointment with Prime Minister David Lloyd-George."

Reginald's eyebrows rose, and he clicked his tongue several times. "That, Mrs. Callahan, may prove difficult to arrange. The prime minister is *very* busy, you see."

"Of course he is. And Tom has nothing but time on his hands, as I understand it. And I, sir, have nothing but a desire to see him freed."

"I cannot promise anything, Mrs. Callahan, but there *is* a senior minister with whom I am closely associated. Perhaps he, in his capacity as Secretary for the Colonies, could be of some assistance. With your permission, I will contact him and request a few moments of his time."

Still standing, Anders turned toward Sir Reginald. "That would be Churchill, would it not?"

"Indeed, Winston Churchill, formerly First Lord of the Admiralty."

"How fitting," Katrina said, rising to stand beside her brother. "Wasn't Mr. Churchill the gentleman involved in the Gallipoli campaign?"

Sir Reginald rose and crossed to the front of his desk. "I see you're well informed, too," he said.

"My eldest son is now a New Zealand citizen, and as I understand it from his account, the Kiwi and Australian boys . . . let's see, I believe he used the expression 'carried the can' in that disastrous campaign," she said, inclining her head and again presenting a broad smile.

"You *have* come prepared, haven't you, madam?" Sir Reginald said, returning her smile. "I will see what I can do to arrange an appointment. My secretary will call your hotel immediately after I am able to arrange a meeting. It has been a great pleasure meeting you, Mrs. Callahan. If you are representative of the Norwegians, I can understand how your country achieved independence. I will be in touch."

"Thank you, Sir Reginald. And by the way, it would be most appreciated if, in addition to Mr. Churchill, Prime Minister Lloyd-George would be able to attend our meeting."

Sir Reginald Hollister paused a moment and then threw back his head and laughed loudly. "Congressman Hansen, you must stay in good stead with your sister. I shouldn't be surprised to see her run for your seat, should you not perform to her expectations."

"How right you are, Sir Reginald. Thank you for your time," Anders said, shaking the older gentleman's hand.

———

Three days later, at exactly 9:30 A.M., Anders and Katrina arrived at Sir Reginald's law office, accompanied by the American ambassador to the Court of St. James, John W. Davis[4] of West Virginia. Katrina had made good on her promise to Sir Reginald that she would invoke every available method to attract the necessary attention to her husband's case. She had as yet not gone to Fleet Street, the center of most newspaper publishing, a restraint for which the American ambassador had offered his sincere appreciation.

Convincing the ambassador to accompany her and Anders to Sir Reginald's had actually not been difficult. During their meeting the previous day, she had merely informed the gentleman that he was welcome to accompany her or not, but that the outcome of the meeting would certainly determine her next course of action. That night, in their hotel suite, Anders had nearly come to blows with his sister over what he had termed her abuse of wealth and position.

"Anders, I have loved you and listened to your advice all my life. But you have fallen under the spell of all politicians. Polite talk and veiled references to nonexistent intentions serve no one other than the politician. It works with the masses and keeps you all in office. Oh, make no mistake, I appreciate all you've been able to accomplish for Utah, along with Senator Smoot, but this time Tom's *life* is at stake. *Fifteen years*, Anders, in that rotten, and no doubt disease-infested jail. Even if he's not hanged, do you really think he can physically stand that length of time under those conditions? I'll not stand by and watch it. Mark my words, if Tom isn't released, I will use every ounce of influence I have, and every dollar Tom has, to publicize the Irish cause and if necessary, I'll give it all to the Irish to buy more guns."

"Katrina, that's not Christian and you know it, and you also know Tom wouldn't want that," Anders pleaded. "I've never seen you like this."

"And I hope you never have to again, but I *will* have Tom out of that dungeon."

Entering Sir Reginald's office with her retinue, Katrina caused quite a stir. When Ambassador Davis appeared along with Katrina, Sir Reginald was immediately summoned from his inner office. As he stepped through the door and recognized the ambassador, Katrina could see his surprise at her startling addition to the party list.

"Mr. Ambassador, I had no knowledge of your attendance this morning."

"I understand, Sir Reginald. Please excuse my impropriety in coming without notification," Davis said.

"Please, come in," he said, ushering the trio into his inner office. As they crossed into the room, another gentleman stood, nodding at the ambassador.

"Good morning, Mr. Ambassador," the other gentleman said and offered his hand.

"And to you, Mr. Churchill. It's my pleasure, sir," the ambassador replied. "Allow me to introduce you. Mr. Churchill, this is Mrs. Thomas Callahan of Salt Lake City, Utah, and her brother, Congressman Anders Hansen."

"My greetings to you, madam," Churchill said, bowing slightly and taking Katrina's hand. He then turned to shake hands with Anders, after which he turned back to Reginald. "This has become a mini League of Nations, eh, Reggie?"

"So it would seem, Winston," Sir Reginald said. "Perhaps if I could have a moment alone with Mr. Churchill," he said to his three guests. "Please be seated. We shan't be a minute."

Churchill and Sir Reginald stepped into a small office just off the main suite while Ambassador Davis, Anders, and Katrina took seats. After several moments Sir Reginald returned and sat behind his desk.

"Mr. Churchill will rejoin us presently. He, uh, had to make another contact. And how have you found London, Mrs. Callahan?"

"London is a lovely city, Sir Reginald, but I've found myself a bit more occupied than on previous visits."

"Yes, yes, of course. And Congressman Hansen, have you been to London before?"

Before Anders had a chance to answer, Mr. Churchill returned to the room, stepping briskly to stand alongside Sir Reginald's desk.

"If I might suggest, Mrs. Callahan, gentlemen, perhaps we can reconvene this meeting just down the street."

"Winston?" Reginald queried, perplexed.

"Congressman Hansen, if you and Mrs. Callahan will please follow me outside, I'll obtain transport for us. Ambassador Davis, perhaps you would be so kind as to accompany Sir Reginald." He then turned to face Reginald. "Ten Downing Street, Reggie," he said, winking.

"*I say*," Reginald responded stiffly.

"Yes, indeed," Churchill replied.

The two hansom cabs arrived in tandem at Ten Downing Street, the residence and working abode of the prime minister of the United Kingdom, and a footman stepped quickly to attend them. Katrina, Anders, and Winston Churchill exited the first vehicle, and Sir Reginald and Ambassador Davis followed quickly behind. Inside the doorway, they were met by a smartly tailored young man who took their coats and asked them to be seated in an antechamber off the main foyer. Presently, he returned.

"Mr. Churchill, the prime minister will see you and your party now, if you please."

They climbed the stairs to the upper level and were ushered into a large room furnished with several desks of various sizes arranged against the walls. A large, rectangular table occupied the center of the room, and a more formal, larger desk was positioned farther into the room on the other side of the conference table. From a doorway toward the rear, a man entered the room and walked toward Mr. Churchill.

"Good morning, Winnie. It's good of you to come," the man said.

"Good morning, Prime Minister. May I introduce you to your guests. Ambassador Davis you know of course, and Sir Reginald Hollister, the barrister of record in this case. This gentleman is Congressman Anders Hansen, and I have the honor to introduce his sister, Mrs. Thomas Callahan, of Salt Lake City, Utah. Mrs. Callahan, Congressman Hansen, may I introduce Prime Minister David Lloyd-George."

Lloyd-George smiled and shook hands all around and then invited everyone to take a seat.

"Now that the formalities are completed, how may I be of assistance?" he asked.

A moment of hesitancy ensued during which the prime minister looked from person to person. Finally, Sir Reginald spoke up.

"Prime Minister, since I am the barrister of record, perhaps I should brief you on the issue before us."

"You are referring, of course, to the incarceration of one Thomas Callahan for surreptitiously providing arms and ammunition to the Irish Republican Army, are you not?"

"Precisely, Prime Minister."

"To my understanding, Mr. Callahan pleaded guilty to the charges, isn't that so?"

"He did, Prime Minister," Sir Reginald replied.

"He pleaded guilty so he wouldn't *hang*," Katrina interjected.

Anders and Ambassador Davis shot her a quick look. Katrina momentarily locked eyes with Winston Churchill and caught from him the briefest hint of a smile.

Lloyd-George nodded toward Katrina. "A wise decision, no doubt, and under the advice of counsel I presume," he said, looking toward Sir Reginald.

"Yes, Prime Minister," Sir Reginald replied, "we discussed the charges at length with king's counsel and reached an understanding."

Again Katrina spoke. "An understanding reached under threat of death is no understanding at all, Mr. Lloyd-George."

"Are you contending, madam," he asked, "that your husband is *not* guilty and confessed only to preserve his life?"

"No, I knew of his activities," she said, slumping her shoulders and nodding her head. "My husband—reluctantly, mind you—told me of his intentions before he left Utah. He also told me that this was to be the last time he would assist the Irish Republican Army. He gave me his word."

"And *that* is the sole basis upon which you have come to seek his release?" Prime Minister Lloyd-George asked, a tone of incredulity in his voice.

"Mr. Lloyd-George," Katrina said, her posture now upright and her green eyes focused on the man seated before her, "as I informed Sir Reginald two days ago, this is a *political* issue, not a criminal one. You, sir, personally approved the release of many political prisoners in 1917, men who had been involved in the Easter uprising in 1916. *After* you had executed their leaders. Nonetheless, some of those men . . . and women . . . had killed British troops in their insurrection. Thomas Callahan has killed no one."

"No," Lloyd-George rebutted, " he merely provided the weapons by which *others* can kill."

"I remind you, sir, these people are Irish. You are killing them and withholding their freedom simply because you currently have the power to do so. You killed the American colonists, too, until they had finally had enough and drove you from their country. Today, tomorrow, perhaps next year, the Irish will do the same thing. You cannot stifle a country's freedom forever, Prime Minister, no matter how you oppress their people."

The American ambassador and Anders sat uneasily, squirming in their seats and slipping, if it were possible, even lower in their respective chairs.

"Ambassador Davis, is this the position of your government?" the prime minister asked.

"Sir, I . . ."

"This is *my* position, Prime Minister, and Woody . . ." Katrina caught herself and gave an embarrassed smile. "Excuse me, gentlemen, I mean President Wilson, has nothing to do with it. I ask no permission of my government to make my case. Since becoming an American citizen, I have learned that the freedoms granted in the British Magna Carta and those derived from the American Constitution are viewed quite differently. Americans are guaranteed their rights, Prime Minister. I'm sorry, Ambassador," she said, looking toward the silent diplomat, "if my comments offend or embarrass you, but I have come to England for a purpose, and I *will* achieve that purpose by one means or another. Should I fail—and to assure that I fail, gentlemen, is certainly within your power—I will have expended every effort and every dollar at my disposal to publicize this issue and, if necessary, to continue the work my husband foreswore."

Lloyd-George inserted a finger into his shirt collar, twisted his neck around beneath the stiff fabric, and glanced at the other gentlemen in the room. A silence ensued for several moments during which Katrina continued to stare at the prime minister.

"Madam," Lloyd-George said, "do I take it that you mean to continue funding *arms* to the rebels in Ireland?"

Katrina exhaled and turned her attention toward Winston Churchill, softening her voice. "Mr. Churchill, I have it on good authority that despite press reports over the past several years—the disasters of the last war included—you are an honorable man. I know my husband to also be an honorable man. Mr. Callahan has often said that the only difference between a traitor and a patriot . . . is who ultimately wins.

"Now, I have been informed that you are currently negotiating with Mr. Griffiths and Mr. Collins of the Irish Republican Army toward resolution of this crisis and that your negotiations are likely to bring about a measure of independence for Ireland."

Churchill blinked twice and looked toward Prime Minister Lloyd-George, then back. "Madam . . ."

"Be that as it may, Mr. Churchill," Katrina continued, "to answer the prime minister's question, I would be very reluctant to continue supplying armaments to the Irish. I would like to avoid bloodshed as much as you would, and as I have indicated, my husband assured me that his involvement was at an end. He did, in fact, for what it's worth, advise Mr. Collins to expend all efforts necessary to negotiate this issue to completion. I want my husband free, Mr. Churchill." She turned her attention back to the head of the British government.

"Prime Minister Lloyd-George, you have the power to free my husband, as you did those in 1917. It *will* happen sooner or later, given my understanding on the progress of your negotiations—negotiations that the press is as yet unaware of, I believe," she added. "I would prefer it to be sooner, of course, to preserve what health my husband may have left after spending six months in solitary confinement, most likely on the traditional British prison fare—bread and water."

Again, both Churchill and Lloyd-George allowed their facial expressions to betray their astonishment at Katrina's understanding of the situation.

"My husband is getting weaker by the day in your rat-infested prison. I will give you one week, gentlemen. If I have not received assurance by then that Thomas Callahan will be released, with your *personal* guarantee, Prime Minister, and yours as well, Mr. Churchill, I will divulge everything I know to representatives from Fleet Street as well as the American news affiliates here in London. And I will also place ads in every major newspaper throughout the continent—ads that will *not* be pleasant or complimentary to your government. Understand me clearly, gentlemen, my husband and I are conservatives, as is your government, Prime Minister—even if *Woody* is a Democrat," she smiled—"but I will have no qualms about funding your opposition in an attempt to bring down this government in favor of Labour. Given the present state of domestic labor unrest and international rebellion across the Irish sea, that should *not* be a difficult task."

Silence prevailed in the room as the six occupants absorbed what amounted to a threat on the sovereignty of the British government, placed before them by a small, extremely attractive, blonde-haired woman from Salt Lake City, Utah. In spite of the weight of the moment, slowly, and with growing volume, Winston Churchill began to laugh.

"Have I said something humorous, Mr. Churchill?" Katrina asked, obviously irritated.

"Quite the contrary, madam. I believe you to be quite serious. But your comments put me in mind of something I read many years ago. Over a century ago, the eminent French philosopher and parliamentarian, Alexis de Tocqueville, wrote about American ways and mores following his tour of the newly liberated colonies. When he returned to France, he addressed the Parliament. He said, 'Were I to be asked to what I would attribute the strength of the American people, I would ascribe it to their women.' I now understand his meaning, Mrs. Callahan, notwithstanding your Norwegian heritage."

Katrina smiled and rose from her chair, followed immediately by each of the men present in the room. She extended her hand to Prime Minister Lloyd-George.

"Thank you for meeting with us, Prime Minister. I trust I will hear from you presently. Mr. Churchill, it has been a great pleasure meeting you, sir. Good day to you both."

With abbreviated salutations around the room, Katrina, Anders, and Ambassador Davis departed the hastily convened meeting, leaving Prime Minister Lloyd-George, Secretary for the Colonies Winston Churchill, and Tom's barrister, Sir Reginald, alone in the office at Ten Downing Street.

Once on the street, Ambassador Davis excused himself and hastened to hail a passing hansom cab.

"Shall I get us a taxi?" Anders asked, smiling at his sister, and shaking his head.

Katrina looked up at the sky, took a deep breath, and slipped her hand into the crook of Anders' only arm. "I believe I'd rather walk," she responded. "It seems such a nice day."

"If you promise not to browbeat any more Englishmen, Klinka," he said, using his childhood nickname for his sister, "I'll come with you. You've threatened to bring down the prime minister of England, offered to fund arms for an Irish rebellion, and held in absolute silence several of the world's most powerful men. All in all, Klinka," he laughed as they started to walk, "it's been *some* day, and it's not even noon. By the way, I have two questions for you. How did you know about the British negotiations with the Irish?"

Katrina pursed her lips. "The morning after we arrived, a man I'd never seen approached me in the hotel lobby and handed me a note. It was from Michael Collins."

Anders raised his eyebrows. "And *Woody?*'"

"I made it up," she said. "The prime minister wouldn't know that I've never met President Woodrow Wilson."

"Klinka, I've often thought of the strength of will you must have possessed to have gotten through your ordeal in the Mexican jungle with Seby so long ago, but until today, dear sister, I had no idea how strong you really are."

"I hope I'm strong enough, Anders," Katrina said. "Actually, I'm very much afraid."

3

JULY, 1920
PORTLAOISE PRISON, IRELAND

The grating of the rusty steel bolt roused Tom from his stupor as he lay on the floor in his cell, staring at the stone ceiling. Other than to make the occasional exchange of his slop bucket for a new receptacle, and to distribute the twice-daily meager ration of bread and water through a small sliding grate, it had been three weeks since anyone had come to his cell door. The bright light that streamed in blinded him, and he shielded his eyes, able only to see the silhouettes of the two men who stood in the doorway.

"On yer feet, Yank," one of the men said, grabbing his arm and jerking him upright. "It's time we get ya cleaned up."

"Where . . . where am I going?" Tom stammered as they dragged him out of his cell and down a dark, damp hallway.

"Not to worry, Thomas, me lad. You'll be told right enough."

The bath facilities, which Tom had visited only once previously during his five months in solitary confinement, consisted of a shallow recess in the rock flooring where water could accumulate. A cast iron spigot dripped cold water into the stone basin, and a rough equestrian curry brush floated in the fetid water. Two additional guards were present when Tom arrived, and they stripped him of his ragged, dirty clothes and made him sit in the cold water. A bar of lye soap was tossed in along with the brush.

"Clean it up, Yank. Time to look presentable if yer gonna meet the constable."

After stepping out of the putrid pool, he was handed the clothes he had been wearing when he had been arrested. Dressed and fed the first proper meal he'd had in months, he was shackled, hand and foot, as he had been when he had arrived at Portlaoise Prison, and then he was loaded into the back of a enclosed lorry. From the sounds he could discern and the shouting of the driver at the prison gate, he assumed the truck was leaving the prison grounds. The meal of old, tough beef, hard corn, and boiled potatoes had hurt his teeth, and as he sat alone in the back of the truck, he could taste blood in his mouth. He had known for weeks that several of his teeth were loose and that his gums were swollen and inflamed.

The truck rumbled through the countryside for the next several hours, stopping only once to allow Tom to step off the road and relieve himself. In the late afternoon, the external sounds and the smell of salt air told Tom that the truck had reached a coastal location. Given the time of their trip, he knew it had to be either Cork or Limerick. When they stopped again, the two guards opened the rear of the truck, and Tom was assisted to step down. He confirmed that he was near the ocean and in fact, on a commercial shipping dock. It looked familiar, and as he was being escorted toward an open, wooden warehouse building, he saw a one stack, medium-sized ocean liner moored to the pier. Suddenly it came to him. It had been twenty-five years, but he now stood on the same dock in Queenstown, near Cork, where, pursued by the law, he had boarded the *Antioch* in 1895 and fled from Ireland.

As they approached the building, Tom and his guards were met by two men wearing suits, one of whom wore a bowler and both of whom Tom instantly took for plain-clothes policemen. Without speaking, one of them motioned to the taller of the two prison guards, and the guard knelt and unlocked Tom's ankle shackles, then removed the irons from his wrists.

"Mr. Callahan, is it?" the other well-dressed man said.

"Aye," Tom replied.

"Good. That will be all, gentlemen," he said to the warders from the prison.

"If you'll just sign this document, Inspector," the tall guard said.

The man in the bowler quickly scribbled his name on a piece of paper, and the two guards departed. Tom watched them climb into the truck and leave.

"Not sorry to be rid of *them,* are you?" the man asked, inclining his head toward the departing guards.

Tom glanced at the back of the truck as it pulled away and then looked back at the inspector for a moment before answering.

"We had an understanding of sorts. They told me what to do, and I did it."

"I see," the man said, smiling and nodding his under-standing. "I'm Chief Inspector Mullins, and this is my asso-ciate, Inspector Harrigan. We're from Special Branch, Irish Constabulary. And will you confirm that you are Thomas Matthew Callahan of Salt Lake City, in America?"

Tom nodded to confirm his identity. "Am I being transferred?"

"You might say that, Mr. Callahan. In three hours you'll be on that ship," he said, nodding toward the end of the pier.

"I don't understand. Am I being transferred to England?"

"You're being released, Mr. Callahan. There's no subterfuge involved. When that ship leaves the dock, you'll be a free man again, on the understanding that you are not to return to the British Isles."

Tom stared at the man, trying to comprehend his meaning.

"Free?"

Again, Constable Mullins nodded. "Indeed, Mr. Callahan. There is someone who would like to speak with you before you board. Oh, and we've placed your luggage— the luggage you had in your hotel when you were arrested— in your cabin accommodations. If you would kindly step this way."

Walking unsteadily, Tom accompanied the two policemen to the warehouse. At the entrance, the two constables stopped, motioning for Tom to continue inside. As he stepped through the doorway, Tom spotted another man across the open space, slowly walking toward him. There was something familiar about the man, but in the gloom of the warehouse, it took Tom several moments to make out who it was.

"Michael?"

Michael Collins, one of several leaders of the Irish Republican Army, the most recent incarnation of the Irish Brotherhood and the '67 Feinian uprising and the chief negotiator in the Irish-British peace talks, stepped close to Tom.

"And how goes prison life, Tom?" the man said, smiling

and taking Tom by the shoulders. "A few pounds gone, I'd say."

"More likely two stone," Tom replied, reverting to the Irish measurement where a stone equals fourteen pounds.

"Tom, I'm sure it wasn't a pleasant ten months, including the time you spent in Mountjoy Prison in Dublin before the trial, but at least it's not fifteen years. It's good to see you, lad."

"And you, Michael. What happened? Did Reggie find a sympathetic ear?"

"It's a long story, but I've left a few letters and documents that will explain things in your cabin aboard the *Annabelle*. She's a good ship, with an understanding captain, if you know what I mean, but she's not what you're used to traveling on," he smiled. "But I suppose right now a dory with two good oars would suit your purposes."

"Aye," Tom laughed, instantly reaching up to hold his jaw as the pain shot through his mouth, "anything to put some distance between me and the bloody Brits. Truth be known, Michael, it was the bloody Irish warders that gave me the worst of it."

"There'll come a reckoning, you can count on it. Are you hurt?" Michael asked.

"Nothing that a few days of soup, soft porridge, and mushy, boiled vegetables won't cure."

Collins nodded knowingly. "Ah, the famous British 'brick-bread and water' diet, I see. Many an Irish lad has lost his teeth and a bit of flab due to that one."

"Did you bring this about?" Tom asked.

"I'd like to claim credit, but all I did was share some inside political information with your wife. As I understand it, your missus went toe-to-toe with Lloyd-George and bested the old sod. She gave Churchill a run for his shilling, too," he smiled.

"You're serious?"

"And here we've been dealing with you for all these years when it's your wife, lad, who's got the stomach for the battle."

Tom smiled and nodded. "Quite a woman, my Katie. Before I leave, there is one thing I've needed to talk to you about, Michael. I've thought a lot about it in the prison."

"You'll not be returning," Collins said, a knowing look on his face.

"Aye, that's the gist of it, but I wanted you to know that the last shipment was to have been my last, anyway, even before the Brits decided it for me."

"I thought as much, Tom. I understand."

"I'd like to see you settle it across the table, Michael. I just feel I can't support the armed rebellion the way I once did. I'm sorry about that."

"Dawn doth break on yonder horizon, Tom. We may be at an end to it, anyway."

"How long now since Cromwell came across the Irish Sea? Three hundred years? Dawn's been a long time coming, Michael. I hope you understand my decision. It has nothing to do with my imprisonment."

"I understand," he said, clamping his arm around his Irish-American visitor. "You've come face-to-face with your epiphany, have you?"

Come face to face with an epiphany? Indeed he had! The long months spent in solitary confinement had given him ample time to think. In the darkness of his cell, he had often reflected on the events of his life, recalling his days as a wild Irish youth, the long months he had spent prospecting for gold in Alaska, and the rescue of Katrina from Mexico.

Katrina. She had occupied his thoughts more than anything else. Visualizing her face and remembering the softness of her body, he had missed her so much that he had often wept.

He had also thought of his children—PJ living in far-off New Zealand, Tess in New York following her dream of being an actress, and Tommy who was still in the Marine Corps. He was grateful that he and Tommy had patched up their differences, and it had provided him much comfort while in prison to remember the day his grown son had come into his arms at Annapolis, and they had been reconciled at last.

To pass the time in prison, he had often played a game in his mind—recalling events and conversations from the past. It had been pleasant for him to remember Sister Mary Theophane, the years of her gentle friendship and guidance, and the bittersweet farewell he had said to her at her grave site.

He had given ample thought, also, to his financial support of the Irish rebellion. The Irish "cause" was just; of that, Tom had no doubt. And following his visit to free his eldest son, PJ, from the British jail after the 1916 Easter Rebellion, it had seemed a reasonable thing to Tom to furnish arms to the rebels. It was clear to him that his countrymen were correct—fighting their way to freedom had been their only option. The Americans had done the same thing, hadn't they, and the British were now close allies of the Americans.

But Michael Collins saw it one way, and Tom's priest, Father Scanlan, as Irish as any of them, had seen it another. And they were both Catholic. They couldn't *both* be right, could they? The one thing he couldn't escape was the knowledge that the arms and munitions had been the cause of bloodshed and destruction. He sometimes awoke from horrifying dreams of women and children weeping over the mutilated bodies of their husbands and fathers.

Waking from those dreams in the dark confines of his cell, his thoughts had often gone to religion. Prayer had frequently been his only solace, but he wondered exactly to whom he should pray. Was it his Catholic God or the God of Katrina's Mormonism? That conflict had plagued him from the moment he had met Katrina and become aware of her faith in the Book of Mormon.

Father Scanlan had told Tom on more than one occasion that in order to receive direction from God, one needed to clear the way—to open the door. Father Scanlan had said that by doing so, God could reach in and touch your heart.

On board the ship, while leaving New Zealand, Katrina had put it another way. Never in their twenty years of marriage had she been so insistent. She had told him boldly that she was tired of waiting and that she was determined to have a temple marriage—either to Tom or to someone else. It was time, she had said, that Tom discover the truth of his relationship with God.

"Epiphany, you say?" Tom said to Michael Collins. "Perhaps so. It's rather personal, though."

Collins nodded. "I've harbored a few ghosts of my own over our past activities," he said. "You've been a good soldier in your own way, Tom, and we've been grateful for your help. But I guess I'm to the point where if we can settle this thing across the bargaining table and can end the bloodshed, I'm ready. I fear, however, that ending our struggle with the British will only lead to further conflict at home. Not all are unified, even within our own ranks[5]."

"As I said, Michael, Godspeed in your negotiations, here and in London," Tom replied.

"And, Tom. I'm truly sorry about Seamus. He was a good lad, he was."

Tom lowered his eyes and was silent for a moment.

"And a good brother, too, Michael. Thank you."

Once on board the *Annabelle*, Tom was shown directly to his cabin by the first officer. The man presented the Captain's apologies and explained that Captain Rugers had gone ashore to take care of some last-minute business before embarking. Alone in his cabin, Tom found his luggage and immediately disrobed, filled the small basin with water, and washed his body, this time using a soft cotton washcloth and considerably milder soap than the lye bar the guards had provided. He put on clean underwear and pulled back the bedding on the single bunk. Slipping between the sheets, he didn't even pause to read the note from Collins he found on the bedstead. For the first time in nearly a year, Tom Callahan felt the comfort of a mattress and pillow, but his joy was short-lived. Within moments he had fallen asleep.

A persistent knock on his door eventually awakened Tom. He emerged from a dream and sat upright in the bunk, momentarily confused by his surroundings. The door slowly opened, and a heavyset man with a thick, dark beard stuck his head through the doorway, then stepped inside and closed the door behind him.

"Mr. Callahan, it's good to see you awake," he said in a thick, Germanic accent. "Would you care for some food?"

Tom rubbed his face and smoothed his hair, gathering his thoughts and quickly recollecting where he was.

"Yes, that would be fine. Something . . . uh, soft, if you

will," he said, running his tongue against the back of his front teeth. "Will we be departing soon?"

"We're underway, Mr. Callahan," the man grinned. "In fact, we've been at sea for almost thirty-six hours. I'm Captain Rugers. Hans Rugers," he said, stepping closer to the bed and offering his hand. "I'm pleased to have you on board."

Tom accepted his hand and shook it briefly. "I take it this is not usually a convict vessel."

Rugers laughed. "We consider you a celebrity, Mr. Callahan. It's my honor to have you on board the *Annabelle*."

"Thirty-six hours you say? Have I been asleep all that time?"

"You have. We've looked in on you, but the doctor thought it best to let you sleep. If you'd like, we have a full bath facility just down the passageway. After you've bathed, I'll have a hot meal for you, either in your cabin, or you can join me in the officers' mess."

"That sounds fine, Captain. I'll join you in the mess, if that's appropriate."

"Not to worry, Mr. Callahan. My officers—two Dutchmen like myself, one Irishman, and an English doctor—know of your recent circumstances and they are quite supportive. Please, there's no need to be embarrassed. Also, the ship's doctor would like to have a look at you, if that meets with your approval."

"Thank you, Captain. I'll take it all—bath, meal, and the doctor," Tom smiled. "It's still hard to believe I'm free."

"I understand," the seaman nodded. "If you have a robe, I'll show you to the bath facility. It's just a couple of cabins down and there's plenty of good, hot water. We have no other passengers this trip. You're actually quite alone in this corridor."

"Where are we bound, Captain?"

"Philadelphia is our first port of call, and then to New York, if you desire to remain aboard. I believe Mr. Collins wired your wife to expect you in Philadelphia. We should be there in about six more days."

"Time for a couple of dozen baths and to get used to solid food, right?" Tom laughed.

"We'll do our best, Mr. Callahan. Again, sir, it's an honor to have you with us."

Tom bathed, a long, luxurious soak, to which he continued to add gallons of hot water. Then he put on fresh clothes from his original luggage and made his way to the officers' mess. Four ship's officers, including Doctor Huddleston, were present, in addition to Captain Rugers. The men all stood when Tom entered the mess, and brief introductions were made all around. The cook had been instructed by the ship's doctor what to prepare, and Tom's meal consisted of a broth, laced with small pieces of boiled chicken meat that Tom was able to savor and slowly chew. He also peeled and ate an orange. The juice stung his gums, but he enjoyed the exquisite sweetness of the fruit—the first he had eaten in many months. The other officers ate silently, and Tom sensed a slight tenseness in the room. When the steward returned to take Tom's bowl, the Filipino man smiled at Tom.

"Me get some-ting more for you? Some-ting you likee?" the steward asked.

Tom looked around the room briefly and smiled at the small, brown-faced man.

"Would you have any hard, moldy bread and a tin of dirty water?"

"Scusee?" the steward asked, bewildered.

The remark cleared the tension in the air, and the men in the wardroom broke into laughter.

"That will be all, Fernando," the Captain said, dismissing the steward.

"I'm sorry," Tom said, "but my changed circumstances, unexpected as they were . . ."

"I understand, sir," Captain Rugers said. "Anything we can do to make your trip more pleasant, please let us know. Now, Doctor Huddleston, I think perhaps a quick once-over would be in order."

"Indeed," Huddleston said, standing. "How about coming down to the infirmary, Mr. Callahan? I'd like to have a look at you if you don't mind."

"Doctor, you'll find skin and bones. Not much more, I'm afraid."

"Sounds to me as if you've retained a bit of *pluck*, as they say."

"That's the Irish in me, Doctor. I'm told it dies hard."

Later that evening, after sharing a few private moments with Captain Rugers, Tom retired to his cabin, content to return to the solitude he had come to accept. Doctor Huddleston had found nothing to surprise either of them. Tom's weight, normally about 190 pounds, had dropped to just below 160, a loss of nearly two and a half stone. His gums and teeth had suffered considerably, but Huddleston informed Tom that eating fruits and vegetables would likely eventually restore him to normal health, although he thought a visit to a dentist would be in order immediately after their arrival in Philadelphia.

Though just forty-five years of age, Tom's hair had

thinned, and his ashen pallor was evidence of deprivation of natural light. His chronic dysentery, Doctor Huddleston said, would likely right itself with a solid and varied diet, as soon as he was able to chew and properly digest food. He warned Tom that some sickness following meals would be normal but should abate within two weeks. Tom's self-imposed prison regimen of physical exercise, extremely limited as a result of his meager food supply and lowered energy levels, had preserved some muscle tone, and the doctor was pleased to see that his heart, lungs, and circulatory system, as far as his on board instruments could detect, were operating normally.

On the bedside, Tom discovered the sealed brown envelope that Michael Collins had informed him was waiting. He slit the envelope and discovered a folded sheet of paper and another envelope inside. The second envelope was addressed in Katrina's familiar hand, simply marked *Thomas*. Saving Katrina's letter for last, Tom unfolded and read Collins's brief note.

> Tom,
> As you journey home, the thought may occur that your support of our cause cost you more than you had bargained for. As consolation, I can only offer my sincere appreciation for your efforts, but I know you are aware that many before you have paid an even higher price. Perhaps, as it is rumored, we are close to resolving Ireland's long struggle. The warrior in me cries out for victory, yet the statesman, a role forced upon me, recognizes the futility of needless

bloodshed and seeks to grasp at the
solution—any solution that allows us all to
return to our loved ones, free of the need to
run, hide, and fear. You now have that
chance, Tom, and I envy you the prospect.
   Godspeed on your journey back to your
loved ones. You have earned your place
among us—by birth and even more by your
generous contributions. When the final
victory—across the table or on the battlefield—is achieved, your name will be
among those honored—legion they are—who
brought Ireland to its rightful place.
   God bless you and yours.
                              As always,
                              Michael

The second envelope contained a single buff-colored
sheet of paper, crested with the Savoy Hotel, London,
England, legend. Tom paused to admire the beauty of
Katrina's script and her practiced hand. With tears blurring
his vision, he read:

My Darling Thomas,
   I do not know how long it will take for
this note to reach you, or if indeed it ever
shall, my beloved. An associate of Mr.
Collins has offered to see this delivered
with all possible haste. I have received
word that it is the intention of the British

government—Mr. Lloyd-George being
in agreement—to release you from your
travail as soon as it is politically
acceptable—thirty days at the most, I am
informed. Mr. Churchill has given his
word on this, Thomas, and I sense that he
is a man of honor.

Come to me, my darling. Let not this
somber memory serve to shake the faith I
know resides in your heart. I know you
have sought our Lord since New
Zealand, and I have taken heart that He
will watch over you and protect you. You
are my life, my darling, and I will be your
light. Until you hold me in your arms, all
my love,

Katrina

Tom spent most of the voyage alone in his cabin or, when the weather was fair, walking on deck. His thoughts ran from Katrina facing down the leaders of the British Empire, as Michael Collins had explained it, to his own epiphany—also described by Collins. He felt as if his life— before his arrest—had been neatly progressing toward a finalization of the religious conflict between himself and Katrina, and he had meant his trip to Ireland to be the final clearance, a washing away of all the things that stood between him and an understanding with God.

The mental and physical shock of being thrown into prison had robbed him for a time of his spiritual focus.

Deprived of his clothing, his freedom, and his dignity, he had gone into a survival mode, striving simply to get through each day and keep his sanity. His first prison infraction, simply not moving as quickly as one of the guards had required, occurred just three days after being placed into the general prison population. It had resulted in his being sent to the "hole," as the prisoners called the solitary confinement dungeon. Time spent in the hole was considered a forfeiture—time not counted against his fifteen-year sentence. Left there for the entire time of his confinement at Portlaoise, Tom still had a fifteen-year sentence on the books when he was finally released. In the hole, he'd realized that his warders could easily have converted his fifteen-year sentence to life in prison simply by drumming up charges against him and keeping him in the hole. Now, here he was, a free man again, albeit one without clear direction or the impetus to pick up where he had left off, spiritually.

God had not deserted him—solitary confinement had convinced him of that. For endless days, he had felt wrapped in a blanket of "cotton wool," as Katrina used to say about the feeling she experienced when Heavenly Father protected her from strong, painful emotions. Still, the fear instilled in him, not so much by the brutality of the guards, but by the thought of an interminable sentence, had taken a mental as well as a physical toll. His confidence, once his greatest asset, or so he thought, was, if not broken, at least diminished by his experience. Lying for days and weeks on end on a cold, concrete floor, hungry, surrounded by the odor of human excrement, and faced with the continual task of fending off the rats and mice that were bold enough to gnaw at his toes or ears while he fitfully slept, was enough to make him wonder how he had come to be so forsaken.

But as Tom reflected on his experience during the return

voyage, the one certainty that overpowered him was the inner knowledge that in spite of all that had occurred, he had *not* been forsaken—either by God or by his family and friends. Regardless the lack of communication, somehow he knew in his heart that his loved ones continued to care and that God had been aware of his plight.

Twenty-four hours before landfall, Captain Rugers told Tom of their anticipated arrival, and Tom began to consider a world beyond his own feelings. How would Katrina respond to him? The entire debacle was of his own making. She had begged him not to get involved in the purchase and shipment of arms, and finally, aware of his determination to proceed, she had told him of her love and of her fear that he would come to harm. Still he had gone—and she had been right.

Now, on the morrow, he would see her again and would hold her in his arms. How could he make it right to her? How could he erase the agony, the loneliness, and the fear she must have felt as she had contemplated fifteen years with her husband in a foreign jail? And how could he tell her of the closeness he had developed with God—a closeness that she had always known in her own life and which she had prayed endlessly would also come to her husband. And finally, how could he explain to her that the God of his sorrows was neither Mormon nor Catholic. He was just God, and He loved everyone equally, even the prison guards, Tom had come to understand.

As the *Annabelle* slowly made her way up the Delaware River, passing the small communities on both sides of the river, Tom stood at the port railing, watching for the first signs of Philadelphia. The harbor tugs came out to meet the ship, and the *Annabelle* was pushed and pulled toward the great pier, slipping into place alongside several other vessels, each flying a flag of its nation of registry. The notion of multiple countries, with diverse beliefs, living together in a single world, suddenly struck Tom as symbolic of mankind. A world where men of all nations worshipped God in one form or another. The name by which He was known was different, the trappings of worship varied, and mankind's understanding of what God required of them was diverse— many of the concepts doubtless self-imposed. But all men sailed on the same sea, and were embraced by the same arms, the arms of a loving God.

Tom descended the gangplank to the dock, where long-shoremen were beginning the process of unloading and preparing to reload the cargo vessel. And suddenly, there was Katrina, standing alone on the dock, alongside the *Annabelle*. Then she was in his arms. The two of them stood for long moments, holding each other without speaking. Then Tom took Katrina's shoulders, stood her at arms' length, and gazed into the face he had tried so hard to recall while in prison, during the endless hours when day and night combined and he was unable to discern one from the other. While on the ship, he had imagined this moment, but not the emotion that now overcame him. It struck him that her eyes, brimming with tears, were startlingly green—more than he had remembered. Then, himself crying, he again took her in his arms, clutching her fiercely.

After a time they separated, and wiping at his cheeks with the back of his hand, Tom looked beyond Katrina toward the terminal building and surrounding pier, seeking other family or friends. Katrina smiled, took his face in her hands, and gently pulled him close to her.

He could smell the scent of her breath as she said softly, "There's only me—only me, my darling."

Tom drew her close again. "Only you, Katie," he said. "I love only you." Then he pressed his lips against hers.

4

"Do you have to go *alone*, Thomas? You always insisted the boys never go up into the mountains alone. What if you're injured or thrown from your horse?"

"Katie, how I do love you," he said, taking her in his arms. "I'll be gone three days, four at the most. And I promise to let the sheriff's office know where I intend to be. There's also old Hank's cabin up there. I'll check in with him if it'll make you feel any better."

"I don't feel good about *any* of it," she argued.

"Katie, I just need a few days to be alone. Please don't be hurt or angry."

"*Alone!* Didn't you have enough *alone* in Ireland?"

Tom bowed his head and nodded. "I did, Katie. This is different."

When Katrina had met Tom in Philadelphia, she had driven him straight to a bungalow that she had rented on the New Jersey shore. Located in a remote place, on a sandy bluff overlooking the sea, the cottage proved a perfect place for Tom to regain his strength. Katrina had stocked the wooden house with food and other provisions and had arranged for a weekly delivery of additional supplies.

They spent several restful weeks there, enjoying each other and taking long walks on the beach and in the nearby rural countryside. They had many long conversations—deep talks such as they had seldom shared, which for Katrina were immensely satisfying. They had also taken advantage of the time alone to renew their physical relationship, and Tom marveled at his wife's passionate response to their long separation.

But, after six weeks, Tom admitted to feeling restless. He told Katrina that he was anxious to get home and back to work and proposed packing up and taking the train to Utah.

The time they had spent together was marred only by a vague feeling of discontent on Tom's part. It was not something he chose to or could have talked about with Katrina. But the fact was that his misgivings over the arms shipments, the trauma of being arrested, and the long period of confinement had exposed in him some emotional vulnerability he had never supposed existed. At nearly forty-six years of age, his body hadn't recovered as quickly or as completely as he had hoped. The truth was he no longer felt invincible, and that bothered him more than he could have said.

Upon his return to Salt Lake, Tom had immediately immersed himself in the affairs of the bank, assisting young Mark Thurston in the daily routine and renewing his many contacts in the city's business community. During the months they had been home, he had been gone a great deal, and, now, here he was again, announcing his intention to go off into the mountains alone. Katrina didn't seem to understand his motivation, and Tom could see that she was annoyed.

49

"You've already resolved most of the things that were bothering you," she said. "You've finally made peace with Tommy, and that business with the Irish rebels is over. I know that you've been distraught over Michael Collins' unwarranted death[6], but what more are you after?"

"Just trust me on this, Katie. It's the final piece of my, well, my *search*, for lack of a better word. And I need to be alone for awhile. Unless you'd like to come," he grinned, trying to ease her concern.

"Twenty miles into the canyons on horseback? No thank you, Mr. Callahan," she rebutted.

"Well, then, since no one else'll have me," he replied, "except the horses, I'd best be on my way out to Seby's. I'll stay at his place tonight and get an early start tomorrow. I promise to telephone you this evening."

Katrina stood her ground. "If you *must*, Thomas, but remember, I said I was against it."

Once again he took her in his arms and held her tight. "I'd not be lookin' forward to being across the bargaining table from you, Katie m' darlin'. You're tougher than any of the union agitators or bankers I have to deal with."

Giving her one final squeeze, Tom gathered up the parcel of sandwiches and fruit she had prepared and started for the door.

"Everything ready, William?" he said to the butler. After nearly eighteen years in their employ, their first and only houseman, Henry, had retired two years previously, and Tom had retained the services of a proper English manservant, recruited on one of his trips to Ireland.

"Indeed, sir. The vehicle has a full tank of petrol, I've checked under the bonnet, and your luggage and supplies have been deposited in the boot, sir."

"Very good, William. Thank you," he said, exiting the

front door and walking down the porch steps toward the circular driveway. Standing at the car door, he paused and looked back to the front door where Katrina stood watching. He smiled and blew her a kiss, but she stood with her arms folded and a determined set to her face. He placed one foot on the running board to enter the car but hesitated for a moment. Then, in one quick motion, he tossed the parcel of sandwiches onto the front seat and came around the car, bounding up the steps to stand in front of Katrina again.

"I'm going on this campout by myself, Katie, but I'm *not* going alone," he said, taking her face in his hands and lightly kissing her lips.

Her face assumed a puzzled look.

"It's Himself who'll be with me this time," he said softly. "Not *everything* is resolved. It's our God, Katie—your God *and* my God—I'll be talkin' to. You must trust me . . . and Him. I'll be in good company," he smiled, pushed back a wisp of hair from her forehead, and kissed her again on the cheek. Then he turned and quickly descended the steps, got into the car, and drove out the circular driveway, leaving Katrina standing on the front steps of *Valhalla*, the home he had built for her on South Temple Street right after their marriage, some twenty years earlier.

Early the following morning, Tom was at the mouth of Little Cottonwood Canyon, where Sebastian Cardenas Stromberg helped him unload two horses from Seby's horse trailer. Seby was the owner of the Hidden Valley Ranch, and after Tom's overnight stay at the ranch, Seby had driven his friend and banker to the graveled road that led into the mountains. After loading the pack animal and saddling his horse, Tom thanked Seby for his assistance, swung into the saddle, and gathered up the pack horse rein.

"You say you are going up to Albion Basin and over Catherine Pass, is that correct, *Señor* Tom?" Seby queried.

Tom nodded and looked up at the granite-walled canyon he was to enter. "I'll camp somewhere between Lake Catherine and Lake Martha until Friday morning, when I plan to come out. I should make it back here by four or five o'clock."

"I'll be waiting," the young Mexican smiled. "And if you don't make it, I'll be in to get you Saturday morning," he laughed.

Tom smiled. "Katrina's been talking to you, has she?"

"*Sì*, Tom," Seby laughed in return, "but in a loving way."

Tom reined his horse's head in the direction of the graveled road, nudged him forward two or three steps, and then pulled up. He turned in the saddle, looking back toward Seby, who remained by the truck and horse trailer.

"May I ask you a personal question, Seby?"

Seby took several steps toward Tom and the horses. Standing alongside and looking up at Tom, he said, "Of course, Tom, anything."

Tom looked at the granite cliffs and towering mountains above them, trying to find the right words to broach the question.

"Seby, I met your grandfather over twenty years ago, as you know. And in my business dealings these past years, I've come to learn something about the strong Mexican traditions—from you," he said, looking down at the young man, "and from the Mexicans who work in our mining operation. Those traditions, including *Catholic* traditions, are strongly honored and are not easily broken. Now this is very personal, Seby, and if you don't wish to answer, I'll understand."

Tom paused again, waiting for Seby to confirm. The young man just nodded and waited.

"Since you were raised Catholic, as I was, can you tell me in just a few words how you came to join the Mormon Church? I mean," Tom added, almost as though he were embarrassed to be asking the question, "you've only been here in Salt Lake about three years."

"In a few words, *Señor?*"

"If you can."

Seby nodded again and looked away for a moment. Several moments passed as both men stood silently, Seby on the ground and Tom in the saddle. The only sound was the creaking of the leather saddle and the horse blowing as he stamped his hooves, anxious to begin the trek.

Finally, Seby spoke. "Three words, *Señor. It is true.*"

Tom contemplated Seby's words for several moments and then nodded.

"That's what Robert always used to say."

"*Uno momento, Señor,*" Seby said, turning and walking quickly toward the truck. He reached in the passenger window, opened the glove box, and retrieved a well-worn book. Returning to the horses, he said, "You told me when you returned from New Zealand that you had read Elder Talmage's book, *Jesus the Christ.* But Grandfather Stromberg, before he died last year, gave me this battered copy of the Book of Mormon. He marked several passages for me but told me that the truth of all that God has told us can be found by following the directions in Moroni, chapter ten, verses four and five. It's well marked, *Señor,*" he laughed, reaching to tuck the book into Tom's saddlebag.

"President Stromberg taught you the truth of the gospel as he saw it, didn't he, Seby?" Tom asked.

Seby reached up and placed his hand over Tom's hands,

which were holding the reins and resting on the saddle horn.

"No, *Señor*," he said, shaking his head. "He told me *where* and *how* to find the truth for myself. You read those scriptures and you'll find out what I mean."

"Thank you, Seby," Tom said, smiling at the younger man. "Friday afternoon," he repeated, spurring his horse forward.

Seby stepped back and allowed the two horses to pass. "*Vaya con Díos, Señor*," he called out, slapping the pack mare on the rump as she walked by. Tom raised his hand in a silent wave and continued up the trail.

Nearly eight hours later, after a long ride broken by two stops to allow his horses to rest, Tom reached his intended campsite. He dismounted in a stand of pines next to one of the small lakes, and after unsaddling his horse and taking the pack off the mare, he tethered the tired animals to graze. As darkness began to gather, he set up his tent, prepared a quick meal, and sat by the fire to eat. After eating, he set his tin plate aside and leaned back against a log next to his crackling fire. Memories of previous camping and fishing trips taken with his sons flooded his mind, and he began to think of them as they were now—as grown men.

PJ, who had remained in New Zealand after his mission, was doing well as the proud owner of Shenandoah Station, a large sheep and cattle ranch located on the Canterbury Plains, east of Christchurch, on the South Island. Tommy, after experiencing combat with the 6th Marines in France, was in his third year as a midshipman at the United States Naval Academy. And Teresa, for reasons Tom had never been able to fathom, was living in New York, pursuing an acting career.

As Tom sat enjoying the warmth and glow of the

campfire, the moon rose slowly above the mountain ridge to the east. Beyond the pop and hiss of the burning wood, it was deathly silent in the forest surrounding the lake. Tom stared at the flames, and ghostly memories of young PJ and Tommy—and even Benjamin, the youngest, drowned these past nine years—danced in his head. In what seemed now to be only an instant, his family had grown, and as Sister Mary Theophane had so often said to the parents of young-sters she'd grown to care for, "They've gone off into the world, and we can only hope that they carry God in their hearts."

Tom wondered, as he had so often, which God—whose God—did they carry? Was it Tom's stern and demanding Catholic God, or Katrina's more personal, almost human Mormon God—or even the God of hellfire and damnation that the Reverend Billy Sunday and other itinerant preach-ers were describing in their revivalist tent meetings across America?

Tom reached into his bedroll and took out a book, simi-lar to the one Seby had put into his saddlebag. At Seby's considerate gesture, Tom had refrained from telling him that he was already carrying a Book of Mormon. Opening the cover, Tom angled the book to reflect the firelight and read the inscription.

> October 5, 1900—For Thomas, on your twenty-fifth birthday—to replace the Book of Mormon I gave you on the Antioch, and which the robbers caused you to lose in Kansas City.
> All my love,
> Katrina

Flipping through the worn and dog-eared pages, he found the Book of Moroni toward the back of the volume and turned to chapter ten. Carefully marked by Katrina in red pencil, the verses stood out on the page, and Tom read them slowly and then again, as he had many times over the years.

And when ye shall receive these things, I would exhort you that ye would ask God, the Eternal Father, in the name of Christ, if these things are not true; and if ye shall ask with a sincere heart, with real intent, having faith in Christ, he will manifest the truth of it unto you, by the power of the Holy Ghost.

And by the power of the Holy Ghost ye may know the truth of all things.

Turning away from the moonrise, Tom looked up through the pines into the darkness of the night. The sky was an inky black, and the stars shone brilliantly. He thought of how often, on their fishing trips, the boys had started counting the stars, asking Tom myriad questions about their origin, how far away they were, and if people lived among the heavens.

He looked down at the scripture again . . . *with real intent.* Had he *ever* asked with real intent? He read further: *Christ . . . will manifest the truth . . .* And wasn't that what Seby and Robert had said? *"It is true."*

Tom placed the book on the log beside him and stood. Extending his arms above his head and then bending, he touched the ground, stretching the muscles in his back. He walked a few steps toward the lake where he stood with his back to the fire. The light of the dancing flames reflected off the nearby trees, creating everchanging odd shapes and shadows. He thought of the twenty years he had lived among the Mormons, both in and out of his household. Through his dealings at the bank, Tom had come in contact with Mormons of every walk of life—church and community leaders and common folks alike. He'd met a few Mormons who were not a credit to their religion, including some business associates who talked a good story, professing belief in the Mormon standards, but whose actions proved far removed from the principles of the gospel as Katrina had explained them to him. *Agency,* Katrina had said time and again. But the one in-depth conversation they'd had about a specific episode had left him confused as to how God could trust such men.

"It doesn't correlate, Katie. He's a bishop, and I'm told a good one, but I've watched him with his employees. It's like he's two different men. He treats them terribly and actually cheats them out of wages."

"He has his agency to fail at his calling, Thomas," she'd said. "A call to be an ecclesiastical leader doesn't guarantee a man success at the calling."

"Well then, why is he called?"

Katrina had just smiled and shaken her head. "Agency. The Lord gave him a chance to progress and he chose not to," she'd replied.

But in the main, Tom had to admit that far and away most of the Mormons he knew were good people—devout and genuine.

He thought too, of D.O., whom he had admired since the day they had met, and of Robert Thurston and his family. Besides serving as a bishop and stake president, Robert had willingly left his place at the bank and his friends and family to serve a mission. Tom thought also of James E. Talmage. While reading *Jesus the Christ,* Tom had constantly marveled at the intelligence of the man. If someone of his ability and understanding could believe the miracles and visions that were at the root of Mormonism, could the religion be founded on a lie?

He thought also of Seby, who seemed to have so easily accepted Mormonism, in spite of his Catholic upbringing. And what of Katrina? No one he had ever met, including Sister Mary Theophane, believed more strongly or had more faith than his wife. It wasn't Katrina's style to preach, but her belief in the origins of her religion and her conviction regarding the importance of the temple were unshakable. She had declared to Tom her willingness to sacrifice even their marriage for her beliefs. Could people such as these be deceived? And all of them—*all of them*—had told him the same thing: Mormonism is true!

"God in heaven," Tom began softly, "I ask thee in the name of Jesus Christ," he continued, his voice growing louder, "to *speak* to me. I *know* you can. I know you have spoken to others. My children are gone now, Father, and my confusion has prevented at least one of them from having the strong, sure witness that their mother possesses. You *can* tell me, I know you can. I've come here to talk with you, and I need you to answer. I'll be here four days, and I'll be pestering you through most of it. Please speak to me, Father. *Please!*"

On Friday morning, the trip down the mountain went much faster than going up. With some of the supplies gone, the load was lighter on the packhorse, but Tom felt it was more a result of their being homeward bound. Horses seemed to sense such things and were in a hurry to reach open pasture and to shed packs and saddles.

The return journey, however, was fraught with disappointment. Tom had not received the answer he had sought. Certain that his sincere quest would bring with it the joy of knowledge, as it had for many of the Book of Mormon characters, Tom rode in silence, brooding over his failure to compel an answer.

He had had a dream. But it had been a perplexing thing that answered nothing. Curled up in his bedroll two nights earlier, Tom had barely fallen asleep—or so it seemed—when he dreamed he was mounted on horseback and making his way along the edge of a deep and rugged ravine. The narrow and rocky trail wound along the edge of the crevasse, providing barely enough room for a horse and rider to pass. Though he was watching his horse pick its way along the narrow path, Tom became aware of the presence of another person across the narrow gulf, walking a parallel trail on the other side. Reining in his horse and raising his eyes from the precarious trail, Tom looked across the canyon and spotted a man. No words were spoken, but Tom understood immediately that it was his youngest son, Benjamin, drowned at age seven on the *Titanic* but now grown to young manhood. The man smiled at Tom and nodded his greeting. Tom's horse twitched nervously, and Tom turned his attention to the animal, stroking its neck to comfort him and ensure that he didn't bolt on the narrow trail.

When he looked again, the young man had been joined by a woman whose long, blonde hair flowed loosely over her shoulders and down her back. The young man and the woman were clearly pleased to greet one another. They smiled and embraced each other. In spite of a slight difference in her appearance, Tom knew the woman to be Katrina, and immediately his chest ached with longing to cross the chasm and embrace both his wife and his lost son.

Tom nudged the horse forward, anxious to find a trail that would enable him to descend the steep side of the canyon and come up on the other side. For long moments he rode, looking occasionally across the space that separated him from his loved ones but finding no way to traverse the void. As his mount became more skittish, frightened by the precipice, Tom's heart beat faster. Turning the horse inward, away from the canyon, he passed behind a clump of bushes that momentarily obscured his vision. When he rejoined the trail on the far side of the brush, the separation across the canyon had suddenly widened and both Benjamin and Katrina were gone. Frantically, Tom turned his horse around and followed the narrow trail backward, but the two had disappeared. He dismounted and, cupping his hands, he hollered Katrina's name across the canyon without response. When he turned back, his horse was also gone, and he was alone on the precipice.

In the morning, when Tom awoke in his tent, he lay for a time in the warmth of his bedroll, reflecting on the dream and the feeling of frustration it had caused. His longing for Katrina and for Benjamin, and his inability to reach them, had left him feeling hollow and weak—even in the light of day. Tom had usually resisted such emotional feelings, preferring instead to rely on concrete evidence of events. But the vividness of the dream and the lonely feelings it caused belied any experience Tom had ever had.

A practical man, Tom had never been able to accept such things as Anders' purported miraculous experience in Cuba during the Spanish-American War, when his brother-in-law, severely wounded, was supposedly rescued by two men who were already dead. Tom had never verbalized his cynicism, but he had wondered for years how Katrina and others could so easily accept something so patently implausible.

By late afternoon, Tom was nearing the mouth of the

canyon, headed for the rendezvous with Seby. All the way down the trail he had continued to rehearse the scripture . . . *by the power of the Holy Ghost ye may know the truth of all things.* Well, why *hadn't* God spoken to him? How did the Holy Ghost work? Was an answer really necessary? Hadn't he always known that some, maybe most, perhaps even *all*, that D.O., Robert, and Katrina had tried to tell him all these years, was true? Certainly Father Scanlan had *believed* all that *he* had told Tom about Catholicism, but had he *known* it to be true? And was the dream an answer? Had God sent Benjamin in answer to Tom's prayer? And why was Katrina in the dream? And if the dream *was* his answer, why had it taken twenty years? But if, as he had read, a thousand years was but a day to God, maybe it had only taken Him ten or fifteen minutes to answer. Was faith alone enough?

When Tom rounded the final turn in the trail, he could see that Seby was waiting at the appointed spot. In addition, another man stood by the horse trailer, and a separate car was parked alongside. Tom waved slightly and was acknowledged by a wave from Seby. Within minutes, he cleared the surrounding brush and guided his two horses into the clearing. Tom swung down from the saddle, removed his hat, and brushed the dust and trail grit from his hair and clothes. Seby approached slowly, his face somber.

"Right on time, Seby," Tom said, grinning. "No need to mount a search party or answer to Katrina," he laughed.

"Tom, there's been an automobile accident."

Tom was instantly serious. "Who was injured?"

"It's Katrina. She's alive, Tom, but it's very serious. She has a severe head injury and has been unconscious since the accident two nights ago. Reed will take care of the horses, and I'll take you immediately to Holy Cross Hospital."

"What about Tess?"

"She's with her mother. Tess wasn't in the car. Katrina was coming back from a concert in Ogden. Tom, Judge Garfield was killed in the accident, and his wife broke both her legs and her shoulder. Katrina has not regained consciousness, so she hasn't been told of the judge's death."

"What have the doctors said?" Tom asked, stripping off his jacket and striding toward the car.

"They've done what they can, Tom. They say all we can do now is wait."

As he climbed into the car, Tom's mind raced with the possibilities and the shock of such news. What kind of a God was He anyway! He had let Tom languish in a prison cell for nearly a year, then, when he had finally gone to plead with that same God for understanding, he returned without an answer, only to find that his wife was near death.

"Get me to the hospital, Seby."

5

Teresa was just about to step back into her mother's room on the second floor of Holy Cross Hospital when she saw her father and Seby hurrying down the hallway. Immediately she ran the length of the hall, falling into her father's arms, sobbing as she surrendered to the emotions she had controlled until that moment. After a few moments in her father's strong embrace, she pulled away slightly and looked up into Tom's eyes.

"Daddy, *why?*"

Tom just shook his head, his emotions reeling with the events of the past hour and the horrifying thoughts that had gone through his head as Seby had raced toward the hospital.

"Let's go see her, Tess," he said softly.

Teresa held her father's arm for a moment, restricting his movement while she wiped her face with a kerchief.

"Dad, it's really a shock," Teresa warned. "Her face is *very* bruised, and they've cut her hair."

Tom nodded and glanced at Seby, inclining his head as an invitation for the young man to join them at Katrina's bedside. As they entered the darkened room, a nurse seated on the far side of the bed got quickly to her feet and stood without speaking. The room was filled with the heavy fragrance of flowers, and the subdued light prevented Tom from clearly seeing Katrina until he closed the distance to her bed. Tom winced with pain as he focused his gaze on his wife. The woman in the bed bore no resemblance to Katrina. Her upper head was tightly wrapped in white bandages, and her eyes were swollen shut. The purple hue of her flesh and puffy features gave her the appearance of having received a frightful beating. Tom was not prepared for the sight, and the shock caused him to groan out loud. His reaction startled Teresa, and she clutched his arm tightly and fought to hold back her tears.

Tom remained standing beside the bed, clasping Katrina's hand for several minutes, not noticing as the nurse quietly left the room. Teresa moved to the foot of the bed and sat in the chair she had occupied almost constantly during the past two days. Seby remained silent and stood against the far wall near the shuttered windows.

When the door opened again, the nurse entered, followed by a man wearing a white smock.

"Mr. Callahan?" the man said, reaching to touch Tom's arm. "I'm Dr. Morgan. May I speak with you for a moment?"

Tom turned his head to observe the doctor and then replaced Katrina's hand at her side. With Teresa at Tom's side, followed by Seby, the small group left the room, and the nurse retook her seat beside Katrina. Tom followed the doctor down the hall and into a small anteroom, where the physician motioned for all to take a seat.

"I am sincerely sorry, Mr. Callahan. I understand you've been away. This situation is never easy to explain or easy for the family to understand, I'm afraid. We just don't know much about head injuries. Perhaps in the future, but, I, uh, I'm afraid all we can do is wait and see how she responds."

"Is she being medicated? For pain, I mean, or a treatment of some kind?" Tom asked. "What *is* being done, Doctor? I mean, surely you're not just . . . *waiting*, are you?"

"Mr. Callahan, I understand your concern. But with injuries to the head, we have to be cautious in administering medication."

Seby came to the far side of the divan and stood beside Tom. He rested his hand on Tom's shoulder, but looked intently at the doctor.

"I'm sorry, Doctor Morgan, I'm just trying to understand what's going on. Tell me about the injury and what's going to happen to my wife."

Morgan nodded. "No need to apologize, Mr. Callahan, I understand your concern. Your wife sustained a severe blow to the side of her head, just above the hairline. Probably from the impact against the side door of the car. We know she has a concussion, but until she regains consciousness, we will have no knowledge of any, uh, the extent, *if any*, of brain damage."

Tom's eyes widened.

"Would her brain damage be severe, uh, in light of her injuries, I mean?"

"We just don't know, Mr. Callahan," he said, shaking his head. "There may be no permanent damage at all, but, I must tell you, the pressure on her brain—from the swelling—is severe. But it's a good sign that she's survived nearly forty-eight hours now."

"You mean her life is still in danger?" Tom said, leaning forward in his seat.

Doctor Morgan nodded again. "I'm afraid so, Mr. Callahan. As much as I regret telling you, there *is* a possibility she might not survive."

"How much of a possibility?" Tom demanded.

"That's difficult to say. We'll know more in a couple of days. It's encouraging that her vital signs have stabilized, and she seems to be in no discomfort. But she is in a state of coma. How much she can hear or understand, well, we just don't know."

"So all we can do is wait, you say?"

"I'm afraid so."

"Is there anyone, *anyone*, who specializes in this type of injury? Could we obtain a referral or bring someone in?"

"I've consulted with Dr. Geoffrey Callister in San Francisco. He has experience in head injuries. We've been conferring by telephone since the morning after your wife's arrival."

"Could he come?" Tom asked. "Would he be able to help?"

Dr. Morgan glanced at Seby. "Mr. Stromberg has already made arrangements. I believe Doctor Callister will arrive tomorrow morning by train."

Tom looked up at Seby and grasped his hand, then returned his gaze to the physician. "Thank you, Doctor Morgan. I apologize for my abruptness. It's just . . ."

Morgan stood, offering his hand to Tom. "There's no need, Mr. Callahan. You and your daughter, and of course Mr. Stromberg, may remain with Mrs. Callahan as long as you wish. We will have a nurse with her around the clock."

"Whatever she needs, Doctor. *Anything*. Just ask, and we will do our best to get it."

"I understand, Mr. Callahan. Now," he said, "I'd best return to my other patients. I'm on duty tonight, and I'll look in on Mrs. Callahan as often as I can throughout the evening."

Morgan left the room and Tom stood, stepping toward Seby. "Thank you, Seby, for your quick action."

Seby shook his head. "I have not forgotten, *Señor*, that it was your kind wife who once preserved my life. I will eternally owe her."

"Thanks again, Seby. Would you, uh, please take Tess down to the room. I'd like to be alone. Just for a minute, Tess, please?" he said to his daughter.

After Seby and Teresa left the room, Tom sat down again on the divan and remained for several moments, his head buried in his hands. Finally, he took a deep breath and leaned back against the backrest.

"Dear God, you cannot take this woman from me," he breathed. "You *can not!*"

———

It took a concerted effort from Tom and Seby to convince Teresa to go home and get some sleep. She had been at her mother's side from within thirty minutes of the hospital calling to inform them of the accident, and she had remained in or near the room for the following forty-eight hours, giving permission for the medical staff to perform all necessary procedures. Tom's arrival had relieved her of that responsibility, but she was still reluctant to go home without a more certain knowledge of her mother's condition. But, as Doctor Morgan had said, that could take hours, or even days. They could only wait and see. Teresa had finally left with Seby, after he promised her that he would return at first light and deliver her back to the hospital.

Accompanied by his young counselor, David Healy, Bishop Ronald Smart entered Katrina's hospital room sometime after 10:00 o'clock that night. Only three other men had served as bishop of the Callahans' ward over the twenty-two years Tom and Katrina had been married. One of their former bishops had been Robert Thurston, Tom's

partner at Utah Trust Bank, who was both a business associate and a close personal friend. Thurston's successor, a
man named Clements, had brought an air of formality to his
office. Lacking the natural warmth of Robert Thurston,
Bishop Clements had always struck Tom as being dogmatic
and a little impatient. He and Tom had been civil to each
other but had never formed a friendly relationship.
However, Tom had immediately warmed to Bishop Smart,
who, like Tom, was a self-employed entrepreneur, a man of
about forty years of age, who had expanded a small, family-
owned freighting business started by his father into a large,
intermountain transportation company.

Tom stood to greet Bishop Smart, first shaking his hand
and then accepting a warm embrace from the man whom
Katrina often referred to as the father of the ward.

"We'd heard you'd returned, Tom. Brother Stromberg
wanted to fly up the morning after the accident, fly over
your camp and drop a note, but we convinced him to wait
until you returned rather than have you race your horses
down the mountain. I hope you don't mind. We were thinking of your safety and perhaps hoping for some improvement
from Katrina. Any change in her condition today?"

Tom shook his head. "None, Bishop. She's breathing
regularly, and the nurse says her vital signs are stable, but no
response yet," Tom said, sitting again and motioning for
Bishop Smart to take a seat.

"Give it time, Tom," the man nodded. "We've actually
come to see you," he smiled, pulling a chair close to Tom's,
then sitting and facing his friend. Brother Healy sat in a
chair closer to the window, although the drapes were drawn.

"To see me? I'm fine, Ron."

"It never hurts to have your friends with you," the

bishop smiled. "Did Brother Stromberg tell you about the accident?"

"He did," Tom nodded, "although he explained that the police didn't know much about what happened. Do you know any more?"

"No," Bishop Smart said. "You do know about Judge Garfield's death and his wife's injuries?"

"Yes. A great loss. He was a fine man. When is his funeral?"

"Tomorrow. We intended to hold it at the ward house, but as the word spread, the expected audience has grown considerably. The service has been relocated to the Assembly Hall on Temple Square at eleven o'clock. He'll be laid to rest in the old Salt Lake Cemetery near his grandparents. I don't know if you knew it, Tom, but the judge was born right here in Salt Lake City, only twenty years after Brother Brigham arrived in the valley. The Garfields have five children. Their youngest son, Jared, has just returned from his mission to the southern States."

"I don't know them well, Bishop. Sister Garfield has occasionally come to our house to practice singing with Katie. She's a very pleasant woman. Is she in Holy Cross?"

"No, she was taken to LDS Hospital. The judge had driven both ladies up to Ogden for a concert, and they were on their way back. For some reason they skidded off the road just north of Layton, maybe to avoid hitting a deer. A following car spotted them in a depression alongside the roadway and summoned help. The judge was dead when the police and ambulance arrived. Sister Garfield was able to give the police an initial report, although she was in considerable pain and almost incoherent. As you know, Katrina has been unconscious ever since. Tom, Brother Healy and I were notified, and when we arrived, Teresa requested that we give her mother a blessing. I hope that's all right with you."

Tom looked over at his wife, her still form lying silently with the sheets tucked up around her neck. The on-duty nurse smiled at him and leaned toward the bed, checking on her patient.

"She would have asked you herself had she been able, Bishop. Thank you." Tom felt a cold chill sweep through him, and he shuddered as he watched Katrina lying so still.

"Ron, the doctor told me that she could still . . . that is, she's still very much in danger."

"Yes, Tom, I've spoken with him," Bishop Smart said softly.

"I saw her, you know, the other night," Tom said, without looking at the bishop.

"You saw her? I don't understand—"

Tom fidgeted his hands. "Two nights ago—in the mountains, I mean. I had a dream. At least I think it was a dream. Isn't that how God speaks to us sometimes? In dreams?"

"He speaks to us in many ways, Tom. Tell me about your dream . . . that is, if you feel comfortable speaking about it."

"In truth, Ron, I don't feel comfortable with *any* of what's happening, but as soon as Seby told me about the accident, I knew for certain it was Katie in my dream. And Benjamin was there, too. I watched as he greeted her and . . ." Tom paused, trying to gain control of his emotions.

Bishop Smart said nothing, waiting for Tom to continue.

Tom took a couple of deep breaths, then turned to look at Brother Healy, who smiled and nodded his assurance. Tom then glanced at the nurse sitting beside Katrina.

"Mr. Callahan," she said, rising, "I'll just step out for a moment and get a cup of coffee. Please call immediately if there's any change," the young woman smiled. "I'll be across the hall at the nurses' station."

"Thank you, Miss . . ."

"Nurse Hughes," she said softly, leaving the room and closing the door.

"Time was," Tom said after she left, "when all the nurses were Catholic sisters. Now of course, with the nursing school and all, they have many lay nurses on staff. What I wouldn't give to see Sister Mary come through that door," he said, breathing deeply and exhaling.

After Nurse Hughes had gone, David Healy stood and said, "Tom, would you prefer to speak with the bishop alone?"

"No," Tom said, shaking his head, "not at all. Please have a seat," he said.

"Bishop," Tom continued, "it all seemed so real, although I know I was sleeping. I dreamed I was on horse-back, riding on a narrow trail on the edge of a deep canyon. On the other side of the ravine, I saw a man, a young man, and I knew immediately that it was my son Benjamin. He seemed as real as you are, sitting here right now. I looked away for a moment, to be sure my horse was staying on the trail, and when I looked back, a woman had joined Benjamin. I didn't recognize her at first, but in a few moments, I knew her to be Katrina. She and Benjamin embraced, and suddenly my heart was filled with the desire to be with them, but I couldn't find a way to get across the canyon. I felt helpless, Ron. I turned my horse around to retrace my steps, but some brush in the trail blocked my view of them. When I got to a place where I could see across the canyon again, they were gone. I called out to her, but no one answered."

"This happened two nights ago, Tom?"

"Yes," he said, reading the bishop's thoughts, "I've thought of that too, sitting here in this room with her, just a little while ago. From what Seby and Doctor Morgan told me, it was about the same time as the accident. Ron, surely that doesn't mean she's . . . that she's gone to be with Benjamin."

Bishop Smart looked briefly at his counselor and then back at Tom. "I don't know, Tom. By all accounts, Sister Callahan is still here with us. Her vital signs are stable, and her breathing is regular. But the spirit has a strong will. I've heard reports of people crossing over and coming back. I personally have never experienced, or known anyone who has, experienced these things, but perhaps there *was* some communication between Katrina and your son. We don't understand these things, I'm afraid. And perhaps we're not meant to, but the Lord *does* talk to us in dreams, of *that* I'm certain."

"But why couldn't I get to them, Ron? I mean, why the separation between us?"

"Bishop," Healy said, "may I speak?"

"Of course, David."

"Tom, I've been sitting here listening to your thoughts and I must tell you, my heart goes out to you. Do you recall last year when the stake presidency asked each bishopric to visit the families in the ward and discuss the plan of salvation and the importance of temple work?"

Tom smiled. "David, you've been in my home dozens of times and brought a good spirit with you each time, but that particular—"

"I know. I'm sorry," he said. "We were talking about genealogy specifically, and I remember Katrina commenting that her greatest joy was knowing that her parents were together and that Benjamin had a family and a home to go to. We talked a bit, Tom, about the Catholic doctrine, too, if you recall, and where in that scheme of things Benjamin would be as a result of his dying before baptism."

"*Now* I recall that conversation, David. I've never found the idea of purgatory acceptable, even when I lived in Ireland as a young man."

"I understand. It doesn't give a parent much to hope for, does it? Still, as you say, you saw Benjamin and knew who he was, right?"

Tom nodded.

"And Katrina joined him, if only for a moment?"

Again Tom nodded.

"Tom," Healy said, leaning forward and looking deeply into Tom's eyes, "I know with all my soul that Benjamin was blessed to enter the celestial kingdom, as are all children who die before baptismal age. And you also saw Katrina join with him and they embraced. We all know your wife to be a fine woman, with a strong testimony of the gospel, trying to live her life so that she can be with her family in the celestial kingdom, isn't that right, Tom?"

"Aye," Tom replied, "I'll attest to hearing over twenty years of *that* testimony, Brother Healy," he smiled. "And I haven't made it easy for her along the way."

Bishop Smart interjected a thought. "Maybe you don't know how much of a support to her testimony you've really been, Tom. Your wife loves you and sustains you as head of the household. Many times she's talked with me about her pride in your accomplishments and how good a father you've been."

"Can she still attain the celestial kingdom if she tells little white lies about her husband, Bishop?" Tom smiled again.

"In all seriousness," Healy continued, "I believe that you

73

were privileged to have a glimpse into the heavens, Brother Callahan, and for one brief moment, you saw your wife together with your son as they will be some day. Bishop Smart will attest that during our blessing of Sister Callahan we felt a complete peace of mind and a comforting feeling of assurance. While that doesn't give us positive answers about her physical condition, I know of a certainty that the Lord is aware of her plight, and that His will shall be done."

"You mean that He told you—"

"No," Healy said, shaking his head, "He didn't tell me anything other than that He is aware of His daughter in peril and that He will be with her. But as regards the great canyon—the separation between you and your family—we are taught . . ." Healy hesitated for a moment, looking toward Bishop Smart for approval to continue. Smart nodded at Healy and looked back at Tom.

"Listen to him, Tom."

"The Lord teaches us these lessons for many reasons. I'm not saying that Sister Callahan's life-threatening injury was brought about to teach you about the gospel—in fact, after all the years you've spent among us, you already know most of it, I'd say—but if, as a result of this crisis, you have a better understanding of this particular principle, this unifying ordinance that holds families together, then it will have been a blessing. If . . . if Sister Callahan were to die as a result of her injuries, she has fulfilled all the necessary earthly ordinances to be with her parents and Benjamin. You understand that, Tom?"

"I know that's the Mormon teaching."

"And you know that by that same doctrine, you have yet to fulfill your part of the marriage vows that would unite you with your wife and children."

"That's pretty harsh, isn't it? I can't believe that God would separate us after all these years."

"I understand. And where would Catholic doctrine have Katrina go, unbaptized as she is?"

"I'm not certain I understand your meaning."

"Tom, according to both religions, you can't be together should either of you die now."

The three men sat silently, contemplating Healy's words. Then Tom stood and stepped to the far side of Katrina's bed. As Tom gazed at his wife, Bishop Smart also rose and came to stand alongside Tom.

"We'll leave you now, Tom. Is there anything we can do for you before we go?"

Tom just shook his head. Across the bed, Healy rose and stepped toward the door. Bishop Smart followed and Tom stood with them near the doorway.

"Thank you, both," Tom said. "Sometimes I think it's easier for someone who hears all this for the first time to accept it. I've struggled to understand your beliefs for over twenty years, knowing perhaps that it was a good doctrine, but not certain how to embrace it without turning my back on my heritage. I suppose I still wrestle with that."

"We understand your concern, Brother Callahan, truly," Bishop Smart said. "Think what Sister Callahan and Benjamin would have you do. I mean, do you suppose for an instant, that as you watched them together across that great canyon—the fondest desire of your heart to join them—that they did not have the same desire—for you to join them? But they can do no more for you, Tom, in this life. While you are still living, only *you* can make that possible."

Tom reached for Brother Healy's hand.

"Thank you, David. I know your heart is true and your

words are sincere. I appreciate your concern. Bishop," Tom said, looking at Smart. "I have always felt your love for my family. Thank you for that. I'll try to make it to Judge Garfield's funeral tomorrow."

"I'll be back either way, Tom. And Tom, talk with the Lord about these things. He *is* mindful of your needs, but His hands are tied to some extent too. We must all make our own choices. That's the plan of salvation."

"Good night, Bishop, Brother Healy."

After the men left, Tom stood silently by the side of Katrina's bed. He looked down at his wife, her once lovely face barely recognizable as the woman with whom he had shared most of his life and all his earthly possessions. *But it isn't earthly possessions she really wanted, is it,* he thought.

"Come back to me, Katie. Please, God, let her come back to me," he whispered.

The door opened and Nurse Hughes entered, walking around to the far side of the bed and reaching to feel Katrina's forehead.

"Any movement, or change?" she asked.

Tom shook his head. "I'm going to step outside for a few moments, in the Rose Garden. Please send someone if Katrina stirs," he said.

"Certainly, Mr. Callahan. I'll be here. Just take your time," she said.

Tom left the room and walked down a long corridor to the east end of the building where he exited the hospital into the cool night air. He followed a walkway into a garden of rosebushes, some of them, he supposed, planted by him many years before, when as a young man he had worked as a maintenance man at the hospital. Lights showed at only a few of the windows in the sandstone building, and the three-story Gothic structure was bathed in moonlight.

When he reached the familiar stone bench, he lowered himself onto the cool seat and read the inscription on the nearby headstone, the only grave marker within the hospital grounds.

"Sister Mary, since you've already gone to your reward, you'd know the answers now too, wouldn't you? But then you always knew the answers long before any of the rest of us. Why can't we learn them here and not have to wait until our turn comes to cross over? Dear God, is it not time for you to speak to me?"

"Did you know the sister?" a voice said, startling Tom. He stood quickly and turned to see a man standing nearby. The man's clerical collar glowed white in the moonlight.

"I'm sorry, my son. I didn't mean to have startled you," he said. "I was just having a midnight stroll in the garden—a little private meditation for a sleepless soul. Did you know Sister Mary?" he asked again, nodding toward the tombstone.

"I did," Tom replied. "I met her when I was very young, many years ago."

"I've read of her efforts here at Holy Cross, and the sisters still speak of her reverently. A fine woman, I understand. I'm Father O'Shea," the short, elderly man said, extending his hand. "I've recently come to Holy Cross from the San Francisco diocese."

"Good evening, Father. I'm Thomas Callahan," Tom said, grasping the priest's outstretched hand.

"Oh, yes, of course," the priest said, his eyebrows raising. "One of the hospital's principal benefactors, as I understand it."

"No, Father," Tom replied, shaking his head. "I give very little. Only money. The principal benefactor lies beneath us here," he said, looking toward Sister Mary's grave marker.

"Quite so, my son, quite so. And did I hear you seeking God's intervention? Are you troubled, Mr. Callahan?"

"Maybe we're all troubled, Father. But yes, I *was* asking God's help—to speak to me, if He would."

"God speaks with us daily, my son, but it's seldom *His* voice we hear. He uses those around us, our friends, our teachers, our clergy, even our own conscience. But still we seek His direct intervention, it seems. Perhaps a miracle, as it were. I must admit, I often seek His counsel myself, only to find that I have already received the answer in some other way. A human weakness, I presume, to seek direct intervention—not trusting our own instincts that are often planted there by God."

"Our clergy, did you say?" Tom asked.

"Among others."

Tom smiled and reached to shake Father O'Shea's hand once again.

"Thank you, Father. You've been a great help."

"A pleasure, my son. Have a good evening, Mr. Callahan. I think I'll just sit here with Sister Mary for a few moments . . . if I may share her," he smiled.

"That's what Sister Mary was best at, Father, sharing herself. A good night to you."

GOODBYE JUDGE, the *Salt Lake Tribune* front-page headlines trumpeted. Beneath the headline was a photograph of Judge Gene Harrington Garfield, presiding judge of the Eighth District Court of Appeals, as he sat on the bench of his courtroom. Inside the paper, in the "Local Scene" section, three separate editorials lauded the praises of one of Utah's longest-serving and most well-respected judicial figures.

With the paper folded beneath his arm, Tom walked west on South Temple toward Temple Square, wondering what the paper would say were it his funeral—or Katrina's—scheduled for today. What would the public say about her? It seemed that whenever the wife of a prominent public figure died, the article invariably covered more of the husband's story than hers.

At about 8:00 A.M., no change having occurred in Katrina's condition overnight, he had left the hospital and walked home to find Teresa preparing breakfast for herself and Seby, who had arrived only moments earlier. Teresa kissed her father and told him to have a seat at the table. When Tom said that he wasn't hungry, Teresa and Seby laughed, and Teresa threatened to give him the same lecture that Seby had just given her about the need to eat and keep up her strength. Succumbing to their arguments, Tom relented and sat down to the breakfast table. Despite her attempt at humoring him into eating something, Tom noticed that his daughter occasionally dabbed at her tears while working at the stove. After picking a bit at a couple of fried eggs, Tom excused himself to go upstairs where he got ready for the funeral service by bathing, shaving, and putting on a suit. While he was doing so, Seby and Teresa left for the hospital, agreeing to meet Tom at Temple Square at a quarter to eleven.

Now, as he approached the south entrance to Temple Square, Tom could see the reason for the change in venue from the ward house. Bishop Smart had been right. Temple Square was awash with people, and the Assembly Hall was quickly filling. He spied Teresa and Seby, standing with David Healy.

"Good morning, Brother Callahan," Healy said. "The bishop asked me to meet you and show you to your seats. Sister Garfield specifically asked that your family be seated close to hers."

"Dad, Bishop Smart and Brother Healy were already at the hospital when Seby and I arrived this morning," Teresa added.

"That's why your mother calls him the father of the ward," Tom smiled. "Shall we go in?"

Considering the number of people packed into their seats, Tom was surprised that the building was nearly silent. The main floor was completely full, except for a few reserved seats near the front, to which David Healy led Tom's group. Upstairs, above the railing, Tom could see that the balcony was also full.

The injured Sister Marianne Garfield was seated in a

wheelchair in the aisle, at the end of one of the pews. She wore a cast on each of her legs, and her right arm and shoulder were immobilized by a sling. As Tom approached, the tearful woman smiled weakly and extended her left hand to him. She drew Tom close and whispered, "Tom, I'm so sorry about Katrina. I'm praying for her."

Tom had intended to say something about Sister Garfield's loss and injuries, but her expression of concern for him and Katrina caused a sudden flood of emotion in him. Unable to speak, he merely squeezed Sister Garfield's hand lightly and nodded his head, then moved past her into one of the rows of benches.

Arriving at the last minute, Tom could feel every eye in the house on him as he, Seby, and Teresa slipped into the pew and quickly took their seats. Flushed and emotional, he glanced at the stand, where Church President Heber J. Grant and several members of the Council of the Twelve were seated, including Tom's longtime friend David O. McKay. Behind the Church leaders, fifty or sixty members of the Tabernacle Choir were assembled, occupying a portion of the choir seats—probably, Tom thought, in honor of Sister Garfield, who, along with Katrina, had been a member of the choir for many years. To the right of the choir were seated a dozen or so judges, appearing as a formal delegation, each of the solemn men wearing his judicial robe.

The casket, draped in an American flag in honor of Judge Garfield's military service during the Spanish-American War, lay beneath the podium in the front of the building.

A moment or two after 11:00 o'clock, and without any announcement, the choir members stood, and, following a brief organ introduction, the soprano section began softly singing the opening bars of "Jesu, Joy of Man's Desiring."

Following that stirring hymn, Bishop Ronald Smart rose to conduct the service, recognizing President Grant, the other leaders of the Church, and the official delegation of judges who were in attendance, before announcing the opening prayer.

The first speaker was the Garfields' stake president, Ephraim Tarkington. The white-haired man began his address in a solemn tone:

"Brothers and sisters, death comes to all men, and from our perspective it comes to some far too quickly. But with our understanding of the plan of salvation, we need not fear death. Our friend, Gene Garfield, did not fear death. Because he knew the gospel plan. He knew, as I know, that through the Atonement and through the ordinances of the priesthood, the Savior has provided a way for us to obtain eternal life. If we are true and faithful, though our time here may be cut short, life will have been profitable. Such is the case with our dear friend, Judge Gene Garfield . . ."

Listening to these remarks, Tom thought of Katrina, hovering near death in the hospital. However comforted the Garfields might be by such remarks, the thought of Katrina lying there in a polished wooden casket filled his heart with a feeling of loneliness and despair. He couldn't imagine coping with such a loss, no matter what eternity might hold. He needed her *now*, not in some distant afterlife.

Two speakers followed President Tarkington, then after another musical number by the choir, young Jared Garfield, barely twenty-two it appeared, stood at the pulpit to eulogize his father.

For several minutes the recently returned missionary recalled experiences he and his dad had shared. He smiled, and the congregation laughed, as Jared said that the judge would occasionally purposely keep his family waiting by coming late to dinner. Then, upon entering the dining room, he would announce in his rich baritone voice, "All rise."

As the quiet laughter subsided, Jared continued: "Just over three years ago, my father went with me to the train station where I was to depart for my mission to the southern states. As the time came for me to board the train, Dad's eyes welled up with tears—an unusual thing for him. He said to me, 'Jared, I have prepared for this day—for my youngest son's mission—from the time you were born, but until this moment, I had no idea how hard it would be to let you go. I release you now into the hands of your Heavenly Father, in the sure knowledge that He will reunite us when you finish your mission. May God be with you, son.'"

Jared was smiling through his tears as he continued: "Those words were with me throughout my mission and are firmly etched in my mind for all time, along with all the other important things my father taught me."

Looking down at the casket below him, the young man paused for a long moment, and in the silence, muffled sobs could be heard in the congregation. Tom could see Elder McKay nodding his head thoughtfully, and to Tom's left, Sister Garfield was dabbing at her eyes with a handkerchief.

Then, taking a deep breath, Jared concluded by saying, "Dad, our roles have now been reversed, and I've not had sufficient time to plan for this moment. I had no idea how hard it would be to let you go."

He paused for a long moment and drew a deep breath. Exhaling it slowly, he said, "But I release you now, as you once released me, in the sure and certain knowledge that Heavenly Father will bring us together again. Until that great reunion, we will work to be worthy and to care for

Mother as she has always supported, loved, and cared for us. In Jesus' name, amen."

Tom sat silently, a lump in his throat and tears burning his eyes, thinking of his own sons and how they might characterize him were he in that coffin.

President Grant made some brief concluding remarks, praising Judge Garfield and quoting from the Doctrine & Covenants: "And it shall come to pass that those that die in me shall not taste of death, for it shall be sweet unto them."

As the choir sang "O My Father," Tom sat listening to the familiar words and melody. Then, in a flash of understanding, it struck him! He, Thomas Callahan, had not yet provided for *his family* the hope of a heavenly reunion, such as young Jared had described. Bishop Smart and Brother Healy were right! Only he, Tom, could take the next step, and it was not up to God or Katie, or even his children. It was not even God's responsibility to show him the way, for in this thing all spiritual leaders were in agreement: one has to act on the basis of faith. It was Tom's responsibility alone. As that reality washed over him, for the first time in all their years together, Tom understood what it was that Katrina had so desperately wanted from him: the certain knowledge that her family was eternal.

We hear the words from our friends, clergy, and our conscience, Father O'Shea had said. And out of the mouths of children or, as Jared Garfield had so ably demonstrated, out of the mouths of young, returned missionaries, who were so confident of their role in eternity.

Later, at the Salt Lake City Cemetery, Judge Garfield's second-eldest son, named Gene after his father, dedicated his father's grave. Then, as the crowd began to disperse, Tom felt someone take his arm. He turned to see Elder

David O. McKay standing next to him. The apostle said, "I was hoping to catch you, Tom. How is Katrina doing?"

"Hello, D.O.," Tom said, his voice cracking. "I don't know exactly how she's doing. When I left her this morning, she was still unconscious. The doctors say it's just a matter of waiting to see what happens."

Elder McKay rested his hand on Tom's shoulder and said, "This is a trying time, Tom, but the Lord is mindful of your fears. If there's anything I can do, you need only ask."

"Thank you, D.O. You've been a good friend to me." Looking about, Tom said, "I'm just about to head back to the hospital now, as soon as I can locate Teresa. She seems to have gotten lost in the crowd."

"I saw her this morning. She's a fine young woman. A credit to you and Katrina," McKay said.

"She's a joy. This accident has really knocked her for a loop, though."

"Have faith, Tom. I believe the Lord yet has work for Katrina, and for you perhaps," he smiled.

"Aye, but if the Lord needs men, D.O., there's surely a long line in front of *me*," Tom said with a smile.

"Perhaps, but if you'll turn around, you'll see the line's a great deal longer *behind* you, Brother Callahan."

"I don't know, David. I look at young men like Jared Garfield, who were brought up in the Church with both parents teaching and guiding them, and I'm astounded. Did you hear how *certain* he was, as he spoke of his reunion with his father. How do they come by such assurance?" Tom said, shaking his head.

"Did you understand and believe what he said, Tom?"

"My goodness, David, who wouldn't *want* to believe it? Is there a parent, or child for that matter, who wouldn't take comfort from the thought that they could always be with those they love? I mean it's just natural that people would want that, isn't it?"

Elder McKay smiled and patted Tom's shoulder. "It *is* natural, isn't it, Tom? Wouldn't any father—even a *Heavenly* Father—seek such an eternity, united with his children?"

"The past forty-eight hours have brought the most intensive . . ." Tom hesitated, groping for the right word, " . . . most intensive mental and spiritual *confusion* I think I've known, and it actually took young Jared there," he said, glancing over at the Garfield family as they consoled one another, "to put simplicity to it. It makes sense, D.O., and to think it's been right in front of my face all the time."

"Life changes for us, Tom, and we move with it if we are wise. I watched you during the service. I noticed you reached for your glasses when you tried to read the program."

Tom nodded and grinned. "*That's* not been a welcome change."

"Nor for me, but we accommodate and adjust. Think about these past years in that way. Maybe you've needed to put on your *spiritual* glasses to bring things into focus. Well," McKay said, reaching to shake Tom's hand, "this is not the place for a sermon, is it? Give my love to Katrina, Tom, and let her know we have her in our prayers."

"She doesn't know I'm there, D.O."

"How do you know that for certain, Tom?"

Tom thought for a moment, considering the question. "I really don't, do I?"

"Maybe she's just wearing a different set of glasses."

"Thank you, David. You have a way about you, and the people around you are always the beneficiaries. The Lord's hand, I suppose," he smiled. "Ah, here come Teresa and

Seby. We'd best be off for the hospital. Good day, David. My regards to Sister McKay."

———✎———

It was nearly 4:00 o'clock before Tom made it back to Holy Cross Hospital with Teresa at his side. Seby needed to drive back to his ranch in Draper, but said he would return late that night, or first thing Sunday morning at the latest. Tom told Seby that he was welcome to use the guest room at *Valhalla* during the crisis, but that he should not put off important business, since Tom and Teresa were there to be with Katrina. Seby politely agreed and said he would return later or in the morning.

When Tom and Teresa got to Katrina's room, Doctor Morgan was present and Nurse Hughes was on duty again.

"Doctor Morgan," Tom said, "any change?"

"Actually, yes, Mr. Callahan, although it's not obvious from Mrs. Callahan's appearance. I've just been reading the chart, and the past two duty nurses . . . umm, let's see," he said, checking the chart again, "yes, here it is . . . about nine this morning it started. Mrs. Callahan *groaned*, I suppose is the best description of it, a low guttural sound is the way Nurse Hughes described it, isn't that right, Nurse?"

"Yes, Doctor. I've heard it two times since I came on duty at noon today."

"What does that mean, Doctor Morgan?" Tom asked. Teresa moved to her mother's bedside and reached down to hold her hand. She could see no physical indication of any change in Katrina.

"The most common reason, Mr. Callahan, is that the patient—Mrs. Callahan, I mean—is experiencing pain."

"*Pain!* Can't you do something?"

"Don't be alarmed, Mr. Callahan, truly. While that

seems a bad thing at first consideration, certainly to her loved ones, from a *medical* point of view, it's quite good. It means she's beginning to recover her senses. Her *brain*, as it were, is beginning to work again. If she shows additional signs of regaining consciousness, we can safely provide medication to relieve her discomfort."

"Two times, you say?" Tom said, speaking to Nurse Hughes.

"Indeed, sir," she smiled in return, giving also a short curtsey. "And two more reported by the earlier shift nurse. It seems she's coming back to you, sir," the young nurse smiled.

Tom smiled back at the young woman and nodded his head, silently mouthing, "Thank you."

"Well, I've finished my examination," Doctor Morgan said. "Once again, I'll be in the hospital this evening. Just call for me if there's any further change, Nurse."

Tom stepped behind Teresa and peered over her shoulder to look at Katrina. Together they contemplated her discolored and swollen face, each searching for any additional signs of consciousness.

After a moment, Tom said, "Tess, can I talk you into going home for a few hours and getting some food and sleep?"

"Dad, I want to—"

"I know you do, Tess. But we still don't know how long this might take. It would be best if we take turns so that one of us is always here with her in case she wakes up."

"I agree, Dad," Teresa quickly said, turning around and facing her father. "And last night, you *forced* me to go home, and you stayed here *all* night, getting *no* sleep whatsoever. Now, *you* go home, eat, and get some sleep and come back about midnight. I'll stay till then."

"Tess, really, I think you should—"

"Dad, do as you're told for once," she smiled.

"Sir," Nurse Hughes interrupted, "you *were* up all night. The young lady and I can watch Mrs. Callahan, and I give my solemn promise that if any developments occur, *anything*, I'll telephone your home immediately."

"Two against one, eh?" Tom said.

"No, Dad, two *for* one."

"All right, Tess, truth be known, I am *very* tired. Perhaps a few hours sleep will do me good. But I'll be back at midnight, and I'll have William come with me to take you home."

"Great, Dad. Thank you."

"Now *call* me, Tess. Any change at all."

"Another groan?" Teresa said, half teasing.

"Perhaps a bit more than a groan. But if she says, 'Thomas, where are you? . . .'"

Teresa hugged her father and held him tight for several seconds.

"Oh, Dad, I pray that's *exactly* what she'll say when she wakes up. I really do."

"I know, Tess. You just sit here and rest. Actually, you can catch a few winks in that old, beat-up, leather chair someone kindly added to the room," he said, smiling at Nurse Hughes.

"It's *very* comfortable, sir. I've used it on my breaks sometimes. It's usually in the nurses' lounge."

"I know," Tom said. "I recognize it."

"Sir?"

"Sister Mary Theophane used to sleep in that very same chair when she stayed overnight for some special patient, which was *very* often, I can tell you. I've caught a few winks in it myself, when I was a lot younger."

"You knew Sister Mary?"

"Probably before you were born, Nurse Hughes. Well, goodnight, ladies. I'll be back around midnight."

"*Eat* too, Dad."

"Yes, *mother*," he replied.

When Tom arrived at *Valhalla*, he found a note from William and his wife, Helen, who served as the Callahans' cook, saying that they had gone to evening Mass at the Cathedral of the Madeleine to say prayers for Katrina and would return later. Not wanting to cook anything, Tom found some cheese and milk in the icebox and took them with a slice of bread up to his room. After eating, though he was tired, he didn't fall immediately asleep. Instead, he lay for a time in the quiet of his empty house, staring at the ceiling, thinking.

Then he slid off the bed, kneeling on Katrina's side and resting his arms and head on the patchwork quilt that his wife had hand sewn some years before. Over the years he had often knelt there with Katrina, but nearly always involuntarily, at her insistence. She had been the one to lead out in prayer, and he wished now that she were there with him. He remained on his knees for several moments, his eyes closed, gathering his thoughts.

Finally, he began. "God in heaven . . ." he said, speaking out loud. Then, not knowing exactly how to continue, he paused for a long moment.

He began again. "Dear God, this has been a long two days, and I need your help. Please, God, bless Katrina to get well."

It occurred to him that God might think him unworthy to make such a request, and with his eyes still closed, he added, "I know I've been stubborn, but I've also been confused. I've wanted to do the right thing, but I needed to know for sure what I should do. It seems clear that you have been trying to tell me to accept the Mormon religion. The dream I had of Benjamin, the words of Father O'Shea, Bishop Smart's caring concern, the counsel of Elder McKay, and especially the thoughts of young Jared Garfield—perhaps all these things have been signs pointing to what I need to do."

Tom paused in his prayer, not able for a moment to define what he was really seeking. Then he continued.

"I guess I'm afraid that if I finally join the Church, Father, Katrina will think I'm doing it only because I was afraid she might die. But that isn't true. It has taken a long time, but at last I'm settled in my mind, and I thank you, Lord. Please bless her to get well, so we can do what she has wanted for so long."

Not knowing what else to say, Tom remained on his knees for a few moments, then got to his feet and began to disrobe. The bedside clock read 5:20 as he set the alarm for 11:30 and then crawled under the covers.

After what seemed only seconds, the alarm rang. Assuming he had set it incorrectly, Tom reached in the darkness of his room to silence the jangling clock. Then, after turning on a bedside lamp, he reached for his vest, lying next to him on the bed, and looked at his pocket watch. It confirmed the lateness of the hour, and he quickly rose.

Hurrying into the bathroom, he splashed water on his face and looked into the mirror at the haggard face of a tired, distraught man.

"Tommy, me lad, another forty-eight hours of this, and when Katrina *does* wake up, she won't recognize you any more than you recognized her yesterday."

He quickly dressed and took the spiral staircase two

steps at a time, bounding down the stairs into the kitchen, intent on grabbing another bite of cheese and a glass of milk.

"You've changed your schedule somewhat, *Señor*," Seby smiled, rising from the table and reaching for a pitcher to pour another glass of milk.

"So, Seby, you decided to come back this evening."

"Yes. I thought you might be taking turns with Teresa and that perhaps I could share in the blessings, if you're willing."

"Thank you, Seby. I know it's only a couple of blocks, but at this hour I'd be less concerned for her safety if you could take me back to the hospital and bring Tess home."

"It would be my pleasure, *Señor*. Was there any improvement when you saw Sister Callahan this afternoon, Tom?"

"As a matter of fact, the doctor said Katrina was showing signs of being in pain, and he was happy about it."

"What do you mean?"

"He said it's a good sign. Supposedly it shows her brain is functioning again."

Seby nodded. "I can see how that would please *him*, but surely he's going to do something to relieve her pain."

"If she wakes up a bit more, I think he said. Shall we go?" Tom said, grabbing two pieces of bread and a hunk of cheese. "I feel like a shepherd, eating bread and cheese all the time."

The hospital corridor was empty as Tom and Seby tip-toed down the hall toward Katrina's room. The door to her room was closed, but as they opened it, they saw the room was filled with white uniforms, gathered around Katrina's bed.

"Dad!" Teresa exclaimed as she saw her father. "She's awake!"

Tom stepped between two nurses who were observing as Doctor Morgan took Katrina's pulse and then pulled back her eyelids, looking closely into her eyes.

"She just opened her eyes, Dad, a few minutes ago. I called, really I did, but there was no answer. You must have just left."

"Is she speaking?" Tom asked.

"Not yet," Doctor Morgan replied.

Tom and Teresa stood at the foot of the bed as the doctor completed his physical exam. Katrina's eyes wavered slightly, her eyelids closing for several seconds at a time, but when she opened them again, her pupils moved from person to person until Tom could see that she was focusing on him. She momentarily looked away toward Teresa and then back to Tom, the hint of a smile on her lips. Teresa leaned into her father and buried her face in his chest, glancing back at her mother several times as Tom stroked his daughter's hair.

"Mr. Callahan, I'd say it's time to relieve your wife's discomfort. Nurse, fill this prescription," he said as he jotted several notes on Katrina's chart. "Immediately, please. And let's clear the room. I think everyone on duty tonight has had a good chance to participate in our miracle and we *do* have other patients. Everyone, if you please," he said to the room in general.

In a moment the room was empty of all but Doctor Morgan, Nurse Hughes, Tom, Teresa, and Seby. Morgan turned his attention back to his patient.

"Mrs. Callahan, are you able to hear my voice?"

Katrina's eyes shifted to her questioner. She appeared to be trying to speak, but her voice was unable to pass.

"Nurse, some ice chips, please. Quickly."

Hughes immediately left the room while Katrina continued to shift her eyes from Doctor Morgan to Tom and then to Teresa. The nurse soon returned with a bowl of shaved ice and a clean facecloth. Doctor Morgan retrieved a few of the ice chips and leaned forward, rubbing the chips across Katrina's lips. She responded with her tongue, licking weakly at the cool moisture. As she did so, her eyes once again turned toward Tom and by a slight movement of her facial muscles gave the impression of understanding. Once again she licked her lips.

"Thomas," the whisper came, "my head hurts."

Doctor Morgan raised his head and looked back at Tom.

"*That* problem, Mr. Callahan, I can treat," he smiled. "I believe our wait is over."

After one more round of cajoling, Teresa agreed to let Seby take her home, and, after gently hugging her mother, somewhere around three in the morning the two young people left. Tom asked the nurse who had relieved Nurse Hughes if she would mind leaving him alone with his wife for a little while, and the young nurse trainee, concerned about her instructions to not leave the patient, agreed only when the shift supervisor, an older Catholic nursing sister whom Tom had known from Sister Mary's time, agreed to give the couple a bit of privacy.

"Thirty minutes, Mr. Callahan, then we'll have that young lady asleep," she ordered, her tone and demeanor reminding Tom of Sister Mary herself. The conspiratorial smile the older nurse gave to Tom as she closed the door was pure Sister Mary as well, Tom thought to himself.

For minutes, Tom just sat by the bedside, content to hold Katrina's hand and look into her eyes.

Finally, he said, "I'm going to talk to you, Katie, and I'd

prefer that you just listen and not try to respond. Is that all right?"

She blinked her eyes and nodded, almost imperceptibly, but before he could go on, she said in a voice that was barely a whisper, "Thomas . . ."

He leaned forward to catch her words.

"I was with Benjamin," she said.

"I know," Tom replied, "I saw him too," he said, squeezing his wife's hand.

"He told me I must come back," Katrina murmured, almost inaudibly. "It was so peaceful, Thomas, I . . ."

"Katie, please be quiet. There's plenty of time. You need to rest, but there's something I want to tell you. Something I need to say. Please try to listen carefully.

"I've been a fool. All these years I've been a bloody fool. The gospel you've tried to teach me is true, my darling. Perhaps I knew it before. I certainly came to understand it in Portlaoise Prison, but now, I *know* it in my heart."

Katrina blinked her eyes as if trying to comprehend his meaning. In spite of her facial deformity, he saw a familiar set come to her jaw and a look of determination sparkle in her eyes.

"Thomas, you can't just—"

"No, Katrina," he said, shaking his head, "just be quiet and listen to me, please. I haven't come to believe in Mormonism because I thought you might *die*. My belief stems from the knowledge that you will *live*—here, *and* in the hereafter. I know that now. I've *seen* it. And so will I. Maybe I *was* frightened by your possible death. *Of course* I was frightened by it. But if I can't stand the thought of being without you *here,* you should be able to understand that I can't stand the thought of being without you *there.* Please don't ask me to explain why it took me so long to understand such a simple principle," he said, shaking his head. "I only know God's hand is in this, Katie. I know that it is. For so many years I sought to hear His *voice*, but I missed the work of his *hands*—his *works* as they were about me every day.

"Just know that I love you, that *God* loves you—loves us both—and that I will *always* love you, in the truest sense of that word."

Having said that much, Tom was overcome by emotion. He struggled briefly to control his feelings, but finally surrendered to them, laying his head on the bed next to Katrina and weeping.

Teresa and Seby left Holy Cross Hospital well after 3:00 A.M., and Seby drove her the few blocks to *Valhalla*. Turning into the circular driveway in front of the great house, Seby stopped the car and turned off the engine. He exited the car and walked around to Teresa's side, where he opened the door for her, then escorted her up the steps to the front door.

"Seby, I almost feel like I'm floating on air tonight," Teresa exclaimed breathlessly, even at that late hour. "Mom is *all right*. She's going to be *all right*," she almost squealed, then covered her mouth with her hand at the sound as it broke the stillness of the night.

Suddenly, she stepped forward and kissed Seby full on the lips before drawing back momentarily and looking into his eyes. Again, without a word, she placed her hand behind his head and stood on tiptoes and kissed him more ardently, holding on to his neck and sustaining the kiss for several moments. His arms went around her and he pulled her to him, returning the kiss and locking her in his embrace.

Then, somewhat embarrassed by her impulsive behavior, Teresa backed away, turned to put her key in the lock, and stepped across the threshold. Before closing the door, she turned back and looked at him once more.

"Seby, I'm so happy tonight. I hope you understand."

"I understand that your mother has returned to her family and that she will recover from a very serious injury. I also understand that you are a beautiful woman, Teresa Callahan, full of passion and life. For me, that is understanding enough for one evening."

<hr />

Tom and Katrina sat in the foyer of the Church Office building and waited until the young Church worker returned. He gestured toward the stairs.

"Elder McKay will see you now," he said.

Following the young man, they walked up the stairs and were ushered into David O. McKay's office. Wearing a light gray suit and a pale blue tie, the handsome Apostle stood from behind his desk and limped toward the couple, his face beaming.

"Please excuse my not coming down to greet you," he said. "My ankle has been giving me fits since I twisted it in a stirrup some days ago."

The two men shook hands, and Elder McKay took Katrina's hand in his and led her to a chair in a small, parlor-like seating arrangement by the window of his office.

"It's wonderful to see you looking so well, Sister Callahan. You gave us quite a scare there for a week or so."

"So I hear, Elder McKay. I recall little of that time, and perhaps that is fortunate," she said, reaching for Tom's hand. "But as for looking well, without this hat to cover my missing hair and the blessing of cosmetics, I think I should look a fright."

"Well, I'm sure you are as beautiful to Thomas as you are to me, and we're grateful the Lord has permitted us to enjoy your presence for many more years," he smiled. "How may I assist two of my oldest friends?" McKay said as he took a seat facing the couple.

"We came to ask a favor, D.O." Tom said.

"Anything I can do, Tom. You know that, I believe."

"I do," Tom smiled in return. "How does your calendar look on Wednesday, the fifth of October?"

"Let me see," he said, rising and stepping to his desk. "That's about three weeks, uh, I'm speaking that evening, at a stake meeting, but the afternoon is free," he said. "Can I help with something?" he asked, limping back and retaking his seat.

Tom smiled again and nodded. "Of course you know that Robert Thurston is still presiding over the British Isles Mission and won't be home for over a year," Tom said. "Robert has spent a lot of time counseling me over the years, D.O. By rights I should talk to him about this request, but . . . well, to come directly to the point, I've come to ask you to baptize me."

Elder McKay instantly looked at Katrina. She responded by smiling broadly, though there was a glistening in her eyes.

"My, this is a pleasant surprise, Tom," the Apostle said, leaning back in his chair. "If I remember correctly, that date would be your birthday, wouldn't it?"

"It would," Tom said. "My forty-sixth. But then Anders always said that the Irish are slow learners," Tom laughed.

McKay chuckled and put his hands together, steepling

his fingers and locking eyes with Tom. "Tom, tell me how, after so many years, you've come to this decision."

"It's a long story, D.O."

McKay nodded. "We're both still young men, Tom. We've got plenty of time," he smiled.

"Well, I guess it all began when this young college kid named Dave McKay pulled me out from under a rampaging horse, on statehood day, down on South Temple . . . perhaps some of the understanding came while I was in a prison cell in Ireland . . . and *most* of it certainly came from watching and learning from this beautiful, spiritual woman as she has showered me with her unconditional, Christlike love for over twenty-five years . . . but it was brought to its conclusion on a mountain top several weeks ago. The years in between, D.O., well, they probably prove the 'slow-learning-Irish' theory," Tom smiled.

Sebastian Stromberg raced into the ranch house. He tossed his hat onto the couch and picked up the telephone on the fourth ring. Then holding the receiver to his ear and the speaker horn to his mouth, he dropped into a chair next to the telephone table.

"Hello."

"Hi, Seby. It's Tess. I hope I didn't bother you."

"Not at all, Teresa. It's very nice to hear from you."

"Seby, listen, Mom asked me to call and invite you to Dad's baptism on the fifth of next month. Do you think you can come?"

"Absolutely. I wouldn't miss it. What time?"

"Eleven, in the Tabernacle. Elder McKay will perform the baptism."

"Fine. That will be just fine. Will there be many people?"

"No, just a few *hundred* close friends and business associates who have been badgering Dad about the Church for over twenty years," she laughed.

"It will be an honor to be there," Seby said. "Thank you for inviting me."

A few seconds of silence ensued.

"Seby, I, uh, about the night you took me home from the hospital . . . I think I made a fool of myself. I'm very sorry."

"Not to me, you didn't, Teresa. But, please, take no further thought. I understand your excitement, that is, joy over your mother's recovery. I'm sorry that you're sorry," he said, wincing at his choice of words.

"Thank you, Seby. Can we keep this between us, please?"

"You have my word, *Señorita*. I'll see you on the fifth."

"On the fifth, then." Teresa paused for a moment, waiting to see if Seby would hang up the telephone receiver. When both parties remained silent, but still on the line, Teresa spoke again.

"Seby, are you still there?"

"Yes."

"I'm not really *that* sorry."

"Good," he said, a small laugh escaping. "Good-bye, Teresa."

7

*You are cordially invited
to attend the graduation ceremony of the
United States Naval Academy,
Annapolis, Maryland,
to be held on the Fifth of June,
in the year of our Lord,
Nineteen Hundred and Twenty-Three,
at ten o'clock a.m.
Following the ceremony,
you are invited to witness the commissioning of
Second Lieutenant Thomas Matthew Callahan III
United States Marine Corps.*

MAY, 1923
NEW YORK CITY

Teresa Callahan put the invitation and the handwritten note from her brother Tommy back into the envelope, slid her chair away from the mirrored table, and walked out of her dressing room. Stepping on stage and standing behind the thick, drawn curtain, she lifted the peephole flap and placed her eye against the soft material and peered out at the rapidly filling house. There, seated in the third row, center aisle, sat five immaculately dressed naval officers.

Well, she thought, smiling to herself, *almost* naval officers. Her invitation had said that the actual commissioning wouldn't occur until after the graduation. But there he was, her brother Tommy and four of his classmates, come all the way from Annapolis to New York to see her debut as the lead actress in a Broadway musical.

Teresa literally tingled with excitement and jitters as she waited for the curtain to go up. It was her first leading role. Prior to now, she had spent three mostly discouraging years, paying her dues by going from audition to audition, winning only bit parts, but in such popular musicals as Jerome Kern's *Hitchy Koo*, then *Sally*, and finally, the *Ziegfeld Follies of 1921*. Having gained a reputation for being a talented singer and dancer and for being dependable, she got her first big break when she was named understudy to one of Broadway's foremost leading ladies. When the actress developed pneumonia, Teresa finally got her chance to shine, and positive reviews had brought her to this current role as the lead in a George M. Cohan musical. She had worked hard and felt that if she succeeded this time, her career was set. At least that's what her agent was telling her, and she was determined to make the most of the opportunity.

Finally the house lights dimmed, the orchestra began playing the overture, and the moment arrived. All of twenty-three years old and with her heart in her throat, Teresa Callahan, who had chosen to retain her real name as her stage name, listened closely for her pitch from the orchestra and waited for the curtain to rise.

———

The knock on her dressing room door after the final act was just one more noise in a cacophony of backstage sounds. The door opened and the stage director stuck his head in.

"Miss Callahan, the fleet's in," he announced in a prissy manner.

Teresa looked toward the door and as the stage director stepped back, a man in a bright white naval uniform with gold trim filled the doorway. The man quickly stepped into the tiny room, followed by four similarly attired young men.

"Tommy!" Tess squealed, bolting from her chair and throwing her arms around his neck. "Oh, Tommy, it's so good to see you."

"And to think, only three years ago you were just a budding ingénue?" he laughed. "I have five votes all lined up for actress of the year," he added.

Teresa released Tommy's neck and stood back, seeking to regain her dignity in front of his classmates.

"Tess, may I introduce First Classmen Hendrick Wilson, Alan Toppins, and Todd Eastman, and my roommate, Sam Fuqua.[7] Gentlemen," he said, bowing slightly with exaggerated formality, "may I introduce my sister, the newest star on Broadway, Teresa Callahan."

Tess felt her cheeks growing warm, and she began to blush. "Tommy, stop it," she laughed. "I'm very pleased to meet you, gentlemen. Thank you for coming to the play."

"Tess, can you join us?" Tommy said. "We're going to the 21 Club for a late dinner."

"Oh, I'm sorry, Tommy. We have a cast party tonight. We always get together on opening night and wait for the early morning reviews. But I'll be down next Tuesday for your graduation," she smiled brightly.

"You'd better be," he said, kissing her on the cheek.

Midshipman Eastman smiled and took a step forward. "Will *all* of the female cast members be at the party?" he asked.

Teresa laughed. "I'm afraid so, Todd. But in *that* uniform, in New York City, at the 21 Club, I don't think you're going to have a problem," she laughed.

"You won't reconsider, Tess?" Tommy asked as they began to depart the dressing room.

"Oh, I wish I could, Tommy. I really do. What girl wouldn't want to go out with five dashing naval officers?" she said. "But I've just *got* to go with the cast. And it's a *private* party," she said, glancing at Todd. "I'm afraid I won't be able to invite each of you, although I'd love to. You understand, I hope."

"I do, Tess," Tommy said, giving a quick nod. "It's their loss, Sis. You'll all sit around reading some literary fob's review, and four *other* New York girls, five actually," he laughed, "will have a great time tonight."

"I'll bet they will," she laughed in reply. "Thank you all for coming, and I'll see you on Tuesday at Annapolis."

Grinning and stumbling over each other to shake Teresa's hand, the four midshipmen and Tommy departed her dressing room, and Teresa closed the door. She took her seat at the dressing table again, thinking that they probably *would* have more fun than she would at the cast party. Tommy had looked great and as for Todd, well . . .

The second knock on the door was perfunctory, as the door immediately opened and a female member of the cast leaned in. "You comin', Teresa? We're ready to go."

"I'll be right along, Betty. Go ahead and I'll follow. I'll be right behind, don't worry."

"Okay. Don't be late," she called out, leaving the door slightly open as she departed.

Teresa turned back to her mirror and finished arranging her hair in a simple chignon, rolled neatly at the back of her head. She looked at herself for a moment in the dressing mirror, wondering again if she should simply take the easy route and cut her hair short in one of the new, fashionable "bobs" and use a wig for her stage performances. In every way, except for her dark hair—inherited from Tom—Teresa looked much as her mother had at her age. She had large green eyes, a petite, finely shaped nose, and a pretty mouth that showed off her white teeth to advantage when she smiled. And from her mother, she had inherited an impressive singing voice, enhanced by nearly ten years of training under one of Salt Lake's finest voice coaches.

After removing her stage makeup, Teresa added a touch of lipstick and placed a dab of perfume on her throat and in the crook of her elbows. As she recapped the bottle, she sensed, rather than heard, someone in the doorway and turned, thinking that one of the cast had returned to tell her to hurry.

"I'll be right—"

The dark-haired, olive-skinned man standing in the doorway took her by surprise, and for a moment she didn't recognize him. He was wearing a dark gray, double-breasted suit, with light gray spats over his highly polished, black leather shoes. Her first impression was of a well-tailored, wealthy Italian, many of whom were frequently backstage. Then it dawned on her, and she smiled broadly.

"As I live and breathe, Sebastian Stromberg! You're a long way from Salt Lake City."

Instantly, she thought of the night, or rather the early morning, when she had impetuously kissed him on the front steps of her home in Salt Lake City. They had had a few flirtatious encounters after that, but her departure for New York the next fall had put an end to any further development in what had appeared to be a mutual attraction. Now, he was standing in her dressing room door, and she suddenly felt strangely foolish.

Leaving the door ajar, Seby stepped into her room, his arms clasped behind his back.

"I am," he smiled. "And your performance, *Señorita* Callahan, was well worth the trip," he said, reaching out to hand her a bouquet of two dozen yellow roses. "Please allow me to present these flowers as a small token of my appreciation for your excellent performance this evening."

"Oh my, Seby, you shouldn't have," she said, taking the flowers from him.

"Yes, I should," he said immediately. "Was that Tommy and his friends I saw going down the hallway?" he asked, inclining his head toward the doorway.

"Yes, it was. They stopped in to say hello. They're going to the 21 Club. You could catch them if you—"

Seby shook his head. "No, thank you, *Señorita*. I think I shall return to my hotel this evening."

"So, what brings you to New York?" she asked.

"Business. I'm buying some property in Mexico."

"Are you leaving Utah?" she asked.

He shook his head. "No. My ranch in Utah is my home now. But I still have interests in Mexico. Well," he said, turning toward the door, "I just wanted to congratulate you on your performance. It was, as I said earlier, excellent and most enjoyable."

Teresa stepped to the door as Seby was leaving. "Will you be in New York long?" she asked. *Why did I say that?* she thought. *Good grief, he's going to think . . .*

"For a couple of days—through the weekend at least. Before I left Utah, your father informed me of Tommy's graduation next week, and I've made arrangements for a car to drive down to Annapolis. I believe your parents will also be there."

"Yes," she brightened, "they will. And I'm going, too," she added.

Seby hesitated for a moment and then looked into Teresa's eyes. "Would it be presumptuous to offer you a ride to Annapolis? That is, if you haven't made other plans."

"No, actually with rehearsals and all, I haven't even had time to think about it," Teresa lied, knowing she had a train ticket to Washington, D.C., with a connection to Annapolis in her purse. "That's very thoughtful. Are you sure it wouldn't be an imposition?"

"It would be my pleasure, *Señorita*. Where may I call for you?"

"Just down the street, actually. I have a suite at the Carlton."

"Wonderful," he smiled. "I'm at the Waldorf, as your father suggested. An excellent hotel. Perhaps, then—if you're not busy, of course—" he said with formality, "we could . . . have dinner some evening this weekend."

"Oh my," she stalled. "We have two shows on Saturday but only a matinee on Sunday. Would Sunday evening suit?" she asked.

"If it is convenient, I shall call for you at eight, at the Carlton."

"That would be nice, Seby. Very nice."

"Until then, *Señorita* Callahan," Seby said, bowing slightly.

"Tess, Seby. Please call me Tess."

"As you wish, *Señorita*," he smiled pleasantly. "Tess it shall be."

"Would you look at these reviews, Thomas?" Katrina said, folding the newspaper to the literary page and handing it to Tom. "You'd think she was Fanny Brice or one of Ziegfeld's leading ladies," Katrina beamed.

The landscape rolled rapidly by as the train crossed through the western Pennsylvania countryside. Katrina had accompanied Tom on a business trip to Chicago, and they were on the way to attend Tommy's graduation in Maryland and to spend a few days in New York to see Teresa's play. Tom had tried to talk Katrina into taking one of the new commercial airplane flights, but she'd have none of it. Seby had even offered to fly them in his newly acquired *Ryan B-1* prototype aircraft, a mono-wing four-seater, and Tom had smiled at the way Katrina adeptly declined the offer, saying she couldn't possibly miss Tabernacle Choir practice and that it would be unreasonable to ask Seby to delay his departure. When Seby had knowingly winked at Tom as he left the house, Tom had barely been able to contain his mirth. So Tom and Katrina had taken the train again, and after several days on the road, with a three-day stop in Chicago, they were now finally nearing Washington, D.C.

"If it hadn't been for that fawning critic at the *Tribune* several years ago, we wouldn't have to travel all the way to New York to see our daughter anyway," Tom groused. "There're plenty of good theaters in Salt Lake City, or in San Francisco for that matter."

"Oh, Thomas, you old stick-in-the-mud. Your daughter's a hit on Broadway, in *New . . . York . . . City,* and you just can't stand it. You've been waiting for her to flop and come crawling home to Utah, haven't you?" she laughed, pulling at her husband's sleeve.

"Well, somewhere closer than New York. I *know* that town, Katie. It's no place for a proper young woman," he blustered.

"You were familiar with New York over thirty years ago,

Thomas. Since then your visits have been to *first*-class hotels, and even more *first*-class banks. Besides, Tess knows how to take care of herself, and she *is* a proper young woman."

"That's just what I mean. She has no place there."

"I *was* surprised," Katrina continued, "when she called us in Chicago and said that Seby had paid her a backstage visit and would be driving her to Annapolis. Do you think she's regaining an interest in him?"

"Humph. At least she'd be in Utah," Tom said.

Sebastian Stromberg handled the rented Dusenberg capably as he steered it along the two-lane, rural roadway in the eastern Pennsylvania countryside, just north of Philadelphia. He drove at a moderate pace—a bit too slowly for Teresa's taste. She'd become somewhat restless and had developed a love of speed—the result of associating with the theater crowd and a couple of hedonistic young men she had dated during the three years she'd lived in New York.

Obtaining her father's permission to attend the prestigious acting school had been hard, and without her mother's support, it would probably have been impossible—that is without overtly defying his wishes and going off on her own. Teresa had been grateful to her mother for making it possible to get her way without the necessity of disobeying her father and incurring his wrath.

Once in New York, she had found work hard to come by, and when she did land a small part, the schedule was demanding. She was surprised, in the midst of so many people, to find herself frequently homesick, and on at least two occasions, she had packed her bags, ready to admit her failure, call it quits, and head back to Utah. On each occasion, some bit-part had been forthcoming, and she had determined to stay "just a while longer." Finally, after having been in the chorus of three successful musical productions, and then watching from offstage as an understudy to the leading actress, her big break had come, and along with it, her temporary downfall.

When Faye Haberstein, a well-established Broadway actress who was starring in Joel Tripland's *Roses of Summer,* had come down with pneumonia, Teresa, on a three-hour notice, had been required to step in. During her first two performances the audience didn't include any critics from the trade papers. Thoroughly frightened, she had performed unsteadily, but on the third evening, when two of New York's biggest literary critics were in attendance, she had performed smoothly and confidently. So well in fact, that in lauding Teresa's performance, critic Lawrence Overshaw wrote: "It is too bad that Miss Haberstein doesn't have mononucleosis instead of pneumonia." Unfortunately, Miss Haberstein found the inference insulting, and upon her return from her illness, she insisted her understudy be fired immediately. A new understudy, less qualified by all accounts, was appointed in Teresa's place.

Certain her career was over, Teresa had once again packed her bags. She was in the midst of doing so when she responded impatiently to a knock on her apartment door, presuming that one more theater reporter wanted to get her response to the firing. Instead, the immensely successful Broadway producer and composer Aaron Copeland smiled back at her angry stare, and within two minutes, had offered her a supporting role in his latest, forthcoming musical. That had led to her starring in the Cohen production in which she was currently appearing.

None of this had been the subject of their conversation as Seby and Teresa drove the hundred or so miles from New

York to Annapolis. Rather, they had discussed the state of cattle ranching in Utah, the financial dealings of Utah Trust Bank, and Seby's love for his Hidden Valley Ranch. Seby had shown little interest in Teresa's life in the big city. His comment was that New York best be left to the New Yorkers.

"So, Utah has grown on you it seems," Teresa said, continuing her subtle probing into the details of Seby's life.

"As New York seems to have favored you," he smiled in return. "Do you find it agreeable, living a public life?"

Teresa laughed out loud. "It's not as glamorous as it seems. This crowd can turn on you in a moment, and in the next evening edition of the *New York Times,* your fall from grace will be headline news. It's a very fickle business, Seby. Better you depend on the cows."

"There is a certain sameness to cattle," he said, shifting down and passing a slow-moving truck. "All in all, though, surely you must be pleased with what's happening—with regard to your career, I mean."

Teresa brightened considerably, turning in her seat to face him. "Seby, it's the most exciting place I've ever been."

"Really?" Seby said.

"Well, there are some rather pretentious people of course, *onstage* all the time would be an apt description."

"Phony, you mean?"

"Exactly. Compared to my dad, for instance. He usually comes straight out and says what he's thinking. Momma says he would be better off *thinking* less or *talking* less." Teresa laughed again. "But I always know where I stand with my dad, and so do those people who deal with him. Here, in the theater I mean, with some people, I never know what they're *really* thinking. What they expect. It's all so . . . so, *calculated.* But the others, goodness, Seby, I've met the governor, the mayor of New York, members of the president's cabinet—it's a whole new world."

"And?" he asked, quickly glancing at her and smiling.

She smiled back. "Well, it isn't *all* fun," she admitted.

"Then why do you stay?" Seby asked straight out, keeping his eyes on the road ahead.

"Sort of like my father, aren't you? Right to the heart of the matter," Teresa said.

"I admire your father, Tess. He is an honest man *and* a banker. The two roles are not always compatible."

Teresa just nodded her head, and they rode in silence for several minutes.

"I don't know why I stay, Seby," Teresa finally answered. "It certainly isn't like Utah. I think you know that Dad made certain we were all financially secure, so I'm not struggling to earn my living. I do enjoy the challenge, perhaps the struggle even, to achieve something. Playing to the audience is . . . kind of a fulfillment of sorts, and I know the thrill of it all is growing on me," she said, her voice now softer as she looked out the open car window at the passing countryside. "They say it gets in your blood, but as I said, it's not . . . uh, *Utah*."

"And that means . . . what?" he asked, giving her a quick smile.

She looked over at him, suddenly aware that he had successfully turned the conversation to an exploration of *her*.

"It means, Mr. Stromberg," she said, sitting up straight and folding her hands properly in her lap, "that I'm hungry, and before I sit down to listen to several hundred names called out for graduation honors, I need something to eat."

"And in that, *Señorita* Callahan. . . ." he said, having gained more insight into Teresa Callahan than she had intended, and having affirmed that she had matured considerably since their last meeting a little less than two years before ". . . we are in agreement. Next stop—food!"

112

8

Over three hundred midshipmen were seated in ranks on the open parade ground at the United States Naval Academy in Annapolis, Maryland. In the guest seats, Katrina and Teresa sat side-by-side, between Tom and Seby. Hundreds of other parents, relatives, and well-wishers filled the seats above and behind the graduates, who were seated in front of the temporary raised dais that had been built on the parade ground.

Tommy sat among his classmates, outfitted in dress whites, his mind racing with the excitement of the moment. As Admiral Wallace Kensington completed his opening address and began to introduce the keynote speaker, Tommy flashed back in his mind to a similar ceremony. Some six years earlier, he, along with Frank Borello and nearly two hundred recruits, had graduated from the Marine Corps Recruit Training Facility at Parris Island, South Carolina. With the horrible events he had experienced in World War I intervening, it seemed almost a lifetime ago.

Now, as then, the keynote speaker was Edwin Denby. Formerly a United States congressman, Mr. Denby now served in President Warren G. Harding's cabinet as secretary of the navy. Denby rose to speak amid polite applause.

Vaguely listening to the speaker, Tommy thought again of Borello and the ultimate sacrifice his friend had made—a sacrifice made in the trenches in France that had saved Tommy's life.

In recognition of that friendship, Tommy had also sent an invitation to his graduation to Mr. and Mrs. Frank Borello in Staten Island, New York. Almost immediately after he posted the invitation, he had wished he hadn't done it, thinking that it would only open old wounds and renew their sorrow at the loss of their only son. They had not responded, and Tommy had not seen them among the guests prior to commencement of the ceremonies.

Most of Secretary Denby's remarks were lost amid Tommy's rambling thoughts, but then a phrase about the current insurgency in Haiti and the Dominican Republic caught Tommy's ear. He instantly riveted his attention to Denby and listened closely. Three days earlier, when initial postings had been received by the graduating class, 2ᵈ Lieutenant Thomas M. Callahan III, had received his orders assigning him to the Second Brigade, 4ᵗʰ Marine Regiment, presently serving in the Dominican Republic.

Through several shifting policy decisions by U.S. presidents, the U.S. Marines had been stationed in Haiti and the Dominican Republic for well over a decade. It was President Harding's decision to keep marines in the beleaguered nations, where they were serving as policemen, rather than front-line troops, a function vehemently opposed by marine commandant General John Lejeune. Supported by the State Department, Lejeune's position was that the Marine Corps was intended to be a fighting unit and should not be involved in a host of civil and political responsibilities in faltering nations. But he had been unable to change the mission assignment, and more marines had been assigned to police duties in the troubled Caribbean West Indies nations.

Enthusiasm over such a controversial posting was hard to come by, and Tommy was not thrilled at the prospect of becoming a policeman. Some of Tommy's classmates had also been assigned to Central American nations, such as Nicaragua, where rebels under the command of General Augusto Sandino were running rampant over Nicaraguan government troops. Lacking a clear-cut foreign policy, three successive U.S. presidents had followed a somewhat nebulous practice of somehow making a stand in defense of these weak nations. Marines had been put in harm's way, and some had been called upon to pay the ultimate price.

It seemed, Secretary Denby said as he concluded his remarks, that the United States was destined to intervene in other nations' politics whenever it was deemed necessary to sustain and support democratic governments in the Western Hemisphere. The Monroe Doctrine, Denby added, provided great latitude for the president to act in situations that threatened peaceful coexistence with our neighbors.

Denby took his seat to a polite round of applause, and Admiral Kensington once again took the podium. In a pre-arranged movement, the Class of 1923 stood. The first two rows executed a smart right face and began to file out of their seats toward the dais. When both rows of midshipmen were aligned, the admiral nodded toward a navy commander standing at a separate microphone off to the side of the stage, near the first graduate in line.

"Midshipman Michael James Adamson," the parade ground speakers boomed.

A round of applause greeted the young man as he adroitly mounted the podium and accepted his rolled parchment from a naval captain standing next to the commander reading the names. Adamson executed a smart salute, turned to his left and took two steps, saluted Admiral Kensington, shook his hand, and then departed the far side of the stage. The procession of graduating midshipmen continued in this manner until all graduates had crossed the stage and filed back into their seats. As the last midshipman in the last row reached his place, on signal, the Class of 1923 took their seats. Admiral Kensington remained behind the podium.

"Mr. Secretary," he said, gesturing toward Secretary Denby, "honored guests and ladies and gentlemen. It is my honor to present to you the United States Naval Academy Class of 1923."

In one swift movement, the midshipmen once again came to their feet.

"Gentlemen," the admiral said, pausing momentarily and looking over the new naval and Marine Corps officers assembled before him, "welcome to the United States Naval Service."

The air was instantly filled with a flurry of white hats as the young men threw their service caps high into the air, shouting and beginning to hug one another. In the guest stands, Tom, Katrina, Seby, and Teresa also stood among the hundreds of guests and proud parents as they too, applauded the scene below. Teresa clung to Seby's arm, and he noticed the tears running down her cheek.

"Proud of your brother?" Seby said amid the tumult as he smiled at Teresa.

"Oh yes," she responded, beaming.

"What say we go find him," Tom said, leaning over Katrina to allow Seby and Teresa to hear him.

Families and friends mingled with their loved ones as the foursome wound their way through the throng. They finally spotted Tommy as he stood talking with a man and a woman Tom didn't recognize. As they approached, Tommy's face brightened, and he turned to give his mother a quick hug.

"Mom, Pop, these are Frank's parents, Mr. and Mrs. Frank Borello from New York. Pop, Mr. Borello is Lieutenant Borello's father—you know, the friend I wrote you about from France," he said, hoping his father would remember.

"Of course," Tom said, extending his hand to the other gentleman. "My son has told us about your son many times, Mr. Borello. I'm in your debt, sir."

Borello smiled briefly and shook Tom's hand. "You, too, should be proud of *your* son, sir," he said.

"Oh, we are," Katrina responded. "And grateful to you," she said, reaching for Mrs. Borello's hand. Katrina pressed her cheek against that of Mrs. Borello in a gesture of appreciation. As she had leaned toward the other woman, Katrina had seen the glistening in her eyes and held her for just a moment as the two women shared an embrace.

"Well," Mr. Borello said, breaking the silence, "this is a fine day, Tommy. My Frankie would have been very proud of you."

"Thank you, sir. Would you consider pinning on one of my bars, Mr. Borello?"

Borello stood silent for a moment, aware of the tradition involved in Tommy's request. His wife slipped her arm into his and leaned into her husband, smiling up at him. The little clutch of people stood quietly as the older man contemplated Tommy's request.

"Son," Borello said, "it would be my honor."

"Thank you, sir," Tommy said, handing one small gold lieutenant's bar to Mr. Borello and another to his father.

Tommy gestured to the position on his right shoulder epaulet where the bar was to be positioned, and Tom pinned it in place. After that, Mr. Borello repeated the action on Tommy's left shoulder and then shook his hand.

"Mr. Borello, I know this is a hard occasion for you, sir. But I'd like you to know that I will honor the memory of your son throughout my career with the marines. He was, and always will be, my friend."

"And you were his, son. You were his." Borello turned to Tom and Katrina, reaching for Tom's hand. "Thank you, Mr. Callahan. It was a pleasure to meet you and the missus. We both have reason to be proud of our sons, don't we?"

"Aye, that we do, sir," Tom replied. "Indeed we do."

The four members of Tommy's family, plus Seby, watched as the Borellos threaded their way through the throng of well-wishers and graduates, disappearing into the crowd. As soon as they were gone, Teresa stepped forward and threw her arms around her twin brother.

"I'm proud of you too, old man," she laughed.

Seby raised his eyebrows, which Tommy saw over her shoulder as he returned her hug.

"Don't let it concern you, Seby," he laughed. "She has this *thing* about our birth dates."

"It's no *thing*, Lieutenant Callahan. You were born in the *last* century. It's as simple as that," Teresa laughed. "Seby," Teresa said with mock sincerity, "while *I* am certainly proud of my older brother, *he* has always had this *old-man* mentality. It's been difficult for me to understand his old-fashioned ways. After all he *is* a product of the nineteenth century."

"Whereas . . ." Tommy started to say.

"Whereas, *I*, on the other hand, am a thoroughly modern product of the twentieth century."

Seby smiled at brother and sister, standing arm in arm, and then he looked at Tom and Katrina, who were also smiling.

Tom held up both his hands. "I told you when we first met, Seby," Tom said, stifling a laugh, "that this family has its own problems."

"Yes, *Señor*," Seby replied, "as I recall, you did. But *Señorita*," he continued, looking toward Teresa, "my grandfather, Don Sebastian, *and* my grandfather Stromberg both taught me an appreciation for the old ways. Perhaps I can learn from both you *and* Lieutenant Callahan."

"Well," Teresa said, "I see that you could easily work for Uncle Anders—Congressman Hansen I mean."

"Enough," Tom intervened. "Are you free now, Tommy? Are we able to go eat somewhere?"

"I am, Pop, and we can. Just let me meet a couple of my classmate's parents. And I'd like you to meet some of them as well. There are some *very* influential families here today. You'd be surprised at the well-known families who send their sons to Annapolis."

"Lead on, Lieutenant Callahan," Tom said.

Throughout the parade ground the graduation scene was being repeated as hundreds of midshipmen were being pinned by parents, girlfriends, and former marine or naval officers who were family members. Tommy's small group wound its way through the people, stopping several times as Tommy introduced his parents to classmates and their families. Finally, they made their way to the hotel where Tom and Katrina had been staying for the past couple of days. A private dinner in the hotel dining room that evening provided congenial conversation and a chance for Tommy to learn a bit more about Seby's ranch in Utah.

"Six thousand head?" Tommy exclaimed.

"Yes," Seby nodded. "And I have a shipment of thoroughbred racing stock enroute from New Zealand," he smiled. "Courtesy of PJ. He tells me the finest race horses in the world come from a little town called Geraldine."

Tommy looked toward his father and Tom nodded. "PJ's raising race horses as well as cattle and sheep. He's become quite the land baron," Tom laughed.

"Tommy," Katrina interjected, "this Dominican Republic thing. Is it safe?"

Tommy caught the quick look from his father. "Of course it is, Mom," he nodded. "The 2^d Brigade is actually serving as a police unit, and from what I've learned this past week, I'll probably be involved in training new policemen from among the local citizenry."

"A waste of our military forces, if you ask me," Tom said.

"I agree, Pop, but we go where we're assigned."

"You could still come into the bank," Tom said.

"Pop, we've . . ."

"I know, Tommy," he smiled, "I just wanted you to know I still think about it."

"One day, Pop, perhaps," he smiled at his father. "So, Seby, are you going back to New York?"

"I'll take Teresa home tomorrow, Tommy. Then I'll fly back to Utah."

"*Fly?*" Teresa asked, surprise in her voice. "Did you fly out on one of the new airplane services?"

"Ah, no, *Señorita*. I flew my own plane."

"*Your* plane?" she asked, incredulous.

"*Sí.*"

Tommy smiled. "You see, Tess, Seby *respects* the old ways, but *practices* the new methods, it seems."

"My, my, Mr. Stromberg," Teresa exhaled, "I'm impressed, and a bit in awe," she laughed.

"There's no need, *Señorita.* It's becoming more common these days. Perhaps you'd permit me take you up some time."

Teresa looked at her brother, who was smiling broadly at what amounted to a challenge from Seby.

"I'm not *that* modern, Seby. That'll take some convincing."

"And how about you, Tommy?" Seby asked.

"Is it safe?" Katrina interjected.

"The plane is very well constructed," Seby said.

Tommy sat for a moment, thinking. "If that's an offer, Seby, I accept. I don't have to report to my assignment till the first of August. And I've thought about the possibility of going back to Utah for a bit. It's been, what, nearly six years since I was home. Pop, what are your and Mom's plans?"

"Up to New York for a few days, Tommy, to see Tess's play and then back to Utah."

"How about a few days of . . ." Tommy made a gesture of flicking a fly rod, suggesting a fishing trip.

"Now that, son, is the best suggestion anyone has made to me in a long time. You're on. We'll be home in about ten days . . . on the train," he said, smiling at his wife.

"Well then," Tommy said, wrapping his arm around his sister who was seated next to him, "I think I could stand to see Tess's play once more, and then, if you're certain it's no inconvenience, Seby, I'd love to fly back to Utah with you."

"I would appreciate the company, Tommy."

"Then it's settled. Pop, I'll take the train to New York with you and Mom. Seby, I'll see you in New York the day after tomorrow."

"Good. I'm at the Waldorf."

Tommy looked toward his father, who nodded. "That's where we're staying, too."

"I have plenty of room in my suite, Tommy. I'd be happy for you to join me."

"Thanks, Seby, you're on."

Leaving the Waldorf Hotel in a cab, Seby and Tommy crossed the Hudson River into New Jersey to the small airfield where Seby had left his plane. They pulled up next to a wooden shed, and a man in overalls came out, wiping his hands on a greasy rag. The cab driver exited the car and began to collect the several pieces of luggage from the trunk of the vehicle.

"All ready, Sam?" Seby queried the aircraft mechanic.

"Gassed up and ready, Mr. Stromberg. Weather looks good," he said, glancing at the nearly cloudless sky.

"That's the variable isn't it, Sam?" Seby replied.

"Yes, sir. Can't control that one, I can't," he laughed. "Let me help you with that luggage," he added.

"Thanks. This is Thomas Callahan, Sam, a newly commissioned Marine Corps lieutenant."

"Pleased to meet you, sir," Sam said, extending his hand. "Do I know you, sir?" he said, studying Tommy's face.

"Don't know, Sam. Where do you think we met?"

"A new lieutenant, you say. Just in the Corps?"

"No, actually . . ."

"That's it, sir," he said, his face brightening. "You're Sergeant Callahan, 6th Marines, ain't 'cha? Private Sam Donaldson, sir—served under Gunny Holloman as a vehicle mechanic, I did. You was at Belleau Wood, wasn't you, sir?"

Tommy nodded. "I was, Sam. I'm proud to make your acquaintance again. Got yourself a good little business here,

122

it looks like," Tommy said, looking around the small airfield and repair hangar.

"Yes, sir. Life's been good to me and the missus. Kinda miss the Corps though, if you know what I mean," he said, a broken-toothed grin highlighting his smile.

"You know what they say, Sam. 'Once a marine . . .'"

"*Semper fi,* sir," he smiled back, giving Tommy a loose salute. "Here, let's get your stuff aboard the aircraft."

The three men walked around the hangar to where a single engine, high-wing monoplane stood, secured by wing ties connected to stakes in the ground.

"I haven't seen many single winged planes, Seby. What is it?" Tommy asked.

"Actually, Tommy, it's a preproduction model. At your father's suggestion, I made a small investment in a fledgling company with a man named Ryan. And then I bought one of his early models. This is what he's calling the *Ryan B-1.* Supposed to be a five-seater, but I've had the backseat removed and an extra fuel tank installed. We can seat three, four in a pinch, if they're all friends," he laughed. "We can cruise at about 180 miles per hour with a range of eight hundred to a thousand miles, depending on winds and altitude."

"How long to Utah?" Tommy asked, walking around the aircraft.

"Two long days if we don't have any trouble. On the westward leg, though, I usually put down east of the Rockies and cross over the next morning, making it two and a half days. Don't want to risk flying in the dark over the mountains. We'll make Indianapolis tonight, or maybe even Springfield, Illinois. Probably stop in Cheyenne the next night and get in to Salt Lake late Wednesday morning. Of course, we'll make several fuel stops each day."

"Actually, not much faster than the train," Tommy commented.

"True," Seby smiled, reaching into the cockpit, retrieving a set of coveralls and pulling them on over his clothes. "There's an extra pair of coveralls behind the front seat on your side, Tommy."

"I'm getting enthusiastic about this, Seby. You know, aviation is becoming a big part of military strategy. Observation, primarily, but there are those who advocate its use on the battlefield to a much greater extent than we did in France."

"You interested in flying?"

"I don't know," Tommy replied, buttoning his coveralls.

"Well," Seby grinned, walking in front and checking the engine cowling, "let me put you in the air for three days, and I'll convince you."

"I'm all yours, Mr. Stromberg."

"Looks good, Sam," Seby said, shaking the man's hand. "Don't expect to be back for a couple of months, but you never can tell. I'll telephone or telegraph if that changes."

"Anytime, Mr. Stromberg. We'll take care of this baby," he said, patting the side of the aircraft.

"You always do, Sam. Take care now, and regards to your wife," he said, climbing up into the pilot's seat. Tommy settled himself into his side of the plane and following Seby's example, buckled a canvas belt around his waist. Sam stood by with a fire extinguisher as Seby set the throttle and cranked the engine. Ryan had installed an electronic starter, eliminating the need to prime the engine and manually crank the propeller prior to start it. With the engine running smoothly, the pressure gauges checked, and the temperature having reached normal, Seby waved off Sam and began to taxi toward the downwind end of the grass strip.

With a wink at Tommy, Seby advanced the throttle, and the small monoplane began to gain speed across the bumpy field, taking two or three bounces as it struggled to gain airspeed and lift. Finally, the wheels left the ground and the *Ryan* gained altitude, quickly rising above buildings of rapidly diminishing size on the ground and crossing over a patch of woods, a narrow rural road, and several cars.

"What do you think, Lieutenant Callahan?" Seby shouted over the roar of the engine.

Tommy continued to look out his window at the diminishing features on the ground, enthralled by the sensation of actually leaving the earth behind. Instantly, he remembered the small biplanes he'd seen over the trenches in France and the one occasion where a platoon under his command had come upon a crashed German *Fokker* tri-wing, its pilot burned beyond recognition.

"Actually, it's a bit frightening, but I think I'm in for an exciting three days, Seby. A *very* exciting three days," he shouted.

"It can get boring," Seby replied. "I'm glad for the company."

"And I'm glad for the invitation," Tommy nodded. "Very glad indeed," he smiled.

9

Upon his return to Salt Lake City from the East, Tom invited Robert Thurston to join him, Tommy, and Seby on their planned fishing trip. But instead of taking a two- or three-day horseback trip to some remote location, as they would have done when Tommy was a boy, Seby flew the party in his airplane to Cody, Wyoming, where Tom had made reservations for them at the Irma Hotel.

Built in 1902 by Colonel William F. "Buffalo Bill" Cody, the Irma was a first-class hotel and a favorite destination for movie actors and other celebrities. Cody had died in 1917, but his reputation and the skill of the current staff of the Irma continued to attract wealthy clientele from all over the world. The hotel, situated on Sheridan Avenue, was the only landmark in Cody and was located in the heart of some of the West's best trout fisheries. Tom and his party planned to take daily trips to the nearby rivers.

Other guests at the hotel that week included celebrities Wiley Post and Will Rogers, who had arrived in Post's airplane a day before Tom and his party. A newly married Oklahoma oil man and his somewhat younger-than-he second wife were also staying at the Irma, but as Rogers and Post enjoyed pointing out, the clean-shaven groom and his

126

comely bride stayed mostly in their room—something the two men found immensely funny.

Also staying at the Irma that week was a British military officer and his entourage, in Wyoming to hunt bear. Brigadier Sir David McIntyre of His Majesty's 60th Regiment of Foot, his manservant, and the brigadier's twenty-four-year-old son, plus several American friends had already been at the Irma for about a week when Tom arrived. The younger McIntyre had been boasting around the bar of his expert marksmanship—something the young man had not as yet demonstrated by bagging a bear, though he had reportedly had a couple of chances.

Following a day of fishing and hunting, the hotel guests gathered each evening in the hotel dining room for dinner and afterward in the adjacent lobby or bar to relax and swap stories.

On the third evening, Tom, Robert, Tommy, and Seby were seated in the lobby, visiting with Rogers and Post about the relative merits of the Gravel, Shoshone, and Clark Rivers as trout fisheries. Rogers changed topics from fishing to the vanishing wilderness in America. He and Tom had engaged in some friendly banter the night before—trading Paul Bunyan-type stories—and the two men, who were about the same age, had become comfortable with each other.

"It's true, Tom," the cowboy humorist said. "Old Buffalo Bill is gone, and about all that's left of the real West is coyote scat, and soon that'll be gone too."

Post chimed in. "Will's right. The only real remaining wilderness is in Alaska, and if we don't get there soon, the Russians will have civilized all the Eskimos." His comment was met with laughter, and as it died down, the conversation turned to world events. Post made a comment about the recent emancipation of the Irish Free State from the British Empire. When Tom's mood became more serious, it was clear to everyone that Post had touched a nerve.

"Why do you suppose it has been so hard to accept the fact that Ireland wanted to be independent?" Tom asked. "The Brits held them in bondage longer than they did the American colonies. And they still control the six northern counties. It's like if America won her independence, but the king kept New England."

"True," Rogers said, setting aside for the moment his characteristic down-home way of speaking. "For some reason, there's always been a reluctance on the part of England to grant the Irish their freedom. They've had their share of oppression, that's for sure."

"Bloody well deserved, I should think, what with their leaders killing each other on their way to the top," a voice said from the entrance to the hotel bar.

The group in the lobby turned their heads in that direction to see a young man, wearing a buckskin shirt, jodhpurs, and leather riding boots, walking somewhat unsteadily toward them. He carried a half-empty beer mug in one hand and a leather riding crop in the other.

"The bloody Irish haven't learned to govern their own appetites, much less their country," the man continued. "And when de Valera had a bullet put through Collin's brain—if the bloody wog had a brain—it was just one less Catholic upstart for His Majesty's forces to deal with."

Robert shot Tom a look that warned "The man's drunk," and Tom nodded in reply.

The six men seated in the lobby remained quiet,

recognizing the potential for trouble should one of them confront the young man.

Speaking more loudly, the man continued. "Are there no Irish among you, then, man enough to defend 'the old sod'?" he challenged.

"And who might you be, son?" Will Rogers asked.

The red-faced man straightened himself as best he could and said, "I am Jonathon McIntyre, Esquire, son of Brigadier Sir David McIntyre of His Majesty's Regiment of Foot. We have come to your country, sir, to bag a few bear as it were." He blinked his eyes and added, "Certainly, if your loud-mouthed, half-blind President Roosevelt can do it, a proper English gentleman can do it better."

Fixing his blurry vision on Rogers, the young man said, "And who might I be addressing, sir?"

"Well, son, I'm Will Rogers. I'm part Cherokee, part German, part likable, and part ornery, but don't let any of that get in your way," he smiled.

McIntyre blinked a few times, then turned his attention to Tom.

"And you, sir, did I hear you speak fondly of the bloody Irish?"

Tom glanced at Robert, who shook his head slightly, again warning Tom not to take the bait. Then Tom looked up at McIntyre.

"Actually, Mr. McIntyre, I *am* rather fond of the Irish, and on occasion, I've even met a few Englishmen I've liked. Just a few, mind you."

Robert Thurston sighed and shook his head, smiling sadly.

"Was that an insult, sir?" McIntyre asked.

"Not unless you take it that way, son." Tom replied, remaining seated. "Why don't you just go on up to your room and sleep it off. I think you've had enough for one evening."

Tom was looking at Robert again, a smile similar to Robert's on his face, when McIntyre's riding crop grazed Tom's face and landed sharply on his shoulder. Tom immediately came to his feet. He grabbed the crop out of McIntyre's hand and flung it across the lobby. The Englishman flinched and backed away. Then, with surprising quickness, given his state of inebriation, McIntyre produced a hunting knife from a sheath on his belt and stepped forward, slashing at Tom. Tom saw the knife, but too late to avoid it, and the blade sliced into the flesh of his upper left arm. McIntyre then drew the knife back, preparing for another lunge.

In an instant, Tommy was out of his chair and moving toward his father's assailant. When McIntyre swiped at Tommy, the young Marine avoided the knife thrust and in a swift movement stepped behind the Englishman and drove his boot hard into the back of McIntyre's left knee. McIntyre's leg collapsed, and he pitched forward, crashing face forward onto a low, wooden table in front of a couch, with Tommy instantly on his back. Stunned, the Englishman didn't resist as Tommy bent the man's arm behind him and wrenched the knife from his grasp, then held the point of it against the side of McIntyre's throat. In seconds, before anyone else could react, Tommy had disarmed the man and now held him helpless.

"Stop!" a man's voice called from across the room. "Please, sir," the man said as he hurried forward. "I beg your indulgence. Do not injure Master McIntyre. I will assume responsibility for him."

"Who the hell are you?" Tommy shouted, glancing up from the man he had pinned to see who had intervened.

"Please, sir, I beg of you. My name is Albert. I am Sir David's manservant. This young man is the brigadier's son."

"Did you see what this drunken fool just did?" Tommy demanded, looking toward his father, whose wound was being attended to by Robert and Seby, who were trying to stop the bleeding with a table napkin.

"I did, sir. I saw the whole incident. I implore you not to call the authorities. Sir David will resolve the matter to your satisfaction straight away, tomorrow, when he returns from Cheyenne."

"Get off me, you bloody wog," McIntyre cried.

Looking down at his captive, Tommy shifted his weight to put more pressure on his opponent's back and pressed the knife point more firmly against the man's neck. McIntyre cried out in pain and fear.

"I suggest you shut up, Mr. *Esquire*," Tommy said, speaking deliberately and holding his mouth just inches from the Englishman's ear.

"Sir," Albert pleaded, "if you will release Master Jonathon, I will warrant his behavior and see that his father is notified of this unfortunate incident."

Hearing the fracas, a large group of men had gathered, and Tommy looked up at his father for guidance. Tom nodded his assent, and Post said, "Let him up, Tommy, we'll help Albert if necessary." As Tommy released his foe, Tom allowed Seby and Robert to lead him away to look for medical aid.

Tommy stared Jonathon McIntyre in the face, the desire to punish the man who had attacked his father not yet fully under control.

"Count your blessings, Englishman. I'd just as soon shove this pig sticker through the back of your neck, but we *are* trying to be civilized here in the colonies."

Stepping to the rock fireplace, Tommy inserted the knife blade into a space between two stones and snapped it off, then tossed the handle into the fire. Then, sneering at the man, Tommy turned on his heel and left the lobby, following his father.

Tom's arm required twelve stitches, administered by the only doctor in Cody, and the foursome didn't return to the Irma until just before midnight. Tommy shared a two-bed room with Seby, and Tom and Robert shared similar accommodations. On their initial arrival at the hotel, they had bantered back and forth with the requisite jokes about old men needing to room together so they could snore in private, and Tom rebutting his son's taunting with stories about Tommy's being afraid of the dark. As they settled into their beds following the altercation, Tommy tossed and turned a bit until, finally, from across the room, Seby said, "It could have been much more serious, I suppose."

"Yeah, I keep thinking that too. If his jab had been a few inches over, he'd have stabbed Pop in the chest."

"I've never seen anyone move as fast as you did, Tommy. You might have saved your father's life. It looked like he was going to stab him again."

Tommy didn't respond immediately. "I could have killed him, Seby," he finally said. "I *wanted* to."

"I think everyone could see that, but they all understood why."

"That doesn't make it any easier to consider. I might have taken another life."

"It was war back then, Tommy," Seby said.

"I know. But the memories are still there. They come when I least expect it."

The two men lay silent, and slowly, as the hour length-
ened, they finally drifted off to sleep.

<hr />

The following afternoon, returning from yet another day
on the river where Robert had bested them all with a
seventeen-inch rainbow trout—a contest Tom had
exempted himself from due to his bandaged arm—the group
was surprised to find Jonathon McIntyre waiting for them
in the graveled car park behind the Irma. Tom took stride
beside his son as they approached the young man. Seby also
moved a bit more quickly to stand between Tommy and
Jonathon McIntyre.

"What can we do for you, Mr. McIntyre?" Robert
Thurston said, taking the lead.

"My business is with *this* man," he said, nodding toward
Tommy.

"I think the two of you have had enough business
already," Robert said.

"Stand aside, sir," he said, abruptly shoving Robert. "Are
you prepared to defend yourself against someone who's not
intoxicated?" he challenged Tommy.

"It appears to me you're always intoxicated—with your
own pompous attitude, you ignorant English twit," Tommy
said, stepping forward to stand face-to-face with Jonathon.
"Where's your knife today, you sniveling coward?"

McIntyre stood his ground and smiled at Tommy.
"Before I'm through with you, you'll eat those words, my
good fellow."

"And you'll be serving the dinner I suppose? And your
keeper—where's Albert today? Did you slip your leash?"

"No weapons, no Albert, Mr. Callahan. A bloody Irish

name, I see. No wonder you have the manners of a cowman."

"The *manners*, Mr. *Esquire*, or lack thereof," Tommy smiled in return, "have been more of your making, I would say. So what's it to be? Knives at two paces," he laughed.

"All right," Tom said, stepping between the two men, "this has gone far enough. *You*, McIntyre, move along and get back inside the hotel."

McIntyre shoved Tom aside as he had Robert and took another step closer to Tommy.

"I'll brook no interference from you, Mr. Callahan, the *elder*," he said. "Fists, I would say," he challenged again, speaking once more to Tommy. "By the Marquis of Queensberry rules."

Tommy just shook his head, sneering at the impudent young man. "You've got guts, Mr. *Esquire*, I'll give you that. Let me get this straight. You come to *my* country, want to kill *my* bears, insult and then stab *my* father, and then challenge me to a fist fight by *your* rules. Only an Englishman would be that cocky. Perhaps it's time you learned a real lesson."

Robert stepped between the two men to separate them.

"It's all right, Robert," Tom said, his anger again kindled. "Tommy can handle himself."

McIntyre smiled victoriously and laughed. "There'll be a lesson taught, all right, and *I'll* be the teacher, Mr. Callahan. I must inform you though, I have held the boxing championship two years running at Oxford. That's fair warning in case you wish to reconsider your decision, although I hope you would choose to continue and prove your manhood."

"Manhood, is it?" Tommy said, dropping his creel and rolling up his sleeves. "Pop, maybe you'd be kind enough to hold my fishing gear for a few minutes. Mr. Esquire *himself*, and Mr. *Queensberry* want to teach me a lesson. Shall we begin, you bloody Brit?"

The quick, sharp jab to Tommy's chin came lightning fast, and, instantly, Tommy found himself sitting on the gravel driveway, gazing through watery eyes up at McIntyre who was prancing around on the balls of his feet, holding his fists upright in front of him.

"Lesson one, never take your eyes off your opponent. Take your feet, Irishman, and we shall move on to lesson two."

"Master Jonathon, *please!*" Albert said as he came around the corner of the building.

"Albert," McIntyre said, continuing to hold a steady gaze at Tommy who was regaining his feet, "you will be silent and keep out of the way. Come now, Mr. Callahan, I thought the Irish had more staying power than one punch."

Fists up, Tommy began to circle as McIntyre danced about, feigning a thrust and withdrawing at each perceived opening. Suddenly, Tommy darted inside and threw an uppercut into McIntyre's body, but he was rewarded with a resounding blow to the side of his head as he retreated. This time Tommy held his feet but kept his distance for the next several seconds, trying to clear his head and moving warily, keeping his eyes focused on McIntyre. Several feints later, Tommy had yet to land another blow, but had avoided absorbing any further *lessons* from the Englishman.

With a smile, McIntyre changed his tactic and instead of prancing, he shifted to a steady pursuit, quickly landing two jabs to Tommy's face, causing Tommy to shake his head to clear his vision. When McIntyre threw his next punch, a looping right hand, Tommy moved quickly forward, stepping inside the punch. The Englishman's arm wrapped for a moment around Tommy's neck, and before he could withdraw for another blow, Tommy grabbed McIntyre's wrist and pulled the Englishman into him, locking the man's arm in the hollow of his armpit. When McIntyre hit Tommy on the side of his head with his other fist, Tommy lifted up hard on the imprisoned arm, wrenching the elbow violently upward. The sudden movement caused a cracking sound that was heard by all. Jonathon McIntyre yelped in pain and stepped back, looking down with amazement at his arm, which hung loosely by his side.

Albert stepped forward, attempting to render assistance and receiving for his trouble a verbal assault from his charge.

"You may consider boxing a game used to teach the lower classes to mind their station in life, McIntyre," Tommy said, rolling down his sleeves, "but fighting is the last resort for a man with a weak mind and should be finished quickly. Albert, I suggest you take Mr. McIntyre to the doctor. Just tell him the stabbing victim from last night sent him. And tell the doc to send *me* the bill."

That evening, sitting around a roaring fire in the hotel lobby, Robert, Seby, Tom, and Tommy were shelling peanuts while drinking hot cider and spending one more evening discussing the day's fishing. Everything had been prepared for their departure the following morning, but the episode with young Jonathon McIntyre had somewhat dampened the mood of the group. While they were conversing, Albert approached the group from the direction of the bar and stood quietly until he was noticed and the men ceased talking.

"Begging your pardon, Mr. Callahan, but Sir David has sent me to inquire if he might speak with you for a moment, that is, if it is convenient." He addressed his remarks to Tom, who considered the request and then nodded his approval.

"Sure, why not?" Tom replied.

Albert left for a few moments, then returned to the lobby in the company of a ruddy-faced, silver-haired gentleman of about fifty, who carried himself with a military bearing. He walked straight toward the group, focusing his attention on Tom.

"Mr. Callahan," he said, stopping directly in front of the small circle of chairs, "thank you for agreeing to my request. I am Brigadier David McIntyre, and I have come, sir, to offer my sincere apologies for the inexcusable behavior of my son, Jonathon. Albert has informed me of the events of last evening, and, unfortunately, this afternoon. I can only offer my most humble apology, sir."

"Things got a little heated, but I think we can call the episode over," Tom said.

"Indeed," Sir David said. "And you, sir," he said, turning to address Tommy, "I am informed, are a United States Marine officer."

Tommy stood and faced Sir David directly.

"Yes, sir. Thomas Callahan Jr., second lieutenant."

"Then you are newly in the service of your military forces?"

"No, Brigadier, I just graduated from the naval academy, but I enlisted in the Corps in '17."

"I see," Sir David said, raising his eyebrows. "And served in France?"

"I did, sir. With the 6th Marines, at Château-Thierry and Belleau Wood."

Sir David nodded his approval. "That would account for the boldness of your actions here."

"Sir, I'm sorry things got out of hand, but your son's attack on . . ."

Sir David raised his hand in a gesture of silence.

"Lieutenant Callahan, I have been reliably informed by the barkeep that over the years many a man in this part of your country has died for significantly less affront than that given by my son to your father. Your restraint in not killing him on the spot speaks highly of your training and your discipline. You owe me no apology. Quite the contrary. Should you ever find yourself in England, and in need of a good reference—and I might add, in spite of my son's behavior, or lack thereof, I do have an impeccable reputation among my peers—please do not hesitate to call on me for assistance. Alfred will give you my card. It may perhaps come in handy someday," he said, extending his hand to Tommy.

"And, Mr. Callahan," he said, turning to address Tom, "I'm sorry for your wound and trust that it will heal quickly."

Tom waived off the apology. "Don't worry about it."

"Yes, well," Sir David continued, "you have reason to be proud of your son, just as I have reason to be shamed by mine. But such is life, as I understand it, and we each must deal with our progeny accordingly. I have had many young men under my command and consider myself a good judge of character, Mr. Callahan, and I would be proud to serve with Lieutenant Callahan, were the occasion to arise."

With that, Sir David drew himself up and said, "Well, if there is nothing else, gentlemen, I will take my leave. Godspeed on your return trip."

Tom got to his feet and stepped toward Sir David and shook his hand without speaking. As the two Englishmen disappeared back into the bar, Robert was the first to respond.

"A true gentleman from the old school," the banker said. "How could you be mad after that?"

"An era that's about gone, I'd say," Tom replied. "But I'll tell you what, Tommy, I *am* proud of you."

Tommy smiled and looked into the fire for a few moments. Then he said, "I hope I can find something more honorable to earn your praise, Pop, but thanks."

During the flight home the next day, Tommy found himself feeling a bit melancholy. Remembering earlier days and thinking how long it might be until the next fishing expedition with his father, he remained quiet during most of the flight. The thought of departing to the marines again, after just rediscovering his home, brought a sense of foreboding and added to his somber mood. His chosen career would, of necessity, send him around the world for the indefinite future, and he'd more than likely meet others like young Jonathon McIntyre, Esquire.

Arriving home, Tommy tried to hide the bruises on his face by avoiding his mother's searching gaze. But she noticed them immediately, and when she was told the story, with Tom omitting the part about having been stabbed, she somehow blamed her husband for permitting the whole sorry mess. When she discovered Tom's bandaged arm later that night as they got ready to go to bed, her exasperation was complete.

"Honestly, Thomas, I don't know what to do with you! You're as irresponsible in these things as one of the children."

Tom only smiled until his wife finished reprimanding him, then said, "You'd have been proud of Tommy, Katie. He handled himself beautifully."

"How are you going to find a nice LDS girl out there, Tommy?" Katrina asked at dinner his final evening at home.

"Mom, you know no one can take your place," he teased.

Her stern look quickly dispelled his humor, and he nodded his head in submission.

"It's not time for that yet, Mom. I'll know when."

The next morning, pleading that she wasn't up to trying to control a public display of emotion, Katrina said her tearful good-byes to her son in the front hallway of *Valhalla*, leaving Tom and Tommy to go to the train station without her. Now, as they stood together, waiting for the train, father and son did so without conversing.

Just before the scheduled departure of the train, Tom finally broached the subject that had been on his mind for some time.

"Tommy, this fishing trip—aside from the McIntyre episode—"Tom laughed, rubbing his upper arm, "brought back all the happy memories of our early days. I want you to know that one of the best things that ever happened to me took place four years ago when you forgave me for being so pigheaded. But I feel there's another area where I've done you wrong, and that's regarding the Church."

"Pop, I—"

"It's my turn to talk, Tommy," Tom said, "just hear me out, please."

Before continuing, Tom was quiet for a moment, searching for the right words. Finally, he went on.

"PJ gave me this same talk when we left him in New Zealand nearly six years ago, at a time when we knew you were going to France. I've lived something of a charmed life,

Tommy, and I've always been surrounded by people who've had an interest in me and watched out for my welfare. When I landed in New York as a brash young fellow with no sense, Father O'Leary helped me see things more clearly. Then when I arrived here in Salt Lake City there were Sister Mary and Father Scanlan to look out for me. Even in Alaska, Uncle John opened a door for me, and, well, you've seen the results of that.

"I've had the friendship of people like Elder McKay and Robert Thurston, and many others, and for years I guess I depended on others. But it wasn't until I began to look inside myself and seek a personal relationship with God that I found any real satisfaction, any peace.

"While I was getting to this point I had your mother's love to sustain me. She's had the faith to believe that I would one day open my heart to the truth and embrace the gospel. Well, I've come to that day, Tommy, but what I'm afraid of is that it's happened too late to help you understand the things that are now most important to me. I'm sorry for all the confusion my doubts must have caused you when you were growing up, but I want you to know that I now have a testimony. God lives, and the Mormon Church is His church. I don't know why it has taken me so long to understand that."

"Pop," Tommy responded, "I remember the feelings I used to have about the Church when I was little. I remember talking to Bishop Thurston and believing in the things Mom told me. It's just that now . . ."

Tom nodded his head and took his son's arm in his, drawing the young marine officer close. "Just don't shut God out, Tommy. It's a dangerous profession you've chosen, and as long as our president keeps sending the marines around the world to fight other people's battles, well, you've got to see the potential dangers. As much as I love you, and as much as your mother loves you, the Lord loves you more, son, and wants you to know that. I failed you for years," Tom said, his face reflecting his sorrow at the omission, "but the Lord has never left you. You said as much in your letter to me from France. God gave you the protection you needed, and He preserved your life. I understand that you feel He took your friend's life, perhaps in place of yours, but as you said to me in that letter, that was His choice to make, not yours or mine. Just give it some thought, Tommy, and don't abandon the principles your mother taught you as you were growing up."

Both men stood facing each other for a long, silent moment, and then Tommy reached out and hugged his father. "You've made Mom very happy, Pop. I'm glad for her, and for you. Thanks for all you've done for me. I love you both very much."

"And we love you, son. Whatever happens around the world, you've always got a home here. Don't forget that. God's blessings go with you, Tommy."

10

On August 4, 1923, three days after he arrived on the island, Tommy stood, sweating profusely but rigidly at attention, in front of Colonel Wilson Rixby, the commanding officer, 2ᵈ Brigade, United States Marine Corps, who was seated behind a chipped and worn wooden desk. The brigade was currently on assignment to the Dominican Republic with the 1ˢᵗ Brigade close at hand on the west end of the island in Haiti.

"Second Lieutenant Thomas M. Callahan, reporting as ordered, sir."

"Stand at ease, Lieutenant," the officer behind the desk said. Colonel Rixby, an up-through-the-ranks mustang who had distinguished himself in the Philippines during the Spanish-American War, slowly riffled through the personnel folder that lay before him on his desk. Tommy snapped to parade rest, waiting patiently in front of the colonel's desk. Finally, the senior officer looked up.

"I swear, I don't know what to make of you, Lieutenant. Most often I get some snot-nosed, wet-behind-the-ears momma's boy out of the academy. They come into *my* brigade, hang up their dress-white ballroom suits, think *they're* marines, and try to command *my* troops."

Rixby's voice was deep, gravelly, and laced with a no-nonsense tone. Tommy instantly understood that Colonel Rixby was not a man to trifle with. He remained silent at his fixed position, his eyes riveted to the wall above and behind the colonel.

"But," and the older man paused again, flicking once more through the papers on his desk, "by all accounts, Lieutenant Callahan, you *are* a marine. And you *can* command troops. So just what in blazes do I do with you in this mosquito-infested, swamp-ridden, tropical paradise?"

Tommy remained silent.

"Have you nothing to say for yourself, Lieutenant?"

"Sir, the lieutenant is honored to be assigned to the Second Brigade and under the colonel's command, sir."

Rixby eyed Tommy and shook his head. "You won't be so honored when you see what we've got to do here, son. We've been assigned to move a pile of manure, and we're flat out of shovels. In short, this is no ordinary marine outfit and you'll be assigned to no ordinary line company. In fact, if I've got one single platoon worth of decent marines on the whole island, I've not yet seen 'em. We've got the dregs here, Lieutenant, and on top of that, we've got the job of turning the meanest bunch of local thugs you can envision into policemen.

"What we *do* have," he continued, rising from his seat and shaking his head as he walked toward the window, "in both Haiti and the Dominican Republic—and I've worked in both—" he said, turning to look back at Tommy "is the worst possible combination of circumstances. The criminals—and I mean hard-core criminals—have been in charge for decades and through intimidation of local politicians, *they've* become the police force. The local population is terrified of them, and to make matters worse, in order to survive, our marines have become just as brutal: summary executions in the field, beatings, rape—you name it and we've followed right along in their footsteps and done it."

Suddenly, Colonel Rixby whipped around and took two great steps to stand eye-to-eye with Tommy. He spoke not a word for several long moments during which Tommy continued to stand at a formal parade rest, his eyes firmly fixed to a spot on the wall behind the colonel's desk.

"Lieutenant, I *know* Colonel Catlin and I *knew* the 6th Marines in France. *Those* men were marines, and if Catlin knew you well enough to recommend you for a field commission and to sign your meritorious commendation, then that's proof enough that *you* are a marine. What kind of marine is yet to be determined, but I'll tell you what General Lejeune used to tell me: 'Marines don't follow orders, they *obey* orders, but they follow leaders.' Do you understand me, son?" he said, his voice rising.

"Sir, the lieutenant is prepared to do all he can to fulfill the orders of the colonel, sir."

Rixby nodded and then stepped behind his desk, taking his seat again.

"Well then, here's what we're gonna do, Lieutenant Callahan. Considering your first assignment some years ago, as a training instructor at Parris Island, I'm going to place you in charge of the training barracks for local police officers. God help you, son, it's a distasteful job, and you'll find the cadets, if they can be called that, the bottom of the barrel. I'll give you two weeks to find yourself a dozen marines and a good sergeant—if you can find a dozen you can call marines on this island—to staff the school. You can take 'em where you find 'em, son. I don't care as long as you think they can do the job.

"We've been at this for about a year now, and the

145

lieutenant you're going to replace gave up after about three weeks. He's been dead weight ever since, but the Corps won't have to suffer his ineptitude any more. I cashiered him, and he's going back to the hardware business in Mineola. I thought I was going to get another feckless officer who didn't want to dirty his whites. You're a pleasant surprise, Callahan, but that won't cut any mustard with me, son, unless you produce results. I want a clean house over there, a new commander—that's you, Lieutenant—new staff and especially, if you can find one, a first-rate, top sergeant. You put that together for me, Lieutenant Callahan, and we just might salvage some degree of success from this misguided effort. You understand me, Lieutenant?"

"Sir, yes, sir."

Rixby smiled for the first time and stood up behind his desk, stretching his hand across the blotched and tattered desk top. Tommy came to attention, then reached out to grasp the colonel's outstretched hand.

"Welcome aboard, Lieutenant. Look, son, for all I know President Harding's unexpected death[8] will have significant repercussions on our mission assignment. Nobody at headquarters knows where President Coolidge stands on these issues, and we'll just have to bide our time until he gets his feet wet. Until then, I have the feeling that Colonel Catlin knew what he was doing when he recommended you for that commission. You may well turn out to be, by all that's holy, a marine officer. My kind of marine. We'll know soon enough, won't we?" he said, looking sternly into Tommy's eyes. "Don't let me down, Lieutenant Callahan. Dismissed."

"Aye, aye, sir," Tommy said, executing a perfect about-face and leaving the colonel's office.

Outside, in the administrative office, Tommy stopped at

the duty noncommissioned officer's desk, and the first sergeant stood to attention.

"Lieutenant. I'm First Sergeant Wilford Cutler. May I be of assistance, sir?"

"That you may, Top. Put in a call to headquarters, 1st Division. I want to know the location and availability of Gunnery Sergeant Rufus Holloman, last known assignment, 6th Marine Training Regiment, Quantico."

The first sergeant nodded slightly, a small smile forming on his face.

"Sir, Sergeant Holloman is currently completing his second year at Parris Island Training Facility where he has been serving as the senior training instructor to the post commandant."

Tommy allowed a grin to cross his face as he looked at First Sergeant Cutler.

"And would it be possible for you to prepare a request for Sergeant Holloman's transfer and to obtain Colonel Rixby's and General Lee's endorsement?"

"You aim to make some changes, Lieutenant?" Cutler grinned.

"Top, I aim to give Colonel Rixby the marine outfit he desires. Are we in agreement?" Tommy smiled.

"*Semper fi*, Lieutenant," Cutler said, snapping a crisp salute.

Five weeks passed before Gunnery Sergeant Rufus Holloman stepped off the boat in the Dominican Republic, his seabag slung over his shoulder. By then, Tommy had scoured the island in search of marines he once knew, finding only two from the 6th Marines, his original outfit in France. One had served as a corporal under Lieutenant

Borello in the closing days of the war. He had selected eight more men from new replacements arriving on the island. These men were untried and unknown to Tommy, but his feeling was that by procuring new men, before they had a chance to be corrupted by local residents or by marines that had already corrupted themselves, it would give him a fighting chance to train them according to his expectations. The arrival of Gunny Holloman meant Tommy's team was in place, and he felt certain that he had at least a chance of accomplishing what continued to present itself as a formidable task.

"Welcome to the island, Gunny. It's been a long time," he said as Holloman tossed his seabag in the back of a dilapidated military truck.

"That it has, Lieutenant," he replied, rendering a salute, which Tommy returned. "I see the Corps has been good to you, sir."

Tommy held out his hand to welcome Holloman and then climbed into the driver's seat and kicked over the engine. They began driving away from the port facility and immediately started climbing into the mountains.

"Gunny, let's cut through the malarkey. I never would have gotten anywhere but for your training and discipline, and probably would be six feet under in France if you hadn't been there to wipe my nose. We both know that, and the bars on my shoulder haven't changed that fact. I still need you, Gunny, and more than anything, I need your ability to put together a training program. The colonel wants me to develop a regimen that will produce policemen—local policemen. It isn't bad enough that the locals can't read or write, but even our marines come from the bottom of the barrel. As for discipline, well . . ." he paused, shaking his head, "if we have any chance of salvaging the *esprit* of the

Corps we know, you're the man to do it. That's why I sent for you."

"I understand, sir. What do we have to work with?"

"I found Corporal Butterman, from Borello's outfit, and Lance Corporal Tims. Other than that, the rest of the platoon is untried. Brand-new privates. In fact you may know some of them because several of them came here straight from Parris Island. Colonel Rixby has given me authority to requisition anyone I think necessary to staff the school. Within limits, of course. I grabbed eight men who just arrived, thinking we could keep 'em clean before the scum got their hooks in 'em."

The truck bounced along the rutted mountain road, and Tommy drove in silence while Holloman looked out over the expanse of jungle below them. Finally he turned to face Tommy.

"Right, Lieutenant. I'll look 'em over and see what we got. How long does the colonel give us to shape up this outfit?"

Tommy avoided a deep rut and glanced quickly at Holloman, grinning from ear to ear.

Holloman nodded. "Yesterday, right, sir?" he smiled.

"Last week," Tommy laughed. "But we can do it, Gunny. Just tell me what you need, and I'll do the best I can. We've got all the support First Sergeant Cutler can muster."

"Yeah," Holloman said, grinning, "me and Cutler go way back, and have I got a bone to pick with *that* pogie[9] marine. I was all set for my last cushy job before retirement. I already had orders cut for Quantico and the rifle team when he got them changed. This here island's not my idea of a picnic."

"Ah, Gunny, like you told me long ago, 'We go *where* we're told, do *what* we're told, and keep our mouths *shut*.'"

"I said that?" the older man smiled.

"And I've been doing it ever since. This is no exception."

"Well, it could be worse, Lieutenant. We could be down in Nicaragua chasing General Santino. He's retired a lot of good marines, *permanently.*"

"Don't say that too loud, Gunny. We could go there next."

"Well, give me a day or two to see what we've got, Lieutenant, and let's get this show on the road."

Tommy pulled the truck onto a side road and drove a few hundred yards into the jungle, pulling to a stop before a small wooden building in the center of a clearing cut out of the brush. A sign over the door read, "Headquarters, Second Brigade Training Platoon."

Tommy shut off the engine and turned to look at the sergeant. He hesitated for a moment and then spoke, his voice soft but serious.

"Thank you, Gunny. I've owed you from the beginning, and if I bear any resemblance to a marine, it's because of what you taught me. I never got a chance to tell you that as I left France, but I'm glad we have this opportunity to work together."

Holloman nodded and held out his hand to his former recruit.

"I knew you had the makin's, Lieutenant, and so did Borello. We lost a good marine *that* day," he said, shaking his head.

"We left some good marines over there, Rufus," Tommy said.

The two men shared the private moment and without further word, the formality returned as two utility-clad marines approached the truck, one of them retrieving Holloman's seabag from the rear. The lieutenant and the gunnery sergeant stepped out of the truck, coming together in front of the two steps leading into the headquarters building.

"Will that be all, sir?" Gunnery Sergeant Holloman said, his posture now rigid.

"Aye, Gunny," Tommy said. "Good luck. Keep me informed."

"Aye, aye, Lieutenant," he said, snapping a salute and turning to face the other marines.

"Corporal Butterman, barracks inspection in thirty minutes," Holloman grunted.

"Aye, aye, Gunny," the younger man replied.

⌘

Teresa rode in the backseat of her father's car, a brand new 1923 Dusenberg, as it pulled out from the car park near the Union Pacific train station at the west end of South Temple Street in Salt Lake City. Tom and Katrina had picked up Teresa after her arrival from the East. Not two months after returning to Utah from New York the previous summer, Tom had ordered the car as an exact duplicate of the one Seby had hired in New York and in which he had driven Teresa down to Annapolis.

"Oh, Dad," Teresa exclaimed as they neared West Temple Street, "could we please stop at Temple Square for a few minutes? I understand they have a giant Christmas tree this year, with lights, and I want to see what it looks like."

"Of course we can," Katrina answered, smiling over at Tom. "It really is beautiful, Tess."

Tom parked the car, and the threesome walked onto Temple Square, stopping at the south entrance to speak with an elderly couple whom Katrina knew. As the couple

151

left, Teresa slipped her arm into Tom's and Katrina's, walking between her parents as they strolled through the grounds. A couple of inches of snow had accumulated earlier in the afternoon, but dozens of people were present on the square, and the temple spires were brightly lit, towering over all of the nearby buildings except the Hotel Utah across the street.

"It's so beautiful this time of year, Mom," Teresa exclaimed, "and so peaceful. New York is such a bustling place. People always seem in such a hurry to get from here to there and then just as pressed to get back again. It tires me out just to watch people moving about on the street," she laughed. "And when I go to see friends across the harbor, you should see them rushing for the Staten Island ferry after work. A real madhouse."

"Are you tired of it, Tess?" Katrina asked.

"Not tired, Mom, just . . . frustrated, I suppose. We had a good run with the play, even though the critics say that Broadway didn't have a very good selection this year. In fact if we hadn't closed when we did, I wouldn't have made it home for Christmas. It's not so much the hustle and bustle of the city as much as it is the . . . well, I just don't deal well with people who can't see past the fact that I don't drink or smoke, or that I won't . . ."

"You mean they're not accepting of LDS standards?" Katrina said, smiling.

"I could have told you that," Tom added, speaking his first words since getting out of the car, but indicating that he had been listening all along.

"All right, Dad, all right," Teresa nodded, acknowledging her father's continuing opposition to her New York residency. "But only one 'I told you so' this evening, please," she said, tugging at his arm. "But I *do* have an opportunity to move closer to home."

"Oh!" Katrina exclaimed. "And what's that?"

"A man named Marcus Loew from Hollywood attended one of our performances about six weeks ago. He came backstage after the show and asked if I could have dinner with him."

Tom raised an eyebrow at Teresa and clucked his tongue as they continued their walking loop around Temple Square.

"I know, Dad," she said, chuckling. "But I'm twenty-three, and I've learned to separate the wolves from the others."

"I should hope so," Tom said, "but you shouldn't be in a place where the wolf pack is so large."

"Thomas, let the poor girl tell her story, *please*," Katrina said, inwardly pleased at the protective feelings Tom had for their only daughter.

Tom grunted his obedience, and Teresa continued.

"Anyway, Mr. Loew is head, or as he said, will soon be the head of a company being formed by the merger of three large film companies. He said that Metro Pictures, Goldwyn Pictures, and the Louis Mayer Company will merge late this year or early next year to become the Metro-Goldwyn-Mayer Corporation. That would put three of the biggest film companies under one roof. He asked if I would be interested in coming out to Hollywood to do a screen test after the play closed."

"And what did you tell him?" Tom asked.

"I said yes, Dad."

"So you're going to Los Angeles after Christmas?" her mother asked.

"I think so, Mom. I called Mr. Loew, and he said late January, when he returns from France, will be a good time."

"Would you live there, Tess?" Tom asked.

"Nothing is certain, Dad. I'll just have to play it by ear, I suppose. I have an offer to do another play in New York, too, starting rehearsals in February."

"You'll know what to do, Tess," Katrina said, hugging her daughter. "Mr. Callahan, your wife is suddenly *very* hungry. I suggest we cross the street and have a nice meal at the hotel."

"*That*, Mrs. and *Miss* Callahan," he added, wrapping his arm around his daughter, "is an excellent idea."

"I'm for that," Teresa said, kissing her father's cheek.

"And, Tess," Tom said, pulling his daughter closer as they exited the south entrance to Temple Square and turned toward the Hotel Utah, "it's *very* good to have you home again . . . where you *belong*."

"Yes, Father."

<hr />

At seven-thirty on a Friday evening, the Roof Garden dining room at the Hotel Utah was not overly crowded, yet a full complement of people were seated at the tables as Tom, Katrina, and Teresa entered the restaurant[10].

"It is very nice to see you, Mr. Callahan," the maître d' pronounced. "And you, as well, Mrs. Callahan. And I see Miss Callahan has returned to Utah to grace our facility as well. We have an orchestra tonight," he said. "Perhaps you will favor us with a number from your musical production?" he suggested, his smile beaming.

"I think tonight, Henri, that we would like a quiet dinner and no ceremony, if you please," Tom said. "Teresa has only just arrived from her trip and . . ."

"Of course, Mr. Callahan," he said, deferring to Tom.

"I meant no offense, Miss Callahan," he added, looking toward the young woman.

"I understand, Henri," Teresa smiled at the man, who appeared to be slightly embarrassed. "I'm honored by the offer. Perhaps some other time."

"Indeed, ma'am. By the window, sir?"

"In the back, please, Henri. Where we can talk without disturbing others."

"Right this way, sir."

The trio followed Henri as he led the way toward a rear window seat, overlooking Temple Square and the brightly lit temple spires. As they passed another window table, a man quickly stood up and reached to shake Tom's hand. Teresa instantly recognized Seby. He was standing in front of Katrina, speaking briefly with Tom and apparently had not seen Teresa yet. Seated at the table was a beautiful young woman whom Teresa didn't recognize. She wore her blonde hair pulled up in a fashionable loose style, and her earrings caught the light from the candle on the table. She was seated so that she could look past Katrina, and she locked eyes momentarily with Teresa. At that moment, Seby glanced over Katrina's shoulder and saw Teresa standing there. He smiled broadly and after pausing to kiss Katrina's hand, Seby stepped toward Teresa.

"Welcome home, *Señorita* Callahan," he smiled. He reached for her hand, bowed slightly and gently kissed the back of it and then stood straight again. "*Señor* and *Señora* Callahan, *Señorita* Callahan, may I introduce my companion this evening, Beverly Walters. *Señorita* Walters is the daughter of a business associate who is visiting in Utah, staying here in the hotel in fact, and she graciously accepted my invitation to dine this evening."

Smiling pleasantly, Katrina extended her hand to the

young woman. "We are very pleased to make your acquaintance, Miss Walters."

"Thank you, ma'am," the young woman responded.

"It will be pleasant to have Teresa home again for the holidays, will it not?" Seby said to Katrina. "Is there any word from Tommy?"

"Yes and no," Katrina laughed. "Yes, it's good to have Tess home, and no, we've heard nothing from Tommy, the scoundrel."

Seby smiled. "Don't judge him too harshly. From what I read in the papers, they have a *very* difficult job down there."

"They certainly do, and Coolidge ought to bring them home," Tom interjected. "A great waste of time and manpower if you ask me," he blustered.

"Thomas, Henri has located our table," Katrina interrupted, "and just in time too, if we're to avoid politics. Very nice to see you again, Seby. You must drive up from the ranch and see us over the Christmas holidays."

"It would be my pleasure, *Señora*. Tom, nice to see you again."

The group began to walk past Seby's table and Teresa smiled politely at Miss Walters again, nodding and smiling at Seby.

"Are you home for long, Teresa?" he asked.

"Probably until late January, I think. Then I have to travel to Los Angeles."

"Perhaps we shall see one another," he added.

"Perhaps," she smiled. "Very nice to meet you, Miss Walters. I hope you enjoy Salt Lake. Be sure Seby takes you on a tour of Temple Square and to see the view of the city from the hills up above the Avenues."

"I will," she smiled back. "And by the way, I was in New

York with my father, and on Sebastian's recommendation, we took in your play. It was quite excellent."

"Why, thank you. Then we have you to thank for ticket sales, Seby," Teresa laughed.

"My pleasure, *Señorita*. Enjoy your meal. I believe your parents are seated."

"Thank you, Seby, and good evening to both of you," she said. Henri waited to seat her, and as the maître d' adjusted her chair, Teresa caught her mother's eye.

"Miss Walters is a beautiful woman," Katrina said, her eyebrows slightly raised, which Teresa immediately noticed.

"Yes, isn't she?" Teresa responded.

"So then, ladies, what shall it be? The prime rib is always good," Tom said, opening the menu, oblivious to the signals passing between mother and daughter about the new woman in Seby's life.

<hr>

"I've invited Seby for dinner on Christmas Eve," Tom said as he walked into the parlor two days before Christmas.

"Oh?" Katrina said, glancing over at Teresa. "And how did *that* come about?"

"He came in to the bank today," Tom answered, draping his overcoat over the back of a chair in the room. William, right behind Tom, immediately picked up the coat.

"Would you like a hot drink, sir?" William asked.

"I would," Tom responded after a moment. "Anyone else?" he asked.

"No, thank you, Thomas. William has already provided for us. We've actually just come in from shopping. It's a shame you don't own stock in ZCMI. I'm afraid we've greatly increased their annual earnings statement," Katrina smiled at her husband.

157

"Hmmm, I'm not surprised. One of you alone can do a great deal of damage to the bank account, but *two* together, well, the store manager was probably wringing his hands in delight."

"Surely you exaggerate, Dad," Teresa grinned as she rose and went to sit on the arm of her father's chair.

"Not by much, Tess, not by much."

Tom removed his shoes, placed them by the side of his chair, crossed one of his legs, and began to rub his foot.

"*Thomas Callahan!* I've asked you dozens of times not to perform your, uh, personal *functions* while downstairs."

Tom glanced up at Teresa, sitting on the side of his chair, and winked. "And I never do . . . *when* we have company. Tess is family," he teased, "aren't you, Tess?"

"Oh, my goodness," Katrina exclaimed, shaking her head in what she knew was a losing battle, "you can take the Irishman out of the country, but you can't take the country out of the Irishman, I guess," she remarked.

"Or something like that," Tom laughed. "Of course, Katie m' darlin', I could come over to the divan, and *you* could rub these poor ole tired feet for me like you used to do when you were less concerned about propriety."

"Don't *Katie m' darlin'* me, Thomas. Just wash your hands before dinner."

"Why?" Tom continued, taunting his wife.

"Enough of this, I say," Katrina said, a smile beginning to cross her face as she recognized that Thomas was, once again, goading her.

"Back to the subject at hand, Thomas. Did Seby have an appointment to see you, or did he just 'drop in'?"

"I think he was just in town, Katie. Why?"

Katrina again glanced at Teresa. "Just wondering. So he

came into the bank to say hi and left with a Christmas Eve dinner invitation?"

"I guess that's what happened," Tom said.

"Well," Katrina said, rising from her chair, "Seby is always welcome in our home. You know that, Thomas, and apparently," she said, touching Teresa's shoulder as she walked by, "so does Seby. I'd best let Helen know that we'll be having another guest for dinner tomorrow night," she said, departing the room.

"What was that all about, Tess?" Tom asked, shifting feet and beginning to rub on the other one.

"Dad, I think Mom is beginning to believe that Seby came by *looking* for a dinner invitation."

"Why would he do that? He has plenty of friends besides us."

"Dad," Teresa laughed, kissing his cheek and sliding off the arm of his chair to stand beside him, "I think Mom may be right," she said, following her mother out the parlor entrance.

"Your hot chocolate, sir," William said, crossing paths with Teresa as he entered the parlor.

"William, does your wife confuse you sometimes?"

William responded without hesitation, his face unperturbed and serene. "No, sir, she does not. She confuses me *all* the time. Will that be all, sir?"

"Yes, William," Tom said, standing from his chair and laughing, "that will be all. I'll just take these shoes upstairs and *wash my hands* before dinner."

"Very good, sir. Cook says dinner will be ready in twenty minutes."

"Fine, William. That's just fine."

Tom, Katrina, Teresa, and Seby were seated in the parlor of *Valhalla* in front of a roaring fire. From where they were gathered a large Christmas tree standing in the foyer underneath the circular stairway was visible through the open doorway. Music was playing softly on the gramophone and light conversation had ensued throughout the evening, following a dinner of roast lamb, boiled potatoes, canned peas and corn, and rice pudding. The dinner was capped by Tom's favorite dessert, prepared by Katrina from a recipe she had brought back from New Zealand: pavlova, a sort of creamy pie with a thick meringue on the top, sprinkled with various fruit slices and chocolate flakes. Ever since their visit to Christchurch, where their niece, Emily Callahan, had introduced them to the fabulous dessert, Tom had often pleaded with Katrina to prepare it. At first, she had been unable to make the recipe work, but after she had fiddled with the ingredients and the amount of time she baked it, based on Salt Lake City's altitude, far different than Shenandoah Station in Canterbury where Emily lived, she had finally found the right combination. Dinner guests at *Valhalla* looked forward to the treat, and New Zealand pavlova had almost become a staple in the Callahans' holiday fare.

"So, Seby, what does 1924 hold in store for you?" Katrina asked.

The atmosphere in the room this evening was markedly different than it had been the first time Seby had sat there years prior, with the exact same occupants. Then, Teresa was going through the trauma of learning some things about her mother's past that Katrina had never shared with her daughter. But this night everyone appeared to be quite relaxed, and Seby was leaning back comfortably in a large leather chair. In spite of the differences in their ages, Seby and the Callahans had become good friends, and Tom often functioned as a financial confidant in Seby's business dealings. Sebastian Stromberg remained, however, as had his Mexican grandfather, Don Sebastian Cardenas, a reserved individual, and, to date, he hadn't revealed to the Callahans anything regarding his romantic involvement or marital intentions, if any.

"Who knows, *Señora?*" Seby grimaced. "The world is changing so rapidly. Even my own country is far removed from the Mexico I knew as a child."

"Change isn't *all* bad, Seby," Tom said.

"*Sí, Señor,*" Seby agreed. "In spite of my original opposition to it, much good has come from the revolution. However, the politicians continue to change as frequently as the seasons," he said, turning his hand back and forth in a vacillating gesture.

"Ha! Mexico doesn't possess *that* distinction alone," Tom laughed.

"No!" Katrina declared emphatically. "I'll have none of this on Christmas Eve. No politics this evening, gentlemen."

Tom winked at Seby and nodded toward Katrina.

"Katie, we bow to your wishes, but, in fact, in that same spirit, I *do* have something we can discuss."

"What is it, Dad?" Teresa said, shifting her position on the divan next to her mother and pulling her legs up underneath her.

"We've exchanged gifts this evening, as is our custom—at least since 'Father Christmas' stopped coming to *Valhalla*," he laughed, pursing his lips and blowing a kiss toward Teresa.

"And as you each know, I recently celebrated my forty-eighth birthday and simultaneously, the third anniversary of my membership in the Church. Last week," he continued, still looking toward Katrina, "Katie and I had a private dinner down in Sugar House to celebrate the second anniversary of our temple vows—our 'eternal anniversary' as she calls it. All things considered, I have much to be thankful for and most of it—with the exception of Tommy and PJ and PJ's family, most of it is right here in this room. My heart couldn't be more full. And so," he voiced a bit louder, "I thought that inasmuch as we have shown our love for each other with our Christmas presents this evening, there is someone who we may have overlooked."

Katrina looked panic-stricken, trying to think who might have been left off their gift-giving list. "Who, Thomas?" she said, "I'm certain we thought of . . ."

"Not to worry, Katie," he smiled, motioning her back into her seat. "It's not *that* kind of gift. Knowing Seby was coming this evening, and that we were *not* hosting the usual large Christmas gathering of family, friends, and business associates that *Valhalla* is known for, I tried to think of how we might make this a more, well, a more *spiritual* experience for each of us. After all, it is *His* birthday we celebrate."

Katrina smiled with relief and leaned back into her seat. Looking across the room at her husband, the thought leapt to her mind that the Thomas Callahan she was seeing this evening, and in fact had seen for the past several years, was a far cry from the Thomas Callahan of years gone by. Always a good husband and a considerate, loving father, despite his temporary failure to show that love to Tommy during those terrible years after the *Titanic*, he had grown quickly in his understanding of the gospel of Jesus Christ. For two years he had been serving as stake financial clerk under Stake President Robert Thurston, his longtime partner and family friend. Tom's commitment was such that he often went to the temple, sometimes alone, as he frequently did on Thursday evenings while Katrina attended Tabernacle Choir practice.

Tom continued his words, breaking into Katrina's thoughts. "So, in honor of His birthday, I propose that we each—"

The sound of the brass knocker on their front door startled all of them. Tom glanced at Katrina as if to ask who it might be, but she only shrugged her shoulders.

Following his first two years of service to the Callahans, their butler, William, had been given a gift of a trip to Vancouver for himself, his wife, and their two grown children, to visit their extended family. They had left earlier in the week, so Tom rose and walked to answer the front door himself. Opening the door, he was surprised to see the Thurstons standing on the porch. Those inside the house could hear the familiar voice of Alice Thurston crying out, "Merry Christmas to all!"

"Well, this is a pleasant surprise," Tom said to the couple. "Please, come in out of the cold. Is it 'Robert and

Alice,' or 'President and Sister Thurston' we have the pleasure of greeting?" Tom laughed.

After stomping their feet on the exterior woven mat, Robert and Alice stepped into the foyer. Upon hearing Alice's voice, Katrina rose from her seat and quickly stepped from the parlor to greet her guests.

"It's Robert and Alice," Robert said, removing his overcoat and shaking Tom's hand. Katrina and Alice exchanged hugs, and Robert and Tom each greeted the wives, then Tom led the couple into the parlor.

"Good evening and Merry Christmas," Robert said to Teresa and Seby as they entered the room. Seby immediately rose from his chair and reached for Robert's hand.

"Good evening, President Thurston—Sister Thurston," he said.

Teresa stood beside the group for a moment until Seby had paid his respects.

"Hi, Uncle Robert," she said, hugging him and then Alice.

After everyone was seated, Tom said, "This is an unexpected surprise, Robert."

"I know," Robert laughed, a bit hesitant, "we were just sitting alone at home, thinking about our kids and the grandkids and wondering how they were doing on their visit to our daughter-in-law's family in California, and suddenly I said, "Let's go see Tom and Katrina. Alice said, 'Well, what took you so long to decide *that*, President Thurston?' I said to her, 'It's not an official visit, Alice.' And then she said, 'Of course it's not. We *love* them, you silly boy.' Then we both started laughing, I got our coats, and here we are."

Everyone in the room laughed, then Katrina said, "And we're very glad you did. With most of *our* kids and PJ's children so far away, we know how you feel. Pretty soon it will be *only* us old folk getting together," Katrina said, bringing another spate of laughter into the room.

"Mother!" Teresa exclaimed, "I'll *always* be here with you," she teased.

"Yes, dear, of course you will," Katrina said in mock agreement. "And you'll *never* get married, and *never* have children of your own, and *never* move away. Right?"

"Mother!" Teresa cried.

"So," Robert said, "are we interrupting anything?"

"Certainly not, Robert. In fact, you've made our evening complete. I was just about to propose that we each offer another gift."

"Another gift?" Robert queried.

"Yes," Tom nodded. "A special gift. We've all exchanged our Christmas presents, and I was just about to challenge everyone in the room to consider what gift they might give if Christ came to be with us this evening. A true gift that we might each feel appropriate for Him."

Robert settled back into his chair. "Now that, Tom, is a tall order."

"Indeed."

Upon hearing Tom's proposal, Katrina quickly stood and said, "How about Teresa and I prepare some hot cider for everyone?"

"Need some time to reflect, eh, Katie?" Tom teased.

She pulled a face at Tom, then said, "You've been thinking about this for days and want us to give an immediate answer. *Of course* I need some time," she said, ruffling his hair as she passed his chair on the way to the kitchen, followed by Teresa.

"I'd like to help . . . *and* have time to think, too," Alice said, also rising and following the two women.

Left alone in the parlor, Tom, Seby, and Robert sat

quietly for several moments, watching the fire blaze, each lost in their thoughts about Tom's challenge.

Robert spoke first. "I would have given second thoughts to popping in had I known you'd be searching my soul, Tom."

Tom stood and walked to the fireplace where he jabbed at the glowing coals with a poker. He then stood straight, leaned against the mantelpiece, and looked at his old friend.

"Robert, do you remember when a young Irish lad came to your home very late one night, or, better said, very early one morning, in the company of your home teacher, Brother McKay, and a Catholic nursing sister?"

"I certainly do, Tom. I believe you were the hospital engineer then. And I also remember the young lad who visited me in the hospital after my appendectomy and who taught me a few things about chess."

"That seems so long ago doesn't it, Robert? Yet tonight's challenge of thinking of a gift for Christ could probably be met just by reading your journal," Tom said, his voice now soft. "As Katrina said, perhaps I've had more time to think of a good answer, but, Robert, *I'm* the one who needed more time. I've only just come to understand Him, to seek Him. You—each of you I mean," he said, gesturing toward the kitchen where the ladies had gone, "have lived your life try-ing to follow Christ."

Robert rose from the divan and came to stand by his friend at the fireplace. "If you think *that*, my friend, then perhaps you're not ready to give your answer either. I've known of your good works, Tom, since those early days when you and Sister Mary used to make your 3:00 A.M. food deliveries. Did you truly think no one knew?"

"But how . . ."

"Do you remember the gentleman who provided the money to Sister Mary to buy the food?"

Tom thought several moments and nodded. "I never met him, but one night when I asked her if we were delivering food to our poor Catholic neighbors, she said she didn't know and it didn't matter what religion they were—that the man who paid for the food was LDS and some of the recipients were Catholic."

Now it was Robert's turn to nod. "That man was my father, Tom—the man who taught me the true meaning of Christlike love. He also knew of your involvement, and before he died some years ago, Dad told me the story. He was part of the bishopric that called Elder McKay on his mission, and when McKay returned, my father told him the story about the Irish lad who had worked with Sister Mary and had run away to Alaska after being hunted on a murder charge. Neither of them believed the story, and then when young David McKay went to see Father Scanlan, the priest was unable to confirm or deny the accusation but left Elder McKay with the impression that he also believed you were innocent."

"I had no idea that so many people knew the story. About the food or the, uh, criminal charges."

"And do you still think that you've never given Christ a present?"

"Well, that's different, Robert. I was just a young kid and was helping Sister Mary to—"

"You were just a young kid who found a way to serve Christ, even if you didn't know you were doing it at the time," Robert said, a smile on his face. "Now tonight, in answer to your challenge, all we are really doing is finding voice for many of the things we try to do every day."

Tom turned to look at Seby who had been quietly

listening to the two older men. "What do *you* think of all this, Seby?"

"*Señor* Callahan, I am in awe of the continuing revelations that come to my attention about your past. The more people I meet who know you, the more I understand why you have succeeded in your business ventures."

"You'd find plenty who'd argue *that* point, Seby. And another thing, while we're *off* the subject, how old are you now?"

"This last summer, *Señor*, I had my twenty-sixth birthday."

"As I thought," Tom said to the younger man, who appeared perplexed by the question. "Robert," Tom said, turning back to his friend, "how old was your son Mark when he returned from Harvard and joined us at the bank?"

"Just twenty-six I believe, Tom."

"Right. At that time I told young Mark that it was time he started calling me Tom. And the same applies here," he said, looking back toward Seby. "From this point forward I would prefer that you call me Tom. Are we in agreement?" he smiled.

"*Señor* . . . Tom," the younger man smiled, "it would please me very much to call you Tom, but if I might be so bold," he said, rising from his chair and taking two steps to stand in front of the two men, "I have another matter I wish to discuss with you. I had intended to ask to meet with you at some later date, but . . ." he paused, glancing out the parlor door toward the kitchen where no sign of the ladies yet appeared.

"And that is?" Tom asked.

"You spoke to me once, a couple of years ago as you took your lone horse trip into the mountains, about Mexican traditions, and how I came to join the LDS Church. Those traditions, as you said, were strongly ingrained in me by Don Sebastian, and they are hard to avoid. In fact . . . Tom, I agree with most of them and do not wish to forget *any* of them. One such tradition is that a male suitor who wishes to call on a young lady with the possible intention of seeking her hand in matrimony should visit with her father in the company of his priest who, hopefully, can attest to his good character."

Seby paused again, and a look of understanding spread across Tom's face. A gentle smile began forming on Robert's.

"In the absence of such clergy, I would ask you, President Roberts," he said, turning his gaze toward the older man, "that, as someone who knows me, you would serve me this evening in such a spiritual capacity."

Robert nodded. "I think I understand, Seby."

"Good. Then, *Señor* Callahan . . . Tom, it is my formal request to you that I be granted permission to attend to your daughter, Teresa Callahan, and that I be permitted to arrange time together, properly chaperoned of course, so that we may determine if the interest I possess and the interest I think, or perhaps hope, she possesses is sufficient to establish a union between us—in due time, of course."

"Whew, Seby, no wonder the Mexicans marry for life. You'd have a hard time saying *that* again, wouldn't you?"

A brief silence was followed by a burst of laughter from all three men. Just then, the women emerged from the kitchen, bringing with them a pot of hot cider and some finger sandwiches.

"Did we miss something funny?" Katrina asked.

"You did," Tom said, continuing to laugh, "but please don't ask us to repeat it. Once was enough. And yes, Seby," Tom said, his laughter subsided and his face now turned serious, "it would be my great honor to approve such a request."

Tom reached out and shook the younger man's hand, and Seby smiled broadly. He leaned a bit closer to Tom and lowered his voice while Katrina set the tray she carried on a nearby sideboard.

"Perhaps, all going well, I may be able to call you something more personal than *Tom*."

"Perhaps," Tom whispered back.

"Wait a minute," Teresa said, "have you guys been sharing your thoughts and conspiring about a gift?" she accused.

"Oh, and we're supposed to believe it was as quiet as a church mouse in the kitchen," Tom said.

"We talked a *little*," Teresa admitted.

"So, are we ready?" Tom asked. "Who's to go first?"

"I'll go first," Katrina immediately volunteered.

"But you were the most reluctant," Tom teased.

"Yes, I was," she said, coming over to stand by her husband and slip her arm into his, "but I also have the most to be thankful for this Christmas."

Tom motioned for everyone to take seats again and assisted Katrina into her chair. After Teresa finished pouring cider and Alice distributed a cup to everyone, the room grew quiet, waiting for Katrina to reveal her intended present to Christ. Katrina sat quietly for several moments, looking into the crackling fire.

"Over thirty years ago, when my parents first investigated the Church in Norway, I found a new meaning in my life. I was not yet fifteen, but I knew from the beginning that the message was true. Many people tried to tell my poppa that what these Mormons asked was far too great a price to pay—that God would never ask so much from His children. But I knew then, and I know now, that what He asks is so little in comparison to what He gives. So if His Son, our Lord and Savior Jesus Christ, entered our home tonight, on the eve of His birthday, I would first hug Him," and at this statement she paused, smiling shyly as if she had erred, "and then I would tell Him that I would continue to do what His Father and my Father had told me to do, so that His sacrifice would not have been made in vain. Just as He had nothing more sacred to give us than Himself, so then, neither would I. And perhaps, in both cases of obedience to our Father's commandments, we would give the gift we most treasured—we would give ourselves."

The only sound in the room was that of Teresa's cup clinking on her crystal saucer as she set both utensils down on the table beside her chair. Then she came to kneel by her mother's chair, resting her head in Katrina's lap. She remained silent for some long moments, as did all the others in the room.

12

Two days following Christmas, 1923, Colonel Rixby, Lieutenant Callahan, and Gunnery Sergeant Holloman drove through a mountain pass toward one of the upland villages on a recruiting mission for the new police academy. Originally called the Guardia, the organization had recently been renamed the *Policía Nacional Dominicana,* and the Dominican government had taken control of the force in anticipation of a U.S. withdrawal, expected sometime in late 1924. Marines, however, continued to provide primary training and, when necessary, the backup support required to assure police control of difficult situations.

The first class of recruits since Tommy's arrival was already in their twelfth week of training. Seventeen of an original class of sixty had washed out by Christmas, and it was likely that about a dozen more would either fail or drop out before completing the course in April. If that happened, the six-month course would have reduced the class size by nearly half before the cadets were supposed to move on to the second phase—a six-month probationary field experience.

The regimen that Gunnery Sergeant Holloman had created included more physical training than the academy had previously offered, and complaints were common among the cadets. But it was the administrative duties—logistics, map reading, and even the menial task of rotational kitchen duty—that were most unacceptable to the recruits, many of whom felt that once in the police, they were above such labor.

In fact, of the twenty-odd dropouts in the first class, nearly half had been self-imposed in response to Sergeant Holloman and Corporal Butterman's demanding daily work-outs. "*Not even fit for pogie marines,*" Holloman had com-plained. The veteran training instructor had seemed quite content with the dropout rate, although Colonel Rixby was pushing for larger numbers of graduates to satisfy the demand from higher headquarters and the State Department for quotas that would show the program to be a success.

The tropical winter brought with it little change in tem-perature but a considerable increase in rainfall, which rendered the muddy mountain roads nearly impassable. Arriving in a small village after a perilous drive on a slip-pery road that was often as not a muddy stream, the three marines had hoped to find fifty or more candidates for the police academy. For two days, Corporal Butterman and two marine privates had scoured the surrounding villages for recruits, but had met with little success. Only a half-dozen men were to be seen, lolling about in the muddy village square.

"Slim pickings, Corporal?" Rixby asked.

"Afraid so, Colonel. The village chief told us that a group of bandits came through about a week ago, threaten-ing any family that provided recruits. It seems to have worked, sir," the corporal said, looking at the small, motley group of men.

Colonel Rixby walked over to the closest Dominican and began to converse with him in Spanish. After several moments, he returned and nodded toward Lieutenant Callahan and Sergeant Holloman who both followed the colonel toward the back of the truck.

"Lieutenant, the job just got a little tougher, it seems. We're going to have to go into each of these villages and counteract the fear presented by the bandits. Look," he said, removing his campaign hat and running his fingers through his thinning hair, "we're about to wrap up this assignment down here. You recall when I went to that meeting at the Constabulary Training Center at Haina?"

"Yes, sir," Tommy replied.

"Well, the State Department had sent Sumner Wells down to negotiate with the Dominican government. By his direction, we'll probably finish this program and get our troops out of the DR by the end of next year. We've got, what, maybe two more classes to train, and then we're gone. The sooner that gets done, the faster we can get back to being marines."

Gunnery Sergeant Holloman glanced briefly at Lieutenant Callahan, and they both looked again at Colonel Rixby.

"Sir," Callahan said, "I was under the impression . . ."

Rixby nodded, anticipating Tommy's question.

"I know, Lieutenant, so was I, but that's the word from upstairs. General Lee wants this job completed. He wants it done right and he wants it done fast. And that's what we're going to do."

"Aye, aye, sir," Tommy replied.

"Now," Rixby continued, "this morning we'll talk with these few recruits," he said, looking at the small group of assembled men, "and then I'll take one of the privates and head back to camp. You and Sergeant Holloman, along with Corporal Butterman, make the rounds of the surrounding villages for the next couple of days and gather what volunteers you can. I want you back at the training center by Friday. Understood?"

"Aye, aye, sir."

"Good. Let's get to it then."

After having transferred the remaining supplies to Corporal Butterman's vehicle, Colonel Rixby and Private Dominguez left the village shortly before noon. Tommy continued with the physical testing throughout the afternoon and was preparing to call it a day when a commotion started in the village. A local boy, about twelve years old, rode into the center of the village on a burro and in short bursts of Spanish, most of which Tommy couldn't understand, began recounting something to one of the village leaders. Corporal Butterman, who spoke fluent Spanish, quickly gained a sense of what was occurring.

"Lieutenant, the colonel's been ambushed about eight miles south, just over the crest of the mountain road."

"How many men?" Tommy asked.

Butterman jabbered at the young lad for a moment and looked back at Tommy, shaking his head.

"The boy don't know, Lieutenant."

Tommy turned to speak to Holloman, but the gunny was already gone and one of the other privates was running after him. Tommy looked back at Butterman.

"Ask the kid if he can guide us back to the site."

"He said it's right on the road, Lieutenant, by the shrine of the Holy Mother. You know, the crucifix station. I know the spot, sir."

"Right. How many rifles did you bring with you, Corporal?"

"We've got our own weapons, sir, plus three rifles for marksmanship testing of the recruits. With you and the gunny, sir, that makes five men with weapons plus the three spare rifles."

Tommy glanced again in the direction Sergeant Holloman had disappeared and saw the sergeant coming back, his arms loaded with several packs. Tommy turned his attention back to Butterman.

"Did you complete rifle testing yesterday, Corporal?"

"We did, sir."

"Fine. Pick the best riflemen and give them the three extra rifles, assure them of a spot in the next class, and tell them they are now officially cadets of the academy. Issue twenty rounds to each man and be prepared to move out in ten minutes."

"Sir, none of these guys is what you would call a 'rifleman,' actually."

"I understand, Corporal; nevertheless, get them ready."

Gunnery Sergeant Holloman arrived just as Tommy was completing his orders. Butterman looked to the gunny who had heard the last of Tommy's orders—to move out in ten minutes—but the gunny remained silent.

"Sir," Butterman said, "it'll be dark in about forty-five minutes. We'll never traverse that road in the dark."

Holloman interjected before Tommy had a chance to respond.

"Who's out there, Corporal?" he demanded.

"Gunny?" he responded, confused. "Uh, the colonel and Private Dominguez, Gunny."

"Would *they* come for you, Corporal?" Holloman asked, his face a stern mask.

The corporal thought momentarily and nodded his understanding.

"We'll be ready to move out in ten minutes, Lieutenant," he said, looking back at Tommy.

"*Five* minutes, Corporal," Holloman added, turning his attention to Tommy. "Lieutenant, I've pulled together about two hundred rounds, plus another hundred for the BAR, and a couple of barrels of water."

"The corporal's right, Gunny," Tommy said. "It will be dark before we can reach them, and we're as likely to get ambushed as the colonel did. The bandits are probably hoping that we'll mount a rescue."

Holloman nodded. "I would if I was them, sir."

Tommy allowed a small grin to cross his face. "Five minutes, Sergeant."

"Aye, aye, sir," Holloman replied and turned on his heel, making for the remaining truck and shouting orders at the two privates who were loading ammunition and water.

Intermittent cloud cover provided only an occasional glimpse of the moon, and in those brief appearances, the light provided enabled the small cadre of men to make their way through the jungle path. One mile short of the crucifix station, a small Catholic shrine where all who crossed the mountain pass stopped to offer their prayers to the Holy Virgin, Lieutenant Callahan divided his small command into two segments. Corporal Butterman waited in the truck with one private and one of the new recruits while Lieutenant Callahan, Sergeant Holloman, two privates, and two of the hastily recruited cadets made their way through the underbrush toward what they presumed to be the ambush site.

Without radio contact, Corporal Butterman was to wait

exactly sixty minutes and then proceed slowly up the road, attempting to draw fire from the suspected second ambush.

Tommy's group of six men made their way to the high side of the road above the crucifix shrine and settled in to wait for the arrival of Butterman and the truck.

Just over an hour later they heard the rumble of the truck engine and saw the headlights round a curve just below the religious shrine. As Butterman crested the high point in the road, the headlights illuminated a newly felled tree blocking their passage. As soon as Butterman killed the lights and the engine and began to exit the vehicle, gunfire opened up from both sides of the road ahead.

From slightly higher, on a rocky outcropping, Sergeant Holloman began to rake the area with the BAR, concentrating on the muzzle flashes. The other five men fired their rounds into the same area, conserving ammunition as Lieutenant Callahan had ordered. As quickly as it had begun, the attack on the truck ended and the enemy fire ceased. The smell of cordite hung in the humid night air following the brief exchange of fire, and then the jungle growth was plunged into a complete silence, broken only by the occasional grunting of what Tommy took to be a wounded bandit lying somewhere up ahead.

One shrill blast of a whistle immediately identified Colonel Rixby's position, and by using hand signals in the moonlight, Tommy directed Sergeant Holloman to move toward the sound. Together with another marine private, Holloman began inching his way in the colonel's direction. In about twenty minutes, two quick blasts of the whistle told Tommy that Holloman had made contact with Colonel Rixby, and Tommy began to move his remaining men toward the truck on the road below.

As they reached the truck, joining up with Corporal

Butterman who was lying in a small depression alongside the road, the moon once again cleared the clouds to illuminate the area. Instantly a burst of gunfire erupted from the hill overlooking the truck, and Butterman, together with Tommy's men, returned fire. As quickly as it had begun, the firing ceased and silence ensued, followed by the sound of a vehicle engine somewhere up the road ahead, which slowly faded as the vehicle, by its sound, raced down the other side of the mountain pass.

Corporal Butterman crouched low and made his way toward the truck. Lying on the ground next to the right front wheel, he found Lieutenant Callahan, unconscious, his uniform shirt soaked with blood.

"Gunny!" Butterman shouted. "The lieutenant's hit."

A whispered order came from the bushes alongside the truck.

"Shut up, Corporal, or you'll be next."

Out of the dark, two figures emerged as Gunnery Sergeant Holloman and Colonel Rixby exited the jungle growth. Holloman knelt next to the prostrate figure of Lieutenant Callahan and pressed his fingers to the unconscious man's neck. Finding a pulse, he quickly opened Tommy's shirt.

"Colonel, he's got a chest wound. He's alive, but he won't be for long unless we can get him down the mountain to a doctor."

The colonel took in the situation immediately.

"Corporal, clear that tree across the road," he commanded, stepping toward Sergeant Holloman. "This is one marine officer I'm not losing. Get him in the truck, Sergeant. Now!"

On the Saturday between Christmas and New Year's Day, 1924, Teresa drove to Hidden Valley Ranch near Draper, where Seby had invited her to join him in a horseback ride. Though the day was unseasonably mild, the accumulated snow had precluded a ride up into the canyon east of Seby's holdings, and they rode instead on the flat below South Mountain.

Cantering some distance behind, in the uncomfortable role of chaperon, rode Reed Warnick, Seby's ranch foreman, who had been introduced to Teresa as a man "who knows more about horses and cattle than their mothers know."

The afternoon passed quickly, and by the conclusion of the day, Seby had explained, in somewhat less formal terms, the request he had made of Teresa's father on Christmas Eve. Startled at first by the official sounding nature of Seby's pronouncement, Teresa was smart enough, and even interested enough, not to respond negatively until she had allowed some time to consider his intentions. She understood clearly that Seby was not offering a proposal of marriage, and for that she was quite pleased, career considerations and all, but she also understood that in Seby's culture such a request was a formality that might well lead to marriage.

"Seby," she said as they rode slowly, allowing their horses to head back toward the main house, "I'm flattered by your request to, uh, what shall we say," she laughed briefly, "*court me*. Is that the way to put it?" she asked.

"That's close enough, Tess," he smiled back. "May I say that I have thought for some time about approaching your father but have hesitated because of the way we first met, that evening in your parlor, when—"

"Seby, I should have said something about that meeting long before now. I've thought about it many times, and, well, I've been embarrassed about the way I behaved. I—"

"You have nothing to be embarrassed about," Seby said.

"Oh, yes, I do," Teresa continued. "I couldn't figure out what my parents were trying to say. That whole thing about Mom being previously married, to a polygamist no less, and then trying to figure out who *you* were! I know now that we aren't related or anything, but when my parents told me that my mother was married for a time to your father, it made it sound like you were my brother. It all came as such a shock. It was more than I could absorb."

"Teresa, it was of no consequence. I can—"

"No, Seby. Let me finish. I need to say this."

Teresa smiled and shook her head before continuing. "That day at the barn, I was awful. You had been a perfect gentleman, but I acted like a fool. I wouldn't have blamed you if you'd never spoken to me again. I'm sorry, Seby, for the way I treated you. You didn't deserve it."

Seby didn't immediately respond, and the two of them rode in silence for a few moments. Finally, Teresa spoke again.

"Seby?"

"Yes?"

"This is the place where you're supposed to say it's all right and that you forgive me," Teresa said, smiling.

The young Mexican reined his horse in front of Teresa's and turned his mount so that they sat side by side, facing one another.

"Of course I forgive you," he said, looking into her eyes.

From his position, some one hundred yards behind, Reed saw the two riders stop their horses, and he also pulled up. He sat his horse, averting his eyes somewhat from the scene ahead.

Seby and Teresa sat quietly for a few moments, looking at each other. Finally, Teresa sat forward in her saddle, leaned toward Seby, and pressed her lips softly against his. After a moment, she broke off their kiss and settled back into her saddle. She smiled briefly at the somewhat startled Seby, then suddenly spurred her horse forward into a gallop, kicking up clods of earth and racing toward the corrals.

Later, at a wooden table in the ranch house kitchen, with Reed seated within hearing distance in the adjacent living room, Seby and Teresa sat across from each other, drinking hot chocolate and conversing.

"Tess, I have often thought of you over these last few years. When your mother's unfortunate accident brought us together again, I realized that you were no longer the young girl I had remembered, and I began thinking of you in terms of being a woman—a very attractive woman, I might add."

"You're awfully bold, aren't you, Mr. Stromberg?" Teresa teased.

"If I recall correctly," Seby countered, "*you* were the one who kissed *me* when I delivered you home from the hospital. Did it mean nothing to you?"

"Well, I was in a state of emotional stress," Teresa explained, laughing. "You took advantage of me."

Seeing a look of protest on Seby's face, Teresa quickly added, "I'm just kidding. Actually, it meant a great deal to me. I've never forgotten it," she confessed.

She went on. "That night, I knew the feelings I originally had for you were real, but I also knew that I was leaving for New York as soon as my mother was fully recovered. Now, after these two years have gone by, I guess I've become a bit more independent—more than my parents would like, in fact. I still have my career to pursue. I'm not certain I'm ready to make a commitment, Seby."

"Do you see no chance for us then, Teresa?"

"I wouldn't say that, Mr. Stromberg. To tell the truth, and in matters of the heart everyone knows that a woman is not required to do so, I still find you a very attractive man. And actress or not, I know that I won't be able to hide those feelings forever. I'm just saying, let's give it some time."

"That's all I hoped for, Tess. And that's enough for now," he said.

When they stepped out of the ranch house onto the porch, the sun had set behind the Oquirrhs to the south and west of where they stood. The winter evening air had turned cold, and a few clouds showed pink in the sky above the western mountains.

Seby walked Teresa to her car, but before she got in, he said, "You say you're going to Los Angeles in a few weeks?"

"Yes, to take a screen test."

"Are you hopeful of having the same success in film that you've enjoyed on Broadway?"

Teresa removed the scarf from her head and tossed it through the open window onto the front seat, then she shook her hair out. She had resisted the urge to cut it shorter into one of the fashionable bobs that were all the rage, and it remained long and, at the moment, windblown and unruly.

"I don't know, Seby. It's still a new industry, and I've talked with a few people who say that you can't tell how the camera will treat you until you see the results. Besides, I have the same reservations I had in New York about living in a world where immorality is so rampant. But I *do* want to see what they say about my chances of being in the movies."

Teresa opened the car door but didn't immediately get

in. "One reason I'm going to Hollywood to take this screen test is that the role I've been offered in New York next season would require me to act the part of someone whose values I would feel uncomfortable portraying."

"Can you not separate the role from reality?"

Teresa smiled at Seby. "Of course, but it feels as though by playing the role that I'm promoting or at least endorsing that lifestyle. Last year, I had quite a lot of fan mail from young women who said how much they identified with my character and wanted to be like her. I had a good role then, but if I play someone sleazy . . . Can you see what I mean?"

Seby nodded. "I can understand that. Don Sebastian used to tell me that the people in Mazatlán looked to our family as an example, and when, as a small boy, I would do anything that was not right, he would take me aside and correct my behavior by saying that as the *patron*, the people looked to him and to our family to uphold the highest standards—that we would be letting them down if we failed to behave properly."

Teresa laughed and ran her fingers through her hair, pulling at some of the tangles.

"That sounds like one of Sister Mary's lectures. She never directly reprimanded me, but she always made me consider how a proper young lady should act. I wonder what she would say about my current situation."

"Do you think she would advise you not to go?"

"No. She was always in favor of our stretching our wings and reaching for higher goals, but she also reminded us to remember who we were."

Teresa got into her car, but before starting the engine, she looked at Seby through the open window. With the daylight rapidly fading, Seby said, "Be careful driving home." Then he added, "Tess, it just so happens that I need to be in

Los Angeles to meet an arriving cargo ship and take delivery of another shipment of New Zealand racing stock I bought from PJ. Would you consider flying down with me?"

"*Flying?* I'm terrified of those things."

"Then this is the way to overcome such fear," he laughed, reaching for her hand. "I promise to be very careful."

"I'll think about it," she smiled and started the car's engine."

"It's been a wonderful day, Tess," Seby said.

She nodded. "Thank you, Seby, for honoring my father enough to seek his permission to, uh, *court* me. I know it meant a lot to him."

"I greatly respect your parents, Tess. They've been very good to me, and I owe them much. By the way, are you free for New Year's Eve?"

Tess cocked her head, then said, "It just so happens, Mr. Stromberg, that I'm *not*."

"Oh," he said, a look of disappointment crossing his face. "I'm sorry to hear that."

"Don't be," she said, smiling. "I'm booked solid for the next three weeks with a very handsome, very respectful, and *very* old-fashioned Mexican-American rancher."

"Oh? Ooooh," he brightened. "I see. Well, I'll be sure he's on time every day."

"You do that," she winked and started her car down the gravel driveway.

Teresa was up long before dawn, but truth be known, she had been awake since shortly after three. How she had allowed herself to let Seby talk her into flying to Los Angeles she couldn't imagine, but as she finished packing the last few items she felt essential, given the limited luggage Seby had said they could take on the aircraft, she knew she would have to go through with her foolish promise or reveal a streak of cowardice to him. A soft knock on her door, followed by a creaking of the old hinges, revealed another coward, one less reluctant to show it to the world—her mother.

"Tess," she said as she stepped into the room, "for the last time, you're not going to go through with this idiocy, are you? You can be in Los Angeles tomorrow if you only take the train this morning."

"Mom, I told Seby I'd go, and, by golly, I'm going to go if he has to blindfold me before we take off."

"Tess, I'm so frightened."

"*You're* not going, Mom, *I* am," Teresa laughed. "Besides, it will impress the studio president when I show up for my screen test by landing on their airstrip in my own plane."

"You call me the minute you land, you hear? The very *minute*. I won't budge from the phone, or feel safe, until you call."

"Mom, it will take most of the day. Seby said we'll stop in St. George to refuel and probably have lunch. We won't get to Burbank until after four this afternoon. Why don't you just go about your normal routine?"

"This *is* my normal routine, my dear daughter. Mothers are supposed to worry. That's what we were created for," Katrina said, smiling through her resistance to Teresa's stubbornness.

"If you insist. Is Dad ready to drive me out to Draper?"

"He's out at the car. He thinks this is great. After flying with Seby up to Wyoming to go fishing last year, he says it's the only way to travel. I think I'll leave it to your generation, Tess."

The blindfold proved unnecessary. Tess steeled herself for the ordeal by employing her acting skills. She tried to imagine herself as an adventurous woman, for whom flying was as routine as riding in an automobile. As for Seby, he seemed oblivious to her fear, going about his normal pre-flight routine and loading the luggage as though Tess were a veteran flyer. Finally, they climbed into the cockpit, buck-led their safety harnesses, and Seby started the engine.

Listening to the coughing and sporadic backfiring of the plane's single engine while it was warming up, Tess forgot her playacting. It was too late to turn back, but she no longer sought to hide her anxiety. Seated next to Seby, who was busy with the instruments, she fought to control a wave of nausea by breathing deeply and keeping her eyes shut tight. When the engine finally smoothed out, Seby began taxiing toward the end of the dirt strip that ran adjacent to his ranch house. After cranking down the flaps, he revved the engine.

"Ready, Tess?" he shouted over the cacophony.

Tight-lipped, Tess just nodded and searched for some-thing to hold onto in the cramped cockpit.

Seby released the brakes and the aircraft began to roll down the strip, bouncing as it gathered speed and fishtail-ing slightly as the rear wheel came off the ground. With a slight pull on the stick, the wheels left the ground and they were airborne, the absence of the bumpy ride being Teresa's only indicator of flight. Seby gained a little altitude and then banked sharply as he approached the county road that traversed his ranch. He spotted Tom's car parked alongside the road with Tom standing nearby, waving as they approached. Seby pointed to him so Teresa could see, wag-gled his wings a bit, and then flew directly over the top of Tom, who had stayed to watch their departure.

Within moments, the aircraft had climbed to 2,500 feet and turned northwest, beginning a large circle so that Teresa could have a view of the Great Salt Lake, Antelope Island, and the downtown area, including Temple Square. Fascinated by the view, Teresa finally relaxed her hands somewhat and studied the landmarks on the ground below. They flew without trying to speak over the noise of the engine, and after making two complete circles, Seby turned the plane southwest to fly over the pass at Point of the Mountain and head down Utah Valley toward Orem and Provo.

"Oh, my," Tess exclaimed. "Oh, my goodness," she repeated as she scanned the horizon and the ground beneath, amazed at how quickly they came upon the familiar landmarks she knew from the many automobile trips she and her parents had taken through the southern valley.

Off their left wing, Mount Timpanogos and the other snow-covered peaks of the Wasatch Range shone brilliantly in the early morning sun. Sunlight reflected off the myriad lakes and streams tucked into the crevices of the mountain range, and as they flew south, passing Lehi and the smaller communities of Utah County, Teresa repeated her exclamation several times. Far below them, the bright blue water of Utah Lake shimmered, providing a beautiful setting. They continued down the valley, finally passing out of residential and commercial areas, and within twenty minutes, they were flying over barren country, the only sign of habitation being the tiny speck far ahead that Seby said was the community of Nephi.

Suddenly aware that she had been completely mesmerized by the perspective afforded by her new, unlimited visibility, Teresa turned to look at her pilot.

"Seby," she said, leaning toward him and speaking loudly, "why haven't you ever taken me up before?"

Seby began to laugh and then he leaned toward her, quickly kissing her lips and tousling her hair.

"Shouldn't you keep driving?" she asked, suddenly frightened.

"It's all right. The plane knows where to go," he teased.

As they flew down the central corridor of Utah, following Highway 91, small communities passed beneath their wings, and Seby commenced to give Teresa a visual geography lesson. Fillmore came and went, then Cove Fort, and later on, Beaver, Parowan, and Cedar City, where the snow-capped mountains gave way to the red rock and rugged terrain of southern Utah.

Just before noon, they glided past Pine Mountain and approached the town of St. George. Before landing, Seby flew over the snowy white temple and then banked sharply to line up with a dirt airstrip, which was located on top of a mesa just west of town. They landed without incident, though Teresa experienced another wave of fear that lasted until they were safely down and Seby had brought the plane to a halt in front of a wooden hangar.

While the plane was being refueled, Seby borrowed the mechanic's car and drove Teresa into the dusty little town where they ate lunch at a small café and stopped briefly in front of an elegant, two-story home, identified by a small sign as "Brigham Young's Winter Home."

Seby then drove them back to the airstrip and again they took off, this time with Teresa feeling considerably more relaxed.

By late afternoon, they had crossed a range of low mountains and were over the Los Angeles basin. On the flight down, they hadn't seen any aircraft other than several on the ground at St. George, but now Teresa spotted a number of other planes in the sky. One of them, an open cockpit biplane, passed by them so closely that she could see the pilot's face, and she was amazed at how much the little craft looked like a kite as it veered up and away from them in the sky. Far below, hundreds of cars, appearing as a file of ants, moved as if in slow motion on the network of roads that overlaid the ground.

Approaching Burbank, Seby lowered his altitude, studying the ground below, searching for the airstrip. He missed seeing it on the first pass, but finally located it—a grassy field, identified by a single orange wind sock suspended from a pole mounted on top of a dome-shaped hangar.

He made a smooth landing on the grassy strip, without kicking up the cloud of dust he was used to causing on the dirt strips he normally used and taxied back to a black automobile parked next to the hangar.

They were met by a representative of the film studio. Teresa introduced herself and her flying companion, and they loaded their luggage into the car. The hotel was located close to the studio, and once they were checked in to their adjoining rooms, an arrangement for which the studio had not been prepared, having reserved only one suite, Seby knocked on Teresa's door.

"Ready for some dinner, Miss Callahan?" he said, freshly dressed in tan slacks, a brown tweed jacket, and open-necked shirt.

"I'm ahead of you this time, Mr. Stromberg," she replied politely. "I've called and made reservations. Actually," she laughed, "I asked the studio man to call for us. There's a car and driver waiting downstairs, or at least he said there *would* be," she said.

"Are you ready for all this, Tess?" he asked, suddenly serious.

"What do you mean? The car, or dinner?"

"All of it. The special treatment?"

"Who *wouldn't* be?" she laughed, closing the room door and taking Seby's arm. "Let's just enjoy the ride while it lasts, and then I can take this so-called screen test, you can fly me back to Utah, and I can come back to earth— literally."

"Dinner it is, Tess, my dear. Oh, did you remember to call your mother?"

"Does Santa come each Christmas? Of course I did. Do you think I want the police looking for us tonight?" she laughed.

"Well, Tess, we have this evening for ourselves, and then early tomorrow I'll fly on to Arizona and check on some cattle. Then I'll come back and meet the ship with the horses I bought from PJ. That should take a couple of days and perhaps you'll be finished by then."

"Let's hope I'm not *finished*," she said, taking his arm and walking through the lobby. "I agree, however, tonight is for us, Seby, and you're looking mighty handsome."

"That's a requisite, I presume, since I'm escorting a famous actress."

"Not out here I'm not. Not yet, anyway. So don't be presumptuous," she laughed.

<hr />

Three days later, after Seby had flown to several ranches in Arizona, he returned to Los Angeles and drove to the port facility where he was advised that the ship was still two days out. He arranged for a local wrangler to pick up the half-dozen purebred horses when the ship arrived and transport them to Utah. Returning to the hotel, he found a note waiting from Teresa.

January 30, 1924

Dear Seby,

A whirlwind of activity. The screen test went exceptionally well, or so I'm told. They have offered me a contract for a film currently being written. I have had to travel to northern Mexico with several of the cast and the crew. Please accept my apologies, but I will not return for two or three weeks, I'm told, and then we will spend several more weeks with inside studio filming. I'll contact you immediately when we return. Thank you for a breathtaking experience. Tell Mom that flying is the wave of the future and that Dad should buy his own plane. See you when I get back.

Love, Tess

P.S.- Please ask Mom to pack some of my clothes and send them down.

Seby folded the note and placed it in his wallet, checked out of the hotel, and returned to the airstrip. The flight to St. George took most of the afternoon, and he remained overnight there, completing the flight to Draper the following morning. When he arrived at his ranch, he telephoned the Callahan residence and was pleased to find Katrina at home.

"Seby, it's so good to hear from you. I'm thrilled you're both back safely."

"I left her down there, I'm afraid," he said.

"Oh? In good hands I hope," Katrina replied.

"Well, I'd rather she be in *my* hands, Katrina, but I have a feeling that I'll be bucking some tough competition."

"Has Tess met someone?" Katrina asked, sounding surprised.

"No," he said, "but I think the film industry has met Tess."

JULY, 1927
OAHU, HAWAII

First Lieutenant Thomas Callahan III checked the gig-line on his summer tans, a cotton-twill tropical uniform, and placed his fore-and-aft cap at a suitably rakish angle on his head. He then stepped through the front door to the porch of his small, palm tree–shaded bungalow. After locking the door, he took the front walk to the street in a couple of giant strides, and without opening the door, vaulted over the side and into the driver's seat of his bright yellow 1927 Essex Challenger, an open-topped roadster.

Assigned to the marine garrison at Pearl Harbor, Hawaii, Tommy had spent the last year enjoying the tropical weather and scenery. He had arrived in Hawaii from the Dominican Republic with a four-inch scar in his upper left chest, a visual reminder of the surgery he had undergone to repair the damage inflicted by a gunshot wound. He had also brought to Hawaii a meritorious commendation for his work in producing what Colonel Buleman, his then commanding officer, had called "a respectable police cadre, complete with competent officers and patrolmen."

The commendation, while limited in its praise of the

new Dominican police force, nevertheless gave high marks to First Lieutenant Callahan's success in filling a difficult assignment, something he had achieved without much local cooperation. Colonel Rixby's after-action report on the nighttime battle with the bandits, wherein he had commended the courage and spontaneous leadership of Second Lieutenant Thomas Callahan, had been forwarded with a favorable second endorsement from the State Department's local representative to the commandant of the Marine Corps. That report and endorsement had earned Tommy a promotion to first lieutenant nearly a year earlier than most of his Annapolis peers.

Tommy endured the good-natured ribbing he received at the officer's club prior to his departure from the Caribbean island in his easygoing, placable way, knowing that the next island he was to visit—a temporary assignment, he was told—would be a darned site more hospitable than the one he was leaving.

He spent most of his thirty-day leave in Salt Lake City, where his mother continued to query him about his plans to "get married and expand the family." Without making any commitment to his mother on that count, Tommy left for his duty station in the Hawaiian Islands, where he found his new assignment physically demanding but very enjoyable.

In 1926, shortly before Tommy's arrival in Hawaii, the Marine Corps had begun evaluating the feasibility of making amphibious assault landings. The remote beaches on the islands provided ample staging areas and numerous "enemy palm trees" for such exercises. Tommy and his platoon had spent most of their duty hours practicing coming ashore and securing a beachhead against an imaginary, unarmed foe. After serving as what amounted to a police academy commandant in his Dominican Republic assignment, his new role of marine platoon leader was more to his liking. It reminded him of his experience in France, and he felt as though he was now more nearly doing a marine's work.

Secondly, the caliber of marines assigned to his new platoon, indeed the entire 1,500 marines shipped over from San Diego and Quantico to participate in the landing exercises, far exceeded the quality of the marines who had been assigned to the Dominican Republic and Haiti. Laboring now without the services of Gunnery Sergeant Holloman, who had recently retired, Tommy was grateful for that.

Due to a lack of adequate landing craft and other equipment needed to ensure that the first wave of marines to come ashore would be adequately supplied with ammunition, food, and reserves, the amphibious training exercises were ultimately cancelled. Following that, Tommy was permanently assigned to the marine garrison at Pearl Harbor, in support of the U.S. naval base.

Hawaii had been annexed by the United States in 1898, and the islands were quickly recognized by the military as a strategic location in a Pacific Ocean that was ever-shrinking due to the range and speed of steam-powered ships. To maintain a naval presence there was the logical conclusion. Initially established during the Spanish-American War in the Philippines, and perpetuated after that as a "forward operating base" by an act of Congress in 1908, Pearl Harbor had become a highly coveted duty assignment for naval and Marine Corps personnel.

The first year of Tommy's permanent assignment to the base rolled by quickly. Then his father's phone call came advising him of Teresa's forthcoming marriage to Sebastian Stromberg. Tommy had not been surprised by the news, though he wondered how his sister would ever balance her love of performing and her budding Hollywood career with the traditional roles of Mormon wife and mother.

With Tommy already in Hawaii, Tom said, it had seemed to Katrina a perfect place to stage a grand family reunion. Following Tess and Seby's marriage in the Salt Lake Temple, they would be honeymooning in Hawaii. At the same time, PJ would bring his family to the islands. Including the time spent there on his mission, by 1927 PJ had been living in New Zealand for nearly ten years. Married and with four children and a successful ranch to show for it, he was by all reports contented to be living there. PJ would also be bringing his business partner and former missionary companion, George Armitage, George's wife, Emily Callahan Armitage, and the Armitages's two children. Emily, Tommy was reminded, was his cousin, the daughter of Tom's long-lost brother John. The two couples from New Zealand were planning to be sealed in the Hawaii Temple.

"And of course," Tom had said, following this lengthy narrative, "your mother and I will come too. Any questions?"

Tommy had laughed at his father's explanation that Katrina had worked it all out and told him, "Come on out. The sun's blazing and the water's warm."

Driving down the mountain road toward the port in Honolulu, Tommy caught glimpses of the city through views framed by palm trees—those his platoon hadn't shot up during their practice assaults. He marveled again at the green foliage and colorful flowers, the white sandy beaches and the ocean beyond and wondered if he would ever tire of such beauty. Enjoying the brilliant sunshine and the scent of tropical blossoms being carried about by the trade winds, he allowed his thoughts to wander.

With Teresa planning to be married, he wondered about himself. The Marine Corps was not an easy life and certainly provided no stability in terms of family. That concern, along with his father's standing offer that all he needed to do was submit his resignation and come home to Salt Lake, where he would have a place on the Utah Trust Bank management team, had often left Tommy in a quandary. If he chose to do so, his future would be assured, and he could get on with the business of getting married and having a family—a responsibility his mother never let him forget. It was something he seriously considered doing while bed ridden in a Dominican Republic hospital, recovering from his wound and wondering whether it would heal sufficiently to permit his return to active duty. However, once he was given a clean bill of health, all thoughts of leaving the Corps vanished.

The banking life certainly offered considerably more money, but money wasn't a factor. His trust fund provided an ample income without even touching the principal. In fact, the annual income from his marine salary was less than a tenth of the interest income that accrued from the investments his father had so carefully arranged.

Tommy took a lot of good-natured flak from his fellow marine officers over how he could afford such things as the off base bungalow, his sporty roadster, and all the other toys he possessed. Without divulging his additional income, he countered their gibes by saying that if they would only manage their pay more carefully, they could enjoy the same benefits.

Financial considerations aside, Tommy wondered how he could ever take on a wife and family. What sane woman wanted to marry a vagabond marine? Though he had met some wonderful wives of fellow officers, some of whom relished the idea of matching up the handsome, clean-cut lieutenant, most of the women Tommy had run into simply wanted a meal ticket and a way out of their destitution— especially some of the women he had met in the Dominican Republic.

No, he thought, shaking his head to himself as he neared the turnoff toward the port facility where the civilian ships moored, the Marine Corps was no place for a married man, and he was not yet ready to make the leap to gray business suits and join UTB's nine-to-fivers.

After parking his roadster and walking to the designated pier, he entered the shipping line's office and asked about the arrival time of the *Southern Winds*, coming from New Zealand. The port director for the Pacific Transport Lines assured Tommy that *Southern Winds* was less than an hour from mooring and, in fact, was already in tow and under the control of the harbor pilot. Outside the office, Tommy negotiated the fee for three Hawaiian girls to be on hand with an armload of leis to greet his family and guests, and then he walked further down the pier to a small café.

He bought a newspaper, ordered a cup of coffee, and then sat at a small, outside table to wait for the ship's arrival. On the front page of the newspaper was a large picture of Charles Lindbergh's recent ticker-tape parade in New York City. *The Lone Eagle* had become an instant hero when he completed the first-ever transatlantic solo flight. America's "melting pot" city had given Lindbergh the biggest parade since the end of the Civil War.

Twenty minutes after seating himself and becoming immersed in the newspaper, Tommy spotted a vessel slowly making her way up the channel, escorted by two harbor tugs.

Uncle Tommy, he suddenly thought as he envisioned a

pack of little kids clambering down the gangway. It would be a new role for him, and he would be seeing a brother he hadn't seen since . . . well, since PJ had slapped him on the back at the train station when PJ had left for a visit to Ireland in 1916. By the time their father had gone to Ireland to get PJ out of a British jail, following the abortive Irish Easter Rebellion, Tommy had left to live with Uncle Anders in Virginia and attend college at Georgetown. Then PJ had gone off on his mission to New Zealand and Tommy had joined the marines, ultimately sailing for France and the trenches. Tommy reckoned it had been eleven years in all since they had seen each other. How peculiar it was the way family members separated and then reunited, bringing with them a spouse, another generation of kids, and often in-laws—or in-law stories.

He downed the last bit of his coffee and then walked to the end of the pier to watch the docking procedure. As the tugs swung the ship broadside in the channel, his mind flashed on the naval hospital ship in March, 1919, arriving at the Brooklyn Navy Yard when he, along with thousands of other wounded marine, army, and navy servicemen had returned from France. Now, as then, the pier was silent except for the general waterfront sounds.

The sound of his name reverberated across the water—a small, echoing sound that startled him from his reverie. *Southern Winds* was primarily a transport or cargo ship, with moderately appointed accommodations for about two dozen paying passengers. Resembling not at all the great ocean liners that plowed the Atlantic between New York and Europe, she still held human cargo that, despite his attempt to minimize his excitement, Tommy now anxiously awaited. His brother and the next generation of Callahans were aboard.

He looked toward the ship, searching for whoever had called out his name. Lining the railing on the port bow stood a small group of adults and children, all waving at someone on the pier. Glancing around, Tommy could see no one else waiting besides the stevedores who stood ready to secure the lines of the vessel.

He realized the passengers were waving at him, and he soon spotted his brother, looking somewhat older but unmistakably PJ even though so many years had gone by. Through pictures sent while Tommy was in France and in the following years, he had been able to keep up with his brother's growing family. Combat-hardened marine that he was, Tommy was surprised that a lump rose in his throat as he watched PJ and his family waving and yelling across the water.

Little Clint, at five, PJ's oldest son, was hollering, "Uncle Tommy, Uncle Tommy," and the young boy's enthusiasm and unabashed greeting brought tears to Tommy's eyes. He quickly glanced around to see who else might be watching the scene.

Within minutes the ship was moored, the gangway lowered, and the three Hawaiian girls were gathered at the bottom of the ramp. A small group of musicians also appeared, and the rhythmic strains of Hawaiian music drifted through the air. The children were first off. Ignoring their mothers' warnings to be careful, they dashed headlong down the gangway with Clint in the lead. Rushing up to the man in uniform, the young lad stopped short of Tommy and looked up at him.

"Are you my Uncle Tommy?" he asked, suddenly shy.

Tommy smiled at his nephew, reached down and picked him up, and held him at arm's length for a moment. The boy had an uncanny resemblence to pictures of PJ taken when he was the same age, and Tommy immediately warmed to him. This was PJ's son. His own nephew. A Callahan of the next generation.

"I certainly am, son, and you must be Clinton Callahan, the leader of the bunch," he laughed. Two smaller children, a boy and a girl, also gathered around Tommy, and suddenly he was standing in front of his brother after so many years.

"You look a lot like Pop," PJ said.

Tommy nodded. "So I've been told." He placed Clint on the ground and took one step toward his brother. "And you favor Mom."

PJ also nodded. "Aye. In temperament too," he grinned. "It's so good to see you, Tommy. Are you well? Do you like Hawaii?"

"First things first, big brother," Tommy said, grabbing PJ and wrapping his arms around him.

After a spate of exuberant hugging and backslapping, PJ stepped back and wiped his eyes quickly with a handkerchief he retrieved from his back pocket.

"I think you've got a good two inches on me, Tommy. I guess I'm not the big brother anymore," he laughed.

"No, but you'll always be 'old brother,'" Tommy challenged with a grin.

A beautiful woman with light-brown skin, long, black hair, and dark, almond-shaped eyes had come up behind PJ, where she stood silently, holding a baby in her arms.

"Might we join in this family reunion?" she asked softly.

PJ whirled around, smiling at his wife. "I'm sorry, Kiri. Tommy, this is my wife, Kiri, and these are my children: You've already met Clint," he said, tugging on his son's ear. "This is his younger brother, Simon, my oldest daughter, Lea, just turned three, and the baby," he said, again looking toward his wife. "We named her Jenny, after Grandma Hansen."

Tommy had known that Kiri was of Maori descent, but he found her more beautiful and exotic-looking than her pictures had suggested. Nearly as tall as PJ, Kiri had a slender, athletic build. Smiling at Tommy, she showed a mouth full of beautiful, perfectly straight, white teeth. She surprised him somewhat after they were introduced by stepping forward and gently touching the tip of her nose against his.

"*Kia ora*, Tommy. I am honored to be your sister."

Tommy smiled at her greeting and then kissed her cheek.

"A fine family, PJ. You've done well, down under."

"Aye, and New Zealand has done well by me, also. Oh, and let me introduce my mate, George Armitage and his family." George had waited patiently, happily watching the Callahans became reacquainted.

"George and I were missionary companions, and now we manage Shenandoah Station together. It wouldn't have become the ranch it is were it not for George. And, Tommy, this is our cousin Emily, now Mrs. Armitage, and their two children, Margaret, named after our other grandmother from Ireland, and Tim. And that about completes the crew," PJ laughed.

Tommy motioned to the Hawaiian girls who stepped forward and draped fresh flower leis around the necks of everyone, including Tommy. Then the party walked toward the customs shed where a couple of uniformed guards were waiting as luggage from the ship began to unload.

"When does the rest of the family arrive?" PJ asked.

Tommy laughed. "Tomorrow. Pop was going to book them all on the same ship, but Mom convinced him that Tess and Seby would be more comfortable traveling by themselves and not having her parents underfoot. She told me on the telephone the other night that all she had to do was remind Pop how he would have felt if Grandpa Hansen had wanted to go with them on their honeymoon to Europe. Pop caved in immediately. They all left San Francisco only hours apart, but on two different ships. When I checked yesterday, I was told that both ships will arrive tomorrow."

"That'd be Mom, all right," PJ allowed.

After clearing customs, the party walked to the car park where Tommy's yellow roadster was standing.

"Well, that'll be a tight squeeze," PJ said, his face beaming.

"Not to worry, old brother," Tommy replied. "I've hired two additional cars." Reaching into his car, he retrieved two sets of keys from the glove compartment. "I've made all the necessary arrangements for accommodations. You'll all be staying in three bungalows out in Laie, a small village on the north shore, right on the beach. The houses are within walking distance of the temple. There're two larger houses, one with five bedrooms for your family and Mom and Pop, one for George's family with two bedrooms, and a small cottage for Seby and Tess, a bit away from the others," he grinned.

"I see the military has organized that disheveled mind of yours," PJ said.

"You could say that," Tommy replied. "Logistics we call it."

"You've done well, brother. Shall we go? How far is it?"

"A couple of hours, around the coast. It's a beautiful drive."

PJ looked up toward the hills to the north and west. "It

all seems beautiful, Tommy. From the way you described the Dominican Republic, this must seem like paradise."

Tommy nodded. "It *is* nice here. I've grown used to it, I suppose. Well, let's load up then. George, you want to take the green town wagon with most of the luggage? And Clint," Tommy said, ruffling the young boy's hair, "how would you like to ride in this hot roadster with your Uncle Tommy?"

Looking at the sporty yellow open-topped roadster, the boy's eyes opened wide, and his face lit up with excitement.

"Oh yes, please. Can I, Dad?" he pleaded.

"He's been over the moon about this trip," PJ added.

"Over the what?" Tommy asked, looking toward his brother.

PJ laughed out loud. "Over the moon. It means 'very excited, or thrilled.' I'm afraid my language has taken on a new dimension. I had to become a Kiwi as best I could, you know."

"Well, take it slow with me, PJ. I'm just a country boy from Utah," Tommy grinned.

Tommy smiled at the lad who was admiring the fancy car, and picking him up, lifted him over the side and set him in the passenger seat.

"I expect you to carry your load, son, and you may have to drive this car part of the way," Tommy laughed and then saw George Armitage struggling with the luggage. "Here, George, let me help with those bags."

With the luggage loaded, the kids installed in the cars, and with young Clint sitting tall in the yellow roadster—to the chagrin of his younger brother who had pleaded to be allowed to also "ride with Uncle Tommy"—Tommy walked around to the passenger side of PJ's car and opened the door for Kiri. She was still holding the baby, and as she approached to enter, Tommy leaned forward and once again kissed her on the cheek, then whispered in her ear.

"Welcome to Hawaii, Sis. You've made a beautiful family, and from all I can see, a fine husband out of PJ."

"Thank you, Tom," she said, "he's a good man."

"Aye. He is that."

<hr />

"I can't remember," Katrina said, "when I've felt so fulfilled or been so happy, Thomas."

"If that's the case, then I'm happy, too."

"You're happy too, and you know it, Mr. Callahan," she teased. "Our family has really grown and just think how long it's been since we've all been together. Or how long it will be until the next time," she added.

"There you go, Katie, already worrying about the next time instead of enjoying *this* time," he said, taking her hand in his.

Katrina pulled at Tom's arm as they walked barefoot along the sandy beach between the ocean and their bungalow. It was nearly midnight, and the moon was full, reflecting off the water and illuminating several of the smaller islands and rock formations just offshore. The walk had been Katrina's idea. For the three days that they had been in Hawaii, PJ's children and even the Armitage kids had clustered around their newly discovered grandparents like bees circling a hive. Katrina relished every moment of it, and even Tom, to his surprise, had enjoyed playing his new role of Grandpa Tom.

The previous morning, after taking a day to settle in to their new accommodations, the four couples had gone together to the temple where PJ and Kiri and George and Emily Armitage were sealed to each other and had their children sealed to them. While the families were in the temple, Tommy had driven back around to Pearl Harbor to complete some military business that he said was necessary, something his mother recognized as an excuse to get away during the temple visit. She had cornered Tommy already and asked him about his activity in the Church, and he had readily admitted that religion was not a priority in his life at that point. He was happy for the rest of them, but he wouldn't be joining them in the temple.

That afternoon, after the sealings, Tommy came back from Pearl Harbor and took the children for a picnic on the beach while Tom and Katrina, Seby and Teresa, PJ and Kiri, and George and Emily returned to the temple to participate in an endowment session. As Tom sat in the temple, glancing back and forth between the women who were seated together and the men who sat side by side with him, he thanked the Lord for what had transpired in his family. Though he and Katrina had walked separately for years, they had come together now, and except for Tommy, they were all united in their faith. At the time Tom had made his commitment and gone to the temple for the first time, Robert Thurston had told him that it really didn't matter how many years were lost in his vacillation about religion, but that his path was set now and all was right with the Lord. Observing his family in the temple, Tom experienced an overwhelming sense of peace and contentment.

Katrina had quickly seen that the two New Zealand women, cousin Emily and PJ's wife, Kiri, were close friends. During the first years they had worked the sheep station together, Emily's new membership in the Church had opened a door for Kiri, a lifetime member, to explain things to her from a female perspective.

Kiri's broad-based Maori family had been members of

207

the Church since before the turn of the century, her grandparents having joined shortly after the Mormon missionaries
first visited New Zealand in 1898. Both of her grandfathers
had been leaders of the Church on the North Island, where
PJ had met her while attending a Church conference. She
was in fact, third-generation LDS, in a land where
Mormonism had yet to really take hold.

In 1921, Elder David O. McKay, in company with
President Hugh Cannon from the Salt Lake Liberty Stake,
had made a worldwide trip, stopping in New Zealand, where
the Apostle had called George Armitage to be presiding
elder on the South Island. Elder McKay had promised the
Saints on the South Island that their numbers would grow,
and that one day a stake would be formed on the South
Island and a temple of the Lord would be built in New
Zealand.

With her heritage of faithfulness and her husband also
serving faithfully in the Church, Kiri's faith was strong. It
was also clear that she and Emily were best friends. Living
together in the isolation of the sheep station and sharing
the hard work of caring for their families and feeding sea-
sonal crews who came to Shenandoah Station to help with
the shearing of sheep and harvesting of crops, Kiri and
Emily had truly become sisters. The bond between the two
was evident, and it was something that Katrina found very
comforting. Having PJ live so far away would always tug at
Katrina's heart, but knowing that he had a loving wife and
close friends made the separation a little easier to bear.

As he and Katrina continued their midnight walk on
the beach, Tom spied another couple walking toward them,
illuminated by the moonlight. Watching them for just a
moment, he quickly determined that it was Seby and Teresa.
Tom didn't say anything to Katrina, who was looking down,

searching the sand for unusual seashells as they casually walked along the water's edge.

As the distance closed between the two couples, Katrina finally looked up and saw Seby and Tess approaching.

"It's after midnight," she exclaimed to Tom. "What are they doing out here?"

"The same thing we are, Katie m' darlin', falling in love all over again."

"Oh, Thomas, don't be silly. We're grandparents now," she laughed.

Tom stopped walking and pulled Katrina around to face him while Seby and Tess were still a dozen yards away. "You can be a *great*-grandmother, Katie, and I'll *still* be fallin' in love with you." He then pulled her closer and kissed her firmly, wrapping his strong arms around her shoulders and holding her tightly.

"Hey, you two," Teresa called out as she and Seby approached, "*we're* the ones on the honeymoon."

Katrina gasped as Tom released her from his hug but stood gazing quietly at her face. Without looking toward his daughter and son-in-law, who had stopped a couple of feet away, Tom said, "and if you're lucky, my precious daughter, you'll never get off your honeymoon."

"I get the point, Dad," Teresa laughed. "We were just about to head back for some midnight lemonade. Any takers?"

"Sounds good to me," Tom quickly replied.

"Thomas, the young folk want to . . ."

"C'mon, Mom," Teresa said, "it's all right. We'd love to have you come back and talk privately. We haven't seen anything of you since PJ's kids got hold of you."

"Well, if you're sure," Katrina said, still reluctant to intrude on the honeymooners' time together.

"*Señora*, we will be sailing to the outer island of Kauai tomorrow anyway. Tess is right. We'd love to talk to you for a while," Seby said.

"All right then," she replied, "but Seby, you've got to find something other than *Señora* to call me, please. I see you've begun calling Thomas, Tom."

"Yes, but—"

"No buts. How about . . . Mom."

Seby smiled broadly. "It would be my honor . . . and perhaps my right."

Katrina smiled at her new son-in-law and linked her arm with his and turned to walk with him back toward their bungalows.

"It is your right, Seby. I was present at your birth, *and* at your marriage. So that settles it."

"Tess, I'll walk with you since it seems your husband has deserted you for an older woman."

"Maybe, Dad, but from what I can see, I think she already has a man."

"You'd be right about that, sweetheart. You'd be absolutely right," Tom laughed.

14

The next afternoon, Tommy helped load Seby and Teresa's luggage into the town wagon as the newlyweds began to bid their farewells to the family. While Katrina was out on the lawn in front of the bungalows, struggling to organize the children for a group photograph, Teresa, PJ, and Kiri stepped away from the confusion.

"It's so far down there, PJ, and it isn't always going to be possible to arrange these family gatherings. It could be years before I see you again," Teresa said.

"I know, Tess. But the world's getting smaller all the time. I'll be back to Utah sometime, and New Zealand's a great place for a vacation. You should bring Seby down," he said, giving his sister a quick hug.

"I'll try," she said, tears continuing down her cheeks. She then made the rounds, hugging all the children and then Emily and George. As Tess was preparing to get into the car, Kiri leaned over to Teresa and hugged her sister-in-law once again.

"Tess, just over a year ago, I took two of my younger sisters to see your movie, *A Gathering Storm*. They were both very moved by your portrayal of the courage of that young woman. Then, when I told them you were PJ's sister, they were in awe. You know, the Church is not well established in New Zealand, and even though the girl you portrayed didn't have any religious affiliation, I want to thank you for showing them that someone can stand up to evil and not always lose. You taught some good principles in that role."

Teresa hugged Kiri again, and the two women rubbed noses in the traditional Maori way.

"Thank you, Kiri. Not everyone is fortunate enough to have such a good role to play. I haven't seen one since," she laughed.

"I understand," Kiri went on. "I read your letter to PJ about how it is to live in Hollywood and about your frustration over the sacrifices so often required. Is it *really* that bad?"

"I can't indict the whole community, Kiri, but young people are quite often exploited and those who have no set standards seem willing to surrender their morals to further their careers or land the next role."

"What's this about careers?" PJ asked, stepping close to the two women.

"Teresa was just saying how hard it is in Hollywood."

"Well, that's all behind you now," PJ said. "You've got a family to create."

Teresa looked at her brother for a moment. "You make it sound awfully easy, PJ."

"Isn't it?"

"No, it's not," she replied. "Few people have the opportunities I've been offered, brother dear. I don't want to just toss it away."

"But you're married now."

"Lots of actors and actresses are married, PJ," she laughed. "It's not a celibate profession."

PJ laughed in return. "I should say not, from what I read. But you'll want a family, won't you?"

"I know Seby will," Teresa responded wistfully. "I'll just have to see how it goes."

"Just remember, Tess, Mom had several opportunities, too, and she chose us—her family."

"And I've chosen Seby, and he's a very understanding man."

Kiri glanced over at the handsome Mexican man who was helping Tommy with the luggage. "He seems a good man, too, Tess." Kiri hugged Teresa again. "You'll know what to do. Just remember, we love you and I'm so glad to have met you. You'd better be going. Tommy looks anxious."

"Tommy's *always* anxious." Hugging Kiri one final time, Teresa stepped back, embraced her mother once again, and got into the car. "We'll see you in a couple of weeks, Mom."

"That'll be fine, dear. Have a good time and take some pictures on that other island."

Tommy slid into the driver's seat and slowly began to inch the car away from the gathered family, all of them waving. Reaching the highway, he gained speed and headed back to Honolulu and the pier where PJ had arrived about a week earlier. After reaching the harbor and parking the car, the three walked toward the shipping office.

"I'll still be here when you get back, Tess," he smiled. "Got to keep Mom and Pop from going native."

Teresa laughed. "No fear of that in Dad's case, I think. He was even wearing a tie this morning."

"He *was* a bit formal, wasn't he," Tommy replied. Turning to his new brother-in-law, he said, "Seby, it's great to have you as a member of the family. I don't know that I ever properly thanked you for coming to my graduation at Annapolis and for the flight back to Salt Lake City."

213

"*De nada*, Tommy," Seby smiled. "I understand you picked up a bit of Spanish while you were in the Dominican Republic."

"Very little," he laughed as they entered the building and approached the ticket counter. "Now," he said, nodding toward the woman selling tickets, "I think I need to learn Japanese."

"Yes, Hawaii seems to have a large proportion of Japanese, doesn't it? A real mixture of races here in the islands," Seby said. "I'll just go see about our tickets and accommodations while you say goodbye to Tess."

"Well, take care, little sis," Tommy said, wrapping his arms around Teresa as Seby walked toward the counter. "Seems you brought a good man into the family."

"Seby *is* a good man, Tommy. PJ told me before we left that I should settle down now and have a family."

"And what do you want?" he said, noticing his sister's hesitancy.

Teresa shook her head. "I want both. I love my career making films . . . and I'd love to have a baby."

"Well?"

"Well, PJ reminded me of what Mom did for all of us— how she gave up her opportunities. He thinks I should be like her."

"And I think you should be like *you*, Tess. Do what makes *you* feel right."

"And if it hurts Seby?"

"I know you don't want to hurt Seby, or anyone else for that matter, Tess. I know you. But you're only going to get one chance at this, and Sis, it looks to me as if you have all the makings of a fine actress. It'll never come again."

"Thank you, Tommy," she said, hugging him tightly. "It's so seldom I've gotten to see you. I wish we were a lot closer."

"No matter how far apart we are, Tess, you and I will always be close. Call on me for anything."

"Thanks, Tommy. Well, here comes Seby."

"Like I said, I'll be here when you get back. Telegraph or call if anything changes; otherwise I'll meet you here on the seventeenth."

"Okay, Tommy. I love you, old man," she smiled, giving him another hug.

"And I you, Tess. Seby," he said, extending his hand to his new brother-in-law, "when you come back and things are a bit settled, PJ and the kids gone and all, perhaps we can get a couple of horses and take a ride on the upper end of the island, play some golf, and get in some fishing. Hawaii's a beautiful place, really."

"Hey," Teresa exclaimed, "this is *my* honeymoon."

"Yeah, but Seby is *my* brother-in-law, Sis."

Seby wrapped his arm around Teresa and pulled his wife close.

"That would be fine, Tommy. I'll look forward to it."

⁂

Tom drove the sporty yellow roadster carefully, following the bends in the road and keeping his speed down to a reasonable thirty-five miles an hour. Convincing Tommy to lend his prize possession to his parents hadn't been all that difficult, but when they had actually driven away from the bungalow, Tom had watched Tommy in the rear view mirror and smiled. The younger Callahan appeared as nervous as a father turning the family car over to his son for his first date. After spending nearly a month in Hawaii, Tom and Katrina were thoroughly relaxed. For several weeks, at Katrina's urging, Tom had not telegraphed his bank, and his only response to Mark Thurston's last telegram was "Use your best judgment. See you in a month." As they drove, Tom felt exhilarated, free of the burdens of business, mergers, and financial dealings of any kind, totally so for the first time in many years.

"Now that we're away from the bungalow and the kids," Katrina said, "why is this little trip so secret, and where have you been each day for the past three days, Mr. Callahan?" she smiled, sliding next to him on the car seat and leaning over so she could be heard against the gentle rushing of the wind.

"You'll see," he grinned.

A mile or so beyond the Mormon temple in Laie, he turned inland, off the main road and onto a red dirt side road, beginning a gentle climb toward the mountains. Cresting one ridge, he descended the other side and made a complete reversal of direction, heading back toward the ocean, the mountains now behind them. Finally, just as the road ran out and the underbrush began, he came to a stop and shut off the engine.

"Taking a girl into the mountains without an escort is *not* proper behavior for a man your age, Mr. Callahan," she teased.

"You're safe enough, Mrs. Callahan," he rebuffed.

"Well, shucks, *that's* not the answer I was looking for," she laughed out loud, removing her scarf from her hair.

Tom came around to Katrina's side of the car and opened the door. Then he assisted her out and took her hand, guiding her toward the edge of the plateau where they had stopped. The view below them was magnificent. To the southeast, they could see the temple and the grounds surrounding it, including a small cluster of neatly arranged houses that had grown steadily each year since President Heber J. Grant had dedicated the temple in 1919. To the north lay the expanse of the Pacific Ocean, displaying an endless variety of shades of blue and green, with white-capped waves breaking on the beach. Immediately in front and below, Tom pointed to a palm-shaded, sheltered cove and its sandy beach, which stretched along the coast for hundreds of yards.

"This is absolutely beautiful, Thomas," she said, leaning against him and surveying the view. "It was well worth the drive *and* the subterfuge."

"There was no subterfuge, Katie. I just wanted to talk to you first without PJ and Tommy being involved."

"Talk about what?" she asked, leaning back and looking into his face.

He looked out over the ocean and scanned the horizon for a few moments, running his fingers through his hair but unable to keep the breeze from immediately displacing it again. Finally, without taking his eyes off the ocean, he spoke.

"How many years have you complained to me about the coming snow and the cold winter walks down to Temple Square for choir practice?"

"*What?* What do you mean?"

"I mean," he said, turning his gaze toward his wife, "that for at least a half-dozen years, and more if I could remember them," he smiled, "you've been moaning about the winter and the cold creeping into your joints."

"I *love* Salt Lake winters," she argued.

"I know," he answered gently, "but you *hate* the cold and the snow."

"But they're one and the same."

Tom laughed out loud, taking her in his arms and pulling her closer.

"Yes, they are, aren't they?"

"So what does that have to do with . . . anything," she said, stretching out the last word as she began to fathom his direction. "Thomas, what have you been up to? What have you done?"

He took a deep breath and exhaled slowly. "Katie, I'll put it to you in a nutshell. It's something I've been thinking about for several years actually, even in Portlaoise Prison where I worked it out in my head, although how I might accomplish it never came to mind, or even if I was going to have a future life to accomplish it with. I'm trying to say that I didn't know how, or when . . . until now, that is."

"What came to mind? How or when to do *what*? Thomas, stop rambling," she demanded.

"All right, Katie," he smiled again. "For several years I've been thinking about . . . retiring—selling the bank or at least turning it over to someone else."

"Thomas, you're not serious," she exclaimed.

"Yes," he answered, nodding his head, "I'm quite serious. I've bought this land, Katie," he said softly, looking around again.

"What land?" she asked.

"*This* land! The land we're standing on. Eight hundred and fifty acres actually, running all the way down to the beach there," he said, pointing toward the ocean.

"For heaven's sake, why?" she said.

"Because I'm ready for it, Katie. I'm ready to stop work-ing, at least in the financial rat race I'm involved in every day. This is kind of a dream, Katie."

"*I'll* say it's a dream," she repeated, "and I wonder if I'll ever wake up."

"Katie, think about it. PJ is in New Zealand, and with his ranch and children growing, his family will *always* be there. Seby and Tess will be in Utah, and Tommy . . . well, if he stays in the Marines, Tommy will be Lord knows where. This is a good spot," he said, again looking out over the land. "We can sail down—probably *fly* down one day—to New Zealand, or back to San Francisco, or have all the kids and grandkids come out here every year. Think of it, Katie. The temple is here, the Church is growing, and who wouldn't want to vacation here in Hawaii? The grandkids will be badgering their parents to come and see Grandma every year."

"Are you serious?" she said, reaching up to hold his chin and turn his face toward hers.

He placed his hand over hers. "I am, Katie. I'm over fifty and you're almost—"

"Never mind what I'm *almost*," she interrupted. "Then you *are* serious."

Again he nodded. "Wouldn't this be a beautiful life?" he said, gesturing toward the beach and the land surrounding.

"Oh, I'll grant you, Thomas, that this is a paradise by anyone's definition. But it's so different from *our* life."

"So was Utah when we arrived, wasn't it? The prophet is counseling new members to stay where they are—in their own countries—and build Zion. We can help, right here."

"So this is your dream?" she said.

"Perhaps I hadn't put thought to the actual site or place, but yes, I *have* thought about selling out and retiring. None of the kids want to run UTB. They don't want to be bankers."

Katie nodded her agreement. "It *has* been a good living for us, hasn't it? But it seems they've all chosen their own way of life, and I suppose we can't expect them to just follow in your footsteps, can we?"

"I have to admit, Katie, they've each made a pretty good way of life for themselves, except for Tommy, of course. His running all over the world playing soldier doesn't sit well with me."

"He's content, Thomas, I can tell that he is."

"I suppose, but he'll never settle down as long as he stays in the marines," Tom said.

"I suppose not, but perhaps to him, he *is* settled down—that frequent reassignment is part of the course in his career."

"Maybe so."

"So you bought this land?" she said, grinning at him as if he were a little boy, caught stealing cookies from the kitchen.

"I did," he smiled. "Do you like it?"

"Who wouldn't? It's beautiful. But it *would* be quite a change for us."

"It would, but wherever you are, Katie, m' darlin', is good enough for me," he said, pulling her closer again.

"Yes, a little soft soap and flattery always brings me around to your way of thinking, eh, Thomas?"

"Whatever do you mean?"

"I mean that I *know* you, Thomas Matthew Callahan. But then, maybe I have a dream of my own."

"A dream?" he asked.

"For after retirement, I mean."

"What dream, Katie?"

"You're not the *only* one who's thought about retirement, Thomas, but I didn't think you were ready. How long will it take you to sell out—to put your affairs in order, I mean?"

"Oh, maybe a year—give or take a few months. If I move too quickly, prospective buyers will think I'm in trouble, and the price will go down."

"Then about a year or so—by the end of '28 at the outside?"

"That's a reasonable timetable, I suppose."

"And then we would move here," she said, looking around at the land, "sell *Valhalla*, build a house here, and live in Hawaii."

"That's right. And travel, too, if you'd like," he said.

"Ah, travel," she nodded. "As if we haven't done enough of *that* in our time. This is all quite short notice, Thomas. You know that, don't you?"

"We've got over a year to prepare, Katie. It's not like we'd be moving tomorrow."

"Alright, Thomas," she said, resignedly. "I'll agree to this plan of yours. Heaven knows it would be wonderful to live here in this paradise. But before we move here, I have one request of my own. Something *I've* been dreaming about ever since Alice and Robert came home from England."

He looked at her without speaking, waiting to hear.

"I want us to go on a mission."

"A *mission?* You mean *Elder* and *Sister* Callahan?" he laughed.

"I mean," she said, a serious look in her eye, "I want to go on a mission *after* you retire and *before* we move to Hawaii."

"A mission! Just think what Robert would say about that?"

"First he'd hug you, and then he'd say, 'God *go with you.*'"

"A mission," Tom repeated, his gaze far beyond the ocean. "Who'd listen to *me?*"

"*I* did," she said, smiling at her husband.

15

APRIL, 1929
SALT LAKE CITY

Rather than taking one year, it took closer to two before Tom was able to conclude several major transactions with Utah Trust Bank's mining interests and stock holdings and to arrange for management of his personal investments during his expected absence. After consulting with Robert Thurston, who had not returned to the bank's employ after his missionary service, and with Robert's son, Mark, now president of UTB, Tom had decided against selling the bank, preferring to leave Mark in charge. With the stock market growing rapidly, all with whom he counseled suggested Tom decide about the bank's divestment after finishing his mission.

That was sound advice, Tom figured, *if* he ever went anywhere.

Nearly a year earlier, when he had finally determined to follow through on his decision to retire, Tom and Katrina sat in front of Robert Thurston's desk in Church headquarters—a strange sensation for Tom who was used to seeing Robert in the UTB setting—and told him of their desire to serve the Lord on a mission. Following his return from service as president of the British Isles Mission, Robert had been called to serve as the director of the Church's missionary committee, under the Quorum of the Twelve, and he had never skipped a beat in his transition from the mission field. During their interview, Katrina had done most of the talking although Tom was clearly supportive. Perhaps aware of Tom's hesitancy, or the underlying reason behind it, Robert did all he could to assure Tom that he was indeed a worthy candidate for missionary service. But nine months had passed since that meeting, and nothing official had been heard from either Robert, whom the Callahans saw at church every week, or from Church headquarters.

Tom's disgruntled attitude about the delay had begun to grate on Katrina's nerves, since the mission had been her idea in the first place. For the first year after coming home from Hawaii, Tom had gently tried every ploy he knew to talk her out of volunteering for a mission, all unsuccessful. When, after nearly a year, nothing had been heard from the missionary committee, Tom felt certain that the mission idea had been scrapped. Still, he bristled at having volunteered and then, apparently, having been rejected by Church authorities.

Then, late on a Friday afternoon, a telephone call came. Brother Farmington, secretary to the Twelve, allowed Tom and Katrina three days to speculate on why they had been summoned to a meeting with Elder David O. McKay. All that was revealed during the conversation was that Brother and Sister Callahan were to meet with the apostle the following Monday morning.

Now, waiting in the Church Office Building foyer, Tom sat impatiently as Katrina tried to curb his nervousness. Finally, Elder McKay himself came down the stairs, and Tom rose from his seat.

"My good friends, good morning to you. And how are you this beautiful day, Sister Callahan?"

"I'm quite well, Elder McKay. Thank you for asking," she smiled.

"And Tom, how are you these days? A little less busy, I understand," he said, reaching out to grasp, and then pump, Tom's hand.

"Oh, Katrina's found a few things around the house to keep me busy, D.O."

The apostle laughed softly, smiling at Katrina. "There's always a list of chores, isn't there? Please excuse the delay this morning, but there is someone I've asked to join us, and he was detained for a few moments in President Grant's office. Please, come with me if you will."

The trio climbed one flight of stairs to Elder McKay's office where he ushered them to seats before taking a seat himself. They chatted casually for a few moments until being joined by another man who came into the room.

"Ah, there you are," Elder McKay said, rising. Recognizing the newly arrived visitor, Tom also stood. "Tom, I presume you know Elder Melvin J. Ballard of the Twelve. Elder Ballard, these are my longtime friends, Thomas and Katrina Callahan."

Elder Ballard extended his hand toward Tom. "It's a pleasure, Brother Callahan. I've been aware of your fine bank for many years and the good work you've done in our community. Sister Callahan," he said, turning his attention to Katrina who remained seated but extended her hand. "I've heard you sing on several occasions, much to my pleasure I might add."

"Thank you, Elder Ballard," Katrina said.

"Well, then," McKay said, gesturing for all to take their

seats again, "now that we're all here, Tom, perhaps you could tell us, how are things at Utah Trust Bank?"

"They're fine, D.O. You know Mark Thurston of course, Robert's son. He's doing a fine job of managing our interests, and I have full confidence in him."

"So you've actually pulled out of management?"

Katrina chuckled softly and reached between their chairs for Tom's hand.

"*Physically*, Elder McKay," she said. "But I still see him with his nose in the paper *every* day, turned to the financial page and reading *every* line."

McKay and Elder Ballard smiled and looked at Tom.

"Guilty," Tom grinned. "But it's been nerve-racking, I suppose, to be so near and to try to remove myself after being so closely involved for, what, thirty years?"

"We can well understand that, Brother Callahan," Elder Ballard said.

"Tom," Elder McKay said, his voice soft yet determined, "Brother Thurston tells us that now that you've removed yourself from the daily operations of your business, you've considered serving a mission. Is that correct?"

Tom nodded. "It is, D.O. It's something Katie and I have discussed for *quite* some time now," a slight tone of irritation at the delay evident in his voice—a tone that earned him a quick glance from his wife.

"I know," McKay nodded. "It *has* been a long time since you spoke with Brother Thurston, but then most things in the Church happen in their own time it seems," he smiled.

"The older I get, the more patient I become," Tom said, "but perhaps I'm just not old enough yet," he laughed, trying to erase his rudeness.

"I know the feeling," Elder McKay responded. "Brother

Callahan," McKay said, continuing a serious tone, "are you in good standing with the Lord?"

Tom remained silent for a few moments, contemplating. He felt Katrina gently squeeze his hand.

"Brother McKay, I've been a member of the Church for just over seven years now, but as you know, I've lived very *close* to a member of the Church for over thirty," he said, looking toward his wife. "If the Lord is displeased with me for any reason, He's not seen fit to display it. For all I know, I'm on the right track. I certainly try to be."

"I believe you do, Brother Callahan, and the Lord is well pleased with your efforts. Perhaps you are aware that Elder Ballard has recently returned from South America—Argentina to be specific."

"I did read that . . . *after*," he said, smiling at his wife, "I finished the financial pages."

"Elder Ballard has done a great work for the Church, opening up the South American continent for missionary work. And that work must continue. In that regard, Brother Callahan, the Lord has need of you . . . and your good wife, Sister Callahan."

Tom looked quizzically at Elder McKay for a moment, not understanding the South American reference.

"Brother Callahan," Elder McKay said, looking directly into Tom's eyes, "we extend a call to you to serve in the South American Mission—to replace Elder Ballard as mission president in Buenos Aires, Argentina."

Tom sat stunned, unable to respond. He looked at Katrina and saw a hint of moisture in her eyes. He then glanced at Elder Ballard, then again at his wife, and then back to Elder McKay.

"Elder McKay," he stammered, "I know nothing of Argentina or South America for that matter. I've been there, of course, inspecting some of the bank's mining interests, but I . . . I don't even speak Spanish or Portuguese."

"That will all come in time, Brother Callahan. Trust in the Lord."

"I don't mean to question the calling, Elder, but . . ."

"I understand," McKay said, "but you have a work to perform—a very important work, I might add. We look forward to the day when the Church will have spread throughout that great continent. Elder Ballard is certain that the Lord is mindful of the people of South America, and that it's time for us to begin in earnest the work of bringing them the gospel."

"Whew," Tom said, exhaling slowly, his eyes flitting back and forth between Elder McKay and Katrina. "I volunteered for a mission, Elder McKay, but a mission *president?* That's for Robert or a member of your quorum."

"Brother Callahan," McKay said, "I've known you for over thirty-five years—as a young Irish immigrant, a hospital maintenance man, a *fugitive* from justice"—at which comment Tom chuckled—"a bank president, lawyer, husband, father, philanthropist—I could go on and on, and you've been successful at all of them, but none of that matters now. The Lord has *always* known you, Tom, and *He* knows your heart."

Tom sat quietly for a few moments, his head lowered in thought.

"I *have* learned one thing in my short time in His Church, Elder McKay—when the Lord calls, we answer."

Elder McKay nodded and looked toward Katrina. "Sister Callahan, how do you feel about your new calling?"

"When do we begin, Elder McKay?" she said, her eyes now glistening with tears.

McKay deferred to Elder Ballard who responded.

"I think you should be in place by August, if possible. We have about forty-eight missionaries there now, and another eight or ten are about to be called. It's a great work, Sister Callahan, and your husband will need all the support you can muster. Outside of the main cities, it's often a very primitive life-style down there, and our new converts come mostly from very humble backgrounds."

"August," she repeated. "That's good. I was hoping to participate with the choir in our first national radio broadcast in July. It will be my last outing as a member of the Tabernacle Choir for some time, I presume."

"I expect so," Elder McKay said, standing and coming out from behind his desk. As Tom rose, the apostle put his arm around Tom's shoulders. "And a great loss to the choir."

"Thank you, Elder McKay," Katrina said, rising from her chair and stepping close, smiling up at the apostle. "Thank you so very much."

<hr />

By July, telegrams and letters had been exchanged with the family, Katrina had found suitable replacements to fill her positions on various charity boards and committees, and *Valhalla* had been sold to an older couple Tom had known for many years. Understanding how hard it was for Katrina to actually put into motion the steps necessary to enable their retirement after their mission, Tom included a clause in the contract, stipulating that the Callahans would have first right of repurchase should the buyers decide to sell *Valhalla*. After having lived over thirty years in the home in which she had raised four children through various stages of childhood and adolescence, the actual signing of the papers with the new owners had been an emotional experience for Katrina. On the morning the moving company arrived to pack and store their furniture, Tom delayed the men with a hastily contrived chore while Katrina cried her way through each and every room in the stately mansion.

The last few weeks prior to their departure for South America were spent in residence at Seby's cattle ranch in Hidden Valley. Seby was very apologetic about the necessity of his spending some time away so close to the Callahans' departure, traveling to New York and Chicago on business, but Tom assured him that his absence provided more time for a long overdue father-daughter reunion with Teresa, who had arrived from Hollywood only two days after Tom and Katrina relocated to Draper.

President Callahan—as Teresa began playfully calling her father—took every opportunity to ride horses in the foothills and up the canyons east of Seby's holdings, often accompanied by Teresa.

The highlight of the time spent living in Hidden Valley was when the family made a trip to downtown Salt Lake City, where Tom and Katrina were set apart for the mission service by Elder McKay. As he sat in the chair, waiting to be set apart, the now graying Irishman held his eyes closed, thinking of Ireland and his dear departed mother. *Be true to the faith*, she had implored. Ever since his baptism into the Mormon faith, this directive from his mother, given thirty-five years earlier as he had fled Ireland, had provided the only guilt he had retained about leaving his Catholic roots. But some time before his baptism, Tom had come to an understanding that he *was* being true to the faith, and surely by now, he hoped, his mother *and* Sister Mary would both understand that.

⸻

Once Seby returned to Utah, the time seemed to disappear, and before the family knew it, only three days remained until departure. After dinner one of those evenings, Tom, Katrina, Seby, and Teresa sat outside the Hidden Valley ranch house on the wraparound veranda, enjoying the sunset and the pleasant air.

Katrina was the first to break the silence. "What a beautiful evening," she exclaimed.

"We have them every night here in Draper. It's only the people in the city that miss out, Mom," Seby teased.

"Is that so? And how about you, Tess? I bet you don't get these kind of evenings in southern California."

"There are some beautiful sunsets, Mom, over the ocean from the studio president's home in Santa Barbara."

"Oh? Do you go there often?"

"He has cast members up on weekends sometimes. We work on dialogue or new ideas."

"I see. When will you go back?"

"Next week, I'm afraid."

Seby rose and walked to lean against one of the pillars supporting the roof overhanging the veranda.

"Will you be going with Tess, Seby?" Katrina asked.

Seby didn't answer for a moment and then he turned his head to face Katrina.

"No. I'll remain here in Utah," he said, looking for a moment at Teresa.

In that moment of visual exchange, Katrina knew all that she had feared was happening. She glanced at Tom who appeared oblivious to the exchange.

"Will you be gone long, Tess?"

This time, Tess glanced up at Seby and then replied to her mother. "I've signed to do another picture, Mom. I've been offered the lead role in this one. It's quite an opportunity. I can't afford to pass it up."

"Katie," Tom said, "how about you take a walk with the old man, so I can be sure to find my way back after dark?"

"A walk?"

"A tour," he said, rising from his rocker, "of Seby's empire before we go down to Argentina to see what a *real* ranch looks like."

"If you wish, dear," she said, placing her glass of ice water on the small table and standing. "You two just enjoy the sunset, and if we're not back by midnight, send the police."

"Okay, Mom," Tess laughed. "Behave yourself, Dad."

Tom stepped toward his daughter, leaned down and kissed her on the cheek.

"That's *President* Dad to you, if you please."

Seby remained standing by the pillar with Teresa sitting close behind him as Tom and Katrina walked down the steps and toward the path leading to the barn and corrals.

"You understand that she knows," Seby said.

Teresa stood and came to stand beside her husband. "I know. Mom *always* knows."

"I think your dad understands, too," he added.

"And how about you, Seby?" she said, facing him and looking up into his eyes.

"I understand that I want a family—children—and that you want another film. Until that's resolved, Tess, I don't really understand *any* of this."

"Seby, you agreed that I should pursue this opportunity."

"No, Tess. I agreed that you should pursue the opportunity that came *before* this most recent opportunity. This is the *next* opportunity, and likely it's only the *current* opportunity, before the *next, next* opportunity raises its head."

"That's not fair, Seby. I've been a good wife."

He looked down at her. "You've been an excellent wife . . . *when* you're here. But I believe we need a family, Tess. Time moves quickly. Look at your mom and dad," he said, turning to watch the couple as they strolled farther from the house and disappeared behind a rise in the landscape. "They once felt young and that life was full of future opportunities too."

"Dad's nearly fifty-five years old, Seby. You're barely thirty."

"*You're* barely thirty, Tess. *I'm* thirty-two, but that's not the point. It's who we are to each other that's important. Nothing on this ranch means more to me than you."

"Are you saying I have to choose?"

"No. I would never say that. But you shouldn't *have* to choose, Tess. You should already know. And when the time comes, you will know. In the meantime, just know that I love you and I want you here with me."

"Oh, Seby, it's so *hard* to let go. I enjoy making movies. I love what I do. Can't you understand that?"

"Yes, I can. But I want you to love what you do *here*, too. That's all I'm asking."

"Just once, Seby. Let me see how I do on this one film."

"Like I said. I'll not ask you to stop. It's your choice."

"Thomas, did you hear what Tess was saying?"

"I did."

"I think their marriage is in trouble. I was trying to find out what she was thinking."

"That's why we're taking this walk. They need to work it out by themselves, my love."

Katrina was silent for several moments as they continued to walk through the pasture surrounding Seby's ranch.

When they crossed another path that led back to the ranch house, Katrina stopped her husband and stood in front of him, looking up into his blue eyes.

"Elder McKay was right. You're already becoming a mission president, President!"

"How about a kiss for the president, Sister President," he laughed, taking her in his arms.

As they had on so many occasions over the years, all family members present in Salt Lake—in this case only two Callahans and two Strombergs—gathered at the Union Pacific train station at the end of South Temple Street to bid the departing missionaries farewell. With PJ in New Zealand and Tommy still stationed in Hawaii, the group was much smaller than on previous family arrivals or departures. Still, as Tom tipped the porter to load their luggage into one of the newly designed Pullman sleeper compartments, the echoes and ghosts of earlier reunions at the same track overwhelmed Tom with a feeling of nostalgia. With his business interests under a blind-trust management agreement—a condition Katrina had requested to enable them to devote their thoughts and energies to their mission calling—their lifetime residence sold, and their children scattered around the globe, Tom had to work hard to overcome the feeling that his world, as he knew it, was coming to an end.

As they waited, they were surprised to see Elder David O. McKay suddenly appear on the platform.

"Elder McKay," Katrina exclaimed, "how thoughtful of you to come and see us off."

"It's a great pleasure, Sister Callahan. And I see the younger generation is hale and hearty," he said, greeting Seby and Teresa. "Who knows, Sister Callahan, by the time you and President Callahan are firmly established in the mission field, you might become a grandmother again."

"There are never enough babies for loving grand-mothers, Elder McKay," Katrina said.

"If there is another addition to the family heritage, the wee thing would be fortunate to have such a wise grand-mother," McKay added.

"President Callahan, may I have a word with you?" McKay said, drawing Tom a few paces away from the group. "President, I presume that at this moment your feelings are varied and perhaps even mixed."

Tom smiled and nodded at the gentle man who stood before him. Over the years they had been acquainted, Tom had watched his friend with growing admiration as the Lord had placed ever greater responsibilities on David O. McKay. Even Archbishop Scanlan, before his death over a decade earlier, had said on more than one occasion that Elder McKay seemed equal to every task laid upon him by the leaders of the Mormon Church.

"Even before joining the Church, I never doubted that the Lord knew what He was doing when He called you to be an apostle, Elder McKay," Tom said. "But your insight continues to amaze me. I *am* confused, even frightened to tell the truth."

Now it was McKay's turn to nod.

"President Callahan, everyone the Lord calls to serve Him retains his agency—to accept or reject the call, or to do it well or even to do just enough to get by. But if you do indeed believe the Lord made the right calling when He called *me*, then know this—He made the right choice when He told me to call *you* to preside in South America. You *will* do a great work there, President Callahan. The results of that work may not immediately be evident and may not be quantifiable in terms of membership and converts, but the Lord will inspire you to add to His kingdom in ways that neither of us now comprehend. Of this I am certain."

"Thank you, Elder McKay. Your confidence in me means a lot." Tom paused for a moment, then added, "I'll do my best to 'act well my part.'" Tom continued to smile for a moment and then reached out to hug his old friend, Apostle David O. McKay.

Three days later, as the train rolled along the west coast of the Florida peninsula, north of Tampa, Katrina sat by the window peering through the dense foliage, trying to catch an occasional glimpse of the Gulf of Mexico. During a brief stop in the small coastal village of Tarpon Springs, Tom and Katrina could see the harbor and the fleet of sponge-fishing boats, said to be manned by Greek immigrants.

Underway once again, Tom studied his wife's reflection in the train window. She sat without speaking, watching the landscape roll by, unaware of her husband's gaze.

"What great thoughts are running through that lovely head this morning?" Tom asked, reaching to gently stroke her hair.

"Hmmm?"

"That far away are you?" Tom laughed, taking his wife's hand.

Katrina smiled at him and laid her head on his shoulder.

"I guess I *was* a bit distant, Thomas. I was thinking of Anders and the time he spent here in Tampa convalescing from his Cuban wound. It seems so long ago."

"I've been to Miami but never Tampa," Tom replied. "It looks and feels much like the rest of Florida does in August—hot and humid."

"I miss Anders," Katrina said softly, laying her head on Tom's shoulder. "Do you think he knows?"

"About our mission?" Tom said, remembering the terrible night in 1925 when they had received the phone call from Utah's outgoing Governor Charles Mabey, advising them of a car accident in Virginia, in which both Anders and his wife, Sarah, were instantly killed. Although Katrina's two sisters were still living and their growing families had often visited *Valhalla,* Katrina had deeply missed her only brother. It was Tom's feeling that she had never fully recovered from the shock of losing Anders at such a relatively young age.

"Ummm."

"I don't know," Tom said, clucking his tongue, "but he's been up there four years with your parents and if no one else has told Lars yet, Anders won't likely be the one to break the news to the old goat."

"Thomas Callahan!" Katrina exclaimed, jerking her head upright and giving Tom a stern look. "*President* Callahan, I mean. *That* was not a kind, Christian remark."

"But true."

"Perhaps," she grinned. "Poppa and Anders didn't often see eye-to-eye, did they?" After a moment she added, "But I'm certain that both of them have a different view of things now."

"Do you think so, Katie?" Tom said, suddenly serious. "Would their, uh, perspective be different, do you think?"

"Well, I would think so, don't you?"

"I just don't know, Katie. Yet I'm supposed to have all the answers for these missionaries we're going to supervise. It's all just too much."

"Elder McKay told you in your blessing—don't try to be

all things to all people. Just do as the Lord inspires you to do."

When Tom didn't respond, Katrina resumed looking out the window. They would soon be in Tampa where they were scheduled to remain for several days, and where they would meet with local Church leaders before boarding the boat for South America.

In Tampa, Tom was astonished that the local Church leaders viewed him as a visiting authority. Though they knew he wasn't a General Authority, his status as a mission president required that he be the principal speaker at every meeting he attended. Katrina also found, to her dismay, that the mission president's wife was expected to preside over all auxiliary meetings and sit on the dais with her husband, speaking each time they were presented to the congregation.

By the time they boarded the steamship *Simon Bolivar*, bound for Buenos Aires, with stops scheduled in Caracas and Rio de Janeiro, Tom and Katrina had begun to realize that their service as a mission president and wife would entail considerably more than they had bargained for. If their experiences in Florida were any indication, it seemed likely that the newer members they would find in leadership positions in the remote areas of the Church would look to them for guidance.

"It's certainly not going to be just a matter of managing young, homesick missionaries, is it, Katie?" Tom joked one evening as the two of them completed their evening stroll around the deck of the ship.

She laughed and held tighter to his arm.

"Maybe when Elder McKay said, 'Don't try to be all things to all people,' he meant 'Try to be all things to most people,' or 'Try to be most things to all people,' or some other variation."

Katrina's twisting of the words got them laughing, but when they saw a passing ship, headed north, in the direction they had just come, they stopped to watch. The other ship was brightly lit, and they could see passengers strolling her deck, some looking back at them. Leaning on the railing, wondering where the other people were going, Tom got a bit more serious.

"Katie, I feel less qualified now than I did back in '98, when I first approached Robert about opening the bank. I don't have the first inkling of what the Lord expects of me, much less what the people will expect."

"Thomas, what do *you* expect of you?"

"Me?"

"Yes. I mean what do you think we should accomplish on this mission?"

He didn't immediately answer, staring instead at the dark sea for several long moments, watching the passing ship fade into the distance. Looking up at the night sky, he said, "There's the Southern Cross again, Katie. Remember when the ship's captain on the *Pacific Princess* showed that to us when we sailed to New Zealand?"

"I do, but you still have to answer my question, President Callahan."

"Sometimes I feel the Lord has had you on a private mission for the past thirty-five years, Katie, just to keep me focused and headed in the right direction."

"Why do you think that?"

"Because every time I've felt confused or misdirected, you always seem to bring me back on track. This mission is really a question of what *I* want, isn't it? It's like D.O. said. Agency. Some accept the call and succeed, and others don't. Some do the best they can and some do just enough to get by. And it all depends on what they want for themselves. It's not what the people in South America want or even need from us, it's what we are willing to offer the Lord. He will never expect more than He knows we can give, will He? All we can do is keep in touch with Him and do our best, right?"

"I'd say you're already growing in this new missionary calling, Thomas. Now if the Lord will only give you . . . oh, say, another twenty or thirty years, just think what you can become," she said, the teasing, tongue-in-cheek look that Tom knew so well written all over her face.

"In another twenty or thirty years, my darling, you will be . . . how old?"

"Thomas," she said with a straight face, "you still don't understand the rules. Making rude, insensitive comments, designed to induce humility in the other party, is a *female* prerogative. Males are not allowed to play, dear, only to function as the target."

Tom laughed at his wife's good-natured impudence. "Oh, Katie," he said, holding her close. "How I would hate to try this alone. What would I do without you?"

16

The broad expanse of the Rio de la Plata didn't look as though it was the mouth of a river, yet Tom had been advised by the ship's officers that, indeed, the 200-mile-wide estuary provided access upstream to the cities of Montevideo, Uruguay, on the north bank and Buenos Aires, Argentina, on the southern bank, where the river began to narrow.

Arriving in Buenos Aires, Tom and Katrina were met at the dock by two of the local presiding elders. The missionaries helped gather their luggage, and President and Sister Callahan were transported to their temporary residence. Elder Melvin J. Ballard had informed them that one of their first assignments would be to purchase a new mission headquarters, which would also serve as home to the mission president and several of the missionaries. It was time, Elder Ballard had said, to begin to establish a permanency to the Church in South America.

The local leaders had arranged a small conference, and all the missionaries in the country had traveled to Buenos Aires to meet with President Callahan. Thirty-two young elders, plus four couples called from local branches, arrived at the temporary mission headquarters to participate in two days of meetings with the new president. The first morning of the conference, Tom's third day in Argentina, he opened the conference and addressed the gathering, which had grown by a few dozen members who, while not specifically invited to what was to have been a missionary gathering, came along to see the new president and his wife.

"Brothers and sisters, my name is Thomas Callahan and this is my wife, Sister Katrina Callahan. I come originally from Ireland, and Sister Callahan was born in Norway. I know that many of you come from Utah, and that's where we've made our home since 1896. That's a *long* time ago," he laughed.

"Each of us has been sent here by the Lord to tell the people of Argentina that The Church of Jesus Christ of Latter-day Saints is no longer a Utah church. It is the *Lord's* church—a worldwide church—and the Lord does not recognize political boundaries among His people. He will reach out and find the pure in heart wherever they are located. Missionary efforts and local branches are springing up in many countries of the world. As we speak, elders are preaching the gospel in Europe, the British Isles, even Ireland and Norway, where they sorely need it, I can tell you," he laughed again. "We send missionaries among the islands of the Pacific and throughout the United States as well. And now, here we are in this great continent of South America.

"Almost four years ago, Apostle Melvin J. Ballard stood in this very city and dedicated the land of South America for the preaching of the gospel. We are about that work now, brothers and sisters, and together we shall strive to do the will of the Lord."

The day was filled with missionary testimonies, talks from local Church leaders, and even a very personal talk from Katrina about facing adversity and building faith in the crucible of life. The second evening, after all the missionaries had returned to their areas, Tom and Katrina were preparing for bed.

"You're awfully quiet this evening, Thomas," Katrina said as she performed her nightly ritual of brushing out her hair. "Thinking about what Brother Juarez had to say?"

"That, and other things."

"He seems a wonderful man, doesn't he. And so new in the Church to be a branch president. But it was clear from listening to him speak that the Lord just reached out and touched him on the shoulder. The Spirit was so strong while he was speaking."

"He seems a remarkably spiritual man, Katie. But, speaking of new members, if you noticed," Tom said as he removed his shoes and placed them underneath the bed, "there's *no one* who's been in the Church very long, except the Utah missionaries."

"I suppose not. Including the mission president," she smiled, slipping beneath the sheets, pulling the covers up to her neck, and turning out her table lamp. "Don't they seem like wonderful boys, the missionaries I mean?"

"Ummm."

"We're really here, Thomas. I still find it hard to believe. It's only been, what, just over two years since we stood on that mountainside in Hawaii and you told me you wanted to retire?"

"I didn't think it was going to happen. This calling, I mean."

"The Lord knows what He's doing, and *when* to do it. You know how patient Elder McKay is, right?"

"Elder McKay's not Irish," Tom replied and then lay still for several moments, staring at the ceiling. "You know, Katie, as I talked individually to each of those young men, I felt . . . I don't know, but I felt kind of like their father, like I was talking to PJ or Tommy."

Katrina rolled over and snuggled close to her husband, laying her head on his shoulder in a manner that had become so practiced and comfortable over the past thirty-two years of their marriage.

"Down here, you're the closest thing to a father they have, President Callahan. That's why the Lord sent you here—to watch over and protect these missionaries."

Managing those missionaries and supervising their labors became Tom's first priority. Returning a few weeks later to the mission home from a five-day tour of mission locations south of Buenos Aires, President Callahan went directly to his study where he pawed through the mail that had accumulated. That was where Katrina found him.

"Thomas, I thought I heard someone come in. How did it go?" she asked.

He turned from the desk and took his wife in his arms. While holding her, he said, "If you want the truth, I'm exhausted. The elders are great young men, but they wear me out. By the time I got there, Barnes and Laycock were ready to *kill* each other—all over some scriptural dispute, if you can believe it."

"I can believe it. Elder Brummer's called every day since you've been gone."

"Still wanting to go home?" Tom asked.

"Not just wanting. Now he's *demanding* to be released."

Tom heaved a sigh. "I thought that assigning him in the city and keeping him close to the mission home would help, but perhaps not. I guess I'll have to bring him in and see if I

243

can talk him out of it. What's today, Tuesday? I'll do it tomorrow."

Katrina winced. "Actually, Thomas, he and his companion will be here tonight."

"Tonight?"

"Well, when I talked to him this afternoon, he was so upset I couldn't stand it. Knowing you'd be back today, I invited Elder Brummer and his companion to come for dinner."

Tom started to say something, then sighed and chuckled. "Do you know what I'd give to be back keeping banker's hours?"

"I hope you're not upset with me," Katrina said.

"Upset? How could I be upset with you, Sister Callahan?" Tom laughed. "It's Elder Brummer who's the problem. Just give me time to get a bath before he comes and I have to take him on."

Following dinner, Tom instructed Elder Farnsworth to make himself comfortable in the living room, then took Elder Brummer with him to his study. Motioning for the tall, gangly elder to sit down, Tom closed the door and sat in his chair across the desk from the missionary.

After a moment of silence, President Callahan said, "Well, Elder Brummer, you've been in Argentina how long now, nearly a month?"

Elder Brummer sat with his head down, nervously holding his hands in his lap. When he looked up, his chin was trembling.

"Yes, sir," he said. "It will be a month tomorrow."

"I believe you're from Cache Valley in northern Utah, is that right?"

The elder nodded his head. "Yes, sir. My dad runs a dairy farm there."

"Are you getting along well with Elder Farnsworth?" Tom asked.

"He's all right."

"How do you find the weather?" the president asked.

"Okay."

"Are you healthy?" Tom pressed.

"Yes."

"But you're not happy, is that right?"

Elder Brummer pinched his nostrils between the finger and thumb on his right hand, then looked for something to wipe the moisture on. Tom handed him his own handkerchief and waited for a reply.

Wiping his nose and eyes with the handkerchief, Elder Brummer mumbled something.

"Excuse me," President Callahan said, leaning forward, "I couldn't hear what you said."

"I said, I want to go home," Brummer said quietly.

Tom considered the remark before saying, "Yes, well, you've said that before. What is it, Elder? What is it that is really bothering you? Do you have a testimony?"

Elder Brummer nodded his head. "I know the Church is true," he said.

"Well, what is it then? Do you have anything you should have confessed before you accepted the call?"

Elder Brummer's head snapped up, and with a look of astonishment on his face, he began to cry. Through his tears, he said, "No, it's not *that!*"

Tom didn't know what to say. Elder Brummer was obviously so offended by the inference that he wasn't worthy that Tom wished he hadn't asked the question. Still, he didn't know what else to say.

The two sat without speaking for a few moments, Elder Brummer crying quietly and Tom feeling awkward, praying

245

silently to know what to say or do. Finally, the young missionary blubbered, "Gol, President! I miss my cows!"

As he said so, Elder Brummer collapsed in tears, holding his face in his hands and rocking backward and forward in his chair, sobbing uncontrollably.

Tom sat for a moment, struggling at first to keep from laughing, but moved also by the young man's agitation and unhappiness, grateful that the problem appeared to be nothing more than simple homesickness. After a time, he stood up and walked around the desk. He rested his hand on the young man's shoulder and rubbed it sympathetically. Then he raised Elder Brummer to his feet and took him in his arms. The slender missionary was taller by a head than Tom, but he bent to rest his head on his mission president's shoulder, clinging to Tom and surrendering to his unhappiness.

"You're going to be fine," Tom said, patting the young man's back. "You're going to be just fine, I promise you. Let's get your companion and you settled into the guest room for the night, and we'll see what we can do tomorrow," President Callahan said.

Upstairs, as they knelt together by the side of their bed, preparing to say their nightly prayers, Katrina anxiously questioned Tom about the fate of the unhappy elder.

"Not to worry, Katie," he smiled, taking her hand. "I met the western region branch president a few days ago, and he specifically asked if I could send a pair of, as he called them, *country elders*, who would feel at home in his rural district. I think I've found just the right elder for him," Tom said, laughing. "Just the man, indeed."

A month after their arrival in Argentina, President and Sister Callahan received an invitation to a dinner function at the American embassy, in honor of the newly arrived American ambassador, Malcolm Foster.

"I don't think we should go, Thomas," Katrina said the following evening after dinner when they retired to the parlor where Katrina had begun writing a letter to Seby and Tess.

"Why not? We'd meet all the local dignitaries and community leaders."

"But we're here to do missionary work, aren't we?"

"Tell me how you think we should best go about that, Sister Callahan," he said.

"Talking to people, telling them about the Church, guiding the missionaries, I guess."

"And won't we be talking to people at the reception? Important people to boot?"

She was silent for a few moments then looked up from her writing. "I suppose so."

"I think we need to let the government officials know they have nothing to fear from the Mormon missionaries, Katie. We're in a very Catholic area here, and our visas only come with their permission."

"If you say so," she replied.

Reluctant though Katrina might have been, on the night of the reception, she looked as stunning as Tom had ever seen her. Dressed in a simple white long gown, her hair shimmered beneath the evening lights that illuminated the embassy grounds.

"Sister Callahan, looking at you tonight, I'd say that any man who can't see the merits of joining this church is a fool. If you're a missionary's wife, you're going to fool any Catholic archbishop who's been invited."

Katrina pulled her arm from Tom's and stopped dead in her tracks.

247

"Thomas, am I not dressed properly? I'm so sorry," she said, her face turning red.

Seeing his wife's embarrassment, Tom instantly regretted his remarks.

"I'm sorry, Katie. I only meant that you look as lovely as always. You look great, really, and your dress is quite beautiful . . . and modest."

Katrina took his arm again, and they continued walking toward the embassy entrance. She took several breaths, and her face began to regain its normal color.

"I'm sorry, too, Thomas. I should have known you were only being yourself and spouting your usual blarney," she said, squeezing his arm. "We're going to have to get used to this missionary role, aren't we?"

"I am truly sorry, Katie. I didn't mean to embarrass you, and, yes, we will need to understand our roles a bit better. But as for the blarney, I have never seen you more lovely, and that, Sister Callahan, is my true word on the subject."

They reached the reception line and slowly proceeded into the building. Introductions were made as they entered and passed through the assembled dignitaries, meeting the new American ambassador and several Argentine officials. As they proceeded into the large ballroom, a man wearing a black tuxedo and white tie approached them.

"You would be Mr. and Mrs. Thomas Callahan, I presume?"

"We are," Tom said, extending his hand in response to the other man.

"Allow me to introduce myself. My name is Richard Van Brocklin of Connecticut. I believe you know my parents, Mr. and Mrs. Henry Van Brocklin. My father is the president of New York First Fidelity Bank."

"Of course, Hank Van Brocklin," Tom smiled, increasing

the vigor of his handshake. "Your father is a fine man, Mr. Van Brocklin."

"Please, call me Dick. Thank you. Dad thinks very highly of you as well. He told me you were coming."

"I wonder how he knew."

"He mentioned in a letter that the president of your bank, Mr. Thurston, I think, told him about your new, uh, appointment, when they met in New York last month. My mother also asked me to pass along her best wishes."

The trio walked through a set of double French doors leading onto the veranda toward a small table overlooking the gardens outside the embassy. A waiter approached and placed three crystal goblets and a carafe of wine on the table, then started to depart.

"Excuse me," Van Brocklin said to the waiter, "could we please have something nonalcoholic? Grape juice or apple juice perhaps?"

"Certainly, sir," the waiter responded, gathering up the wine.

Katrina caught Tom's eye momentarily and raised an eyebrow.

Dick Van Brocklin noticed the exchange and smiled.

"No," he said, shaking his head and laughing, "I've not yet been persuaded to your religion, but I am familiar with some of your tenets. In fact, Father advised me that in his bank dealings with you, he always admired your presence of mind and your fortitude in light of some of the other banking participants' after-hours behavior."

"That's very kind of him," Tom said, "but actually, it's merely a health consideration. So tell us, how are your parents? Did your mother ever tell you how we met? Before I met your father, I mean."

"Yes, indeed," Dick said, his smile disappearing. "It's a

very special but sad memory for my mother. She told us that when you left her that morning on the train to New York, upset over the newspaper story of the *Titanic*, she wondered for a long time what had happened and if your family was safe. Eventually, she read the casualty list in the newspapers. It was a tragic event."

"It's been a long time, Dick, but thank you for your concern. I was so pleased to receive your mother's wonderful letter back in Salt Lake, several months later. She was very understanding. It seems everyone has difficulties to overcome."

"You're referring, I presume, to my sister's fatal accident so many years ago. Yes, that was a tough time for my parents. You're right, I guess we all have to deal with tragedy in life."

"So, what brings you to Argentina and how long have you been here?" Tom asked.

Dick smiled and started to explain, but paused when the waiter returned with three glasses of sparkling cider.

"I've been here two years, Mr. Callahan. Just after I turned forty, my father . . ."

"Tom. Please, call me Tom."

"Of course, thank you. As I neared forty and had put in fifteen years with the New York branch of the bank, Dad felt it necessary that I experience what he called the new frontier—international banking. New York First had developed an affiliation with the *Banco de Nationale* here in Buenos Aires. I've come down as vice-president. Dad was right. It's been an eye-opener."

"That's excellent, Dick. I wish you well."

"Am I correct that your bank still has significant mining interests in South America?"

"Less than we did some years ago, but yes, we still maintain a presence, especially in silver. Is your father still running the New York branch of the bank?"

"No, he's not. In fact, a couple of years ago, he purchased a seat on the New York Stock Exchange. Most likely I'll stay here for a few years and then maybe take over his seat when he retires. I think you'll like it here, Tom. It's a beautiful country and once you learn the language, quite easy to travel. There's a large European influence and population, especially Germans and middle Europeans."

"Do you have a family, Dick?" Katrina asked.

He nodded. "Yes, my wife's name is Cassandra, and we have two daughters. Cassie went back to Connecticut a couple of weeks ago. Our oldest daughter is about to enter Vassar, and the youngest attends high school here in Buenos Aires. Cassie should be back in about two weeks."

"How nice," Katrina said. "Two of our children are married, one son living in New Zealand, and one daughter trying to balance her new marriage between Salt Lake and a film career in Hollywood. Our other son is a lieutenant in the Marine Corps. We seldom know *where* he might be at any given time. Last we heard, he was in Hawaii," she laughed.

"That's quite a spread, Mrs. Callahan. And I thought my parents had it bad with my family down here in South America. We'd be glad to show you around and help in any way we can."

"Well, we're grateful to have met a friend already, Dick. Your parents hold a special place in my heart. I'm indebted to your father for some good advice on many a deal over the years."

"The way he tells it, Tom," Dick laughed, "*you* advised *him*. If there's anything I can do to assist you here in Buenos Aires, please don't hesitate to ask."

"Let's try you out," Tom joked. "Does your bank have a real estate department? We're going to need a formal residence. A large place actually. Not a ranch—we don't need acreage—but plenty of bedrooms and office space. Room for a household staff as well."

"That shouldn't be too difficult. Come see me on Monday. I'm sure we can help. By the way, Cassie and I have an excellent stable at our place, just outside of town, if you like to ride."

"Well, Dick, our *appointment,* as you called it, will take up a great deal of our time. It's not the banking kind of job, I'm afraid. Do you know much or anything about the Mormon Church—besides our stance on nonalcoholic cider," he said, causing a ripple of laughter from all three.

"Not much, Tom. My oldest daughter, the one who just left for Vassar, met a couple of missionaries in Connecticut several years ago. She was quite favorably impressed, but you know young people. She thought the young men were handsome and that *might* account for her interest. Then a member of your church—out of Yale, I believe—hired on with the bank a year before I left. A fine fellow. But as to doctrine, I can't say as I know much at all."

"I see. Your horses, uh, do you ride every day?"

"Oh, no. This bank has long hours, too," he grinned. "My father demanded them of his Yankee staff assigned here and that hasn't changed since he left for the stock exchange. But I find time. Are you interested?"

"It might be a fine way to see the countryside, wouldn't you say, Katrina," Tom asked.

"Certainly, dear," she said, a quizzical look on her face.

In the car on the way home, Katrina leaned her head on Tom's shoulder and stifled a yawn.

"Tonight reminded me of the old days, Thomas, when

we hosted the governor's reception and attended a couple of the receptions Anders took us to in Washington. Did you see the diamonds dripping from the French ambassador's wife at the dinner table?"

"A wide range of society, wasn't it?"

"Not like the people we met in church the other day, were they?" Katrina said. "Are you really going to go horseback riding with Dick?"

Tom looked out the window of the taxi as they sped down the boulevard alongside the river.

"At first I thought not, Katie. But then, something inside me said yes."

"I thought so when I saw the look on your face. The mantle is settling on you, Thomas. And the Spirit is whispering. Listen to it, my dear, listen to it."

SEPTEMBER, 1929

MALIBU, CALIFORNIA

After spending three years assigned to the marine garrison at Pearl Harbor, Hawaii, newly promoted Captain Thomas M. Callahan III was selected for a two-year advanced degree program with a follow-on assignment to Marine Corps headquarters, Washington, D.C. He left the lush, tropical environs of the Pacific islands, headed for Stanford University in Palo Alto, California, and a doctorate program in international economics.

There was considerable opposition to a junior grade lieutenant receiving such a plum assignment, and, in fact, some voiced their opposition to a rich banker's son being assigned to pursue an economics degree at the expense of the Marine Corps. In the end, obtaining approval over many senior officers had not been easy, and, in fact, it had required that Tommy's slot be added to the three other higher education approvals granted during 1929. His approval, and his promotion—arranged to silence the critics who complained that he was only a lieutenant—had been personally signed by General John A. Lejeune, commandant of the Marine Corps, who had been one of Tommy's commanding officers in the 6th Marines in France.

When his ship from Hawaii, a commercial liner rather than a military transport, docked in Los Angeles in late August, he was met by Teresa, who drove him to her seaside bungalow on the cliffs above the beach in the small village of Malibu, west of Hollywood.

"Now *this* is the life, Tess. Can you get me an acting job, so I can live this way?"

"Oh, I'm sorry, Tommy. All of our leading men are good-looking," she said, deadpan.

"I see," he replied, "I guess you're grateful that doesn't apply to the actresses, huh?"

Teresa called for her housekeeper to bring a few sandwiches and cold drinks, and took Tommy's hand, leading him out onto the deck. The ocean view was panoramic.

"What say we skip the traditional sparring this time, dear brother?" she said, taking a chair.

"That would be fine with me, Sis. I'd rather hear the truth anyway," he laughed. "What do you hear from Mom and Pop?"

"Got my first letter yesterday. They think the country is beautiful, the people are friendly, and they are both in good health."

"Aha, another missionary, 'we-are-so-excited' tourist brochure, eh?"

Teresa laughed again. "Just about. Mom did say that they

met the son of an old friend of Dad's. Richard Van Brocklin is his name. From Connecticut. His dad owns a bank in New York, and the son is in Buenos Aires working for an associate bank."

"That's what Pop would have me doing if he could— traveling the world in banker's clothes. Poor Richard. I wonder if his father pushed him into the banking world?"

"There are worse occupations. And you *already* travel the world."

"Can you imagine Pop as a mission president? That's not the Pop I know," Tommy said. "From a gun-runner, ex-convict to a missionary."

"Tommy Callahan, you stop it right now! You promised that you would never let on that I told you about all that. Besides, we all change, Tommy."

The housekeeper arrived and placed a tray of freshly pre-pared sandwiches and a pitcher of lemonade on the table. "Will there be anything else, *Señora?*"

"No, thank you. We'll be fine." Teresa poured them both a glass of lemonade and looked out over the ocean as Tommy consumed a sandwich.

"Actually, Tommy, I think Dad will do very well as a mission president. We all need to adjust to our differing roles in life."

"Don't get me wrong, Sis. I admire Pop's decision. But he's probably more uncomfortable in this role than he's ever been."

"As I said, we all change as we grow older," she said.

He nodded, wiping his mouth with a napkin. "Do I detect a subtle shift to the serious?"

Teresa turned her head to look at her brother. "You like this place, Tommy? The house and the ocean, I mean?"

Tommy rose and stood by the railing, looking out over

255

the beach and the breakers rolling in. "It's magnificent, Tess. What can I say?"

"And what if I said it was lonely?"

Tommy turned around, leaned back against the railing, and stared at his sister.

"Then I'd say sell it and go home before you find a way to end that loneliness. You telling me you're not happy?"

"I *love* my work. I love the public relations and the press coverage. I'm selfish, Tommy. I want it all, I guess. And Seby . . ."

"And Seby just wants you?"

"But he has his other life, too. He manages the ranch, he's investing heavily in the stock market now, making tons of money, but he's not pleased to have me living away from him, down here."

"Can you blame him, Sis? You married the guy, and here you are, living a thousand miles away from him and hanging around the best looking men in America."

"Why haven't *you* found someone, Tommy?"

"My turn, huh? We're not that much different, Tess, in spite of our *century* difference in age. My career is not exactly compatible with being married. That's all there is to it. I'm a marine. I like it. I want to stay a marine. And I don't think that asking a woman to take on the life of a 'Mrs. Marine' is fair."

"Are many of your friends married?"

"They are," he said. "And many of them are gone half the time. Some wives are faithful and some, well, some are not, Tess. I see it all the time, but neither are their husbands quite often, so it's only fair, I suppose. But that isn't what I want, Tess, a part-time marriage. I would imagine Seby feels the same way.

"Do you know, Tess," he said, turning around again and

scanning the coastline and ocean, "it was a real eye-opener to leave Utah and begin to see how things are in the real world. What's amazing to me is that I don't think that Mom has ever even *considered* that Pop might be unfaithful to her. And what's more amazing, I don't think that *Pop* even considered it. That's one thing I've always admired about them."

"They love each other, Tommy," she said, coming to stand by him at the railing.

"And you think that makes the difference?"

"It's a large part of it. And the Church's teachings, of course."

"What about you, Tess?"

"What do you mean?"

"You know what I mean. Living down here, alone and all. How have you handled it? Do you love Seby? Are you faithful to him?"

Teresa didn't answer, and for a long moment, she stood silently staring out at the ocean.

Tommy slid down the railing, closer to Teresa and wrapped his arm around his sister, pulling her closer. "What does Seby think, Tess?"

"I don't really know. He's quiet about it. I think he's trying to let me come to some decisions. Before Mom and Dad left, they stayed at the ranch in Draper. Seby said they could tell we were having problems."

"That doesn't surprise me," Tommy laughed. "Mom could tell if one of the bishopric had drunk a cup of coffee. Did she talk to you about it?"

"No, but I think Dad kind of restrained her."

"*Restrained* Mom?" he asked, incredulous. "Maybe his new calling *has* impressed her and she's assumed her rightful, subservient place."

"*Tommy!*" Tess exclaimed, laughing and poking at her brother's ribs.

"Just joking, baby sister. So how are you and Seby going to resolve all this?"

"I wish I knew. I'm under contract with the studio."

Tommy looked down at his sister, tilting his head slightly, his face questioning.

"I know, I know . . . I *know*," she cried, shaking her head. "It's only an excuse and no reason to jeopardize my marriage."

"You just needed someone to listen, Tess. You already know all the answers."

"In Hawaii, PJ told me I was married and that was it as far as he was concerned—that was my only job from there on out. On the other hand, *you* said, 'Go for it, Sis.' I listened to my two brothers, and so, here I am—married *and* going for it."

"And you're afraid you're going to have to choose?"

"Well, aren't I?"

"Of course you are," he smiled gently, nodding at her. "I love you, Tess, and *I'm* not going to be the one to try and tell you how to resolve this. But you know what Mom and Pop would say—'Go home and have babies.'"

"I *want* babies, Tommy," she smiled.

"Then that's a big part of the decision. I have learned *one* thing in my short life. To have babies takes *two* willing participants. Surprisingly, Tess, that also takes care of the loneliness."

"You think you're so smart," she said, jabbing at his chest with her finger. "Have another sandwich and tell me about this doctorate program you've entered at Stanford. I thought you told me that marines didn't know how to read and that they didn't *need* to, anyway."

"Don't start, Tess, just don't start with me," he smiled, grabbing her and hugging her close.

———◈———

The next morning, an hour before dawn, Tess was up and back on the deck of her beach house, sitting in her chair wrapped in a blanket, sipping a cup of warm cider. She had tossed sleeplessly throughout much of the night, her thoughts ranging from giving up Hollywood and returning to Utah to a brief contemplation of divorcing Seby and putting her complete energy into acting—a momentary thought that left her shaking in her bed, her tears flowing.

Tommy had struck home so easily, so offhandedly, that it had taken her by surprise. *Was* she faithful to Seby? *Had* her thoughts and even her intentions been honorable? Nothing had come of her flirtation with the director of her last picture, but, she thought to herself, she *had* accepted his invitation to his estate for the weekend and she *had* considered being unfaithful, hadn't she? It was not a pleasant thought in retrospect and even the memory that she had considered such an action had left her lying in bed, ashamed.

And as to the deeper meaning of the word, as Tommy had so casually voiced it, any way you looked at it, she was not *truly* faithful, remaining separate from her husband and allowing their marriage to struggle on with both parties essentially carrying on separate lives. Leave it to Tommy to strike at the heart of the matter, she thought as the sky slowly began to take on an amber hue. Throughout their lives only Tommy had been able to gain such an insight into her soul, and, she smiled to herself, she in his. *Twins*, they had always laughed to each other. Born a century apart, as she never let him forget, but twins in the true sense of the word.

As if on cue, she heard the French doors open just as the first distinct rays of morning light began to clear the hills to the east, illuminating the surf rolling in below the house.

"Doesn't anyone sleep around here?" Tommy smiled, reaching to take her empty cup from her.

"I used to, and very well, thank you very much, *before* you started analyzing my life and my marriage, *doctor*," she said.

Turning serious, Tommy said, "I don't mean to pry, Tess. Really."

"I know, Tommy," she said, rising and wrapping the blanket around her shoulders as she moved to the railing.

"You asked me last night if I'd been faithful to Seby."

"Tess, I don't—"

"It's all right," she smiled over at him. "But the answer is no, I haven't, Tommy. Now don't let your mind run wild, big brother. I haven't taken a lover or anything like that, but when I *married* Seby, I promised to love him and I promised to . . . to be with him. If surrendering to the seduction of my career is a form of infidelity, then, yes, I've been unfaithful."

"And what are you going to do about it?"

"I don't know yet, Tommy. I just don't know."

He moved closer to her and took her in his arms, holding her closely for several moments. "This advice may seem a bit out of character, coming from me, Tess, but I think this is one of those situations when Mom would say: Pray about it."

"Yes, she would," Tess said softly, "and she'd be right. And I'd quiver to think what Sister Mary would say," Tess laughed, trying to ease her brother's tenseness. "And another thing, Captain Callahan, tough combat marine, I know the person *inside* that handsome uniform, and the advice is not out of character at all. In fact," she said, smiling up at him, "you could use some of it yourself."

"Thanks, Sis," he smiled. "Drive me to the train station?"

"With pleasure," she laughed, stretching up to kiss his cheek. "And thanks, Tommy. For everything. Every girl should have such a brother."

⁂

The first day of the new term at Stanford, Tommy felt self-conscious among the other students and a bit out of place in civilian clothes. For over a decade, each workday he'd donned either his khakis or field utilities and headed out for another day of *marineing,* as he had come to call it. Few women were on the campus, so in some respects it was still an all-male world he occupied.

Professor Theodore Wallington, a man who Tommy took to be in his eighties, stood before the class, comprised of graduate students enrolled in master's and doctorate programs, intent on making their way in the financial and banking worlds. After a few moments of looking around the class, nodding to those he recognized from previous classes, Professor Wallington turned to the blackboard and wrote one word in large script: MARGIN.

"Would anyone care to venture a guess about what I mean?" he asked, again facing the class.

A hand went up.

"Mr. . . . uh, Johnson, is it? What are we talking about?"

"The grading structure for the class? A grading curve, or perhaps the margin between high and low grades?"

"Nope, anyone else?"

He continued to look around the room and another hand went up, more confident than the first. It belonged to one of only two women in the class.

"Miss Prisman, if you please."

"Are you referring, Professor Wallington, to the practice of buying stocks on a thin margin of payment? The underlying strength, or weakness, of the current market valuation?"

"Exactly, Miss Prisman. Thank you," he smiled. "Does everyone understand what Miss Prisman has just explained to us? And she *is* quite correct in her statement about 'the underlying weakness' of the market. Mark my words, ladies and gentlemen," the old man said, picking up a piece of chalk and drawing a large circle around the word MARGIN on the board, "this practice will be the downfall of the market one day."

"Professor," one of the students said, "everyone is making money in the market nowadays. It's the wave of the future."

Wallington smiled at the young man and held his hand, palm down, beneath his chin. He slowly raised his arm until his hand rested between his nose and his eyes.

"Just don't get drowned, young man, when the wave comes tumbling over you and your friends. There are cab drivers making tens, even *hundreds* of thousands of dollars in the stock market. It just can't sustain such growth—not with a 10 percent underlying cash basis."

"Well, my father says . . ." the student continued.

"No disrespect to your father, young man, but this marginal purchase power will be the downfall of the world's economic system, and we will likely see it in *my* lifetime. Now *that* should tell you something," he said to the class.

The class laughed in return, and Professor Wallington

commenced his opening lecture on the interlocking relationships of the world's economy.

That afternoon, Tommy walked to the economics department in hopes of catching Professor Wallington in his office. He knocked lightly on the door and received a muffled "Come in." As he entered, the old professor turned to see who his visitor was and smiled at Tommy.

"Mr . . . uh, . . ."

"Callahan. Thomas Callahan."

"Of course, our sole military doctoral candidate this year. So what brings you to Stanford, Mr. Callahan, and not to one of the prestigious eastern Ivy League colleges so favored by your naval associates?"

"*You*, Professor Wallington."

Wallington's bushy eyebrows shot up, and Tommy noticed a look of disbelief cross his face. Tommy smiled at the old man and inclined his head toward a chair in the corner of the crowded office.

"May I?"

Wallington nodded assent, and Tommy sat in the chair after removing several magazines first and placing them on the floor. The floor of the office, the window sills, and all the flat surfaces in the room were littered with piles of books, magazines, stacks of students' essays, and copies of the *Wall Street Journal*.

"I don't mean to sound ingratiating, Professor, but it's true. My father has spoken of you many times and attended several lectures, mostly when you were visiting at the University of Utah. When I was growing up, we lived in Salt Lake City. Since then, we've scattered around the world. But Utah is still home."

Professor Wallington thought for a few moments and then his eyes lit up.

"Thomas Callahan, Utah Trust Bank. Of course, now it makes sense. I know your father, and we have corresponded several times. But you're in the military, right?"

"Yes, sir. I'm a captain in the Marine Corps."

"Why not into banking with your father?"

"That's a very long story, Professor," Tommy replied, a bit hesitant.

"Another time, young man. I understand these family things don't always go as planned by the parents. So, what can I do for you today?"

"I thought that you might recall my father, Professor, and I came to ask you to assist me in a little subterfuge."

"That would be in the political science department, Mr. Callahan," the old professor smiled. "But seriously, how can I help?"

"I'd like to keep my relationship, that is my father's banking interests, a private affair if that's possible."

"I see. You know, there are some students here whose families are considerably wealthier than yours, if that's your concern."

"Partly, sir, but since I am a marine officer, I'd rather just appear as such, and not from any particularly wealthy family."

"That should pose no problem," Wallington said, stroking his neatly trimmed, fully gray beard. "Captain Callahan, is it, or would you prefer Mister?"

"I'll be a civilian for the next two years, I think, Professor."

"Done. Now, tell me, how is your father?"

"He's presently in Argentina."

"Argentina? Mining ventures?"

"No, sir, he's serving as a missionary for the Mormon Church."

"My goodness, a man of varied talent, I can see. A banker, a missionary, a son in the marines."

Tommy laughed. "Yes, sir, we've gone in all directions, I guess. My sister, Teresa, is acting on Broadway and in films, and my older brother, PJ, owns and operates a sheep and cattle ranch in New Zealand."

"I repeat myself then, *my goodness*. No bankers besides your father?"

"Not yet."

"So you intend to enter the world of finance after your time with the marines?"

"I don't know, Professor, truly. This opportunity to acquire a doctorate in economics is part of the overall plan, I suppose, but I still have ten years or more with the marines."

"You'll never make any money in the marines, son," he said.

"No, sir, that's a certainty," Tommy laughed. "But my father saw to it that we were all assured of a good future. I've followed the market for some years now, adhering, mind you," he said, smiling broadly at Wallington, "to your very sound principle of 100 percent cash equity. My father always stood by your principle of not buying on margin, and his bank has not loaned money to people who bought in quantity on margin."

"Well, good for him. It's a shaky situation at the moment, and banking institutions are the most vulnerable, besides the individual investor, of course. The market is supported by less than 15 percent cash valuation, with well over half of outstanding common stock supported by less than a 10 percent equity base. It's a house of cards back there on Wall Street, and the fools don't even care. And what stocks have you speculated in, Mr. Callahan?"

"Mostly mining, some transportation. I've generally followed my father's advice."

"And your portfolio is significant?"

Tommy hesitated a moment. "My father set aside a trust fund for each of his children and gave us control when we were, as he put it, 'mature enough to handle it.' I was the last to receive mine," he laughed again, "and only when I had graduated from the naval academy in 1923."

"Another point for your father," Wallington smiled.

"My sister and I have always combined our investments, but now that she's married, I've been going it alone. I would say the portfolio is upper seven figures now, Professor. But that too, I'd like to keep confidential."

"Of course," Wallington again nodded. "Imagine, a marine captain with seven or eight million dollars in stocks. What's the world coming to?" he laughed. "I've met New York cabbies at my lectures who have five million, but always on a 10 percent margin. A charade, a foolish charade. They'll rue the day. And you say you hold a 100 percent equity position?"

"My father wouldn't have it any other way," Tommy laughed again.

"Well, young man, I'm suitably impressed. I hope that we can teach you something here at Stanford. What do you plan for your off-time?"

"I don't understand, sir."

"I've just graduated my teaching assistant with his doctorate. Would you be interested in serving as my teaching assistant? You'd be lecturing to undergraduates and grading papers—tasks like that. It's about twenty hours a week."

"Would I be depriving some other student of the income, Professor?

"Not likely at Stanford. Not too many needy students here at the moment, Tommy, if I may call you that."

"Certainly, sir. If you're sure I can be of assistance, I'd be pleased."

"Excellent," he said, standing and reaching to shake Tommy's hand. "You'll be working with Susan Prisman, the young lady in our class this morning. Her family owns a fleet of freighters and oil tankers. They live just north of San Francisco, in Marin County."

"Very impressive and knowledgeable young woman," Tommy said.

"And beautiful," Wallington added.

"I think I *did* notice that, Professor," Tommy replied, a grin on his face.

"Captain, I'd be disappointed in the United States Marine Corps if you'd missed that piece of national intelligence."

"Something tells me you haven't spent all your life on campus, Professor."

"I've led a varied life myself, Tommy. My father was an army officer with Winfield Scott in the war with Mexico. Then, he rode with Jeb Stuart and didn't come home. I got my first lesson in military tactics when Sherman burned his way through Georgia, right past our plantation. Now *that* was economic warfare at the grass roots. Our southern way of life changed forever in those flames, I'm afraid. But perhaps slavery wasn't any more of a solid foundation for a strong, lasting national economy than buying stocks on margin is today."

This time Tommy's eyebrows rose, realizing for the first time just how much the professor had seen in his lifetime.

"That was back in '64, and I turned fifteen that year. I

came west, and I've never looked back," he said, a nostalgic look crossing his face, which he just as quickly erased.

"I presume that you would like to keep your, uh, financial status, confidential from Miss Prisman, too?"

"Yes, sir. Thank you for your consideration."

"I'll see you tomorrow then," Wallington said. "I'll arrange with the front office to have your name added to my list of teaching assistants. I'm happy to have you on the team."

"And thank you, Professor Wallington. It's an honor to finally meet you and attend your classes."

"It'll be two long years to obtain your doctorate, Mr. Callahan, and the enemy is a bit more abstract than you might be used to fighting."

"Yes, sir," Tommy replied, "but I'll be serving under a good general."

17

The rural countryside outside of Buenos Aires was as beautiful as Utah, Tom thought as he rode slightly behind Dick Van Brocklin. Tom had taken Dick up on his offer to ride on two previous occasions, and despite Dick's being fourteen years younger, the two had struck an immediate friendship—in some respects a tutelage—with Tom serving as mentor to Dick.

Their wives had remained in the house, preferring to fuss about the kitchen in preparation for the evening meal. Katrina had also quickly become friends with Cassie Van Brocklin. With Cassie being twelve years Katrina's junior, they'd formed an almost sisterly relationship. They had commiserated together over the 'growing up and disappearing' of their newly adult children, and Katrina had advised Cassie to hold on to Peggy, the youngest daughter who still resided at home, as tightly and for as long as she could.

The estate that Dick's people had located had immediately satisfied all of Tom's requirements. Katrina had loved the house and the grounds from the moment she and Tom first viewed them. It had once belonged to the president of a Belgian corporation with a branch in Argentina, but when the Belgian executive died while traveling in South America, the company had put the estate on the market.

Surrounded by a stone and wrought-iron fence, the three-story brick and stucco residence was palatial. With ten bedrooms, four complete bathrooms, including the one in the master suite, a living room and a large, formal dining room, an expansive kitchen, as well as a wing containing a study and library, the home provided ample room and facilities for a combination mission home and office.

Tom saw the residence as giving the Church a legitimate presence in Buenos Aires, but Katrina fell in love with the home for its charm. She was especially taken with the park-like grounds. A seventy-five-year-old, massive oak tree spread its branches over a formal garden and a terrazzo patio and fish pond. With its wrought-iron tables and chairs, the shaded patio provided a comfortable setting for the missionaries staying in the home to take their meals. The study, which Tom utilized as an office, opened on one side to a glassed-in atrium, in which a tree, flowers, and shrubbery grew in profusion. It was a residence that met the Church's needs perfectly, and Tom had recommended its purchase to Church headquarters without reservation.

During the first two months of their residence in the new mission home, Tom and Katrina spent time touring several of the outlying branches of the Church, meeting with the people and struggling to learn the language. Tom could see that Katrina would be the one to most quickly pick up Spanish, and almost immediately, he came to rely on her to communicate. It was evident, too, that it was most often the poor and humble who were willing to investigate and accept the gospel. The middleclass and wealthier families had much to lose by affiliating with a religion outside the Catholic mainstream, and with rare exception, did not entertain even a second visit from the missionaries.

Whether out of a desire for friendship or an interest born of sincere curiosity, Dick had asked many questions of Tom about the Mormon Church. The Callahans and Van Brocklins enjoyed a comfortable and friendly relationship, something made easy by the Van Brocklin's gracious and well-mannered New England courtesy.

Back in the stables following their ride, Tom unsaddled his horse, and Dick put feed in the individual cubicles. Then the two men busied themselves, currying their mounts. As Tom worked the brush, a memory flashed through his mind, and for an instant, he was back in Portlaoise Prison, under the watchful eye of his warders. He glanced at Dick, but the moment of reflection had gone unnoticed by the younger man.

"We'll probably have potluck for dinner," Dick announced. "Cassie didn't have anything particular in mind when we left this afternoon."

"After eating here a couple of times, I'm confident we're in good hands," Tom replied. "Dick, you mentioned that you'd be interested in going to church with Katie and me. How about joining us this coming Sunday, if that fits with your schedule? Katie's going to be singing."

"That's fine with me, Tom," Dick said, continuing to rub his horse. "Let me just check with Cassie. I've been reading in the book you gave me. Quite a family saga, isn't it?" he said, smiling at Tom. "I mean the brothers really didn't like each other, it seems. I remember the story of Joseph from Bible School when I was young. If the Lord can choose anyone He wants, I wonder why He simply doesn't choose the oldest son and avoid all this anger when the younger sibling is chosen to rule over the elder. I'd be angry too, I guess, if I had a younger brother."

"Me too," Tom laughed in return. "But then I was second-oldest. There," he exclaimed, patting his horse on the rump and closing the stall gate, "now I need to wash up a bit before Katie finds a stall for *me*."

"You know where the facilities are, Tom. Right around the end of the stable. I'll be right behind you. I'm starved, whatever we're having."

On Friday evening, October 25, Katrina picked up the telephone in their third-floor residential quarters and answered in her ever-improving Spanish.

"*Hola?*"

"Katrina, it's Dick Van Brocklin. How are you this evening?"

"I'm fine, Dick. Looking forward to Sunday. Thomas and I are so glad you can come with us."

"That's actually what I'm calling about. I'm afraid we're going to have to cancel. We're sorry, but I've been unavoidably called away. Would it be possible to speak to Tom for a few minutes?"

"Of course, and we'll miss you, Dick, but perhaps another time. Just a moment, I'll get Thomas."

Tom was just climbing out of the bath. Wrapped in a towel, he picked up the receiver in the bedroom.

"Dick, how are you?"

"I'm well, Tom, but I'm afraid Cassie and I will have to postpone going to church with you on Sunday. We're very sorry."

"So are we, Dick. Is there anything I can do to help?"

"No, thank you. My father sent a telegram this afternoon.

He wants me to fly back to New York in the morning on the *Commodore*.[11] Tom, there's apparently been a dramatic reversal in the stock market, starting yesterday. Father is concerned that it will spread further. Have you heard anything from your bank?"

"No, I haven't, Dick, but I've got my portfolio in a blind trust with Mark Thurston at UTB, and I've given him full authority regarding the bank. I wouldn't expect to hear from him. How serious is it? Katrina and I have been out in the countryside for the past few days, and I've not seen the papers."

"I don't know, but Dad is never excitable. Having me come home immediately . . . well, I'd think it was serious. Would you like me to do anything for you . . . if it comes to that?"

Tom was silent for a moment, collecting his thoughts.

"I trust your father's judgment, Dick. You say you're leaving tomorrow?"

"The *Commodore* leaves early in the morning and we'll overnight in Caracas. I'll arrive in New York Sunday night, the twenty-seventh."

"Right. Depending on your father's decision, please telephone or telegraph Mark Thurston and tell him I've approved his following your father's instructions with my entire portfolio. I've maintained full equity position, Dick, but if we crash, it could be disastrous, of course."

"I'll contact Mark first thing Monday morning. Oh, and Tom, we still want to come and hear Katrina sing. I'm very sorry about this, sincerely. We'll come to your church with you after I return."

"That's great, Dick. We'll keep an eye on Cassie and Peggy while you're gone."

"Thank you, Tom. 'Bye."

Tom hung up the receiver and resumed toweling his hair, thoughts of what Dick's news might mean during a time of his absence from the bank swirling in his head.

"Is something wrong, dear?" Katrina asked as she came back into the bedroom.

"He's flying home in the morning."

"A problem with his family?"

"No, his father telegraphed, concerned about the stock market. It seems it's falling dramatically."

"Oh?"

"Don't worry, Katie, Mark will handle things, and I've asked Dick to call him if things are actually getting worse. We've weathered these crises before."

"Yes, but Mark hasn't," Katrina said, sitting on the bed and folding her hands in her lap.

"I know. As hard as it is to stay out of it, that's not our job right now. That's exactly why you had me put the portfolio in a trust with Mark, right?" he said, smiling at her. "We'll just have to leave it to his good judgment."

The following Saturday, after spending a full day visiting members and teaching missionary lessons with two of the young elders, Tom and Katrina drove through the streets of Buenos Aires, headed back to the mission home.

"Thomas, do you think Sister Hortensia will get her husband's permission to be baptized?" Katrina said as they drove into the circular driveway of the mission home.

"He's a firm figure in the household," Tom replied, "but I think he's fair. It's not easy for him to see his wife go against his wishes and his family traditions."

Tom parked the car and came around to open Katrina's door.

"Do *you* think he will?" Tom asked, smiling at his wife as he opened the front door.

"I hope so, Thomas. She's so sincere in her belief. Why is it that so many of our new members are women whose husbands show no interest?" she asked.

"Dick called it the Latin macho image. Praying or showing humility goes against generations of breeding. Oh, would you please check the hall table for mail, Katie," he said as he hung up his coat on the front hall clothes tree.

"Great!" Katrina exclaimed. "A letter from Tommy. That's the first since we arrived. And a telegram as well."

Tom came to stand beside his wife and look over her shoulder.

"You read Tommy's letter, and I'll deal with the telegram," he said, reaching for the yellow envelope.

Katrina sat down at a small secretarial desk, took a silver letter opener, and slit the envelope containing Tommy's letter. Tom tore open the telegram envelope, and each read silently for several moments.

"He's met a girl!" Katrina exclaimed. "That's the first time he's ever written about a woman, Thomas." When Tom didn't respond, Katrina looked up at him, standing alongside her chair. "Thomas?" she said, noticing the look of concentration on his face. "What is it?"

"It's from Mark Thurston."

"About the stock market?" she asked.

"Yes," he said quietly.

"Thomas?" she said, frightened by his sudden pallor.

Slowly he read to her.

"*Market began dropping Oct 24th–Stop–Van Brocklin advised sell all immediately, Monday, 28th–Stop–Total market collapse, 29th–Stop–Completed sale of your portfolio Nov 2nd–Stop–Total losses 80–85%–Stop–Hoover closed banks this week pending government action–Stop–Will wire more info as received–Stop–Regards, MT."*

"Oh, my goodness. What does that mean, Thomas?"

"It means we've lost most of our money, and the bank is in jeopardy of going under," he said, his eyes scanning the telegram for the third time. "President Hoover is trying to halt the slide it seems, but it looks like it's too late. If I've lost 85 percent of my holdings with full equity, the exchange will have issued a call for margin and the majority of the stockholders will lose everything they own, including those assets they own outright. It appears to be a catastrophe."

"Do you need to go home?" she asked, her mind reeling with the events.

Tom walked through the foyer and into the parlor, where he dropped heavily into his favorite leather chair in front of the unlit fireplace. Katrina rose and followed him, sitting on the arm of the chair. Tom remained quiet for several moments, and Katrina sat without speaking, her arm draped around her husband. Finally, Tom spoke.

"What did you say Tommy wrote?"

"Excuse me?"

"Tommy's letter. What was he saying?"

"He's, uh . . ." she stammered, "he's met a girl."

"At Stanford?"

"I suppose so. I didn't finish reading it."

"That's wonderful," Tom continued in a monotone. "It's about time he met a nice girl."

"Thomas, what about—"

"Do you know, Katie, when I met you on board the *Antioch*, I had a total of twelve pounds, nine shillings in my pocket, and no prospects when I reached New York." He paused, staring above the fireplace at a painting of a Napoleonic cavalry officer on horseback, his saber glistening and the horse's eyes flashing with terror amidst the cacophony of the battle.

"It's been a good life, hasn't it, Katie?"

"I don't understand, Thomas."

He patted her hand and abruptly stood from his chair, taking her hand and walking toward the stairs.

"Let's go upstairs and get ready for bed. I'm really tired, and tomorrow I'm going back to speak with Mr. Hortensia. I just *know* I can talk some sense into him. He seems a fine man."

"But, Thomas, what about the bank? Our finances?"

"That's not my job now, Katie," he said, absentmindedly, "and there's not one thing I can do about it. The Lord called us here for a purpose. I've got to believe He knows what He's doing. How about some hot chocolate before we go to bed?"

Katrina stopped halfway up the stairs and watched her husband continue to the top, turn toward the next landing, and continue walking up toward the third-floor residence. Then slowly, she descended the stairs and went into the kitchen. After taking a bottle of milk from the icebox and lighting a burner on the large, gas-fired stove, she poured the milk into a saucepan, added cocoa powder, placed the pan on the flames, and began to slowly stir the milk.

In early December, Seby flew from Salt Lake City to Los Angeles to attend the premiere of Teresa's latest film, *Angry Is the Night*. For nearly two and a half years, they had weathered a stormy marriage, not so much in face-to-face confrontation but rather in the quiet, unspoken knowledge that each was not happy with the decisions of the other. When, on her last visit to the ranch, Teresa had asked Seby how hard he had been affected by the market collapse, he had advised her that his stock holdings had been eradicated, but that he still owned the ranch, several thousand acres in Wyoming and Mexico, and had just completed a large sale of nearly six thousand head of cattle to a processor in Chicago. He was worse off than some, he said, but not as devastated as many others. Tess told him that following her father's and Tommy's advice, she had kept her trust fund in less volatile municipal bonds and U.S. Treasury notes. It was diminished, but intact.

"We've grown apart these past two years, Tess," Seby said as they rode toward the theater where the premiere was to be held. "We have to ask each other how much money we have."

"Are you unhappy, Seby?"

He drove silently for a few moments and then answered.

"My happiness has always been in knowing that you are happy, Tess. Doing what you love to do, enjoying the results—that has always been my joy, however much it requires our separation."

"And you're willing to continue that way?" she asked.

"You are my wife. I will support you as best I can."

"But what about *you*, Seby? What do *you* want? What makes *you* happy?"

Again he drove in silence, the traffic increasing as they reached the downtown area. As they neared the theater they saw the garish lighting towers, the blinding lights blistering the announcement of yet another Hollywood premiere.

"Are you asking what I want you to do, Tess?"

"Yes."

"That's not fair," he said, shaking his head. "You need to do what is best for you."

"And what about *us?* What's to become of us—our marriage?"

"What do you *want* to happen to us, Tess?"

"Damn you, Seby!" she shouted. "Why do you have to always be so gracious? Why can't you just tell me what you want? Tell me you *love* me! Tell me you *need* me! Tell me you can't *live* without me!"

He pulled the car to the curb, short of the theater, and shut off the engine, then he smiled sadly at his distraught wife.

"All of those things have been true since before we were married, *Señora* Stromberg. And they are no less true now. But if you need a lesson in human relations, perhaps it is *I* who should be asking you the same questions. Do you love *me?* Do you need *me?* Can you live happily without *me?*"

The tears in Teresa's eyes flushed through her carefully applied mascara and formed two dark, vertical streaks on her face. Her dark hair, cut short in a moment of frustration over her loneliness, framed her beautiful, alluring face, reminding Seby of the young college student she had been when he first felt the stirrings of affection for her. She held her head in her hands for several moments and then Seby put his arm around her, pulling her toward him and holding her close. After several long moments, she raised up, opened her silver compact mirror and gasped at the sight she beheld.

"I think I'm going to *have* to come home, Seby," she laughed through her tears. "No one at the premiere will recognize me as Teresa Callahan."

Seby took a handkerchief from his suit pocket and began dabbing at the dark stains on her face, cupping her chin in his free hand. When he finished, he leaned forward and kissed her gently, then held his face mere inches from hers.

"I will *never* be fully happy, Teresa, until we are husband and wife, living together and raising more than cattle. And as for happiness, I have not believed for one moment that *you* have been happy here in Hollywood, either. Professionally challenged, pleased with your success, and perhaps even amazed at your own talent, but not happy. Is that not true?"

Teresa looked into her husband's eyes, blinked to stem the next onslaught of tears, and slowly nodded her head. She looked ahead toward the gathering crowd of spectators, each hoping to catch a glimpse of their favorite movie star, Teresa Callahan included, and then she looked back at Seby and smiled at him.

"It's time, Seby," she nodded. "I need to come home."

It was April 1930, nearly six months after the stock market crash, before Cassie advised the Callahans that Dick Van Brocklin was returning to Buenos Aires. She said they would only remain long enough for Dick to close out his interests in Argentina and arrange for his family's return to New York. By that time, Mark Thurston had provided Tom a full accounting of the extent of his personal losses and the precarious position of Utah Trust Bank.

Through the holiday period and the early months of 1930, Tom's financial concerns put a tremendous strain on him, yet he continued to work tirelessly in his missionary efforts, conducting conferences, interviewing each missionary at least twice a month, and constantly visiting newly baptized members to fortify them in their decision to join the Church.

After having observed her husband's near total, thirty-year involvement in the affairs of Utah Trust Bank, Katrina was astonished at Tom's seeming ability to focus now on the work at hand. Even with the prospects of a personal financial disaster and the possibility of his bank's collapse, Tom's work as mission president remained his foremost interest. As a result, the South American Mission was prospering.

This prosperity was occurring in the face of what was becoming a worldwide financial calamity. President Herbert Hoover had assured the nation and the world that all would be well and warned that hysteria would only exacerbate the situation. Even so, frenzied depositors had made a run on hundreds of banks in the United States, resulting in the closure of many. Utah Trust Bank had not escaped the effects of the panic that gripped frightened depositors, who could only think about getting their cash in hand and who lined up daily, seeking to withdraw funds.

When Tom left Salt Lake in August 1929, his financial position had seemed secure. He had full confidence in Mark Thurston's abilities and the judgment of the bank's board of directors. His personal portfolio, consisting of stock, real estate, and commercial property, was valued at that time at nearly 155 million dollars and had been growing at about 6 percent annually. It was fortunate that in 1927, shortly after returning from the family reunion in Hawaii, he had begun divesting himself of any stock holdings that required close, personal scrutiny and had reinvested nearly a third of his capital in real estate and commercial properties. In light of the crash, doing so had saved him several millions of dollars.

As majority shareholder in Utah Trust Bank, his wealth had been further decimated in the run on the bank. UTB had always catered to personal rather than corporate depositors, and the bank held nearly eleven million dollars in personal savings and checking accounts, all of which had been frozen by presidential order. By February of 1930, banks were operating regular schedules again, but hundreds of smaller banks across the country had gone under and thousands more were threatened, including UTB.

At what amounted to fire-sale prices, Tom had instructed Mark to liquidate most of his commercial holdings, and from the proceeds, Tom had personally made good on every customer's deposits. His instructions to Thurston, that no public notice be given of how the payout was accomplished, left Mark unable to explain to his Utah banking associates how, and in fact why, in light of presidential decree, UTB was honoring 100 percent of its customer withdrawals.

Tom gave Thurston one final instruction. Utah Trust Bank held 174 home mortgages valued at some three million dollars. Knowing that the bank's home mortgage customers were likely to lose their jobs and be unable to meet their mortgage payments, Tom instructed the board of directors to use money from his personal account to clear all the home mortgages—essentially forgiving the debt owed by the bank's customers. At the same time he directed that the bank's remaining stock holdings, which had lost much of their value in the crash, be liquidated and that the proceeds be distributed to the members of the bank's board of directors for their long and faithful service.

When all was finally valued and totaled, Thomas and Katrina's net worth amounted to about four and a half million dollars, about half of which was tied up in real estate, including the eight hundred acres Tom had purchased in Hawaii. They had lost or given away nearly one hundred and fifty million dollars in the worst financial crisis to ever beset America.

One evening shortly after he had confided his intentions regarding the bank to Katrina, they sat alone on the veranda, sipping lemonade and discussing their situation.

"Thomas, has it not entered your mind that all this happened shortly after we answered the Lord's call?"

"I've considered it," he said, picking up a small piece of cake. "It's not His doing, Katie. I've never thought that."

"I've always told you that the Lord blesses those who serve Him. It confuses me. How can you be so . . . stoic?" she asked.

"When I stepped off the boat from Alaska in '98, I felt like the richest man in the world, Katie. I'm far richer now," he said, reaching across the space between their chairs for her hand. "If I learned nothing else in that dark cell in Portlaoise, I learned the truth of the teaching, 'You can't take it with you.' My wealth meant nothing in there."

"And all the customers of the bank? They don't even know what you've done. What it's cost you."

He shook his head. "Sister Mary used to tell me on our evening food deliveries, 'It doesn't matter whether they're Mormon or Catholic; They're all God's children.' I don't presume to be like Sister Mary, Katie, but do you remember the week we were married when we rode the train from San Francisco to Salt Lake and I asked you about the name of the bank—what the customers would want the most?"

"Vaguely," she replied.

He smiled at his wife and squeezed her hand. "You told me they would want to *trust* a bank where they kept their money. Utah *Trust* Bank, Katie. We've honored that. I feel good about it. So," he said, rising and finishing the last of his drink, "I'm for bed. It'll be good to see Dick and Cassie again tomorrow. I'm sorry they're leaving so soon."

"They have two weeks till they leave," Katrina said, an impish grin on her face.

Tom looked at her and squinted his eyes for a moment.

"Katie, you've got that look."

"They'll be here for dinner tomorrow, Thomas. My lips are sealed till then."

"You women have always got something cooking, don't you? Always a bit mysterious," he said, raising her up out of her chair. "But know this, Katie m'darlin'," he said, pulling her closer, "the Lord gave me you, and with His assistance, you gave me the gospel of Jesus Christ. I'm far richer than I could ever have expected to be for a sod-buster, part-time store clerk from Ireland."

She looked up at her husband, his temples now completely gray and his thick, dark hair streaked with silver, yet his blue eyes still vibrant and piercing. She laid her head against his chest and wrapped her arms around his back, squeezing tightly.

"I love the Irish larrikin you've always been, Mr. Callahan, and I love the man of God you've become. We *are* rich, Thomas. By any man's standard, we are *truly* rich."

Dick looked older somehow, Tom noticed. Throughout dinner at the mission home, the conversation had been casual, the Callahans and the Van Brocklins preferring, perhaps, to defer any serious subjects until after the pleasantries of dining had been completed. As they walked out onto the terrazzo veranda behind the main house, the lights of Buenos Aires and the shipping traffic on the Rio de la Plata provided a beautiful backdrop to their evening.

"Katie tells me," Tom began, "that your father has retired to Connecticut and is doing a bit of yachting."

"It was too much for him, Tom," Dick replied. "His brokerage, Van Brocklin, Holcomb, and Evanston, never had a chance. He lost his seat on the exchange and most of his clients lost everything, too."

"That wasn't Hank's fault," Tom said. "They should have known the risk of buying on margin."

"I know, but that didn't change their opinion. They felt the brokerage should have warned them ahead of time. They'd made money hand over fist for so many years that they couldn't believe what had happened. It *had* to be someone else's fault, or that's how it seemed to them."

"Is he well?" Tom asked and could see Cassie shake her head at the question.

"He's eighty-two and a broken man, Tom," Dick said. "His life's work was gone in less than a week. But I don't want to dwell on that tonight. Dad's always been strong-willed, and with Mom's help, he'll recover his priorities," Dick added, his face brightening. "I take it you've come through the crisis, not unscathed, of course," he laughed, "but solvent at least."

"Katrina and I will be fine, Dick. How about you and Cassie?"

"We'll be okay. I've taken over the New York branch of the bank, and we should survive the onslaught. Now, tell me, how's the missionary work going?"

Tom looked quizzically at the two women who appeared to be trying hard to maintain their composure and keep from laughing.

"It's struggling, Dick," he said quietly, still confused by the women's restrained actions. "We have a dedicated group of missionaries, but still, it's . . ." he paused, looking again toward his wife. "What *is* it with you, Katie? Am I missing something?"

"It's my fault," Dick said, also beginning to laugh. "Cassie—against my better wishes, mind you—confided in Katrina several weeks ago, but the two of them agreed to keep it secret until I returned and could speak with you."

"Keep what secret?"

"Tom, you remember when you first gave me the Book of Mormon to read."

"I do."

"And you were surprised, or at least I *think* you were surprised, when I told you I'd read it."

"I remember that, too," Tom said. "You said you read it all."

"I did, Tom, front to back," he said, his demeanor turned serious. "And I've read it again since then, while I was in New York. What I didn't tell you before I left, President Callahan, is that not only have I read the book, I believe it to be true—to be the word of God."

Tom looked at Katrina who was holding Cassie's hand. "You knew this?"

"I did, Thomas. Please don't be angry with me. I was sworn to secrecy, under penalty of . . . of, well, of breaking my word if I confided in you. It was Dick's right to talk to you first."

"And you, Dick. What's your excuse?" Tom asked, beginning to enjoy the conspiracy to keep him in the dark.

"My excuse, Tom, is that I came to know of the truth of your message before I left Buenos Aires for New York, but I wanted to return and ask you to baptize me. Once I knew I had to stay in New York longer than I planned, I feared that if Cassie told you, you'd demand that I be baptized in New York and not wait a minute longer. I wanted to wait until you could do it, Tom. Don't be upset with Katrina. We forced her to go along."

"*Forced*, my eye," he said, looking again toward his wife. "She *loves* this sort of subterfuge. And what about you, Cassie?" Tom asked. "How do you feel about Dick's decision?"

"I believe it with all my heart, Tom," the petite, strawberry blonde woman said, her eyes sparkling. "It's *our* decision. The very first time Dick and I knelt in prayer, the Spirit flooded my heart and I knew. I would like you to baptize me, too, President Callahan, and Peggy as well. We'll discuss it with our older daughter, Margaret, when we get back to New York. You've changed our lives, you and Katrina. And considering what we've all just experienced financially, it's been so comforting to know that there's something more to this life that is worth so much more. From the bottom of my heart I will always thank you, Tom. You and Katrina. I love you both," Cassie said, tears forming in her eyes.

Later that night, long after the hugs and tears had ceased and the Van Brocklins had departed, Katrina sat in a chair in front of the bedroom mirror, completing her nightly ritual of combing out her hair. Tom came and stood behind her, looking at her reflection in the mirror.

"As long as I live, I'll never *fully* understand the Lord, Katie. It took me well over twenty years to understand what he wanted me to see, and Dick and Cassie simply read the Book of Mormon and believed it."

"He knows us all, Thomas, and he loves us equally. Some children take longer to learn how to walk. Others, well, they know Him instantly. Knowing Him is what

287

matters, President, not how long it takes to recognize the truth. Aren't you happy for them?"

"Dick will be the first person I've ever baptized, Katie. Personally, I mean."

"But he won't be the last, President Callahan. Mark my words," she said, reaching her hand out to hold his. "He won't be the last."

18

The Prisman estate was located north of San Francisco, across the bay in Marin County, and as Tommy drove his new roadster onto the ferry at the foot of the Embarcadero in San Francisco, he felt a moment of fear at the decision he had reached. Susan clung tightly to his arm as they stood on the foredeck of the ferry during the windy crossing, and Tommy could sense her tension as well, although he had not discussed his intentions with her.

To say their relationship had been a whirlwind affair would not do it justice. It had not gone well at first. Susan had resisted all of Tommy's overtures, both subtle and direct, for all of the first year of their doctoral programs. Despite the fact that they worked in close proximity as Professor Wallington's teaching assistants, the beautiful, intelligent, confident woman had for some reason determined to pay Tommy no heed.

Then, without warning, shortly after New Year's Day, 1931, when Tommy had returned to Stanford from a quick holiday visit to see Seby and Tess, and with less than four months left until they graduated, Susan Prisman had reversed the order of battle. Tommy had fallen as if to the advance of the combined European armies, allied against his single outpost.

His surrender had been pleasant enough, and convincing Professor Wallington to retain two new teaching assistants a couple of months early so as to free up their time had not proved difficult. In fact, the old man had seemed quite enamored to play a role in furthering the romance.

Spending weekends in San Francisco, taking day trips to Half Moon Bay, Carmel, and Big Sur, and simply lounging around whichever of their apartments was the closest, gave them ample time to discover the joy young love brings. Tommy's reservations about having a *Mrs. Marine* disappeared within weeks, and suddenly he found himself thinking about his graduation, departure for his new assignment in Washington D.C., and a world without Susan Prisman at his side.

It was not a pleasant prospect. Though he had not yet discussed the possibility of marriage with her, it was an assumption he had begun to make. He had never had such feelings for a woman. Knowing and being with her had provided him a zest for life he had not thought possible. He anticipated their every meeting—even study dates—and when they were not together, she dominated his thoughts.

The trip to Marin County to meet her parents presented no particular challenge to Tommy. Full of youth and confidence, he crossed San Francisco Bay arm in arm with his lady love, anticipating a warm reception from the kind, caring, and always gracious Anthony Prisman that Susan had so lovingly described.

The Prisman estate was much as Susan's photo album had depicted—a Spanish-style adobe castle, replete with archways and with formal gardens surrounding the main house. From the expansive backyard, the view carried across the bay to Alcatraz and the city of San Francisco beyond.

As Susan had explained, her father had lost well over half of his fortune in the great crash, yet he had maintained a large share of the American-Japanese ocean freight market. His fleet of freighters and tankers had survived the financial disaster mostly as a result of their foreign flag status, and his quick manipulation of stock holdings from U.S. to foreign exchanges had preserved his wealth. As the effects of the collapse of the New York Stock Exchange rippled around the globe, Anthony Prisman had simply transferred title to his ships to several foreign government officials, mostly African, with whom he had often shared "special knowledge" about market conditions. In the midst of the furor, Prisman Enterprises was back in business and making money faster than it had prior to the crash.

Dinner was as formal as Susan had advised Tommy to expect. Several servants hovered around the table, instantly retrieving plates, cups, and glasses as the family members completed each course of the meal. Mrs. Prisman was a woman Tommy instantly took to be a socialite of the first order. Completely detached from the conversation during dinner, she excused herself immediately following the final course. Susan also rose and with a quick wink toward Tommy, followed her mother out of the dining room.

"Shall we have coffee in the library?" Anthony Prisman said, rising and raising a finger toward one of the servants.

Tommy stood and followed as the elder Prisman led the way through the corridor into a room filled, quite literally floor to ceiling, with hundreds of books of all types.

"Have a seat, Mr. Callahan. Care for a cigar?" he asked, raising the lid on a humidor and looking briefly at Tommy for a response.

"No, thank you, sir. Just coffee will do fine."

Prisman inserted his cigar into a small, sterling silver cutter and removed the end, then twirled it between his fingers, striking a match and taking a few moments to be sure it was well lit before resuming.

"It was good of you to bring Susan home for the weekend. We haven't gotten to see much of her since she enrolled at Stanford. Do you know my daughter well?"

"Well, sir, we've been enrolled in the same graduate economics program for nearly two years, and I've worked with her as one of Professor Wallington's teaching assistants, but we've actually only recently spent much time together. She's a wonderful woman, sir. I'm sure you and Mrs. Prisman are very proud of her."

"Indeed," Prisman said, blowing a cloud of smoke toward the ceiling. "And what are your plans after graduation? Back to the army?"

"The marines, sir. I'm a captain in the Marine Corps."

"Yes, yes, of course. And you'll return to that, uh, occupation?"

"Yes, sir. I've been assigned to Marine Corps headquarters in Washington, D.C. I'll most likely be there several years. Mr. Prisman, I'd like to talk to you about Susan, if I might, for a moment."

Prisman looked up from admiring his cigar and glanced toward Tommy.

"About Susan? What do you mean?"

"Sir, I don't know what Sue has told you about us, but we have spent considerable time together lately, and, frankly, sir, I've come to love your daughter very much. I believe the feeling is mutual. With your permission, sir, I would like to speak to her about marriage, but I felt it important to discuss the issue with you first."

Tommy began to feel a bit uncomfortable as the look on Prisman's face turned to what could only be described as shock.

"I gather, sir, that she has not addressed the subject with you," Tommy said.

"Absolutely not," Prisman replied, rising from his chair and moving to stand by a large globe of the world. "I'm afraid that's not possible, young man. I'm surprised you would raise the subject."

"Sir?"

"You can see, Mr. Callahan," he said, pointing around the room with his cigar, "that my daughter is used to the finer things in life. Now, I can admire your, uh, *pluck*, son, but you and my daughter come from two very different worlds."

"I still don't understand. We haven't discussed my background very much, I'll agree, but I'm certain we can find common ground for a good marriage, sir. I mean—"

"I know you mean well, young man, but it is out of the question. Absolutely impossible."

"Sir, with no disrespect, I think Susan should have something to say about that decision."

Prisman's face turned darker and a scowl crossed his eyes. He fairly glared at Tommy.

"Let me be blunt, Callahan. My daughter has had the best of everything in life—education, privileges, European vacations. All the things money can provide. Now from what little I do know about you, I don't think you can offer her that kind of life."

"Sir, I think my assets are perhaps greater than you have been led to believe."

"Yes, yes, I know. You'll have a doctorate and probably obtain a fine professorship at some small college, but that isn't what I'm talking about." Prisman took a deep breath and exhaled loudly, an exasperated look on his face.

"Mr. Callahan, here it is in a nutshell: you're a soldier, a poorly paid soldier at that. The military is sending you to Stanford, paying your costs and all, and you've taken a teaching assistant's position to put a few bucks in your pocket. Your father, from what I understand, is a dirt poor missionary looking after the needs of peasants somewhere in a South American jungle. Now that's all fine and good. The world needs such people, but from what you have seen here, surely you can understand that such a life would not suit my daughter."

Tommy stood from his chair, his own blood beginning to rise. His determination to keep his family status from his classmates and even from Susan Prisman had not changed when he began to develop feelings for her. He could see that the description of his family that Susan had provided to her parents did not present a flattering picture.

"Wouldn't that be up to Susan, Mr. Prisman?" Tommy asked, his voice a bit more rigid.

"No, it would not."

"I don't agree, sir. Not meaning to be disrespectful, I came here with the intention of obtaining your permission to speak with your daughter about marriage, and that is exactly what I intend to do, with or without your permission."

"Tell me, Mr. Callahan, is Susan aware of your feelings or this discussion?"

"No, sir, I thought it proper to discuss it with you first."

"And you suppose she feels the same way about you, do you?"

"I believe so, sir."

Prisman stared at Tommy for a few moments. When he

spoke again, his voice was icy. "You're in way over your head, Mr. Callahan. If you don't understand that now, you will soon."

With that, the older man turned his attention to the ash on his cigar, essentially dismissing Tommy who stood across the desk from the arrogant man, struggling to control his anger. For a moment, Tommy considered telling Susan's father that Prisman wasn't the only wealthy man in the room, but pride prevented him from doing so. If he wasn't a worthy suitor on his merits, he for sure wasn't about to plead his case on any other basis. Surely, Susan would see things differently than her father.

After a time, Mr. Prisman said, "I assume you'll be leaving in the morning, Mr. Callahan, but of course you're welcome to stay the night."

A servant was summoned to the study, and Tommy was shown to his room, where he spent the rest of the evening alone, feeling like a whipped pup and wondering why Susan didn't come to see how the meeting went.

When he awoke in the morning, Tommy found an envelope that had been slipped under the door during the night. It was a note from Susan, thanking him for bringing her home and advising him that she wouldn't be returning with him to the campus. Twenty minutes later, embarrassed and frustrated, Tommy loaded his luggage into his roadster, and after standing for a moment, looking up at the blank windows in the mansion, drove away from the estate to the ferry terminal in Sausalito.

Susan didn't return to Stanford for the remainder of the term. She mailed a formal note to Tommy explaining that she never meant to harm him, that she had no idea that he had been so serious about their relationship. He didn't respond.

In the final months of the year at Stanford, Tommy threw himself into completing his doctoral dissertation, "Sherman's Rampage through Georgia: Economic Warfare or Punitive Assault?" In May 1931, he completed the requirements for his doctorate three weeks early, and, foregoing the traditional graduation ceremonies, bid farewell to Professor Wallington, whom he had come to admire. He left Palo Alto the following morning. He drove alone over the Sierra Nevada Mountains and across the desert toward Utah, driving through the night. After making excuses to Seby and Teresa about not staying longer than one night in Draper, Captain Thomas Callahan commenced the long drive across the country toward Washington, D.C., and his new assignment.

The first of the next generation of Strombergs appeared early on a crisp winter morning with fresh snow blanketing the ground around the ranch house in Draper. Jessica Marie Stromberg, born February 13, 1931, quickly became the special treasure of her admiring father, with Teresa being allowed only to feed, bathe, change, and cuddle the infant when baby Jessie was not otherwise occupied with her father. Teresa watched with mild amusement as Jessie, tiny as she was, proceeded to captivate her father. Teresa voiced no complaint and, in fact, verbally acknowledged to her husband—tongue-in-cheek, of course—that his devoted parental involvement was a wonderful gift and would allow her time to return to Hollywood and star in a few more movies.

Instead, Teresa stayed at the ranch in Draper and produced, in 1932, Sebastian Cardenas Stromberg III, and was well into her third pregnancy, when, in February 1933, President and Sister Callahan returned to Salt Lake City from their mission in Buenos Aires. While determining where they would eventually live, the Callahans stayed for several weeks at the Stromberg ranch, where to Seby's dismay, he was, by his own *mi casa es su casa* house rule, required to turn over all cuddling and cooing chores for both children to the doting grandparents.

The first time Tom drove past the building that formerly housed Utah Trust Bank, he pulled his car to the side of the street and sat watching as people entered and left the law firm of Watson, Hodgekiss, Macklin, and Fritz. While in the mission field, he had disciplined himself not to think about financial concerns. But since his release, his losses—simply numbers on a sheet—had caused him moments of sadness that a way of life had gone. He was grateful, though, to have retained the wherewithal to provide for his family. In the midst of the deepening, worldwide economic depression, he was not without resources. Now, sitting in front of the new occupant's law firm, he was forced to concede that Utah Trust Bank was yet another memory. He reminded himself that he had retired and that the warmth and beauty of Hawaii beckoned.

During the final months of their mission, Tom had begun to think about their moving to Hawaii, but in keeping with his resolve to concentrate on his work, he had not spoken of it to Katrina. However, once they were released, he felt at liberty to broach the subject. He did so one evening during the second week of their stay at the ranch.

"More snow tonight," Tom said, reading to her from the newspaper as they sat in the living room in Draper. Seby had enlarged the original ranch house, building on a new wing, complete with a massive stone fireplace, in which a fire now roared, spreading its warmth into the rustic but comfortable room. Katrina had convinced Seby to take Teresa out for the evening. It was a transparent ploy calculated to give Katrina exclusive access to the grandchildren, and Jessie, who had just celebrated her second birthday, was playing on a rug on the floor in front of the fire, but under the watchful care of both grandparents. Little Seby, not yet one, was sleeping in a crib in the corner of the room.

"Always ice and snow. I guess we'll miss the mild winters in Argentina," Katrina said.

"They're a lot milder in Hawaii," Tom said, grinning broadly at her.

She lowered the Book of Mormon she had been reading into her lap and looked over at him, peering over the top of her reading glasses.

"We just got here, Thomas."

"I'm just saying, we need to consider what we intend to do. We can't stay at the ranch indefinitely. I did hear that Moses Vanderberg has taken seriously ill. Mary may want to sell *Valhalla* again."

"Really?" she said.

"I still think we should go to Hawaii, Katie. The plans we made when we were there are still valid. It's halfway, almost, between here and New Zealand and PJ's kids . . ."

"I know, I know, it's a good plan and certainly better weather for two old goats who are otherwise going to be sitting in front of a fire four months out of the year."

"Just *four* months?"

"Well, six then," she said, laughing at her husband. "But look at her, Thomas. How could we leave little Jessie?"

At the sound of her name, Jessie looked up from her toys

and toddled toward Tom. Raising her arms, she begged to climb up on his lap.

"Katie, if I didn't know better, I'd think you *trained* this kid to tug at her grandpa's heart," he laughed, reaching for the little girl and lifting her high above his head, causing her to squeal with delight.

"Shhh, the two of you. Do you want to wake Sebastian, *again?*"

"We wouldn't want to wake little Seby, would we, sweetie?" he cooed to Jessie. "Then we'd have to give him one of the cookies you and grandpa are going to have right now."

"Thomas, it's almost bedtime," Katrina complained, halfheartedly.

Tom stood and boosted little Jessie over his head and onto his shoulders.

"Katie, we need to consider this seriously. PJ was thrilled about the prospects of our being in Hawaii, you know that. He felt he could bring his family for a visit every two years or so, and if we were there, we could go down to New Zealand the in-between year. What can I say? It's time to make that decision. And you can't ask Tess her opinion. That's not fair to PJ," he said, raising and lowering his shoulders several inches, keeping Jessie in squeals.

"I'll pray about it. And you do the same. How's that?" she smiled.

"Cookie, Gwampa," Jessie said, putting her little hands over his eyes.

"Okay, big girl. Cookies it is. How about you, Grandma?"

"No, thank you. I've had sufficient for tonight. And just a little bit for Jessie. It really *is* close to bedtime. And after the children are in bed, President Roosevelt is coming on with tonight's fireside chat."

"No bed, Gwamma. Wead me a stowy."

"I can do that, sweetheart."

Thirty minutes later, Jessie was sound asleep in her room, and Tom was dozing in his chair while Katrina continued to read her scriptures. She glanced at the clock on the mantel and called out softly to Tom who opened his eyes slowly.

"It's time for the president," she said.

Tom nodded and rose to turn on the radio, waiting while it warmed up and the static cleared. He adjusted the dials as Seby had shown him and just as he found the right station, the front door opened and Teresa and Seby entered.

"The president is about to talk to us," Katrina said, smiling at the couple.

They hung up their overcoats and came over to stand by the fireplace, warming themselves in front of the flames.

In a crackly voice, interrupted by occasional bursts of static, President Franklin Delano Roosevelt quickly warmed to his subject. The federal and state governments had declared bank holidays, the nation's unemployed were destitute, and Americans everywhere were looking for solutions to the great problems that beset the country. "But, my friends," the president said, "the only thing we have to fear, is fear itself."

After the president's address, the foursome talked for several minutes about how national conditions were affecting Utah and Salt Lake City. Agreeing among themselves that it was a long-range problem, which most individual Americans could not solve, they retired to their respective bedrooms.

As had become his habit long before his mission, Tom arose before dawn. He stepped into his slippers and pulled on his robe, then descended the stairs to Seby and Teresa's living room. Embers from the previous night's fire were still glowing in the hearth, and, adding some kindling, Tom quickly fanned the coals into a flame. As it took hold, he added a couple of logs and watched with satisfaction as the fire grew, casting its glow and warmth into the room.

Tom padded quietly through the house into the kitchen, where he cut some bread and propped the slices up against the electric toaster. While waiting to turn the bread, he turned the radio on and adjusted the volume down, so as to not disturb the children and the rest of the family. KSL Radio was reporting that it had been the coldest night of the winter and that two men had been found frozen to death in a hobo camp on the west side of Salt Lake City.

Read by a newscaster, the report of the two deaths was delivered in an impersonal and matter-of-fact tone. In these hard economic times, such occurrences were taking place with some frequency and rarely merited much more than a perfunctory statement on the radio or a brief mention in the back pages of the newspaper.

Turning off the radio, Tom took his toast and a glass of milk into the living room, but before eating, he knelt down to offer his morning prayers. After rising, he sat munching his solitary breakfast and staring into the flames.

He thought about the news report. *Two men were found frozen to death in a hobo camp on the west side of Salt Lake City . . .*

He also thought of Father O'Shea, whom Tom had met in the Rose Garden of the Holy Cross Hospital, that night when Katrina lay so badly injured. He remembered what the Catholic priest had said to him: *God speaks with many voices and none of them are His.*

After a time, Tom downed the rest of his milk, rose from his chair, and quietly made his way back to the bedroom. Fumbling around in the remaining moonlight, he found the shoes and clothes he had taken off the night before and slipped quietly out of the room, somehow managing to do so without waking Katrina. When he reached the kitchen, he quickly dressed and pulled on his overcoat. He scrawled a note to Katrina, saying he would be gone for a time, then, with a glance up the stairs to see that no one had yet awakened, he opened the door and stepped into the winter morning air.

It was long after dinner before Tom returned to Draper to find the family gathered in the living room, where the two women were seated on the floor in front of the fire helping Jessie cut out paper dolls. They all looked up as the door opened. Tom stomped the snow off his overshoes and removed his overcoat before stepping into the living room.

"Where in the world have you been, Thomas? I was about to call the police," Katrina said, frustration in her voice.

"I've never gotten lost in Salt Lake," he said, smiling as he leaned down and held her cheeks in his nearly frozen hands.

She squealed at the shock and Jessie quickly stood, reaching up her arms for Grandpa to pick her up. Instead, he sat on the floor beside the three women, touching Jessie with his cold fingers and nodding briefly at Seby who remained silent.

"Well, where *have* you been, President Callahan?" Katrina pressed.

"I've been all over town, actually," he said, drawing out the question without answering. "I've been to the hospital to see Moses." His face saddened for a moment. "It's not good, Katie," he said, shaking his head. "They're going to have to place him in a long-term care facility. Mary was actually pleased to see me. She's still a strong woman, but she's going to live with one of her daughters."

"Is she all right, Thomas?"

"Not really, but we'll keep watch on her, and she has many friends."

Katrina looked at him for several seconds, and he knew from her look that he could postpone the issue no longer. It had been many years since Tom had been able to actually get away with keeping secrets from his wife.

"I bought a large warehouse," he blurted out, and even Seby leaned forward in his chair, laying aside the book he had been reading.

"A *what?*" Katrina exclaimed. "What in the world do we need a *warehouse* for?"

"For the soup and the beds," he answered.

"Thomas Callahan, stop that this *instant!* Tell us the full story and stop playing your silly little games," Katrina demanded.

"I also arranged to buy *Valhalla* from Mary. She was thrilled. She couldn't think of living in that big house with Moses in a hospital."

Katrina just sighed, a deep exhale escaping her lips, and her look growing firmer each moment. Teresa glanced at Seby and gave him a knowing smile and a wink, which said this was a game her father loved and seldom had the opportunity to play.

"Katie, I'll take you there for a nice vacation, in fact, I'll take all of us, if you can get away, Seby, but Katie, you and I are *not* going to *retire* to Hawaii."

Katrina's eyes grew wider.

"I'm not yet fifty-eight, Katie. UTB is gone. I saw that firsthand the other day, and it hurt to see it. But I'm not ready to retire. I thought I might be, but I'm not. And you know the Brethren," he smiled. "They aren't going to let me retire at such an early age. And I'm not *bishop* material, we all know *that*," he laughed, receiving a peck on the cheek from Teresa for his candor. "So I needed to find something to do—something of my own choosing." He paused, glancing around the room.

"Katie, we're going to move back into *Valhalla*, and I'm going to open a rescue mission—what the papers are calling a 'soup kitchen' for the homeless."

The three other adults seated around the room were silent for long moments with only Jessie, holding Tom's hand and trying to climb in his lap, making any noise.

"What do you know about soup kitchens and homeless people?" Katrina asked, her voice incredulous.

"Only what Sister Mary taught me, dear Katie. There are *always* people who need them. And now, from what I read in the paper and see on the streets, that's a growing number."

Within two weeks, Tom had acquired about seventy-five cots, bedding, two commercial-grade stoves, and a kitchen full of dishes and utensils gathered from various sources, including—Tom thought most appropriate—from several restaurants that had gone under as a result of the gathering economic depression.

The word spread quickly around Salt Lake County, and almost from its inception, the soup kitchen began the daily feeding of several dozen men.

At first, Tom had not wanted his wife to work in the facility, which the vagrants began calling Seagull Inn in honor of the divine rescue of Salt Lake City's original inhabitants. But one afternoon, when several workers were held up by transport problems, Katrina accompanied Tom to the facility and was treated so respectfully and courteously by the visitors, who appeared so grateful for her efforts, that she insisted Tom allow her to participate in his work. He agreed.

Where most of the men—and an occasional woman—came from was an eye-opener to Tom and Katrina. Expecting to find mostly rural Utah men who were out of work and gathered in the big city seeking employment, they quickly discovered the men were from a variety of places and circumstances. As the transients passed through the food line, hat in hand, they almost all mumbled words of appreciation to the ladies, including Katrina, who were serving their food. Many had heavy accents. There were southern men, Yankees from New England, Texans, and perhaps most surprising, quite often English, Scottish, Irish, and European immigrants, who had come to America in search of opportunities, much as Tom had done several decades earlier.

When Tom sat at one of the tables, having soup and bread with the men, he was told that the same conditions existed all over America and that Seagull Inn was only one of hundreds of similar facilities, some of them government sponsored, located in cities across the nation.

How Seagull Inn had become occupied so quickly also became readily apparent as the men chatted with Tom and his staff. Without thought to a specific location, when Tom had sought out a large, open-area warehouse, he had obtained a building two blocks from the terminus of the Union Pacific Railroad yards, not far from Temple Square. Railroads, the men informed him, were their primary source of transportation and—not that they didn't like Utah, they'd laughed—those unlucky enough to hop a freight headed north during the winter months ended up in the hub of the Intermountain West: Salt Lake City. Tom discovered that if they were unsuccessful in finding work, most men would head south during the winter months, seeking a more hospitable climate.

Perhaps the most depressing aspect of Tom and Katrina's discoveries was the knowledge that, by far, the majority of those traveling in search of work had left families—wives and children—someplace "back there." It ate at these men, and drove them to fits of depression to think that they were unable to obtain work sufficient to send money home. The little work they *were* able to find—day laborer jobs for the most part—barely provided for their own sustenance. How their families were surviving at home was something that collectively, almost to a man, they could not bring themselves to dwell upon.

In the fall of 1932, the American public had turned President Herbert Hoover out of office, blaming him in large part for the economic woes of the nation. It was hardly his fault. Greedy men seeking a fast buck on the basis of little investment were ultimately responsible for the depressed state of the economy. Even so, Hoover was defeated, and the charismatic former governor of New York, Franklin Delano Roosevelt, a man of immense personal charm and wealth, was elected. Like Winston Churchill in England, Roosevelt had come up through the privileged classes and had served in functionary roles in government most of his life. Churchill and Roosevelt were alike in that each had been involved with their respective nation's navies, with Roosevelt having served President Wilson as Assistant Secretary of the Navy.

By early summer 1933, Seagull Inn had established itself as a respite, and while the overnighters diminished with the advent of good weather—Seagull Inn had facilities for 175 overnight residents—the soup line remained a popular and busy daily scene, far beyond the departure of winter.

Tom spent much of the summer of 1933 visiting old banking and business associates, committing them to donations for Seagull Inn operations and the purchase of food supplies. He made several presentations before the Salt Lake City Council and the Salt Lake County commissioners, finding that with government support came government regulations. No one disputed the volume of traffic in the city and the need for such services, but committing public funds to the support of welfare projects brought with it a host of demands that the recipients provide some form of labor for their meals and lodging. The local city council seemed determined to follow the national trend of establishing work camps and putting the nation's unemployed to work doing public service jobs. President Roosevelt's Civilian Conservation Corps (CCC) and Works Progress Administration (WPA) legislation had become the model for the nation.[12] Tom was determined that Seagull Inn would remain merely a temporary safe haven for those who needed a meal, a bed, and perhaps several days of rest before moving on in their quest for permanent work.

One noontime in October 1934, when Salt Lake City was suffering through a rather warm Indian summer, Tom was in Ogden to see about opening a second Seagull Inn. Katrina was working behind the serving line in the Salt Lake facility, dishing up meals and helping out the full-time staff. They had served over a hundred meals, and she was trying in vain to push a wisp of loose hair back beneath the hair net she was wearing when she looked up to see two well-dressed gentlemen in the food line. One of them was David O. McKay, newly called second counselor in the First Presidency of the Church.

"President McKay," she exclaimed, trying to remain composed. "To what do we owe the honor of your visit?"

"Good day, Sister Callahan," he smiled. "The President and I thought we would try out the newest hot lunch spot in town. We hear the food's mighty good," he said, his pleasant smile revealing his joy at the charade.

Katrina looked to the next man in line and lost all her ability to cover her surprise. President Heber J. Grant accompanied Brother McKay, and both men stood, each holding a tray, waiting to be served.

"Hello, Sister Callahan," President Grant said. "Brother McKay insisted that we needed to eat at Salt Lake's finest new establishment, and here we are," he smiled.

Katrina quickly filled their trays and then came out from behind the serving line to escort them to a table where a half-dozen somewhat disheveled men already sat.

The two Church leaders greeted each of the men and shook their hands before sitting down.

"We're so glad to have you here, President and Brother McKay," Katrina said. "I'm sorry that Thomas is gone. He's in Ogden. He thinks we need another soup kitchen before winter sets in."

"And he's probably right, Sister Callahan," President Grant said as he started in on his potatoes, mixing a spoonful with the day's vegetables. "It's a wonderful work you and Brother Callahan are doing here with these men. We're living in very difficult times."

"Thomas will be disappointed that he missed you," she said.

"Give him our love and tell him the Brethren admire the work you and he are doing here. I'm sure the Lord is pleased with your efforts," President Grant said.

19

In the early 1930s, United States Marine Corps Headquarters, Washington, D.C., was an efficient, if not well-staffed place, manned by career marine officers in a corps greatly diminished by the "between-wars" reduction-in-force mandated by Congress. The total strength of the Corps had been reduced to roughly 1,200 officers and 16,000 enlisted marines.

From 1931 through 1934, Captain Callahan was assigned to the War Plans Section, Pacific Operations Division, working as executive officer to another naval academy graduate who had chosen to be a marine, Lieutenant Colonel Hanscomb, Class of 1915. Two other junior officers and nine enlisted men comprised the remainder of the division.

Working on the U.S. military color-coded contingency war plans, Tommy was assigned specific duties in refining "Plan Orange," the battle scenario for a hypothetical war between the United States and Japan, to be fought primarily in the Pacific Ocean through naval engagements. A half dozen other color-coded war plans divisions existed, each designated to prepare U.S. forces for potential conflict against multiple enemies, both European and Asian.

By 1935, after Japan had begun her conquest of weaker Asian nations, Plan Orange took on a more urgent status. Then, when President Roosevelt appointed General John Russell the new commandant of the Marine Corps, the War Plans Section acquired a heightened sense of mission, and Tommy received a new assignment: to accompany a select group of navy and marine officers who were assigned to reconnoiter a number of Pacific islands that had been recommended as potential forward base deployment sites. For the next seven months, from January to July 1935, Captain Callahan took a tedious tour of the out-of-the-way scattered islands, traveling by ship and by *PBY*, the navy's new, long-range flying boat. Built by Consolidated Air, the *PBY* extended the range of flight to over 2,500 miles, and throughout 1935, it was extensively tested, officially becoming part of naval aviation in 1936.

Upon the team's return to Washington, D.C., the plans they presented to the commandant and chief of naval operations were well formulated, and according to Lieutenant Colonel Hanscomb, Tommy was in line—as Tommy had requested—for assignment to what had been designated as Forward Defense Battalions, which would man the outposts.

But early one Thursday morning in August 1935, Tommy was called in to see Colonel Hanscomb and that order was changed.

"Sir, Captain Callahan reporting as ordered," Tommy announced formally as he stood in front of the colonel's desk.

"Stand easy, Captain. I've received a call from the commandant's office. We've been directed to see the general at sixteen hundred hours."

Tommy stood silently, his hands clasped behind his back. Hanscomb looked up from his desk, shook his head and proffered a slight frown.

311

"The commandant's gunny gave me a head's up on this one. I'm sorry, Captain, but I'm afraid you've been passed over for command of one of the defense battalions."

"Sir?"

"I know that's what you wanted, but apparently the commandant has other plans. Exactly what those plans are, we'll have to wait until this afternoon to find out."

At fifteen-fifty-five, Lieutenant Colonel Hanscomb and Captain Thomas Callahan were in the outer office of the commandant of the Marine Corps, General John Russell. At precisely sixteen hundred hours, they were shown into the general's office.

"Sir, Lieutenant Colonel Hanscomb and Captain Callahan reporting as ordered," Hanscomb said.

"Stand easy," General Russell said. He looked both men over and then motioned to a small cluster of chairs in the corner of his office. Hanscomb and Tommy sat but remained rigidly upright, a holdover from their academy days.

"Did you enjoy the Pacific tour, Captain?" Russell asked.

"I did, sir."

"And what did you learn?"

Tommy glanced quickly at Hanscomb, then back at General Russell.

"Sir, as the colonel indicated in our final report, the primary sites for strategic defense were determined to be Wake Island, Midway . . ."

"Captain, I asked what did *you* learn?"

Tommy hesitated for a moment, shifting nervously in his chair. It was most unusual for a general officer, much less the commandant, to ask the opinion of a lowly captain.

"General, in my uneducated opinion . . ."

"Captain, I'm going to ask you once more," the general said, fixing Tommy with a withering stare, "and if you

312

consider the education provided to you, free of charge I might add, by the United States Naval Academy as having left you 'uneducated,' then perhaps we need to reconsider your commission as a marine officer," Russell said brusquely.

"Aye, aye, sir," Tommy replied. "In my opinion, sir, the islands chosen are the only logical choices, *geographically* logical that is. However, sir, I submit that they are indefensible without a naval task force standing by to aid in their overall defense."

Russell nodded. "Go on."

"Sir, the islands are remote and would be totally dependent on outside supply. There are limited water resources, and the lines of supply for food, ammunition, and other matériel, are long and vulnerable to enemy interdiction. The logistics of supporting a battalion of marines on each of those locations would be staggering. I must assume, sir, that the marine battalions would be positioned to provide a delaying action in the event of attack and that a naval fleet arriving to join the battle would be the only hope such a unit would have of surviving."

"That's very astute, Captain. Anything else?"

"Well, sir, it would seem that lacking such support, the battalions must be viewed as, uh, expendable, sir, in the interest of achieving a strategic delay."

Colonel Hanscomb raised his eyebrows and glanced once between Tommy and General Russell, wondering at the brashness of Captain Callahan.

"That, Captain Callahan, is the *exact* conclusion reached by the navy and marine joint committee after reading the travel team's report to the joint chiefs. Yet, as I understand it, you still aspire to command one of the defense battalions. Is that correct?"

"Yes, sir. I believe they will play an important role in Plan Orange."

Russell shook his head. "I'm afraid it's not your time, Captain," the general said, summarily dismissing the subject.

"Do you know a British brigadier named McIntyre?" General Russell continued.

Confused by the sudden change in topic, Tommy didn't immediately answer, thinking about the name. *McIntyre. McIntyre.*

"Sir, I don't recognize the name . . ."

Then he remembered.

"Excuse me, sir. I do recall someone by that name, a man I met many years ago, while on a fishing trip in Wyoming."

"And?"

Determined not to be chastened again, Tommy simply said, "There was a bit of trouble, as I recall, with McIntyre's son. That was the only time I met the brigadier, sir. I've had no contact with him since."

"I see," Russell said. "Well, he apparently remembers *you*, Captain. And, it would seem, he has followed your career, too, including your doctorate. Using the British embassy military attaché in Washington as his conduit, Brigadier McIntyre has asked that you be assigned as a visiting lecturer on the effective use of economic warfare in the modern age."

"Lecturer, sir?"

"At Sandhurst. The Royal Military Academy at Sandhurst. The British West Point, actually."

"I don't understand, sir."

"Little wonder, Captain, it's most unusual. But the Secretary of the Navy has forwarded the request, and we're all marines here. We go *where* we're told and do *what* we're told."

"Aye, aye, sir," Tommy replied.

"You're to be in place in September."

"A *visiting* lecturer, sir?" Tommy questioned.

"It's more than a simple lecture, Captain. The brigadier is now commander of the Royal Academy. He's requested you be posted for a multiple year assignment, the length of assignment to be determined by the needs of the Corps. Good of him to give us *some* say," General Russell said, a bit sarcastically. "The defense battalion concept will still be here when you return, Captain, and, if I read the world situation right, it will be even *more* important.

"One more thing," he said, rising and walking toward his desk. When General Russell stood, both of the other officers stood immediately. The older man returned to the group carrying a small green case that Tommy and Colonel Hanscomb instantly recognized.

"To properly represent the Corps, we feel that this assignment should be filled by at least a field-grade officer. Upon my recommendation, the secretary has also approved your immediate promotion. Congratulations, *Major* Callahan," he said, handing Tommy the insignia case containing two gold oak leaves.

"Thank you, sir," Tommy replied.

"You'll report directly to the military attaché at our embassy in London—a navy captain at the moment, I believe. It goes without saying that you'll be expected to represent the highest traditions of the Corps, Major. That will be all, gentlemen," Russell said, returning to his desk.

Tommy arrived in Southampton on the *Bergensfjord,* a Norwegian liner that made the crossing from New York in just over eight days. As the ship made her way up the River

Test toward her berth, Tommy found himself immersed in a flood of nostalgia.

Though twenty-three years had passed, he remembered the morning in 1912 when, as an eleven-year-old boy, he had boarded the *Titanic*, along with his mother, grandparents, and Benjamin and Teresa. The huge ship had filled him with awe, and thinking of the tragic events that followed, he experienced a sense of melancholy that he couldn't shake.

In spite of the lateness of his arrival at Southampton, Tommy chose to forego his prearranged accommodations there and, instead, press on. He took the midnight boat-train to London where he hired a taxi to take him to the Savoy. Arriving at the upper-class hotel after 2:00 A.M., Tommy was too tired to be impressed by the night clerk's attempt at *hauteur*. The bedraggled-looking and unshaved American marine officer responded without comment to the snooty clerk's request that he pay his bill in advance, then carried his own luggage to his room where he promptly fell asleep.

The following afternoon, he went to the American embassy in London, where he had an impromptu meeting with a Captain Tolbert, the naval attaché. Tolbert had a vague recollection of having seen some notice of Major Callahan's assignment to Sandhurst. Clearly, the elderly naval officer was well overdue for reassignment, or perhaps even retirement, and his admonition that Tommy "put on a good show for the limeys" was delivered so indifferently that Tommy concluded it would be unnecessary for him to report to the embassy on a regular basis.

Victoria Station, London, reminded Tommy of Grand Central Station in New York City, except there were no winos on the street outside the British rail terminal and no vagrants sleeping on the benches beneath the marbled arches inside. Tommy upgraded the second-class rail ticket provided him by the U.S. Embassy to first-class and made his way through the bustling crowd of people toward the trains. Stopping once to ask track assignments, he found the British Rail train destined for Camberley and Aldershot, located some thirty miles southwest of London, and climbed aboard.

After a pleasant ninety-minute trip through the Surrey countryside, the train conductor announced Camberley. Tommy had arranged to have the bulk of his luggage shipped straight through from Southampton to the academy and was carrying only a single bag with him. He retrieved it from the overhead rack and before the train stopped, stepped to the door of the compartment, and prepared to descend the metal stairs to the station platform. The train came to a halt, but as Tommy was taking the first step down, the car was jostled, and he lost his footing, pitching forward and falling facedown toward the wooden platform. Instinctively, he dropped his bag and threw his arms out in front of him to cushion the fall, but his left hand twisted beneath him, and when he hit the ground, his body landed heavily on top of his folded hand.

Instantly, a pain shot up his arm, and his wrist began to throb. Embarrassed by his public display of awkwardness, he immediately got to his feet but winced again at the pain in his wrist. Not wishing to make a further spectacle of himself, he reached with his good hand to pull his bag from where it had fallen, beneath the wheels of the train.

"You all right, Guv'ner?" a voice called out. An older man dressed in a porter's uniform strode quickly to his side, hefting the bag from Tommy's hand and guiding him away from the edge of the track.

"Just a fall, but I think I've probably sprained my wrist."

"Here, we better get you to hospital," he said, continuing to use Tommy's elbow as leverage to guide the younger man toward the car park beside the station platform. He whistled and gestured toward a taxi stand, and a car immediately pulled alongside.

"Prince Albert Hospital and be quick about it," the porter said to the driver.

Tommy hesitated entering the cab. "I don't think I need—"

"Better the doctor 'ave a look, Guv'ner," the man admonished. "Never can tell about these things."

"Right," Tommy conceded as the pain jolted through his arm again. "I need a taxi anyway. How far is it to the RMA?"

"Not far, Guv'ner, and Prince Albert's on the way."

As the porter handed Tommy's bag into the cab, Tommy tried to reach into his pocket to tip the elderly man, but the helpful porter shook his head.

"No need, sir," he smiled, showing several missing teeth. "Welcome to Surrey. We're very sorry for your troubles."

"Thank you," Tommy responded as the cab rolled away.

Tommy waited nearly two hours in the stark hospital corridor for someone to attend to him. White-clad nurses, orderlies, and other patients moved up and down the corridor, seemingly oblivious to his need. Finally, a male orderly he had watched taking care of other patients for the entire time he had been waiting stopped in front of him and lifted Tommy's arm, feeling not so gently around his swollen wrist.

"Right then, wha' ha' we here?" he asked, his speech scarcely resembling English to Tommy's ear.

"I hurt my wrist," Tommy replied, retrieving his

appendage and cradling it in his other hand. "I'd like not to make it worse," he added.

The young orderly grinned at Tommy, a supercilious look that failed to instill confidence in his American patient.

"Follow me, Mate, and the x-ray blokes'll 'ave a go."

Have a go, Tommy thought as they walked down the hallway. *If that's anything like the 'go' you just had, I'll pass, thank you very much.*

Forty-five minutes later the x-rays had been taken and the orderly had installed Tommy in an examining room, where he once again roughly handled Tommy's injured wrist while placing the arm in a temporary sling.

"You wait right 'ere, Mate. The doctor'll be along directly," he said, laying the x-rays on a bench next to the examining table.

Another twenty minutes passed while Tommy sat perched on the edge of the wooden examining table, trying to hold his arm immobile and grimacing at the pain, which by now was radiating all the way to his shoulder. The door opened abruptly, and a young woman dressed in a white uniform walked into the room. Picking up the x-rays and turning on a lamp, she held the pictures up to the light, examined them briefly, and then laid them back on the table.

"Well," she said, smiling brightly at Tommy, "let's have a look. How did you say this happened?" she asked as she reached to undo the sling around Tommy's neck.

Tommy drew back, shielding his injured wrist.

"If it's all the same to you, ma'am, I'd just as soon not be prodded again until the doctor comes. No offense," he added, "but I was beginning to wonder if the last orderly might break the other wrist as well."

"And how did you come by this injury?" she asked, ignoring his remark.

"If you must know, I fell off a train at the station this morning. Some *four hours* ago," he added, permitting his exasperation to show in his voice. "Look, miss, whatever your name is, I said I'd like to wait for the doctor and get a *professional* opinion. One that will cause less pain than the original injury, if possible. From what I've seen of British medicine so far, that may be asking too much."

"Mister, uh," she hesitated, looking down at the hastily scribbled patient chart, "Callahan, if you wish to wait for a *doctor*, the next one will not be on emergency shift until after six this evening. However, if that's your preference . . ."

"I don't mean to be rude, miss . . ."

"Rossiter," she said calmly, her face stoical, "Elizabeth Rossiter. *Doctor* Elizabeth Rossiter."

Silence filled the room as Tommy contemplated his mistake. Doctor Rossiter lifted the x-rays and glanced again at the clean break revealed by the negative. She looked back at Tommy but didn't speak.

Tommy smiled thinly at her and squirmed a bit on the table.

After a time, he said, "Actually, *Doctor* Rossiter, while my wrist hurts considerably, perhaps you could have a look at my foot first."

"Your *foot?*" she asked, glancing at the chart she held in her hand and then down at the floor beneath the examining table.

"Yes, ma'am. The one firmly embedded in my mouth, I mean."

"Oh, *that* foot," she chuckled. "I've found it's generally best if the patient performs self-extraction in such cases. It can be *very* painful, and often humiliating, but in the end

. . . well, I'm sure you understand," she said, suppressing a laugh.

"All too well," Tommy replied, allowing his own smile to break through. "So, what's the verdict on the wrist?"

"A clean break, I'm afraid. We'll have to plaster it."

"*Plaster* it? The way it hurts, Doctor Rossiter, I think it's already been *plastered*."

The young doctor laughed again, and Tommy noticed her even teeth, the laugh lines around her green eyes, and her jet black hair, which was she was wearing pulled back into a bun.

"There's our bilingual problem again," she said. "I believe you Yanks call it a *cast*. It won't take long. We should have you out of here in time for dinner."

While Doctor Rossiter completed the wrapping and plastering of Tommy's wrist and lower arm, he studied her face. She went about her task confidently but gently, something Tommy appreciated after the rough treatment he had received. He found himself admiring the set of her pretty mouth as she worked, and, thinking about the assumption he had made in the examining room, he once again winced with embarrassment.

"Well, that should do the job," Doctor Rossiter said, smoothing the wet plaster one last time. "Will you be in Camberley long?" she asked.

Tommy could see from her expression that she suddenly realized her question sounded personal. It would have been impossible for her *not* to have noticed his constant stare during the plastering operation, so again he felt responsible for her predicament.

"What I mean is, will you be able to return in about four weeks so we can have another look at your wrist?"

"I understand," he smiled. "Yes, actually I'll be here for a few years. I've been posted to the Royal Military Academy as an instructor. I think it's a bit late to arrive today, however," he said, looking at the clock on the wall, which showed the time to be nearly 5:00 P.M. "Is there a good hotel nearby?"

"There is," she said, drying her hands after washing off the plaster. "The Star and Garter is just two blocks north. You can walk there, and they have a fine restaurant as well."

"Excellent. I think I'll just get a room for the night and report in to the school tomorrow." Standing down from the table where he had been seated, Tommy said, "Doctor Rossiter, you mentioned that another doctor comes on about six. Does that mean that you're *off* duty at six," he said, hoping that the absence of a ring on her finger indicated she was single.

She glanced up from drying her hands for a moment and then turned away to hang up the towel. She reached into a cabinet above the sink and withdrew a large brown bottle. Without answering him, she shook about a dozen tablets onto a platter on the sideboard and replaced the bottle. Then she scooped up the tablets into a small brown envelope. Turning back toward Tommy, she said, "Take a couple of these tablets when you reach the hotel, and then every four hours as required for pain. And yes, my shift is finished at six," she smiled pleasantly.

"If it isn't too presumptuous, *Doctor* Rossiter," he shrugged, "could I interest you in dinner and some conversation this evening? Sort of a 'welcome to Camberley' tourist-guide duty? I'll do my utmost to keep my foot out of my mouth. Roast beef and potatoes sounds so much better right about now."

"It does, doesn't it," she laughed. "But the Star and Garter has an excellent rack of lamb, boiled potatoes, and asparagus that I can highly recommend."

"Served for two?"

"It *can* be served for two," she said, giving herself a moment to make a snap decision, then continuing with confidence. "Eight o'clock, Mr. Callahan. I'll meet you there," she offered.

"Great," he said. Gathering up his bag, he turned to leave but then looked back.

"And Doctor Rossiter, I . . ."

She smiled broadly at Tommy and shook her head, wagging her finger in mock admonition.

"You promised, no more foot-in-the-mouth, if you please. I'll wait for the lamb."

"Thank you," he laughed, gently waving his new cast and grimacing at the surge of pain. "And thanks for the *plastering*."

Tommy's room at the Star and Garter was not quite as elegant as the one at the Savoy in London, but the staff were much more cordial. The old English atmosphere appealed to Tommy, and in some ways the quaint old Tudor-style inn reminded him of his childhood home, *Valhalla*.

Laboring to keep his cast dry, he showered with a hand-held wand in his tub, and then dressed casually in slacks, shirt, a tie, and a tweed sport coat that was badly rumpled from being packed away. From somewhere he remembered that even casual dress in England usually included at least a coat and tie for men. More formal dress differed only in what *kind* of coat and tie.

At seven forty-five, he was seated in the pub in the entry to the Star and Garter, trying to get used to the taste of a cup of English tea, when Elizabeth arrived. Wearing a plaid skirt, a white blouse, and a soft pink cardigan sweater, she scarcely resembled the professional-looking woman he had met a few hours earlier. Her dark hair, which had been pulled back into a tight bun earlier in the day, was now loose and worn at shoulder length under a silk scarf, which she removed as she walked toward Tommy. He took a deep breath and stood to greet her.

"Doctor Rossiter was supposed to meet me here this evening," he said, his face straight. "Have you come in her place?"

"She couldn't make it, but asked me to represent her," Elizabeth answered, picking up immediately on Tommy's game.

"Excellent. Would you care to join me in a glass of wine before dinner?"

"No, thank you, Mr. Callahan. I'm on duty again in the morning at six."

"Wow. They certainly get their pound of flesh, don't they?"

She tilted her head and looked puzzled.

"I don't quite understand your meaning."

"Twelve-hour shifts it would seem," he answered.

"Oh, yes," she laughed, "resident doctors are fair game for exploitation."

"Shall we go in?" Tommy asked. "I've reserved a table, although I think they were simply being kind. It doesn't appear to be crowded."

"No," she said, "a Wednesday night would be light dinner traffic, I think. I'm ready if you are."

"Fine."

Tommy nodded and glanced at a pleasant-looking woman who stood in the doorway to the dining facility, located just off the entrance to the hotel lobby. The hostess smiled at the couple as they approached.

"Good evening, Doctor Rossiter," she said. "It's nice to see you this evening."

"Thank you, Mrs. Proctor. And how is little Sarah?"

"Just fine, Doctor. She responded to the medicine like a duck to water, that is, once I got her to swallow it."

"That's good. Have you met Mr. Callahan?"

"Just briefly, when he registered for his room this afternoon. Welcome again, Mr. Callahan. Would you like to be seated close to the fireplace?"

"Before arriving, I wouldn't have imagined a fire in August, but England has a unique climate, doesn't it?" Tommy replied.

"We do, indeed."

Tommy stepped aside so that Elizabeth could follow Mrs. Proctor, who seated the couple at a stout wooden table slightly to the side of the large fireplace where a small peat moss fire burned slowly in the center of the hearth.

"May I get you something to drink before you order, sir?"

"What would you like . . . Elizabeth?" Tommy asked, shifting to her first name.

"I'm famished. I'm ready to order if that suits you," she said.

"Yes, fine," Tommy said, looking up at Mrs. Proctor. "I'm reliably informed that your rack of lamb, for *two*," he emphasized, glancing at Elizabeth, "is without peer. That would be our choice of the evening if it's available."

"The specialty of the house, Mr. Callahan. And your usual drink, Doctor Rossiter?"

"Yes, a nice mug of hot apple cider sounds just fine, thank you, Mrs. Proctor."

"And you, sir?"

"The same, please."

Mrs. Proctor walked toward the kitchen doors, and suddenly Tommy and Elizabeth were the only people in the room, and the only sound was the soft hiss from the compressed peat moss burning in the fireplace. They each started to speak at once and then both laughed nervously at the attempt.

"Ladies first?" Tommy offered.

"No, sir. *You* are the guest and *I* am the tour guide if I recall the invitation correctly. Who, what, where, when, and why, if you please?"

"My," Tommy exclaimed, exhaling a deep breath. "All right. As succinctly as possible. Who: Thomas Callahan; what: Major, United States Marine Corps; where: currently arriving for posting to the Royal Military Academy, Sandhurst; when: starting tomorrow if I can make it to the grounds; and why: because it sort of took over my life at an early age," he finished, taking another deep breath.

"That was succinct as claimed. And you answered all five questions," she smiled, the glow from the fireplace reflecting off her face. "And I know little more than your patient chart told me this afternoon."

"Right," he grinned. "Your turn."

"All right, you asked for it. Elizabeth Rossiter, Doctor of Medicine, resident at Prince Albert Hospital, Camberley, Surrey, England; two more years until completion of an orthopedic residency; and because my older brother said I'd never make it."

"*Touché*," Tommy said. "Now we both know little more than when we started. Let me revise the rules, please."

Elizabeth nodded, resting her chin on both hands with her elbows on the table. They were interrupted momentarily by Mrs. Proctor returning with two mugs of hot cider, a loaf of bread, and a small pottle of whipped butter.

326

"First, Elizabeth, let me sincerely apologize for my behavior and attitude this afternoon. There's no excuse and as to mistaking you for an orderly or a nurse, well, I plead guilty. It is after all, 1935, women have the vote, and I've previously known several female doctors and lawyers and everything in between, I suppose. It was rude of me to make such an assumption. Can you forgive me?"

"You've made a good start, but I'd like to hear more." She smiled coyly, her laughing eyes barely visible over her hands.

"My father's name is Thomas Callahan. My mother calls him Thomas, everyone else calls him Tom, and so I became Tommy at an early age and it stuck."

"I like Tommy."

"The name or the man?" he teased.

Again she smiled but didn't respond.

"And what would you prefer to be called? Besides *doctor*, Doctor?"

"My parents named me Elizabeth after my great-aunt. My mother called me Elizabeth, my father called me Lizzie, and my brothers called me . . . other things. I prefer—"

"Bess," Tommy interrupted.

She paused for a second and then shook her head.

"No one has ever called me Bess."

"Good. Then that's what I'll call you."

"Why Bess?" she asked.

"Something I recall from history. Elizabeth the First was often called Good Queen Bess, wasn't she?"

"Yes, she was. But we don't have the same royal lineage."

"My mother used to tell us that we were all of royal lineage," Tommy said.

"Not in England," Elizabeth laughed.

"Are you from Camberley?"

"Oh, no. Not even from England, although both my parents were from Manchester originally."

"And where do they live now?"

"New Zealand."

"*New Zealand!* I've got a brother living down there. He's been there since 1917 or '18, I think. Somewhere on the South Island, near Christchurch."

"Have you ever been there?" she asked.

"Nope. Most everywhere else, though. Why did you come to England, Bess?"

She paused at the sound of the new name, smiled again at Tommy, and continued.

"My father is a lawyer in Dunedin on the South Island. That's about a hundred miles south of Christchurch. It's mostly a Scottish community. I was born there shortly after they arrived. I have four older brothers, all born in Manchester, and one younger, born in New Zealand. I attended Canterbury University in Christchurch and was accepted to medical school here in England. Then Prince Albert Hospital took me into its residency program. Two more years, and I'll be certified in orthopedics and likely return to Dunedin."

"Here we are, then," Mrs. Proctor announced as a young girl of about sixteen came out carrying the tray of food. Conversation ceased while plates and a platter of lamb were arranged on the table, cider mugs were refilled, and Mrs. Proctor and the girl departed.

"This is truly a wonderful lamb, but don't ever tell Mrs. Proctor," Elizabeth said, leaning forward in a conspiratorial whisper, "that nothing on earth compares to a tasty New Zealand roasted lamb with mint sauce."

With the cast on his wrist and arm inhibiting his dexterity, Tommy awkwardly cut off a morsel of lamb and raised the fork to his mouth. "Your secret is safe with me, Doctor Rossiter," he said. "Ummm, if you're telling the truth, Bess, and if New Zealand lamb is better than this, then I can see why PJ stayed in Christchurch. This is marvelous."

"Take my word for it. Good as this tastes, it runs a distant second to a Kiwi lamb, properly cooked, of course."

"Is that a *home*-cooked lamb you're talking about?" he said, tasting the boiled potatoes.

"Of course."

"And you brought the secret with you?" he asked, giving away the game.

"Ah, yes, but these are *English* lambs. They're not the same."

"But surely you can do them more justice with Kiwi cooking? In your own kitchen, I mean."

Bess cut another piece of lamb and held it up on her fork in front of her.

"This really is good, isn't it," she said, dodging the question. "But perhaps, with a bit more practice, I could do it justice."

"If that's an invite to a home-cooked, Kiwi-method lamb, I accept your invitation."

"The Brits are right, you know?"

"About what?"

"You Yanks are brash and pushy."

"Only if we don't get our own way," he countered.

They were silent for a few moments, concentrating on their food. Then, pausing mid-bite and smiling, Tom said, "Bess, I would have never thought I would be so grateful for a broken wrist."

After dinner, Tommy walked Bess to the front door of the hotel, intending to see her to her car.

"Did you park close by?"

She laughed. "I have no car, Tommy. That's not part of a resident doctor's budget. I walked. It's not far, really."

"May I walk you home?"

"I'd like that."

Several blocks from the hotel, Bess turned into a smaller side street and stopped in front of her building.

"This is a large home for a single woman," Tommy observed.

"I have a small, cold-water flat on the third level, Major Callahan. Nothing so grand as it appears."

"I see. Third level, you say. That means fourth floor, right?"

"No, it means third level," she replied, smiling.

"But we are now standing on the ground level and one flight up is the first floor, right?"

"Right. And you thought we spoke a common language," she laughed.

"I've been disabused of that notion ever since I set foot on the ship in New York. Too many Brits on board."

"I've even found differences between here and New Zealand," she said.

"Bess," Tommy said, turning serious, "may I see you tomorrow evening?"

"I'm afraid not, Tommy, but thank you."

"Is my *tour* over?" he asked, grinning at her.

"The pound of flesh you mentioned earlier—at the hospital, I mean? We don't have twelve hour shifts. We have *thirty-six*-hour shifts, catching catnaps when and where we can. I'm on at six tomorrow morning and not off again until six Friday night."

"Man, and I thought the Corps got their money's worth. What happens to the patient who comes in during your thirty-fourth hour, when you're exhausted?"

"Oh, he dies," she grinned at him.

"And how long does this schedule continue?"

"For two years."

"*Every week?*"

"We have some breaks. In fact, I have two more shifts and then five days off. I was planning to travel down to Brighton and see if England really has any sun, but I've not yet made arrangements. It's probably too late to book anything. I never have time to properly plan."

Tommy reached out and took her hand.

"Thank you, Bess, for a lovely evening. You've made my welcome to England all the more special. I truly hope we can see one another again."

"You'll be pretty busy at Sandhurst. The new class will be arriving soon."

"You know about the academy?"

"I work the clinic there sometimes during the school year, to make a few extra pounds."

"And sleep? Is that part of your routine?"

"Not often. I enjoyed tonight, too, Tommy. Thank you for inviting me."

"Goodnight, Doctor Bess Rossiter. I'll be back."

"And a goodnight to you, Major Tommy Callahan. For a brash Yank, you show some promise."

Smiling at him again, she let herself in the door. Tommy stood, staring after her for a moment, then crossed the street, retracing his steps to the Star and Garter. Before turning the corner, he stopped to look back toward Elizabeth's flat. Then, whistling a tune, he walked on into the damp English night.

The following morning, after spending a restless night thinking about the woman who had just entered his life—a woman who was so different from Susan Prisman—Tommy telephoned the administration office at Sandhurst and arranged a late-morning appointment with Brigadier David McIntyre. The corporal who took the call said he had been told to expect Captain Callahan's arrival and that he had arranged a billet until the captain could make his own arrangements. Tommy thanked him and disconnected. Struggling to keep the cast on his left arm dry, he shaved and put on his tropical khaki uniform. Then he repacked his small bag and went downstairs for breakfast.

Mrs. Proctor was on duty again in the kitchen and greeted him at his table.

"Good morning, sir. A cup of coffee?"

"Yes, please, and some breakfast."

"What would you like, Mr. Callahan? Porridge? Bangers and eggs? Perhaps just some toast and marmite?"

"*Bangers?*" Tommy asked, screwing up his face.

Mrs. Proctor laughed. "Little sausages, sir. Quite nice, actually. We usually have them in the evening as bangers and mash—potatoes. We're a world apart over here, aren't we, sir?"

"A very pleasant world, Mrs. Proctor. Bangers and eggs it is, then. You were here last night when we left and again this morning. Quite long hours for English workers, it seems."

"Ah, well, me and Albert *own* the Star and Garter. We'd never work this hard for wages, I can tell you," she laughed. "I'll be just a moment with your coffee."

When she returned, pouring Tommy a cup of steaming black coffee, she stood by his table for a minute, observing his one-handed balancing act while he added a dash of cream and sugar and stirred the contents. Again he was the only occupant in the dining room.

"How did you come to meet Doctor Rossiter, if I might be so bold?" she asked.

Tommy held up his cast. "I fell off the train yesterday."

"Fortunate, that," she smiled.

"That's not how I saw it at first," he joked in return, "not until *after* I met the doctor. Do you know much about Doctor Rossiter?"

"She's been here in Camberley about six months, I think, only been here to dinner with a man once, afore you that is. A very pleasant woman. She worked wonders with my Sarah, so's I can't complain."

"She's got the '*touch*,'" he said, again holding up his cast. "Now, what can you tell me about the RMA?" he asked.

"A bunch of the aristocracy's 'ne'er-do-wells' if you ask me, the disdain evident in her voice. "Are you bound for there?"

"I am," he answered, sipping his coffee. "And a right proper 'ne'er-do-well' I'd be, too, I suppose," he said, smiling at her.

"Not a Yank, sir," she smiled. "You'll see what I mean. Well, I'd best be off to the kitchen. Bangers and eggs it is."

After Tommy had finished breakfast, a taxi driver parked down the street from the Star and Garter agreed to take him out to the academy for two and six. Tommy had yet to figure out the pounds, shillings, and pence, and simply held out a handful of coins.

"This one'll do, sir, 'alf a crown."

As they drove through the grounds, the area seemed absent of much activity, and Tommy assumed that the students had not yet arrived for the new term. At the administration building, he introduced himself to the corporal to whom he had spoken on the phone and asked if he could be shown to his quarters. After seeing the gold oak leaves on Tommy's uniform and apologizing to the major for mistaking him for a captain on the phone, the corporal summoned the brigadier's "batman" and directed him to escort Major Callahan to his quarters.

"Your batman is on a day trip to London, sir. He'll report as soon as he returns."

Tommy waited until the brigadier's batman had taken the one small suitcase and left the room to ask his question.

"Corporal, just what *is* a batman?"

"An orderly, sir," he replied. "An enlisted man who's assigned to look after senior officers—their needs and such. He'll do the whole kit and caboodle for ya, Major, right as rain."

"And you say I have such a person assigned to me?"

"Yes, sir. By all means, sir. The brigadier saw to it himself. Corporal Townsend is a good man, Major. He'll watch out for you, help you learn the ropes here at Sandhurst. Spent a bit of time in the states, he did, sir."

"Thank you, Corporal. I'll be back at one o'clock to meet with Brigadier McIntyre. I appreciate your help."

"Not a'tall, sir. My pleasure," he said, coming to attention as Tommy left the office.

After checking out his new digs, Tommy walked around the academy grounds, encountering very few people in the process. At ten minutes to one o'clock, he was back in Brigadier McIntyre's office foyer, sitting in a chair and flipping through a magazine, when the brigadier walked in with another gentleman. Recognizing McIntyre's florid face and upright military posture, Tommy stood.

"Good afternoon, Brigadier."

"Ah, yes, *Major* Callahan, you're early I see. We didn't expect you for another week or so. Welcome to Sandhurst, and congratulations on your promotion. We were expecting a captain."

"The commandant felt—"

"And rightfully so," the brigadier said. "Major, allow me to introduce Winston Churchill. Mr. Churchill is one of Sandhurst's illustrious alumni and will be our first guest speaker this coming term. Coincidental to your own instructional portfolio, he'll be speaking on the economic turmoil in Europe, especially Germany and Chancellor Hitler's proposed solutions."

Tommy put forth his hand to greet Churchill.

"It's my pleasure, sir. I've heard much about you."

"Callahan? Which state are you from, Major?" Churchill asked.

"Utah, sir. But I've lived all over the world since leaving there just before the last war."

"Your father wouldn't also be named Thomas Callahan, would he?"

"He would, sir. And I've heard my mother speak of you fondly."

A smile of recognition crossed Churchill's face and he nodded. "A *remarkable* woman, Brigadier," Churchill said, speaking to McIntyre. "Absolutely remarkable. And your parents are well?" he asked, looking back at Tommy.

"Quite well, sir."

"That's fine. Well, David," Churchill said to McIntyre, "I'd best be on my way. I'll be back on the eighteenth. It was good to meet you, Major Callahan. Please pass along my regards to your parents, and the best of good fortune to you here at the RMA."

"Thank you, sir. I'll inform my parents."

Churchill left and Brigadier McIntyre led Tommy into his office, where they took seats facing one another.

"How are you finding England, Major?"

"A lovely country, Brigadier. Apart from my clumsiness," he said, holding up his cast.

"Is that recent?"

"Yesterday, as I arrived in the village. I fell off the train, actually," Tommy said, a sheepish smile on his face.

"And you were well taken care of, I presume?"

"Yes, sir. At Prince Albert Hospital."

"Good, good," the older man nodded. "I presume also, Major, that you are wondering why in the world an old British goat would seek an American marine instructor at Sandhurst," he smiled.

"It *had* crossed my mind, sir."

"Do you know General Archibald Vandegrift?"

"I've not had the pleasure of serving under the general, but I've met him in Washington, at marine headquarters."

"He and I were comrades-in-arms in the Great War, so you see. Through him, I've kept track of your career. It was through Archie that I learned of your posting to Stanford, your doctoral studies in economics, and your assignment to marine headquarters."

Tommy remained silent, but his face still reflected puzzlement. McIntyre watched him for a moment and then nodded.

"That still doesn't answer the question, does it, Major? I don't know that there is an answer, actually. I've lived for many years under the curse of my son's belligerency. His conflict with you was not the first unpleasant incident . . . or the last. But because you were the first person to really stand up to him and actually best him, I had hoped that perhaps he would take a lesson from the experience. Unfortunately, he didn't." McIntyre paused before adding, "He was killed some three years ago in a row in a pub on the east end of London. Shameful waste, that," the old man said, shaking his head.

"I'm very sorry, Brigadier. I've regretted that incident myself. It was not my finest hour," Tommy said.

"Nevertheless, we're here now, and we shall make the best of it, shan't we?" McIntyre said, brightening a little.

"Indeed, sir. Though I'm not entirely sure what's expected of me, I'm honored to be here. I've heard a lot about Sandhurst."

"The history of the academy dates back to the 1700s. Actually, we have two colleges—the RMA at Woolwich, where we train engineers and artillery officers, and here at Sandhurst, where we produce the world's finest infantry and cavalry officers—with the possible exception of the American Marines, of course," he laughed.

"Thank you, sir," Tommy said, waiting for the British officer to say more.

"Have you thought about your syllabus for the coming term?"

Tommy laughed out loud. "Nothing else, Brigadier, since receiving the assignment. I'm still stumped."

"I'm sure it will come to you. Actually, this first term, your schedule will be light—only two classes, three times a week. Perhaps some of the other time you could sit in on a couple of other lectures and see how we do things here. I don't mean to direct your instructional methods, but our lads are used to a different set of rules, I presume. However," he said, using his arms to assist in rising from his chair, "the term doesn't begin for nearly three weeks. Plenty of time to get 'squared away' I believe is the term General Vandegrift used. Marine jargon I would suspect," he smiled. "Take some of that time to see the countryside, learn a bit about the mother country, so to speak."

Following McIntyre's lead, Tommy stood immediately.

"Actually, my 'mother country,' sir, is across the Irish Sea," he laughed.

"We'll have some Irish lads in the class for certain. Oh, one more thing, Major. How might your parents have met Winnie? Mr. Churchill, I mean?"

Tommy stroked his chin for a moment, delaying.

"Sir, as I understand the story, my mother met with Mr. Churchill and Prime Minister Lloyd-George some years ago."

"And your father was with them?"

"No, sir. They met to talk *about* my father."

It was McIntyre's turn to look puzzled.

"Sir," Tommy began, taking a deep breath, "it's not an admirable family story. When you met my father in Wyoming in 1923, it had been about three years since his release from Portlaoise Prison in Ireland."

"I thought he was from America."

"He is, sir, but he was born in Ireland and became involved in providing arms and ammunition to the IRA before the Free State was formed. He was captured and sentenced to fifteen years in prison. My mother met with the prime minister and Mr. Churchill to demand his release."

"*Demand?*" McIntyre said.

Tommy smiled. "All I know, sir, is that my father served slightly less than a year and was out of prison within six weeks after my mother's visit. Mr. Churchill's comments this morning have convinced me that my mother did, in fact, *demand* my father's release. Successfully, it would seem."

McIntyre's eyebrows rose. "As Winnie said, she must indeed be a remarkable woman."

"She is that, sir. If that will be all, Brigadier?"

"Yes, of course. We'll convene a staff meeting of instructors on the fourteenth. Corporal Hendriks will provide you with all the information you need, and your batman, Corporal Townsend—don't hesitate to ask his assistance. He'll become invaluable to you."

"I'm not used to having a batman, sir. It's not standard Marine Corps issue," Tommy laughed.

"Well, then, enjoy it, son. A fine old British custom. Good to see you again. You have an excellent career ahead of you, it would seem. And regarding your syllabus, take a hint from Winnie—study a bit of Hitler's work in Germany. The economic conditions there are providing fertile ground for his ideas, and Winnie is convinced the Germans are moving toward a war footing. Chancellor Hitler is taking advantage of the political and economic situation to further his military objectives, and the German people are seemingly buying the whole lot. It's a situation that will bear some watching."

Tommy returned to his quarters and found that Corporal Townsend had arrived. The sandy-haired, slightly built young man was unpacking Tommy's luggage, which had arrived that morning from Southampton. He quickly came to attention as Tommy entered the room.

"A good morning to you, sir," Townsend said.

"And to you, Corporal. I'm Thomas Callahan; good to meet you," Tommy said, extending his hand. "I guess we'll be working together."

"As you wish, sir," Townsend replied, tentatively accepting Tommy's hand. "I took the liberty of unpacking your things. Will you be maintaining your quarters here on the grounds or would you prefer I seek accommodations elsewhere in the community?"

"I think here will do fine for the present, Corporal."

"Right. Is there anything I can do for you, Major Callahan, to help you settle in?"

Tommy thought for a moment, considering the two-plus weeks he had free until the term commenced and thinking about Bess's comment about her having five days off.

"Corp, what do you know about obtaining accommodations for a brief holiday in Brighton?" he smiled.

"Leave it to me, sir. When, and for how long?"

"Monday through Friday of next week. *Two*, separate rooms, Corporal."

"I understand, sir."

"And first-class accommodations, if you please," Tommy added.

"A lady is it then, sir?" Townsend asked.

"A recuperative trip to the English seashore with my doctor," Tommy replied, holding up his cast and smiling broadly.

Monday morning at seven o'clock, Tommy drove his new MG Roadster, British racing green in color, to the apartment building where he had left Bess Rossiter the previous Wednesday. As Corporal Hendriks had said, Corporal Townsend was indeed very resourceful. He had immediately proven himself invaluable by obtaining, on short notice, two adjoining rooms at the Fluted Unicorn, a small seaside bed-and-breakfast establishment in Brighton. Then Tommy had penned a note to Bess and asked Corporal Townsend to deliver it to Prince Albert Hospital. Bess telephoned her reply the following day, accepting Tommy's invitation. After writing the note and sending it off, Tommy had wondered at his boldness. When Doctor Rossiter called to say she thought the idea was smashing, he breathed a sigh of relief. The idea of spending nearly a week with her was very intriguing.

He had barely parked the car and stepped out onto the street when she appeared in the front door, briskly coming down the several steps, carrying a single, smallish bag.

"Five days, *one* bag? You *are* an unusual woman," he teased.

"I'm counting on sunshine," she said, crossing her fingers.

He opened the door, and she entered the low, open-topped sports car, doing so gracefully by sitting sideways on the passenger seat and simply pivoting her legs into the car. After putting her bag into the boot, Tommy squeezed himself into the driver's seat.

"This may take some getting used to," he said. "I feel like *you* should be driving from over there. I suppose most Americans have the same reaction. My father said he had a hard time adjusting to driving on the left-hand side of the road in New Zealand, and those roundabouts you insert at each road crossing were nearly the death of him. He said you could spend an hour driving round and round the circle, looking for a way out."

Tommy started the engine and slowly pulled onto the road, looking both ways twice at the joining of Bess's small street with the main thoroughfare. He shifted gingerly, using only his fingers and thumb, which Bess had left as mobile as she could when casting his wrist.

"A lovely motorcar," Bess said, wrapping a scarf around her hair. "Did you borrow it from someone at the academy?"

"Nope. My *batman*—I don't think I like that term—has proven very helpful, in all respects. He and I took the train into London and bought it on Saturday."

"He sounds very helpful, and rich, too," she smiled.

Before he realized Bess was making a joke, Tommy almost said he had used his own money, but catching himself, he said instead, "Oh, yes, very rich, indeed."

Bess laughed and said, "When he brought me your note, he said you seemed like a *right enough bloke*, to use his words."

"Were you surprised?" Tommy asked, glancing at her as the roadster gathered speed and Tommy shifted into high.

"Quite."

"Perhaps I should have asked, were you *pleased?*"

Bess smiled back at him, the wind blowing wisps of hair from beneath the scarf.

"I'm here, Major."

"So you are. Five whole days . . . in the sun, as you predicted."

"We can always hope."

The good news was that it didn't rain until late afternoon, after they had arrived at the Fluted Unicorn. Tommy sensed that Bess was a bit apprehensive about the arrangements, but she seemed to relax when what Tommy had promised in his note proved true—that they would each have their own room.

Her room overlooked the ocean and had a small fireplace along one wall. Tommy's, across the hall rather than adjoining, had a wonderful view of the English countryside and the small village of Brighton—a resort that had been a traditional holiday spot ever since the Prince of Wales, who later became King George IV, had visited it over a century earlier.

After settling into their rooms and borrowing a large umbrella that the innkeeper referred to as a *brolly,* the couple walked two blocks to a tavern called the Pig's Snout. Tommy made a remark about the unappetizing name, but Bess said that her associates had assured her it was not to be missed. And this time, she said, roast beef and not lamb was the main fare.

Unlike the Star and Garter, the Pig's Snout was full of people, and several young girls scurried about tending to the needs of their customers. Tommy and Bess ordered the roast, boiled potatoes, and creamed cabbage, recommended by their waitress.

"Would you care to choose from our wine list, sir?" the girl asked.

"Bess," Tommy said, "no work tomorrow. Have you a favorite dinner wine?"

"I think I'll just have cider again, thank you," she replied to the waitress.

Tommy looked at her for a moment and nodded to the waitress, holding up two fingers.

"I'm sorry, Tommy, I didn't mean to imply that *you* shouldn't have a glass of wine," Bess said.

"It's all right. Actually, I rarely have wine and even then, only with dinner. Cider is fine. So," he smiled brightly, "here we are, and you've got five full days with no patients, no thirty-six-hour shifts, and I have almost three weeks until the next term starts."

"Since you mentioned it, how did it go at the academy?"

"Great. They've done their best to make me feel welcome. I met Winston Churchill the first day."

"Really?" she said. "What's he like?"

"Friendly enough, I guess. We spoke for only a few minutes. He's an old associate of Brigadier McIntyre's. He said they were fellow lieutenant colonels in France during the Great War."

Tommy consciously decided not to tell Bess that Churchill had also met his mother some years ago, feeling that it would invoke the expected question, "Why?"

The proximity of other people and bustling waitresses combined to keep the dinner conversation light. On the walk back to the hotel, in an attempt to stay dry beneath the single *brolly,* Bess tucked her arm into Tommy's, and they walked close together.

"Before we left for dinner, the hotel clerk told me that there was a picture show in town. It's either the hotel lobby or the film," Bess said, squeezing Tommy's arm.

"The film it is," he said. "Where is it playing?"

"Two blocks past the hotel, the man said. Can't miss it."

"Let's do it," he said, enjoying Dr. Rossiter's proximity as they walked through the steady rainfall.

A small cluster of people stood outside the theater,

huddled beneath the small marquee that read *A Gathering Storm*. Tommy was surprised to see the title but managed to keep his face calm.

"That's ten years old. Are you sure you want to see that old film, Bess?" Tommy asked.

"I've never seen it," she replied. "Have you?"

"I'm not sure," Tommy lied, knowing full well it was his sister, Teresa's, first starring role in Hollywood.

"It's still the only alternative to the hotel lobby and a couple of old gents with cigars," she laughed.

"Right," Tommy said, stepping to the box office and purchasing two tickets.

They found seats several rows from the back, and, in a few minutes, the newsreel came on showing hundreds of workers in Germany rioting outside a closed steel factory. Other story clips from England filled the remainder of the news, and then the film began. When the name Teresa Callahan appeared on the screen, Bess leaned closer to Tommy and said, "I'm meeting Callahans everywhere, it seems." Tommy just smiled and nodded.

When they emerged from the theater nearly two hours later, the rain had stopped, and they strolled along a rain-wet pathway leading to the ocean wall that fronted a portion of Brighton.

"I felt so sorry for Abigail," Bess said. "All she wanted to do was keep her promise to her father. And look at all she lost."

"It was just a movie, Bess," Tommy said, putting his arm around her and pulling her closer as they walked.

"But it was like life, don't you think? Many of us are unable to keep our promises, and it's not always our fault. Circumstances sometimes combine to prevent us from doing what we know we should."

"Maybe it works the other way, too. Take you for instance. You said you became a doctor because your brother said you couldn't."

"Oh, that was just a family rivalry. He didn't mean it. Maybe you're really thinking about yourself?"

Tommy thought silently for several moments about why he had originally joined the Marine Corps and how it had ultimately shaped his life.

"We take different paths, I suppose, Bess, perhaps as a result of what others wanted or didn't want for us. Take that actress, for instance," he said, smiling at her. "What did you think of her?"

"A beautiful woman, but more than that. You could almost see her soul. She was beautiful *inside*, if you know what I mean."

"I do. But, of course, she's a Callahan," he laughed.

"Right," Bess laughed in return. "And what about *your* soul, Major Callahan? Is it beautiful, too?"

"Marines don't have souls, Doctor Rossiter. They're not standard issue, I'm afraid. And if they were, they would probably need to be polished and readied for inspection twice each month."

"C'mon, no more evasion, if you please. What *do* you believe, Tommy?" Bess asked as they continued walking along the ocean front.

"About what?"

"About things, people, medicine, war, the hereafter, love . . . anything that matters in this life."

"Introduction to philosophy, you mean?"

"I *mean* . . . what do you *believe?*" she repeated.

He stopped walking and turned to face her, lifting her chin so that she faced him directly. He leaned down and tenderly kissed her lips, then pulled his face back and looked into her eyes.

"I believe that you are an extraordinary woman, Elizabeth Rossiter, and that I've never met anyone quite like you. I believe that you are beautiful, intelligent, conscientious, caring, spontaneous . . . and that you have *excellent* taste in men," he added.

"Wow! Flattery *and* conceit in one sentence. I'm impressed."

"By the kiss or by the words?" he teased. "Or would you prefer a chance for a second opinion?"

Instead of answering, Bess turned and started walking again, pulling Tommy along by wrapping her arm inside his. They walked for a couple of minutes, saying nothing but watching the cluster of stars that occasionally broke through the intermittent cloud cover and enjoying the sound of the waves. At the end of the walkway, they turned inland and headed back toward the hotel.

Entering the lobby, Bess stifled a laugh at the sight of two elderly men, who were seated in front of the fire in a dense haze of cigar smoke. Both men looked up at the younger couple and then resumed their conversation.

"I think I'd best get some sleep, Tommy. I got off shift this morning at six, just before you picked me up. Sunshine tomorrow, I'm sure of it," she smiled.

They walked up the staircase and stopped in front of Bess's room. With only a slight hesitation, Tommy leaned to kiss her again, holding her cheek in his hand.

"As they say, you Yanks really are a brash lot," she said, a slight smile on her lips.

"I guess we are, especially with a beautiful woman. Oh, and regarding what I believe. I believe much the same way Abigail did in the film tonight. We *do* have an obligation to honor our promises and to do right by others. In fact, Abigail learned that from me."

"Oh, *really?*" Bess said, her tone mocking.

"Yes, really," he smiled. "You see, Teresa Callahan, *Abigail*, is my younger sister. My twin sister actually. I taught her everything she knows, though she probably wouldn't agree."

"You're joking," Bess said, her sleepiness suddenly gone.

"I seldom joke about anything to do with Teresa. Her married name is Stromberg, and she has three children."

"Why didn't you tell me during the movie?"

"I didn't think it was important," he said.

"Of course it's important," Bess said, punching his arm.

"Maybe that's not quite true," he laughed. "I wanted to see if you liked the movie and the actress before committing myself."

"How devious. If I'd said the film was terrible and the actress dreadful, you'd never have told me she was your sister, would you?"

"Probably not," he admitted. "See you for breakfast?"

"Not too early. These lazy mornings are quite rare. When I can sleep in, that is."

"Goodnight, Bess. Thank you for coming."

"Other than the rain, it's been perfect, Tommy," she said, inserting the skeleton key into the lock while Tommy stood close behind her. She opened the door and then turned quickly, kissing him lightly on the lips, smiling at him, and then just as quickly stepping inside and closing the door behind her.

Inside her room, Doctor Elizabeth Rossiter leaned against the door frame and breathed deeply, clutching her hands against her chest.

"This *cannot* work, Lizzie," she said softly to herself.

"You're on a path to nothing but heartache, and you've got to get control of yourself and stop it while there's still time."

She undressed, pulled on a heavy, flannel nightgown and climbed between the cold sheets. She pulled the down comforter up around her neck and turned on her side so she could look out the small window toward the ocean.

"A second opinion he wants," she chuckled. "Hmmmph."

⊰⊱

At eight o'clock sharp, Bess was roused from a deep sleep by a gentle but persistent knock on her door. She rose, pulled on a bathrobe and slippers, and went to the door.

"Yes, who is it?"

"Breakfast call," a familiar voice called out.

"Tommy, I'm not properly dressed."

"Nevertheless, bangers, eggs, and hot chocolate are standing here on a tray waiting for someone to devour them."

Bess cracked open the door and peeked out. Tommy stood in the hall behind a small wheeled cart and a tray containing several dishes of food, cups and saucers, and a small silver pitcher.

"Thomas Callahan," she laughed in spite of herself, "a man is supposed to know that a woman needs time to herself in the morning."

"I could leave the tray, ma'am," he grinned.

"Five minutes, Major Callahan, if you please."

"The hot chocolate will get cold."

"Too bad. You should have thought of that before launching your assault. Five minutes I said, and I mean it."

"Yes, ma'am," he replied. "I'll just nibble out here in the hallway. Oh, and by the way, the sun is out."

"You're impossible," she said, closing the door.

In about three minutes, a touch of lipstick on, her hair hastily combed, and her robe adjusted properly, Bess reopened the door . . . to an empty hallway. She looked up and down but there was no sign of Tommy. Then she stepped across the hallway and knocked lightly on his door.

"Yes, who is it?"

"Tommy," she said, looking about to see if anyone was in the hallway to see her in her robe, knocking on a man's door, "open up this minute."

The door opened and Bess quickly stepped in to see that the food had been placed on a small table next to the window.

"Breakfast is served, madam," he said, closing the door. "It's not often I have a beautiful lady demanding entry into my room so early in the morning."

"Even with only one good arm, you're a handful, Thomas Callahan."

"I hope so, Bess," he said, sliding the chair back for her to take a seat. "And by the way, you look absolutely beautiful this morning. And I need no second opinion."

On Friday morning, after spending four days in Brighton, they checked out of the hotel, loaded the car with their few possessions, and drove away from the seaside village. The weather had cooperated for the final three days, and they had enjoyed their stay. On one of the mornings, with the sun out, they even ventured to go swimming in the ocean. Given that all the other people on the beach were bundled in sweaters and jackets against the coolness of the breeze, they should have known better. In a show of bravery, and holding his cast out of the water, Tommy took a brief plunge in the frigid water but quickly came sputtering back to shore, shivering uncontrollably. They'd only been able to tolerate an hour on the beach, during which they kept themselves swathed in towels, trying to imagine the air was getting warmer.

During their stay in Brighton, they did manage to get in two picnics, one horseback ride, and even a short trip out into the English Channel, made possible when Tommy chartered a small fishing boat, complete with a two-man crew.

On the last night of their holiday, following dinner and a long walk, they had paused in the darkness before going into the hotel. With Bess leaning against a tree, Tommy had kissed her softly, then more urgently. Yielding to the moment, Bess at first responded ardently, but then suddenly broke off their embrace and pushed past Tommy toward the hotel entrance. It provided an awkward moment, and knowing he'd somehow offended Bess, Tommy followed her.

He caught her inside the hotel, where a number of people sitting in the lobby turned to look at them. Taking Bess's arm, Tommy turned her toward him. Not wishing to be overheard, he said quietly, "What is it? Are you all right?"

Glancing at the hotel guests who were staring at them, Bess said nothing but shook her head. Then she pulled out of his grasp and quickly went up the stairs to her room.

Wondering what had happened, Tommy could only stare after her.

Bess was quiet during most of the drive home, responding to Tommy's questions or comments, but remaining silently contemplative the rest of the time. As they neared

351

the village of Camberley, Tommy asked if she would like to stop at the Star and Garter for dinner before going home.

"I don't think so, Tommy. I've got to wash my hair, finish a few things, and get ready for another shift starting at six tomorrow morning."

He drove straight to her apartment where he lifted her bag out of the boot and saw her to the door as he had the first night he had walked her home.

"Tommy," she said, her voice sounding hesitant and tentative, "I've had a wonderful time this week, truly. But perhaps we should take time to consider where we're headed."

"I'm headed right here, every chance I get, Bess. What do you mean?"

"Well, this is all so sudden. I've still got two years of long hours and hard study if I'm to get through this residency."

"I don't mean to interfere with that, Bess. What do you *really* mean," he asked.

She looked directly at his face, then lowered her eyes.

"That *is* what I mean, Tommy. I've had a good time, but I can't, uh, I just . . ."

"Are you telling me you don't want to see me anymore, Bess? I thought we had a good time and liked each other. If it's about that kiss, I—"

"It's not that. At least not *only* that," Bess said. He could see that she was struggling to say what she was feeling, but the implications did not seem to be favorable.

"I'm tired. I really need to get upstairs. Please understand."

"Bess, if you want the truth, I don't understand at all."

"I'm sorry, Tommy. Really. We're from two different worlds. I've been thinking about it all the way home. Since the first day, actually. I *do* like you, but—"

"Two *countries*, Bess, not two worlds. And I admire your

country and its people. My brother even lives there, and he married a Kiwi."

"But I think we're moving in two different directions . . . in life, I mean."

"I really don't understand that. But if that's what you really want, Bess, I'll not call you again, but it doesn't make sense."

Again she glanced at him, and he could see the glistening in her eyes as she appeared to fight off the tears. She touched his cheek with her hand and then opened the front door and quickly stepped inside. After the door closed, Tommy stood there for a moment before returning to his car, starting the engine, and driving down the street. On impulse, he stopped at the Star and Garter and went inside, where he was met by Mrs. Proctor.

"Good evening, Mr. Callahan. Just one for dinner tonight?"

"Just one, Mrs. Proctor. And I'll have a bottle of your best red wine if you please."

"Certainly, sir. I'll bring it right out."

21

In late September 1935, The Royal Military Academy at Sandhurst commenced a new term, and Winston Churchill gave the opening address. Since 1933, when Adolph Hitler first came to power as chancellor of Germany, Churchill had been voicing a warning to the British people about Hitler and his intentions, but many of those in power, including some in his own conservative party, pooh-poohed Churchill's concerns, dismissing his warnings and calling him a warmonger.

Major Thomas Callahan listened intently while Churchill recounted the history of European nations and their ascendancy and decline. The quest for economic power, Churchill admonished those present—some new students as young as sixteen—was the driving force in the modern world, and to achieve or retain such power, nations had gone and would go to war.

Churchill's concluding remarks struck Tommy as prophetic in that he strongly advocated building a superior base of air power to supplement the ground soldier. Sandhurst, long a bastion of infantry training, had traditionally given little credence to the importance of air power. Churchill, one of Sandhurst's own, was now supporting the mission of the Royal Air Force, and Tommy smiled to himself at the cool, provincial reception his message was receiving.

After the opening exercises concluded, a small reception was hosted by Brigadier McIntyre for guests and members of the faculty. Standing in a small cluster of officers, Churchill saw Tommy across the room.

"Ah, Major Callahan," Churchill said, waving him over to join the group. "Please be good enough to join us if you will. Gentlemen, this is Major Thomas Callahan, recently seconded to Sandhurst from the United States Marine Corps. Major Callahan will be instructing our young cadets about economic warfare in the modern age."

Several field grade officers shook hands with Tommy, and a lieutenant colonel from the Royal Fusiliers said, "Major Callahan, we were just discussing Mr. Churchill's advocacy of air power. How does the American Marine Corps view his proposition?"

"Quite favorably, I think, sir. It's going to be essential in the order of battle in any large-scale future engagement."

"That's a rather definitive statement for an unproven and often unreliable component of modern warfare."

Tommy glanced at Churchill, who was listening intently.

"Colonel, General Mitchell of the American Army proved, in 1925 I think, that airpower can disable the strongest battleship. In '26 and '27, I participated in amphibious landing exercises in Hawaii, part of our overall strategy for a hypothetical engagement in the Pacific against a well-entrenched foe, bunkered down on one of the islands. We quickly saw that a landing force from seaward has no hope of establishing a beachhead against an enemy with superior airpower."

"Balderdash, Major," the lieutenant colonel continued.

"Give me a finely tuned regiment of artillery, and I'll keep your ships well back and your men off the beaches."

"Yes, sir," Tommy nodded agreement. "But if *my* airpower has already destroyed *your* artillery, then I'll storm ashore and capture every fortified position you hold, using airplanes to keep your nose in the dirt while I do it."

"Is this is the view of the Marine Corps, and is that what you'll be teaching here at Sandhurst? Airpower?"

"No, sir. My role is not that of a military strategist or tactical operations instructor. As Mr. Churchill said, economic warfare, especially preliminary to actual combat, is the essence of military preparedness. That's the concept I hope to explore with your students."

"And *that*, gentlemen," Churchill interjected, "is exactly what Mr. Hitler is accomplishing in Germany at this very moment, with the acquiescence of our own government, I might add."

"Good lord, Winston," the lieutenant colonel sighed, "let's not get on that subject again, if you please. The prime minister has assured us Hitler is only trying to bring some prosperity back to Germany. Can't blame the man for that, even if he was only a corporal in the last war."

"Mark my words, Johnny, the Hun will be back, and his ships, tanks, and steel factories will be of the finest quality. And his *airpower* will be second to none . . . including the RAF, unless we wake up to the threat."

"I don't agree, Winston, but, there you are. Major," he said, turning his attention back to Tommy, "am I correct that you served in the last war also? Doing what, specifically?"

"Nothing important, Colonel. I was only a corporal," Tommy replied.

Churchill coughed a bit too much, just as Brigadier

McIntyre joined the group and quickly moved to defuse the argument.

"Gentlemen," McIntyre said, "with the advent of the air arm, perhaps our traditional division of engineers and artillery over at 'the shop' in Woolwich, and infantry and cavalry here at Sandhurst will have to be supplemented by a third RMA for fliers, eh, what? What say we adjourn to the drawing room for a bit of brandy and cigars?"

"Finest suggestion all afternoon, David. You've saved the day again," Churchill said, stepping away with McIntyre and inclining his head for Tommy to join them.

"You've got a solid head on your young shoulders, Major. My compliments," Churchill whispered to Tommy. "What was your last assignment?"

"Sir, I was executive officer in Pacific Area War Plans, Marine Headquarters, Washington."

"David, you need to extract every bit of wisdom the marines can provide it would seem. I'd say this young man has a grasp of *total* warfare, including economic preparedness and the use of all of the military elements," he said as they crossed the room.

In late November, Tom and Katrina braved the fresh snow in Salt Lake and walked the several blocks to Church headquarters to keep an appointment with President Heber J. Grant. On several previous occasions, the President had called them in to discuss the needs of transients and local unemployed workers and the status of Seagull Inn. This visit, however, was out of the ordinary in that rather than calling a committee meeting, President Grant's executive secretary had called and scheduled an individual appointment with Brother and Sister Callahan.

They followed the young man toward President Grant's office where President Grant came forward and greeted them with a warm handshake and a hearty welcome.

"I believe you know President Harold B. Lee, president of the Pioneer Stake."

"I do, sir. We've met on several occasions. Good morning, President Lee. May I introduce my wife, Katrina Callahan."

"I've attended several of your concerts, Sister Callahan. It's a pleasure to meet you in person," Lee said.

"Well, then, shall we all have a seat?" President Grant said, gesturing to the chairs in front of his desk. "Brother Callahan, perhaps you are aware of the fine work the Pioneer Stake has been doing providing welfare assistance to the members of the stake."

"I am, President Grant. Brother Lee has even helped us over some rough times at Seagull Inn, occasionally providing vegetables from his stake farm."

"Brother Callahan, you know more than most that we are living in very difficult times. The work you and Sister Callahan have done to aid those in need has been invaluable. All across the country caring people such as yourselves have opened their doors and, more importantly, their hearts, to the destitute, the homeless, and the hungry. The Lord has told us time and again to care for His poor. It is now our intention to formalize that effort, and to accomplish our objectives we have taken a leaf out of Pioneer Stake's handbook, so thoughtfully and prayerfully developed by President Lee. We've asked you in to seek your help in that regard."

"Whatever we can do, President," Tom replied.

"Good, very good. During our April conference next year, we intend to announce the formation of a new Churchwide welfare program, called the Church Security

Plan. It will be a full-scale operation, providing food, clothing, and even employment training, under the direction of
Brother Lee, who has been called as the first managing
director.[13] He has asked that you be called to work with him
as director of operations. Your work has become widely
known, Brother Callahan, and the Lord has need of your
skills," President Grant said, peering over his glasses at Tom.

"President Grant, Brother Lee, I should remind you that
I've recently turned sixty, and I'm not as young and ener-
getic as I used to be."

"I see," Grant said, a slight scowl crossing his face. "Now
that *could* be a problem," he continued, looking toward
President Lee. "What do you think, Brother Lee? Is Brother
Callahan too young and inexperienced for the job?"

"Well, it is a concern, but we could bring him along
slowly, President, until he learns the ropes," President Lee
replied, going along with President Grant's joke.

"Point taken, President," Tom laughed.

"In all seriousness, Brother Callahan, I learned as a
young man that in the Lord's work, it's nearly impossible to
ever consider yourself too old to serve. Generally, and certainly in this case," he smiled, "the person extending the
call is far older. But the Lord needs you, Brother Callahan,
and I'm calling you to serve as the director of operations for
the Church Security Plan, working under the direction of
Brother Lee."

Tom looked at Katrina who smiled back at her husband,
extending her support.

"President Grant, I'd be honored to serve with President
Lee. And thank you, Brother Lee, for requesting me to work
with you."

"Good, then it's settled. Please keep this meeting confidential until the announcement is made at conference. In

the meantime, I believe Brother Lee will want to initiate some planning meetings." President Grant stood. "Welcome to the beginning of a new era, Brother Callahan. It is well overdue that we care for the needs of our people during this difficult time. And Sister Callahan, thank you for supporting your husband in his efforts. I have heard some rumor of your plans to retire to the balmy Hawaiian Islands. But the Lord doesn't always arrange things as we would see fit, does He?"

"No, President," Katrina said, "but He always arranges them the way they *should* be."

"Indeed, He does," Grant replied.

Two weeks before Christmas, Tommy received a letter from his brother, PJ, with the recently released New Zealand airmail stamp in the upper right-hand corner. Six months earlier, in the summer of 1935, Pan American's new *Clipper* had opened commercial air routes to the Far East and had begun carrying mail across the Atlantic to Europe. Within a year, letters that had previously taken three months to transit from New Zealand to England by ship through the Panama Canal were making the trip in three or four weeks. The world was getting smaller each year, it seemed.

PJ's letter was full of family news, including details of his oldest son's riding exploits. At fifteen, Clinton Callahan had taken the Canterbury equestrian trials championship, and PJ took the opportunity to skite[14] a bit about his oldest son. But it was the brief comment toward the end of the letter that caught Tommy's full attention. He read PJ's statement several times, finally understanding what had eluded him ever since Bess had declared they should no longer see one another.

. . . regarding the young woman you mentioned in your last letter, Elizabeth Rossiter, I do indeed know the family. In fact I met her father, Trevor Rossiter, some months ago at a gathering of priesthood leaders in Christchurch. He's been the branch president in Dunedin for well over ten years, and . . .

Tommy set the letter on the table and stood by the window of his quarters, gazing out at the parade ground and the cadets forming up for evening assembly.

What had she asked me in Brighton . . . What do you believe, Tommy? Clearly that's the problem Bess was having with me. Not knowing where I stand on religion, she was trying to give me an opening to discuss my beliefs and convictions. She was trying to do some missionary work on me.

Suddenly Tommy was sure of it. Bess felt she couldn't pursue a relationship with a man who had no interest in her way of life. Any committed LDS woman would hesitate to allow herself to fall in love with a nonmember. Even his mom had initially rejected his father for the same reason.

He shook his head as he remembered what had happened—his drinking coffee, offering Bess a glass of wine, and his not responding when she asked him what was important to him in life. There was no way she could have known that he had any knowledge of Mormons—that he was himself a Mormon! He smiled to himself. He couldn't blame her. What were the odds of meeting another Mormon in England, outside of actual Church activities? Especially if that man was a career marine?

Thinking about what Elizabeth had done, Tommy found all the more reason to admire her, for sticking to her convictions, in spite of the fact that she was strongly attracted to him. Was she strongly attracted to him? he wondered. Of course she was, he assured himself. Why else had she responded so warmly to him at first?

Since September and their return from their trip together, Tommy had written two brief notes to Bess and mailed them to the hospital. Only one had been answered, and that only to thank him again for his generosity in their holiday in Brighton. She had not been unkind, but it had been clear—she was focused on completing her residency and then returning to New Zealand. There was nothing to indicate any further interest on her part in seeing him.

Tommy left his apartment, taking the steps to the lower level two at a time. He hurried across the quadrant toward the officers' dining hall, continuing around the side of the building to the enlisted side of the facility. He stopped two sergeants who were entering and asked them to please locate Corporal Townsend. In a few moments, Townsend came outside.

"Sir, may I be of assistance this evening?"

"Sorry to interrupt your tea, Corporal, but I need you to do something for me."

"At your service, sir."

Tommy explained his request and Corporal Townsend nodded compliance.

"I'll get on it immediately, sir. Shouldn't be too difficult, actually. I have a suspicion it will be down to Aldershot though."

"That'll be fine, Corporal. Thanks, and my apologies again."

"Not to worry, sir," Townsend said, coming to attention and saluting.

The Sunday before Christmas, Tommy was wearing a civilian suit and tie and was on the road in his MG just after 7:00 A.M. He drove the fifteen or so miles to Aldershot where he located the address Corporal Townsend had written down. It was a small union hall with a couple of offices downstairs and an upstairs meeting room. Tommy entered the building and climbed the creaky wooden stairs to the second level. Opening the door and stepping into the dimly lit room, he saw two younger men who stopped what they were doing and turned to face him. Instantly, Tommy knew he was in the right place.

"Good morning," the shorter of the two men said. "Can we help you?"

"Maybe I can help you," Tommy smiled. "What time does your service start?"

"At eight-thirty, sir. Will you be joining us this morning?"

"I will, after I help you sweep up. Looks like someone had a party in here last night."

"They did," the young man laughed. "Every Saturday night the worker's union has a dance and a booze-up. Sunday morning we collect the beer bottles and sweep up the mess before services. We're glad you could join us. I'm Elder McTavish from Glasgow, and this is Elder Honeycutt from Ephraim, Utah. Are you familiar with the LDS Church, sir?"

"Yes, I am, Elder McTavish," Tommy said. He hesitated a moment, then added, "But I've been away for a while. Thomas Callahan is my name."

"You're most welcome here, Brother Callahan. The members should start arriving soon. Brother Albert usually comes early to help us clean up. We've got about thirty members in the Aldershot Branch, but they come from several surrounding villages."

"Well, let's get cleaning, what say?"

By eight-twenty, two dozen or so people had gathered,

most of whom greeted Tommy and welcomed him to their branch. Christmas greetings were exchanged by the adult members, and the children ran around the room, their excitement at the approaching holiday evident. Finally, Elder McTavish asked the members to be seated so they could begin their service. Tommy sat on the far side of the room toward the back, away from the entrance.

At eight-thirty, Elder Honeycutt opened the meeting, and the small congregation began to sing "Joy to the World." As they completed the second verse, the door opened and Elizabeth Rossiter quietly entered, immediately followed by a man and woman in their forties, accompanied by three children. Attempting to keep their children quiet, the couple took vacant seats near the entrance, toward the front of the room, and Bess sat down next to them.

At the conclusion of the song, an older teenage boy stood and walked to the front of the room where he offered a brief opening prayer. Elder McTavish then rose to stand behind the small, portable podium.

"Good morning, brothers and sisters. We welcome you on this beautiful Sabbath morning. There are a few announcements. On Tuesday evening, the children's Christmas party will be held at the home of Brother and Sister Henderson in Aldershot. Check with them for directions if you've not been to their home, please. Also, the group that is going caroling to the hospital needs to have one more practice, according to Sister Bailey. That will be right after church this morning. She encourages everyone who can, to please attend. And before we have the sacrament song, I'd like to welcome a visitor to our branch. Thomas Callahan from, uh, Brother Callahan, where are you from?" the young elder asked.

All heads turned toward the rear of the room and for an

instant, Tommy locked eyes with Doctor Rossiter. Her face reflected her astonishment at seeing Tommy in this setting.

"Utah, Elder McTavish. I come from Salt Lake City."

"We're very pleased to welcome you to our branch, and if you're going to be in the area for a while, we hope you will return. Now, for our sacrament song, let's sing . . ."

Tommy returned his gaze to Bess who was still staring at him, her eyes wide open but a smile beginning to form on her pretty mouth. She turned back to face the front and began to sing, but Tommy continued to stare at the back of her head. As the sacrament was passed by two of the young men, Tommy participated in the ordinance. Memories of his youth flooded his mind, and he calculated that it had been almost twenty years since he had taken the sacrament—not since he had lived with Uncle Anders and Aunt Sarah and attended the branch with them in Washington, D.C.

Throughout the meeting Tommy glanced at Bess, although she continued to look forward. He wondered, had he been seated toward the front, if he would have been able to resist the urge to turn around and take another look at her, but Bess appeared to concentrate intently on the message being delivered.

After the service concluded, the members rose and several came to greet Tommy, welcoming him to their branch and encouraging him to return the following week. One elderly couple invited him to a Christmas dinner should he still be in the area. Finally, most members having departed, Bess approached Tommy and stood silently in front of him for several seconds, smiling at him and slightly shaking her head.

"So, *Brother* Callahan, do you have any other surprises?"

"I hope so, Bess," he grinned sheepishly.

"Well, this is enough of a surprise for quite some time, I should say. Why didn't you *tell* me you were a member?"

"I don't know, Bess. Perhaps because I haven't been as active as I should have been. Why didn't you tell *me?*"

"Hmmm," she nodded. "I'll have to give *that* some thought."

"May I take you to dinner this evening? Maybe the roast lamb at the Star and Garter?"

"No, Tommy, I have a better idea. I'm cooking Kiwi roast lamb for the elders and an older missionary couple. If you would consider coming . . ."

"Wild horses couldn't keep me away, Bess. I've missed you," he said, touching her cheek.

She placed her hand on his arm and smiled softly at him, slowly nodding her agreement.

"Six o'clock. I think you know where to come."

22

On Saturday, July 25, 1936, President Heber J. Grant officiated at the wedding of Major Thomas Matthew Callahan III and Doctor Elizabeth Hawkins Rossiter, in a ceremony in London.

Elder and Sister Thomas Callahan traveled to the British Isles to be present, combining their trip with an assignment from the First Presidency to conduct training sessions among the local brethren regarding the newly introduced Church Security Plan.

Prior to the wedding, President Grant had traveled throughout northern Europe where he visited Church branches and missions and met with thousands of members in many countries. In late July, he arrived in England and, a week after the Callahans' wedding, on August 1, he presided at the British Mission Centennial Conference in Rochdale, England.[15]

Bess's parents were unable to come from New Zealand, but Katrina did all she could in the final days before the wedding to act in Sister Rossiter's stead as a mother to Bess.

Seby and Teresa Stromberg also made the trip, leaving three of their children at home and bringing the newest Stromberg baby, Matthew. When she first met Teresa, Bess told her sister-in-law-to-be the story of her first date with Tommy to Brighton, where they had gone to see *The Gathering Storm* and Tommy had purposefully left Bess unaware of his relationship to the actress.

"He's always had this devious streak," Teresa said to Bess. "I think it's because he was born in the last century. If I were you, I'd run away right now and never look back."

"But I love him, Teresa," Bess laughingly replied to Teresa's mock taunt.

"Heaven help you, Doctor Rossiter," Teresa warned, an impish grin on her face. "Now he'll have to answer to Bess *and* Tess. Perhaps we should ask heaven to help *him*," Teresa said, as both ladies broke out in laughter.

The two women made an immediate connection, as if they had known each other throughout their lives. Teresa served as matron of honor, and, together Katrina, Bess, and Teresa spent three days in London prior to the wedding, shopping for Bess's wedding trousseau.

Tommy rented a reception hall in London and invited several members of the faculty at Sandhurst. The highlight of the reception was when Winston Churchill, who had agreed to attend, along with Brigadier David McIntyre, came face-to-face with Thomas and Katrina Callahan following the ceremony.

"Good afternoon, Mrs. Callahan," the portly gentleman said, bowing slightly and accepting Katrina's proffered hand. "I'm pleased to see the intervening years have done nothing to diminish your beauty, nor, hopefully, your ardor for a good cause," he smiled, taking her offered hand between both of his.

"It's been *many* years, sir, and I have changed a great deal," Katrina said, blushing slightly. "But it is indeed a real pleasure to see you again. May I introduce the subject of our previous meeting, my husband, Thomas Callahan."

"Good day to you, sir," Churchill said, reaching to shake Tom's hand. "I trust you are enjoying your trip to England."

"It's been seventeen years since the last trip, Mr. Churchill, and the accommodations this time are much better."

"I can well imagine, Mr. Callahan," Churchill chuckled. "My compliments on your son's wedding. I've had several chats with young Major Callahan. He's a fine soldier, well educated and a credit to his country, and, of course, to his parents."

"Thank you, sir," Tom said. "His finer attributes come from his mother, I'm pleased to admit."

Churchill chuckled and winked at Katrina.

"It wouldn't surprise me, sir, to find a bit of the Irish in there somewhere."

"I'd like to think so, Mr. Churchill," Tom smiled.

After circulating throughout the room, the two newly-weds joined the small group, and Katrina gave Bess a quick hug and a kiss on the cheek.

"Thomas, we now have a doctor in the family," Katrina said.

"And not a moment too soon, since I'm getting so old and decrepit. Do you know much about geriatrics, Elizabeth?" Tom teased.

"Not yet, Brother Callahan. Do you think I should learn?" she smiled.

"You'll be better off, dear," Katrina said, "if you call him Dad or Pop. He'll feel much younger, I think."

"Major," Churchill said, "Brigadier McIntyre tells me you and your lovely bride will be taking some time to tour the Continent. Will you be visiting Germany or Italy?"

"Yes, sir. We'll take the night train to Dover and the ferry over to Calais."

"If it wouldn't be an imposition, Doctor Callahan, I'd very much appreciate a word with your new husband before you leave this evening."

"You may have him, sir, for a brief moment, but then he's mine, and I'll not give him up for an instant."

"Well said, madam," Churchill smiled. "And, Mrs. Callahan," he said, turning back to face Katrina, "it was a pleasure to meet you again. I have fond memories of our meeting with Mr. Lloyd-George that eventful day. And you, sir," he said to Tom, "have reason to be very proud of your wife. She took the British lion by his mane and tweaked his nose, as it were. I've not seen the like before or since. By all rights, I should take her to Germany where she could speak some sense to Chancellor Hitler."

"I've more cause than that to be grateful to her, Mr. Churchill, but that's high on the list, I can assure you. The accommodations at Portlaoise left much to be desired."

"Quite right, I'm sure," Churchill said to Tom. "Now, if you'll excuse me, ladies and gentlemen, as I have another engagement, I'll take my leave. Major Callahan, if I might speak briefly with you before I depart."

"Certainly, sir. I'll be along in just a moment."

"Mom," Tommy said, "don't forget that you promised me a dance. And Pop, Bess said she wouldn't mind taking it easy on you if you'd care to wiggle your feet."

"I'm not *that* old, Major Callahan," Tom rebutted. "Your mother could tell you stories about the old days at Saltair."

"Oh, no," Katrina laughed. "Some of those stories, Thomas, my dear, we've kept from the children for many years. Even at his current age, he'd best not hear them, don't you think?"

"Hmmmph! If you'd be so kind, Elizabeth," Tom said, taking his new daughter-in-law by the arm, "there are people here who would spread malicious stories if I let them. Let's just go off by ourselves and *I'll* tell you the truth."

"I'm all yours, Dad," she said, winking at Tommy as he left to speak with Churchill.

In mid-September 1936, Tommy and Bess returned from their honeymoon on the Continent and moved into a small thatched-roof cottage in Camberley. The new term at Sandhurst was about to begin, and Brigadier McIntyre had increased Tommy's teaching load. Bess returned to Prince Albert Hospital to complete the six months remaining of her orthopedic residency.

The second day of the term, Tommy arrived at their cottage to find Bess home early, preparing dinner. He came up from behind and wrapped his arms around her, pulling her into him and nuzzling her hair.

"Do you know, Mrs. Callahan, I can't think of when my life was more pleasant or when I was happier."

Bess turned from the sink and wrapped her arms around his neck. "I agree wholeheartedly, Major Callahan. What should we do about it?"

"How would you like to go away for the weekend?" he asked. "Another honeymoon is in order, I think. It's been three weeks since we got back. Don't you think we owe it to ourselves?" he laughed.

"I'm on shift this weekend."

"Any chance you could swap with someone?"

"Is it that important?" she asked, moving toward the table and laying the place settings.

Tommy held up a small, hand-engraved invitation card,

waggling it back and forth, teasing her. "This *might* convince you."

She took hold of his wrist and tilted her head slightly to read the card. "*Chartwell?* We've been invited to Chartwell for the weekend?" she exclaimed.

"It would seem," he smiled.

"Why would Winston Churchill invite us to his estate?"

"If I were to guess, I'd say he wants to speak with me about our trip through Germany. Remember when he pulled me aside at our wedding celebration? He asked me to keep my eyes open as we traveled through the Continent. And just last week when the term started, the brigadier told me that Churchill is building a private intelligence-gathering network."

"He doesn't have a position in Chamberlain's cabinet, does he?" Bess asked.

"Not at the moment, but apparently he plans to," Tommy smiled. "So, can you get relief for the weekend?"

"I wouldn't miss going to Chartwell for the world. Perhaps Doctor Henderson will stand in for me. He owes me several weekends, in fact. Now, how about some dinner?" she smiled up at him.

"*After* I get a kiss."

"Brash Yank," she teased, standing on her tiptoes to kiss him. "And as to another honeymoon at Chartwell, I suspect I'll be lucky if I even *see* you after we arrive."

"Churchill couldn't drag me away from you, and besides, I've got my own intelligence to gather," he said, taking her in his arms and pulling her close.

Bess was right.

After their arrival on Friday evening, a late dinner was

had by all, including the ladies. And then while Clementine Churchill entertained the women in the drawing room, the men—eight military officers and senior government officials, plus Tommy and Churchill—sequestered themselves in the library[16].

The only officer Tommy knew well was Brigadier McIntyre, although Churchill made it a point to personally welcome the young American as the group was assembling in the library.

"I'm pleased that you and your wife were able to attend, Major Callahan. I trust you'll make yourself right at home."

"Thank you, Mr. Churchill," Tommy said. "It was most kind of you to invite us, sir."

"Not at all. You'll fit right in among this lot. Some of the "old breed" are here as well," he chuckled, "but speak your mind nevertheless," the politician said.

"Well, then, gentlemen, port or brandy are on the sideboard, cigars as well," the portly politician announced.

At sixty-two, Winston Churchill had not lost any of his fire for political battle. He continued his quest for a greater involvement in the British government. In doing so, he was not above opposing his own party leadership, whenever he felt it in the best interest of England. In this he was seen as something of a maverick, and he had managed to irritate some high-ranking people in the government.

Amidst some good-natured bantering and laughter, the men filled their glasses, and cigar smoke began to cloud the room. But as the gentlemen took their seats, there ensued a few moments of silence, and all eyes turned to their host. Looking like the bulldog he was often compared to by political cartoonists, Churchill stood beside a large globe of the world, positioned some feet from the elevated writing table on which he often prepared his speeches, following his habit of writing while standing, as opposed to being seated behind a desk.

"Gentlemen, I've made no secret of my feelings about what I perceive to be the growing military and political threat on the Continent. But, tonight, I have asked you all here to discuss, nay, *analyze*, the information that has been forthcoming as each of you, through your own channels, has gathered information of import. Admiral Benchley, as senior officer present, perhaps you would be so kind as to enlighten my guests regarding your recent visit to the Bremerhaven Naval Base."

"I'm pleased to say, Winston, that the German Admiralty kept me wined and dined and fully feted during my entire stay . . . but far away from the shipyards. It was the most social military visit I can recall," he laughed, holding up his brandy snifter.

Churchill frowned, his pugnacious face wrinkling at the effort. "You mean to tell us that you were unable to obtain any strategic knowledge of the Hun's naval capacity other than our current intelligence?"

Benchley swirled his brandy slowly, took a sip, and raised his glass slightly in the gesture of a small toast toward Churchill.

"My dear, Churchill," he smiled. "It's always been my belief that those of you who obtained your military education at Sandhurst," he said, pausing and smiling at McIntyre, "with all possible respect to you, Brigadier, have always underestimated the value of a good military aide. A *junior* aide to be specific. While Admirals Raeder and Doenitz were holding my hand and assuring the blindfold was securely in place, Lieutenant Commander Curtis spent three days among his peers in the, shall we say, less-formal establishments to be found along the waterfront in

Bremerhaven, near the Krupp Shipyard. The first evening, when he discovered himself—quite to his chagrin, mind you—" he smiled, conspiratorially "without quarters for the evening, the noted German hospitality was immediately forthcoming, and he was secreted aboard the *Stuttgart,* a German ship-of-the-line for the evening and afforded quarters suitable to his station, without official sanction, I might add."

Winston also smiled. "He got *inside,* you say? Jolly good for him."

"He did, indeed," Admiral Benchley replied. "And before the captain of the *Stuttgart* became aware of his presence and summarily, but quite politely, mind you, had him escorted off the post, Curtis counted fourteen new keels underway, three of them capital ships-of-the-line."

For nearly three hours the conversation continued, each participant contributing what he had learned in one way or another about the current state of affairs in Germany and Italy. During all of this, Tommy sat silently in a corner of the room, fascinated to watch the way Winston Churchill led the discussion, orchestrating it much as a conductor might direct a symphony orchestra. Just as Tommy was beginning to feel relaxed, his role being limited to that of an observer, Churchill looked his way.

"Gentlemen, we have another *foreigner* in our midst this evening," Churchill said, smiling and nodding at Tommy. "A junior aide, as you mentioned, Admiral Benchley, is often very valuable indeed, in this case, Major Thomas Callahan, of Irish-American extraction via his father's birth. I will not regale you with an episode I was privileged to witness some seventeen years ago regarding his mother's tenacity, but suffice it to say, gentlemen, that were she to don the uniform, Herr Hitler would think twice about his plans for the future.

"As to Major Callahan, he comes to us from the United States Marine Corps, seconded to Brigadier McIntyre's faculty at Sandhurst, where, I am told, he has performed admirably. He is a graduate of the United States Naval Academy, is possessed of a doctorate in world economics from the illustrious Stanford University, comes from a successful banking family in America, served three years in Washington on the war plans staff, and, as young as he appears," Churchill smiled again at Tommy, "I am reliably told, that at eighteen years of age, he held his own as a sergeant with the 6th Marines at Chateau-Thierry during our last bout with the Hun. Have I missed anything, Major?"

Tommy shifted his position, suddenly uncomfortable, totally unprepared for Churchill's comments and uncertain how to reply.

"I'm sure you understand, Major Callahan, that as you are unknown to most of the officers present, I thought it appropriate to introduce you properly, and, ah, yes, there is one further item," Churchill went on. "It should come as no surprise, Major Callahan, but your President Roosevelt and I have become, shall we say, supportive of one another's objectives. The president was kind enough to have your marine commandant provide a dossier on those American military personnel currently stationed in England. You come highly recommended, Major, including Brigadier McIntyre's strongest endorsement. Nonetheless, I sincerely apologize for any embarrassment I have brought to your threshold this evening. There is, however, one other thing. The commandant of the Marine Corps has authorized me to announce this evening, the promotion of Major Thomas Callahan to the rank of Lieutenant Colonel, effective immediately, and to advise that your follow-on assignment has been approved to become the assistant military attaché to the American embassy at the Court of St. James. It would seem, Colonel Callahan, that you and your lovely New Zealand bride will continue to enjoy His Majesty's hospitality for some time. Gentlemen, I think a toast is in order concerning Colonel Callahan's promotion, what say?"

Brigadier McIntyre was the first to stand and raise his glass, followed by each of the officers gathered in Winston Churchill's library at Chartwell that evening.

"Now, with the social graces completed," Churchill went on, "what do you make of this evening's intelligence, Colonel?" he said, addressing Tommy. "Bear in mind, that what is said in this room is strictly unofficial and although we have combined here tonight some of the best analytical military minds in Great Britain, we are gathered informally. That said, what did you observe on your trip to the Continent?"

"Mr. Churchill, I feel it would be presumptuous of me—"

"Colonel, speak your mind," Churchill directed, his face suddenly serious.

With a quick glance toward Brigadier McIntyre, Tommy nodded.

"Yes, sir. Gentlemen, during the several weeks I toured the Continent, I observed a great deal of random military movement and facility construction going on. Given the German people's unrest and Hitler's growing consolidation of political power, along with the movement of the mark in comparison to international currency, it seems evident to me that Mr. Hitler is preparing his country, that is his people and his military, for war."

Churchill puffed on his cigar and glared around the room at the assembled senior officers.

"There you have it, gentlemen, from the most junior officer present. Is anyone in disagreement with Colonel Callahan's hypothesis?"

"Winnie," Admiral Benchley began, "Chamberlain assured us only last month that—"

"Poppycock, Admiral," Churchill interrupted. "We are going to war and sooner than any of us expects. And if the navy is not ready, Admiral, it shall be a long and very costly war. Mark my words."

Silence followed Churchill's remarks, and Admiral Benchley stood to refurbish his brandy glass.

The meeting broke up about 2:00 A.M., and Churchill said his farewell to several officers, who were not staying the evening at Chartwell, while seeing them to the door. Tommy remained in the library, conversing with Brigadier McIntyre, until Churchill returned.

"Well spoken, Colonel," Churchill said as he entered the room.

"I think it's not what they wanted to hear, sir."

"You're right about that, but what they want to hear matters little now. How familiar are you, Colonel Callahan, with William's Crossing?" Churchill asked, completely catching Tommy by surprise.

"I guess you're referring to William the Conqueror's invasion of England in 1066," Tommy said, "but I don't know what you're driving at."

"As I read your dossier, Colonel, you participated in the Marine Corps' beach assault landing exercises some years ago. Is that correct?"

"Yes, sir, in Hawaii in '26 and '27. They didn't work out very well."

"But the Corps learned from them?"

"We did, sir."

"Good. I've asked the brigadier to schedule a senior-level staff seminar next month on amphibious landing techniques . . . using your expertise, of course, combined with our chaps. Before this is over, I'm quite certain we're going to have to reverse William's route and land a major force on the Continent, contending—as William did *not* have to do—with the enemy's airpower." Churchill was silent for several long moments, and Tommy and Brigadier McIntyre sat quietly as well. Finally, the old gentleman spoke again. "Well, David, I think that should be quite enough for one evening, wouldn't you say?"

"Indeed, Winnie," McIntyre said, standing and stretching. "Thank you for a very informative evening."

Leaving Churchill alone in the library to finish his third cigar and a final brandy, the Brigadier and Tommy said goodnight to their host.

"Well done this evening, Tommy," the old brigadier said as they exited the room.

"Nothing like any marine briefing sessions I've ever attended, I can assure you, Brigadier."

"As I told you, son, Winnie has formed a shadow government of his own, in preparation, mind you, for his anticipated return to power. And don't count him out."

"I wouldn't think of it, sir. Goodnight, sir."

"Goodnight to you, Colonel, and congratulations again on your well-deserved promotion."

Tommy climbed the stairs toward his room and slipped as quietly as he could into their assigned bed-sitter. Silently undressing in the dark, he was surprised when Bess switched on a small bedside table lamp.

"So, my husband has returned from the halls of power,"

she said, smiling at him. "Whew, and smelling of cigar smoke, I might add. Any startling developments?"

"Not much," Tommy said, sitting on the edge of the bed and removing his shoes. "Mr. Churchill told us all we're going to war, but otherwise it was just a pleasant evening," he said casually.

"To *war!*"

"Not tomorrow, but not long either. Oh, and I've been promoted to lieutenant colonel and we've been reassigned. We're moving to London where I've been posted to the embassy staff."

Bess sat upright in the bed. "Just a pleasant evening, you say? You've been promoted, transferred, and we're going to war. The next time we attend a 'pleasant evening out,' would you consider giving me advance notice if anything of *real* import is likely to happen?"

"You'd be the first to know, sweetheart," he said, slipping between the sheets and rolling over to snuggle his wife.

"I doubt it, *Colonel* Callahan. I sincerely doubt it."

In the fall of 1938, Doctor Elizabeth Rossiter Callahan completed her orthopedic residency at Prince Albert Hospital and accepted a surgical staff position at the Royal London Hospital. Lieutenant Colonel Thomas Callahan assumed his duties as assistant military attaché at the American Embassy, London, leaving the Sandhurst faculty after three years. Tommy and Bess thoroughly enjoyed their working environment and the social whirl of London.

Then things changed—rapidly.

In late August 1939, Benjamin Arthur Callahan was born in London. On September 1, the German army invaded Poland, and on September 3, Great Britain and the

Commonwealth countries, including Bess's homeland of New Zealand, declared war on Germany.

While Bess was still in the hospital following the birth of Benjie, Tommy was manning his duty station at the embassy nearly twenty-four hours a day as political and military message traffic increased dramatically. Within a week, Prime Minister Neville Chamberlain named Churchill First Lord of the Admiralty, a position Churchill had held during the Great War. In September 1939, Sandhurst closed its doors, and the faculty and current students entered active duty service. Anticipating widespread conflict, the First Presidency of The Church of Jesus Christ of Latter-day Saints recalled all missionaries serving on the Continent.

By May 1940, following the surrender and occupation of Norway, France, and Denmark, and with fear of a German invasion sweeping England, Chamberlain resigned, and Winston Churchill was asked by King George VI to form a new government. At sixty-five years of age, Winston Spencer Churchill became the Prime Minister of Great Britain at a time when the Empire was on the verge of collapse.

To establish their military supremacy, in the spring of 1940, German aircraft began indiscriminately bombing residential districts in London, and civilian deaths mounted daily. Tommy pleaded with Bess to take their son, Benjie, and relocate to Salt Lake City with his parents.

"Tommy, we've talked about this before. I'm not leaving until you can come with us, and we can be sealed in the Salt Lake Temple. We both know that's impossible during this crisis."

"Bess, please, be reasonable. This war has taken a turn no one expected. If the RAF can't keep German aircraft at bay, their army will be on the beaches by late summer, and

England will be an occupied country. Then, as a New Zealand citizen, you won't be able to get out no matter how hard you try. Even the British are evacuating their children to Australia or Canada."

"What chance do you have for a reassignment?" she asked.

He shook his head. "I can't leave now, Bess; you know that. If I asked for a reassignment, it would be viewed negatively, possibly even considered cowardice. Despite what President Roosevelt says publicly, America will eventually be in this war. In the meantime, I've got to stay in place."

"And so will I," Bess declared, stepping close to her husband and placing her hand on his cheek. "We'll be all right, Tommy. The Lord will watch over us."

Tommy exhaled a long sigh and took his wife in his arms. "Why in the world I fell in love with a headstrong woman, I'll never know."

"Because if I wasn't headstrong, Colonel Callahan, you'd wish I were. Remember, Tommy, my country is at war too, and most of the Kiwi men are already in North Africa, including two of my brothers. We'll get through this, I just know it. At least you have a relatively safe assignment."

"I'm a marine officer, Bess. I'm not supposed to seek a safe haven."

"But America's not at war. At least, not yet."

"That won't last long. Promise me you'll at least take Benjie down to the air raid shelters when the siren sounds."

"Of course I will," she said, again stroking his cheek in an attempt to ease his concern. "Now get back to the embassy. I know you're not supposed to be here. We'll be fine."

Three weeks passed with Tommy spending nearly all of it on twenty-four-hour duty at the embassy. Twice he had made it home, and on one occasion, he had been unable to find Bess in the confusion of yet another air raid. He'd left her a note, expressing his love and indicating that he hoped to get a forty-eight-hour pass over the weekend.

On July 18, at about two in the afternoon, the embassy's Marine duty officer entered the secure crypto area where Colonel Callahan was working and came to attention in front of Tommy's desk.

"What is it, Captain?" Tommy asked, looking up from a series of messages he was reading.

"Colonel, the ambassador has asked if you would have a moment to meet in his office."

"Of course," Tommy said, standing and grabbing his tunic. "Did he say what it was about?"

"No, sir. Just that he needed to see you."

"Fine. Thank you, Captain."

In 1938, President Franklin Roosevelt had appointed Joseph Kennedy of Massachusetts as the American ambassador to the Court of St. James in London. Buttoning his tunic, Tommy entered the stairwell and climbed two floors to the ambassador's level, where he knocked on the outer door.

"Ah, Colonel Callahan, please come in," Ambassador Kennedy said.

Tommy entered the office where the ambassador stood talking with a uniformed police constable and another man dressed in civilian clothing.

"Colonel, this is Chief Inspector Mulligan and Constable Higgins."

"Colonel Callahan," the inspector said, "your residence is located on Chidester Place, in Kensington, is it not?"

"It is," Tommy replied, immediately wondering what this was all about.

"And you live with your wife, uh," he consulted his notes, " a Doctor Elizabeth Callahan?"

Tommy looked at the ambassador for a moment and then looked back toward the inspector.

"Yes, and our son, Benjamin, an infant."

"Colonel, I'm sorry to inconvenience you, but I'm going to have to ask you to come with us, if you will."

"What's the problem, Inspector?" Tommy asked, fear rising in him.

"Tommy," Ambassador Kennedy said, "there is no easy way to say this . . . the, uh, the inspector came to inform me that a block of flats on Chidester Place, including your particular address, was the impact site for a cluster of bombs just after midnight. He, uh, the inspector, I mean," Kennedy stammered, "needs to ask you to accompany him for identification purposes."

"Identification?" Tommy asked, his heart rate suddenly accelerating.

Kennedy stepped closer and lowered his voice. "Tommy, the inspector has informed me that a woman they believe is your wife and a male infant were killed early this morning in an air raid.[17] I'm so sorry."

Tommy stood stunned for several moments, staring at Ambassador Kennedy.

"We have transport, Colonel, if you'd be so kind as to accompany us," Mulligan said.

"I'll . . . I'll, uh, meet you in the foyer, Inspector. If you'll just excuse me for a moment," Tommy said, turning and slowly walking out of the ambassador's office.

Ambassador Kennedy followed Tommy into the hallway, motioning for the marine captain who stood at the end of the corridor.

"Captain," he said, as he watched Tommy retreat down the hallway, "go with Colonel Callahan and see if you can be of any assistance. He's had some rather bad news, I'm afraid."

"Yes, sir. I'll remain with the colonel."

Other than the morning of the funeral service and the burial, it had been three weeks since Tommy had left the embassy. He immersed himself in work, but had difficulty concentrating. When he slept, it was only infrequently and fitfully on a cot in his office. Using the marine ready room to shower and shave, he depended on the embassy housekeeper to wash and care for his uniforms. He recognized attempts by the ambassador's wife, Rose Kennedy, and others to console him as heartfelt and sincere, but what could anyone say to alleviate such a loss or relieve the ache in his chest?

His parents had responded to his telegram informing them of Bess and Benjamin's deaths by declaring their intention to immediately fly to London on the Pan Am *Clipper*. But Tommy wired back that the funeral was to be held too quickly and that he would have no time following to spend with them. Besides, the emergency situation and the danger inherent with the bombings made their coming to England a risky thing. Acquiescing to Tommy's arguments against their coming, they had reluctantly telegraphed their acceptance of his request and cancelled their bookings.

When Ambassador Kennedy appeared in his office one morning, an unusual occurrence, Tommy rose to stand behind his desk.

"Just an informal call, Colonel," the older man said. "Please be seated," he said, patting the air with his hand and taking himself a chair across the desk from Tommy.

"To be quite candid, Colonel Callahan, I'm here at the direction of Mrs. Kennedy."

"Sir?"

"You know women, Colonel," he said, trying to smile and shaking his head gently. "They always think they know best in matters of the heart . . . including a broken heart, son," he added softly.

"Mrs. Kennedy has been very kind," Tommy said.

"Yes, well, that's her way," the ambassador said.

Waiting for Kennedy to continue, Tommy sat quietly.

"Actually, Colonel, I do have something of importance I would like you to do for me."

"Yes, sir," Tommy responded.

"It will entail your leaving this, uh, your quarters, as it were," he said, looking around the office that Tommy had turned into a bed-sitter.

Tommy remained silent.

"I think you know that Mrs. Kennedy and I will be departing England shortly, and I'd like to obtain a first-hand report of morale in fighter command before I go. In RAF High Wycombe, specifically. President Roosevelt will surely ask my opinion of the current situation, and . . ."

Tommy remained silent, but his face betrayed his thoughts, and Kennedy just shook his head again. "You're not buying any of this, are you, son?"

"Sir, I know you and Mrs. Kennedy mean well, but I'm doing okay, really."

"That's just it, Colonel. You're not doing okay, at all. I want you out of here for a few days at least," the ambassador said with sudden firmness. "Now I can send you on a fool's errand and have you gather useless information, or you can just jump in that little roadster of yours and drive to a place of your choosing. One way or another, you *will* leave London. What's it to be, Colonel?" the older man smiled.

Tommy sat silently for a moment, then smiled sadly at the ambassador, slowly nodding his head.

"Please thank Mrs. Kennedy and your housekeeper, Mrs. Winston, for their kindness. I've been rather reclusive, I know. And thank you, sir, for your thoughtful offer. I'll leave tomorrow morning if that suits, Ambassador."

"That's fine, Colonel," Kennedy said, standing and stepping toward the desk. "Can I be of any assistance, with reservations or accommodations?"

"No, sir, thank you. I believe I'll just head down to the coast."

"Tomorrow's Thursday. I don't want to see you back here before Monday morning. Is that clear, Colonel Callahan?"

"It is, sir," Tommy responded, also standing and accepting Ambassador Kennedy's handshake.

Kennedy stepped toward the door but before leaving, turned to face Tommy.

"You've just been through the toughest thing a man can endure, Colonel. In this abominable war Mr. Hitler has started, I think there will be a great deal more of it before we can bring it under control. Our own sons will likely be involved. Perhaps that's what Mrs. Kennedy sees in you—a reflection of the future and the pain they—we—might be called upon to bear."

⁂

Not consciously certain of his destination, Tommy drove into the countryside of Kent, heading southeast from London. Within twenty minutes he found himself behind a convoy of British military vehicles, traveling only twenty to twenty-five miles per hour. Unable to legally overtake the outrider motorcycles, he followed the line of trucks for some forty miles before he was able to circle through a few roundabouts in a small village and leapfrog the convoy. Immediately, he found himself behind yet another cluster of military lorries heading southeast.

By dusk he was on the outskirts of Brighton, a destination he had discovered some miles back was at the end of this particular road. Remembering the last time he had crossed the same terrain, he experienced a renewed ache in his chest. The trip had taken over seven hours this time—courtesy of his military escort—considerably more than the three-hour trip when he had first brought Bess to Brighton on the holiday they had shared.

As he drove through the narrow, winding streets, the windows on each of the buildings were shuttered for the evening and the street lamps were unlit. Stopping in front of the Fluted Unicorn, he parked his car and climbed stiffly out of the driver's seat. Then he walked into the darkened lobby and to the reception desk.

"Any chance for a room for a few days?" he asked the clerk.

"Your choice, sir. We've few guests in these troubled times."

"Something upstairs, then. Facing the ocean."

"How many nights, sir?"

"Uh, three. Through Saturday, please."

"Right. Sign here, please, sir," the man said, turning a large registration book toward Tommy. "Number seventeen, top of the stairs. A good view of the ocean, sir, but nothing to see this evening, I'd say, and even in the daylight, it is, uh, different."

"That's fine. Thank you. I'll just get my luggage."

"I'll have the boy—"

"Don't bother. I've only got one bag. Thanks again," Tommy said, retracing his steps through the front door and retrieving his bag from the car.

In his room, the darkened curtains adjusted to block the light from his bedside lamp, Tommy stripped his uniform to his trousers and lay on the bed, his hands folded on his stomach. After some minutes, he reached down to his bag and withdrew the letter he had received from his mother the day before his departure from London. He lay back on the bed and unfolded the letter and read it again, slowly, pausing occasionally to consider her thoughts.

July 22, 1940

My dearest Tommy,

Your father and I were devastated to hear of your terrible loss. I was for coming to you immediately, despite your plea for us to remain in Utah. It was your father who thought that your advice was best and that you needed to consider this yourself and find a way to accept what has happened. I must admit, privately of course, that he is usually wiser in these things than I am. The mother in me simply wants to hold you and love you, my darling.

When your telegram arrived, I felt as if my heart had broken quite literally. Your father was in Denver on business, and I immediately drove to Draper to see

Teresa. After telephoning your father, Tess and I cried through the night, aching for your grief.

I have never told you this, Tommy, but on many occasions I have remembered the morning when my lifeboat pulled alongside the *Carpathia* and I heard your small voice calling me from her decks as you stood with the other survivors of the Titanic. Never has my heart been so filled with joy. Throughout that long, agonizing night, I had imagined that both of my sons, as well as my parents, had perished in the sinking of that great ocean liner. Our grief at Benjamin's loss was great, but I have often thought how unbearable it would have been to have lost all of you. I had actually considered slipping over the side of the lifeboat in the quiet of the night and joining you. It was Teresa and her belief that you were alive that kept me from the dreadful act.

And now you, Tommy, must understand that Bess and Benjamin—your Benjamin—await you in our Father's house. I know that is true, Tommy. I know it with all my heart. With your permission, your father and I will accomplish the necessary work in the temple as quickly as possible.

390

I know that such knowledge does not fill your arms, or warm your heart, or greet you with a tender kiss. I know it does not replace the little hand of a son who sees in his father a hero of giant proportion. And I know that your heart aches for the tenderness you shared with your beloved Bess. But you will hold her again, Tommy. As God is my witness, you will hold her again, and your father and I will be reunited with your brother Benjamin.

We are often reminded by our Church leaders of the sacrifice made by our Father in giving up His Son. Perhaps it is only when we have truly felt the pain of such loss in our own lives that we can understand the depth of His love and the true meaning of the plan of salvation. He does love us, Tommy, as you love Bess and your tiny son. Live well for them, Tommy. Don't let your grief overwhelm you and cause a loss of the testimony and caring that Bess helped to restore to your life. Turn to your Heavenly Father, my son, and cry unto Him.

I love you as only a mother can, my dearest Tommy. May God wrap you in His arms until I can hold you again in mine.

All our love,
Mom

The following morning, Tommy rose at dawn and dressed in his uniform. Leaving the hotel, he walked away from the village toward the cliffs overlooking the sea. Wartime Brighton bore no resemblance to the bustling, cheerful village he had once explored with Bess. Now it seemed almost deserted. Where bathers had once frolicked, barriers of concertina wire had been stretched along the beachfront, and the hillsides were pocked with dark brown depressions where hasty embankments had been thrown up against a pending invasion.

As Tommy walked further, toward the high cliffs, he encountered a large lattice work of metal stringers rising above the landscape, capped by several hundred crisscrossed cables and pipes. Tommy recognized the conglomeration as the newly installed, long-range air detection system that was being referred to as radar.

Avoiding the entanglements of wire on the beach, he climbed a green hill overlooking the harbor and sat on a small pile of flat stones. Obscured in the bright, early-morning haze, the English Channel stretched before him. He sat there for more than an hour, staring at the ocean, occasionally catching sight of a patrol boat scouring the water for mines or imagined infiltrators. As the morning progressed, the haze gradually burned off, providing an unusually clear day, with only a few high cirrus clouds brushing the sky.

The chirping of a pair of scissortailed swallows, flitting about in the low-growing brush, oblivious to the new starkness of their surroundings, reminded him of the happier time he had spent there earlier with Bess. They had tramped together in this very spot, but if he had supposed coming there would be a comfort to him, he was mistaken. Though the birds continued to sing, for him the magic had gone out of the place.

He gradually became aware of the distant droning of engines, and as the sound grew louder, Tommy turned and looked up to see a squadron of British *Spitfire* fighter planes suddenly upon him. He came quickly to his feet as the sleek planes roared over his head. Flying at an elevation of only a few hundred feet, in an instant they had left the cliffs and beach behind and were out over the channel, flying in formation toward the Continent.

The British were fighting for their lives, and these courageous, mostly very young pilots and their comrades were all that stood between England and a German invasion. It was of these British airmen that Churchill would one day say, "Never in the field of human conflict was so much owed by so many to so few."

Tommy watched as the planes grew smaller in the unusually bright blue English sky. Great Britain had already been at war for nearly a year, and it promised to be a long, difficult time that would require sacrifice from everyone. Every day, these brave, young pilots went up, and every day, fewer of them came home.

It was clear to Tommy that in the not too distant future, America and her sons would join the fight. It would be a brutal, bloody conflict. Once again mothers would weep for their sons, wives for their husbands, and in some cases, as Tommy had so painfully learned, husbands for their wives and children, who would be caught up in the maelstrom of inhumanity and violence.

Tommy shielded his eyes against the glare of the sun and watched as the squadron of fighter planes became a mere speck in the sky.

Then he straightened, put on his cap, and rendered the now distant warriors a loose, informal salute.

"Godspeed," he said softly. "Godspeed to us all."

Thomas Holcomb, General
Commandant of the Marine Corps
Marine Corps Headquarters
Eighth & "I" Streets
Washington, D.C.

2 September 1940

Ref: USMC Requisition Notice—Raider Battalion

Sir:

In response to USMC Directive 40/1621, soliciting
marine officers of appropriate age and experience for
voluntary hazardous duty consideration, the under-
signed hereby submits application for immediate
reassignment and subsequent transfer to the proposed
1st Marine Raider Battalion, now forming at Camp
Pendleton, California.

Respectfully submitted,

Thomas M. Callahan, III
Lieutenant Colonel, USMC
Assistant Military Attaché
American Embassy, London

Epilogue

From the Salt Lake City Cemetery, located high on the Avenues, heat waves could be seen shimmering in the valley below. In the annual changing of the seasons, all vestiges of snow had disappeared from the surrounding mountains, and summer had transformed the city into a breathless cauldron.

In spite of the heat, well over a thousand people had attended the chapel service, and most of those, it seemed, had also come to the graveside service. The people at Larkin Mortuary had observed to the family that it was an unusually large crowd for so elderly a decedent, given that most of his peers had already passed on.

The grave having been dedicated and the formalities completed, the majority of the people hastened to leave the cemetery, retreating to the air-conditioned comfort of their cars as quickly as diplomacy and propriety allowed. Now, only a few stragglers and the members of the immediate family remained.

An elderly woman sat apart from the others on a marble

bench in the shade of a large sycamore tree. A man of about forty approached her but stood a few paces away, as though reluctant to intrude on her solitude.

"May I have a word with you, ma'am?" he finally asked softly.

Looking up, she nodded and extended her hand in greeting.

"Certainly," she said, smiling at him.

The man shook her hand, then said, "You wouldn't know who I am, Sister Callahan, but my name is Parker, and I want you to know how much I admired and respected your husband. He forgave the mortgage on my father's home back during the Depression. That is the home I grew up in, and I have raised my own children there. That wouldn't have been possible except for your husband's generosity. I just want you to know how grateful we are. God bless you, ma'am," he said, then turned quickly and walked away.

While others greeted Katrina, a white-haired, distinguished looking gentleman stood nearby, watching as the remaining people stopped to pay their respects. When there was a moment, the man approached slowly. Two much younger men, dressed in suits, stood to one side, carefully observing the older gentleman but not interfering with his movements.

Katrina recognized him and smiled and held out her hand, which he accepted and clasped gently between his own.

"You're looking well, Sister Callahan," he said.

"Thank you, President, but a man in your position ought to tell the truth. When a woman gets to be ninety years old, there's not much that looks well at all," she said, smiling.

He laughed and shook his head. "No, Sister Callahan,

I can't recall a time over the seventy-odd years we've known each other when you *haven't* looked well."

"Well, thank you, President. And thank you for coming. It means a great deal to me, and I'm sure to Thomas as well."

The president looked toward the mountains to the east, and a warm breeze ruffled his white hair. "Do you recall the time many years ago when I asked you if you thought your Thomas to be a good man? At your brother's wedding, in the Salt Lake Temple?" he asked.

She nodded thoughtfully. "I do, and I replied, *by any man's standard*, I believe."

"Yes," he laughed. "You bristled slightly at the question, as I recall, and I hastened to add that if he was a good man by any *man's* standard, then perhaps he was a good man by God's standard as well.

"I want to tell you today, Katrina Callahan," he said, patting her hand gently, "that both statements are true. And now Thomas Callahan will receive the reward of his labors, for both God *and* man will forever hold him in high esteem. That's evident in what we've seen today," he said, gesturing at the line of cars still departing the cemetery.

"His works are known and his legacy has spread far beyond this valley, into the world. I used to tell my missionaries that it is better to be trusted than loved. I believe Thomas was both trusted *and* loved by most of the people he dealt with. And what more can we ask than that?" he said, inclining his head toward Katrina and smiling kindly.

"What more, indeed?" she replied. "Thank you again, President McKay, for taking the time to come today."

He released her hand, nodded his respects to Teresa, who was standing nearby, then made his way to his car, followed by the two men who had remained discreetly distant. One of the men opened the door to the dark sedan, and President McKay entered the car, which then slowly left the cemetery.

Almost immediately, a young man of perhaps twenty quickly approached Katrina. He carried a small notebook in his hand and seemed nervous.

"Excuse me, ma'am. My name is Michael Murphy and I'm with the *Tribune*. Might I have a word with you, please?" he said.

The elderly woman looked into the young man's deep blue eyes and took note of his thick, dark hair, a distant memory flashing through her mind and a smile forming on her face.

"Are you Irish, Mr. Murphy?" she queried.

"Yes, ma'am. That is, my grandfather was, originally." Nodding toward the departing vehicle, he asked, "Wasn't that President David O. McKay?"

She glanced toward the car, now exiting the circular drive, and nodded. "Yes, it was. How may I help you, Mr. Murphy?"

"The gentleman who was buried, uh . . ." he paused, checking his notes, "Thomas Callahan. Were you a close friend of the family?"

She smiled gently. "A very close friend."

"Mr. Callahan was . . ." he referred to his notes again, "over ninety. Is that right? And he originally came from Ireland?"

Glancing beyond the reporter at the workmen who were removing the chairs and canopy, and preparing the grave for final closure, she responded softly.

"He died peacefully in his sleep, August 24, 1968, six weeks short of his ninety-third birthday, and, yes, he was born in Pallas Grean, County Tipperary, Ireland, October 5, 1875."

"Can you tell me a bit about him, ma'am? Did he come from a wealthy family? How did he start in business? Was he from one of the pioneer families?"

She could tell he was new at his job, asking so many questions before allowing time to answer any of them. She smiled and patted the bench beside her, offering a seat to the young man and looking toward her daughter, Teresa, now sixty-eight, quietly standing off to one side, waiting for her mother.

"You go ahead, Teresa. You and Jessie take the smaller children out of this heat. I'll stay for a while and speak with Mr. Murphy, and Seby can return for me later, after he's taken you back to *Valhalla*," she instructed.

Teresa frowned, concern written on her face.

"Don't be too long, Momma, it's very hot. Are you sure you'll be all right?"

"Yes, of course, dear," she replied, returning her attention to the reporter. "Now, Mr. Murphy, you were saying?"

"His family, ma'am. Did they provide his start in business, and how did you come in contact with the family?"

The elderly woman smiled wistfully, and her green eyes took on a faraway look. She shifted her gaze out over the valley, to the growing community with residential neighborhoods spreading to the south, and to the west toward the Great Salt Lake. Her mind raced through the events of the years, and a warm, pleasant memory of her youth suddenly filled her chest with longing.

"It was the spring of 1895 as I recall . . ."

———— ⊛ ————

Late that evening, in the quiet of her bedroom, sleep eluded Katrina, as it had for the past several nights. Four days earlier, when she had awakened to discover Thomas's still form lying peacefully next to her in their bed, her own chest had constricted at the shock. But she had mentioned her discomfort to no one, determined to carry on, giving her family the care and attention that ninety-odd years of living and seventy-odd years of mothering had ingrained. But in the quiet of those following nights, as her breath came in short, ragged gasps, she had been haunted by the image of a young, dark-haired, blue-eyed Irishman.

She rose from her bed quietly, so as not to awaken her daughter across the hall. Teresa had gently chided her mother into allowing her to stay with her for a few days following the funeral. "*Just until we get things settled, Momma,*" the concerned daughter had said.

Katrina slowly descended the spiral staircase in the dark, holding onto the burnished oak banister, so well worn through the years. She padded in her slippers toward the kitchen, where she turned on the light and took a glass from the cupboard. After pouring herself a tumbler of milk, she moved to the kitchen table, pulled back a chair, and carefully sat down.

She sat there for several long moments, listening to a house that, after so many years of laughter, so many parties, so many memories of children and grandchildren, and so many thoughts of . . . Thomas, was agonizingly silent.

She remembered the times he would come home after work, and, never mindful of her sense of propriety and decorum in front of the servants or the children, he would sweep her up boisterously into his arms, kissing her without restraint, and whispering in her ear. She wondered how she had gone all those years without confessing how much she looked forward to and desired his embrace.

Random thoughts of events and times and places they

had shared swirled through her mind, conjuring up happy memories of their years together.

Her breathing suddenly became labored, and she pulled her shawl closer around her shoulders to ward off a sudden chill. As she lifted her head to look toward a calendar on the wall, she gasped. The image of the young man who had haunted her thoughts for the past few nights stood in front of the kitchen cabinets, a loving smile on his face.

"Oh, Thomas," she breathed, her chest once again tightening.

He held out his hand, his countenance radiant and his smile beckoning.

The pain in her chest instantly subsided, and a warm sensation coursed through her body. Her face softened, and she nodded, slowly raising her hand toward the man she had loved for nearly seventy-five years—the young man to whom an immigrant girl of sixteen, standing on the deck of the *Antioch*, had pledged her heart and her destiny.

"You've come for me," she whispered.

He continued to smile, his hair once again dark and his shining blue eyes so like her memories.

Upstairs in the bedroom, Teresa awoke at the sound of breaking glass. She threw on a robe and quickly began to descend the stairs. From the first landing, she saw a light shining in the kitchen and a puddle of milk spreading on the floor. She hastened her pace down the stairs and called out.

"Momma? Are you there, Momma?"

Notes

1. Michael Collins was one of two prominent leaders of the Irish Rebellion against British rule.
2. Portlaoise Prison is located about fifty miles west of Dublin and has been the site of British incarceration of prisoners since the last century. It still functions as an Irish prison to this day. It is pronounced "port leash."
3. Eamon de Valera was one of the leaders of the Irish Revolution arrested after the abortive Easter Rebellion in 1916. He was born in America and his family had moved to Ireland early in his life, but his American citizenship saved his life when the other leaders of the uprising were executed. Later he became the president of the Irish Republic. After Ireland was granted independence, he had a falling out with Michael Collins over the terms of the treaty Collins had negotiated.
4. John W. Davis, a noncareer diplomat, served as the American ambassador to the Court of St. James in London, from 1918 until 1921.
5. As quickly as the agreement was reached with the British, allowing a measure of sovereignty for Ireland but not full independence, a civil war broke out, with

Michael Collins leading one faction and Eamon de Valera another.

6. Collins was assassinated in 1921 while returning to his home near Cork, Ireland. Most historians attribute the killing to the de Valera faction.

7. Samuel Fuqua was an actual member of the United States Naval Academy, Class of 1923. On the morning of December 7, 1941, Fuqua was a lieutenant commander, serving as the duty Officer of the Deck onboard the battleship USS *Arizona*, berthed at Pearl Harbor, Hawaii. When Japanese naval aviators attacked the base, Fuqua not only survived the sinking of the ship but was awarded the Medal of Honor for his heroism in rescuing several of his shipmates. Over 1,100 of his fellow crewmen were not so fortunate and lost their lives when they went down with their ship.

8. On August 2, 1923, President Warren G. Harding died of a heart attack in San Francisco.

9. A "pogie marine" was the name given to marines whose responsibilities usually restricted them to administrative duties. Candy or snack food came to be called "pogie bait."

10. Built between 1909 and 1911, in a joint effort by local community leaders and The Church of Jesus Christ of Latter-day Saints, the Hotel Utah was widely thought to be the finest hotel west of the Mississippi River. It cost approximately two million dollars to build, a sum that was considered impressive for that time.

11. In 1928, Pan American Airlines pioneered a flying route down the west coast of South America to Chile, and then to Buenos Aires by flying east over the Andes Mountains. Eventually, Pan Am merged with the Grace Corporation, a competing airline, because of

their air routes, to form a short-lived company called PANAGRA. In February 1930, four months after the stock market crash, a new company, New York, Rio and Buenos Aires Airlines (NYRBA) initiated service from New York through Miami and down the east coast of South America to Buenos Aires. They flew a twenty-two passenger, four-crew *Consolidated Commodore* flying boat with a 1,000-mile range. By the mid-1930s, Pan Am had bought out NYRBA and began flying the South American route in the Pan Am *Clippers*, which had increased their range to 2,500 miles and eventually to 3,500 miles. This aircraft became the mainstay of the Pacific, Atlantic, and South American routes for Pan American Airlines until well after World War II.

12. By late 1933, President Roosevelt had put his New Deal legislation in place and had created a system of national camps, similar to military installations, for the purpose of housing and feeding men hired to work on federal public works projects. The Civilian conservation Corps (CCC) and Works Progress Administration (WPA) had been created by Congressional acts, and for the next decade these government agencies would be the primary source of employment for hundreds of thousands of otherwise unemployed American workers. Their work left a legacy of improvements that are still evident in dams, national parks, and federal highways. The nation's financial recovery began in earnest only during and after the next Great War.

13. In 1936, Harold B. Lee was, in fact, called as the first managing director of the new Church Security Plan, which later became the Church welfare program.

14. *Skite* is a New Zealand slang term for bragging on one's exploits.

15. In actuality, this visit by President Heber J. Grant and the British Mission conference occurred August 1, 1937, not 1936. The author has taken the liberty of moving the event up one year to coincide with fictional events in the story.

16. In an interview (*Newsweek*, March 8, 1999) Churchill's youngest daughter, Mary Soames, indicated that in the late '30s, senior British military officers often visited her father at Chartwell. Risking their careers if Prime Minister Neville Chamberlain discovered their communication, they were nevertheless in agreement with Churchill's position that war was imminent. Once war broke out and Churchill became prime minister, some of these officers led the defense of England and were instrumental in achieving the final victory over the Germans.

17. In one of the inexplicable tragedies of war, thousands of civilians—men, women, and children—were killed during what was called the "Blitz of London." Many of Britain's airmen actually lived at home or near their homes and fought air battles during the day, returning to their families each night. There are innumerable reports of military men surviving their daily combat experiences while members of their families suffered and died during the ravages of Germany's air raids.